Beautifully Absurd

by

Robert Ashley, MD

Chapter 1

Where am I?

"Dr. Kubler 8219, Dr. Kubler on 8219"

"Dr. Kubler 8219, Dr. Kubler is on 8219."

"Katie, did you page Dr. Kubler?"

"No, I paged Dr. Ross 30 minutes ago and she still hasn't called back."

"Dr. Kubler 8219, Dr. Kubler on 8219."

You got to be kidding me. Where are you, Paul? I remember sitting on the toilet at home, but this isn't home. I'm lying down in some kind of bed, looking up at a generic particleboard ceiling, the same type that I've seen at work, or at the bank, or lying down in a dentist's chair. The square particleboards are filled with perfectly aligned holes. What the hell are the holes for? Do they somehow allow for better ventilation?

I can't move; nothing's moving and I'm barely able to move my eyes to look around this room. There's a generalized heaviness, as if I were water in a deep lake. Did I drink too much last night? My breathing is strange, like someone's forcing air into my lungs, then having that air pushed out of my chest, like someone opened up a balloon, and suddenly, at what seems in inappropriate moment, another forced inhale. Each time I try to fight this controlled breathing I hear a loud beeping; an officious, mechanized sound that tells you, you've done something wrong.

What's that blue plastic tube on my left? It seems to be coming out of my mouth, extending to somewhere behind me. Drops of water cling to the lower section of the tube. There's an intermittent soft compression on my right leg. It's soothing. My left leg? I don't feel my left leg. Was I in an accident? Am I in a hospital?

Time seems to have passed. How much time's passed since I last closed my eyes? My stomach's rumbling and it distends with pain. There's a slow ooze of warmth coming from my groin releasing the pressure from my stomach, dreadfully reminding me of when I was potty training but didn't quite have the hang of it and a mistake would happen. Am I shitting myself? My groin feels coated, but I can't smell a thing and the warm liquid that was there is starting to cool. I got to close my eyes. I must be dreaming.

I'm looking at blue tile and a sink. Where am I?

"You have him, Tracy?"

"Yeah, I have him." Someone's wiping my backside with warm water, wiping away the slimy stuff in between my legs.

"I've been doing this job for so many years. But no matter how many years I've been doing it, the shit still smells."

They're turning me to look up at the ceiling again and there's someone hanging over me, adjusting the blue plastic tube. She has red hair and a rounded, earthy face. She looks like a nurse...so, I *must* be in a hospital. What am I doing in a hospital? Hey, lady! Talk to me! I can't move my lips to talk to her. Her ruddy face looks tired, forlorn and is covered with a thick coat of makeup and eyeliner. Yuck! She's not smiling and appears in a hurry, adjusting something on the blue tube. The beeping returns for a second, then stops and my breathing suddenly gets easier. Is this some kind of messed up dream? I got to close my eyes, and hopefully the next time I wake up I'll be back at my condo and not in this place.

Ouch! Someone is putting a needle in my right arm, causing my breathing to stutter which causes an alarm from the machine.

"It's OK, honey. I'm only taking some blood for the morning." Where's the voice coming from? Warm fluid ebbs from my groin uncontrollably. The evacuation is marvelous, but then the fluid turns cool and slippery. I cannot smell a thing. Holy crap! I don't think I'm dreaming.

"Nurse, we have a problem here." My mind wanders behind my closed lids and I see Sarah smiling at me. That time we were with Jacob in Disneyland, the happiest place on earth. The sunshine mixing with the haze of Southern California as we're all circling on the merry-go-round and there's me trying to take a picture of Jacob and Sarah with my new Polaroid. I remember. They're sitting on different horses, bobbing up and down, each with a happy smile. The bobbing slows as the ride ends.

"Let's go on the Dumbo ride," Jacob saying as I lift him off his horse. We step down from the merry-go-round and see Mickey Mouse, waving. Hordes of children and parents surround this large human-like rodent. "Mickey!" Jacob runs toward the clothed mouse, Sarah trailing behind. I stop a second to look over at the crowd, take a deep breath in and all seems to be right, all seems to be in order and somehow, I joke to myself, this really is Mickey Mouse, an animal with a heart of gold; a Christ-like figure with apostles of Pluto, Goofy and Donald, animals that will diffuse the pain of existence. I walk over, with Jacob along, to take a photo.

I remember the image of little Jacob, looking up in disbelief, watching the huge smiling mouse above him. Where is that picture? I think Sarah had it. Sarah. I wish I could see that picture again. For God's sake, I need something now to make me happy.

Pictures? They now seem like such a waste, all those pictures shot over my life, hundreds of them; my desire to chronicle my family life and somehow give me meaning. All those pictures, what becomes of them? Do they just go in the trash? Hey, what's going on with my condo? Who's taking care of my stuff? My car? The battery will die. And the novel. It's just sitting there in the drawer of my desk. That damn book! Did anyone call Jacob?

"He's getting agitated."

"Let's give two of Ativan." Is that Dr. Gellman? Doctor Gellman! Where are you? I don't see him. Where is he? I can't keep my eyes open.

There are distant, high-pitched voices, singing what sounds like a jazzed up version of that old Coke commercial. *"I'd like to teach the world to sing, in perfect harmony. I'd like to buy the world a Coke, and keep it company."* The sounds of the television are comforting.

An arm crosses in front of me, and a gaunt man with a moustache is fiddling with something below what I can see. He smells like cigarette smoke and I want to ask him, "Hey buddy can I bum a cigarette off you," but all I can do is bite down on this tube in my mouth. What wouldn't I do for a cigarette now? The machine starts beeping again and I feel as if I can't breathe.

4

A woman's voice comes from nearby. "He gets agitated easily, Steve."

"I think he needs a bite-block so he doesn't bite down on the tube," Steve answers. "He's still on assist control and he's waking up, so you can't adjust the pressure when he gets agitated like this."

The smell of cigarettes reminds me of my first cigarette. I stole those cigarettes from Dad and shared them with Jon Matlin and Jeff Jensen, under a sycamore at Rustic Park. It was like some clandestine operation, made all the more delicious by our camaraderie and the knowledge we were doing something wrong. When the smoke came deep into my lungs it burned inside my chest, which made me want to cough, but I didn't. I exhaled slowly, deliberately and watched the smoke rise up against the blue sky. Jon and Jeff smoked in the same deliberate manner and the way we copied each other made the whole adolescent scene seem ritualistic, like Plains Indians in a teepee sharing a peace pipe. I couldn't do a whole cigarette. My mouth and lungs couldn't handle it, but it wasn't too long before I was able to smoke more than one. So addicted, I'd crave a cigarette like a newborn craves its mother's tit, especially in college, smoking while I read Emerson, Kerouac, Ginsberg, Baldwin. My cigarette was a symbol of the rebelliousness of the authors I liked, the rebelliousness of my generation. So cool I thought I was, hanging out at coffee houses with friends and drinking my cup, cigarette in hand, while we discussed the plight of man in the realm of an increasingly restrictive society. What bullshit! We would change the world with our Luckys or Marlboros, listening to Mick Jagger sing, *"He can't be a man because he doesn't smoke the same cigarettes as me."* It was only later, that I understood the irony of that statement and how I, too, identified with brands. "I only smoke Camels," I'd say loyally.

"Paul, can you hear me?" Is that Dr. Gellman? I try to open my eyes. "Paul, it's Dr. Gellman." Dr. Gellman! What's happened to me? Dr. Gellman? I'm beginning to recognize his chubby face, his spectacles, his curly grey hair, his light skin speckled with red blotches, and that perpetual sardonic look. Shoot, every time I went in his office that look of disdain would be on his face, as if to say, "You again!" Yeah, I messed up again, Doc. He moves his head close to the right side of my face.

"Paul, I don't know if you can understand me. It's Dr. Gellman. Paul! Paul!" He's shaking my right shoulder. "Paul, you've had a severe stroke. It's involved a large portion of your brain. You've been here for two weeks now and we have you on a respirator to breathe for you." Two weeks? "We also have a tube going from your nose into your stomach that's feeding you. Paul, do you understand me?" He talks slowly and loud as if this will make me understand. "You've been here for two weeks. You've had a stroke. We're going to get you better." I can see more of him now, his large upper body leaning in.

Better? I can't move, Doc. I'm like a tree and my arms and legs are roots digging deeper into the soil of my bed. All I can do is change my breathing pattern. Don't give me that look of concern, Gellman! It reminds me of that time three years ago when I came to the hospital with my heart attack and you were looking up at the monitor then looking down at me as my heart rate was going really slow and those light bluish-grey eyes conveyed a sincere fear that something was going wrong. You didn't want me to die. I'm not sure why. You never really seemed to like me, were perpetually frustrated with my lack of health and more so with my lack of enthusiasm.

"Paul, you have to change your diet." Or "Paul, you have to take your medication every day. Do you understand? Every day!" Or "Can't you see that your legs are giving you pain because of your Diabetes?" And of course "Are you still smoking?" I did stop smoking after that heart attack. That didn't take much convincing. Your look was enough. You didn't want me to die. Maybe my survival had a direct relationship to your ego. The look on that day was the look of inadequacy. If I died, you would consider yourself a failure.

"Paul, you might not hear me, but you've had a large stroke. It was caused by a blood clot in your heart that traveled to your brain. Paul, do you understand me?" He looks at me, waiting for me to say something, but how can I say a god damn thing with this big tube in my mouth? He nods, pats my chest as he says, "O.K. Paul,

I'll see you tomorrow," and turns away. I hear his voice in the distance.

"Marge, who am I kidding, he can't understand a single word."

"But he is looking around. He's trying to understand, no?"

"I know, but the CAT-scan showed a large stroke on his right side. If the stroke weren't enough, he also had a period of time in the field when he was hypotensive and hypoxic. I don't know how much he'll recover. I don't know what to do with him."

"This is my first day with him. What exactly happened? The sign out said he had a stroke, but I don't know much more."

"What I got from the ambulance report was that his neighbor downstairs heard a groan and a thud from above. When nobody responded to her knock, she called the police and they found him unresponsive, barely breathing. We were going to remove him from the ventilator after the sixth day because he showed little sign of brain activity, but one of the nurses saw that he started to move his right hand when she was checking his blood sugar. Since that time I've been trying to speak to him, but it's like talking to a wall. He opens his eyes, which is some consolation, but I don't know if that means he understands anything. Or if he'll ever recover."

"He's pretty bad off... But you never know."

"On top of that, he didn't give any indication of what he wanted us to do if anything like this happened and I have no family to consult with."

Am I going to die? Is this the end?

"He's got no family?"

"He lives alone. He has a son, but I have no current information about him. His chart has an old phone number for his son and that number doesn't work. I've had Social Services looking for the son's current number, with no success."

"Well I'm sure his son will turn up. After not hearing from his dad for two weeks he's bound to realize something's wrong," Jacob......Jacob? How would he know?

I'm coughing, then, hear the beeping. Although I try to please the machine by changing my breathing, the beeping doesn't stop and the machine keeps pushing air into my lungs. "Beep! Beep! Beep! Beeeeeeep!" The monotonous sound is driving me to lunacy.

7

"Marge, give him two of Ativan." Is this really the end? Stroke? Am I going to make it? The beeping continues as air is being forced into my chest.

A black woman hurriedly walks past my left side. "We're going to give something to calm you down, Mr. Mathews."

"Beep! Beep! Beep!" The ceiling is getting darker and darker.

Where is my son? Where's my mother?

I wake to a pain in my right arm. "It's OK honey, I'm only taking your blood." I cannot see the face of my benefactor. There are the sounds of a television overhead. "Consonants are worth 300, vowels cost 150." "May I have an S?" There is applause, like someone has just won and there are screams of happiness that sound almost like the cries of mourners. Wheel of Fortune. That show came on at 7:00 pm, sort of a no man's land for a sports fan when all sporting events, at least the local ones, begin at 7:30. Oh the ritual! Sitting down on the couch, drinking a beer, watching this game show and eating something out of the microwave. Afterward I'd watch sports, and, if there were no sports, I was fair game for anything that came on prime time. It was sort of a lame existence, but it was my way of interacting with the world, watching those people on television, absorbed in their predicaments. After dinner I would have a cigarette and would savor it. If I found time, sometimes late into the night, with caffeinated attention, I would work on the novel. That damn book!

Evenings with Sarah were different. The washing of my hands prior to dinner, the warm water cleaning off my day, the anticipation of sitting down for a good meal, sitting at a table with my family. Sarah was a good woman and made it a point to have home cooking even though she worked. I remember Jacob in his high chair sitting with us, making a constant mess, the food displayed all over his face, arms and chest. We'd nearly have to hose him off after.

We'd argue though at that table, like opposites on the ideological spectrum, especially after Jacob was born. But sometimes it was just mundane conversation about her day hairdressing or my day at the store. Boring and different from the first time we met, when she came into the record store wearing that

8

white embroidered blouse, buttoned up to the top and seemed to glide around in her white Keds, light as a feather, as she looked through the records. And I was pulled towards her and her innocence.

"Can I help you?" She turns toward me.

"I was looking for this one band. I can't remember the name. Do you know who sings the song 'Come On People'?"

"It's actually called 'Get Together.' That would be the Youngbloods."

"Funny name," she giggles like a schoolgirl. How old could she be? Nineteen?

"The Youngbloods are a pretty good band, but that song is the only good one on the record."

"Have you listened to the record?"

"Many times."

"So you don't think I should buy the record?"

"No, it's OK, but if you really dig that type of music you should buy some Buffalo Springfield." I walk backward to the B line of the store.

"What kind of music do you mean?"

"Huh?"

"What type of music do you think I would dig?"

"Hippie music."

"And do you think I'm a hippie?"

"No, not exactly. I'm not saying anything is wrong with being a hippie. In many ways I'm a hippie."

"In many ways so am I," she smiles.

Wow! I'm walking backward and I'm looking at her blue eyes, which surprisingly seem to be interested in what I'm saying. There's something magical about her and I feel like we're connecting.

"Here we go, Buffalo Springfield."

"Do I know any of the songs they sing?" Her breasts bulge through her quaint top.

"Oh yeah, you know that song, *'Think it's time we stop. Children, what's that sound? Everybody look what's going down.'*"

"Hmmm, I know that song. I don't know if I like them."

9

"But they have other ones too. Like," I clear my throat this time, making sure there's nobody else in the store. *"Sit down, I think I love you. Anyway I'd like to try. I can't stop thinking of you. If you go, I know I'd cry."*

"That sounds really pretty."

"Really?"

"Yeah, you have a nice voice. You know, I want to be a singer. When I was sixteen I did background vocals for the New Christy Minstrels when they came to my home town?"

"Where's your home town?"

"San Luis Obispo."

"How long have you been down here?"

"About six months."

"You want to be a singer?"

"I'd love to be a singer, but I've only had one audition so far."

"So how do you make money?"

"I cut hair. I'm pretty good at it. I know it's not what I really wanted to do, but I like it. I mostly work on women, but maybe one day you'll let me cut your long hair."

"Not a chance. And it's not that long. I haven't cut my hair since returning from Vietnam."

"You were in Vietnam." She moves a little closer, this beauty from some small town I've never been to. I think she digs me. Why does she dig me? There's an awkward silence as I try to rouse something to say about Vietnam.

"Yeah, I just got back six months ago. It's a stupid war."

"I've no idea what we're doing there."

"We need to protect our capitalist markets."

"It doesn't seem right with all those soldiers dying."

"No, it's not right to die for an unjust cause."

She appears saddened by the conversation and looks down at the floor.

"Don't worry, um... What's your name?"

"Sarah."

"I'm Paul. Don't worry. The war will be over soon."

"A boy I used to know died there."

"I'm sorry."

10

"I used to have a crush on him. Gosh…" She looks away, bringing her hand to her mouth. "You know you never get over a crush."

"I know what you mean."

I'm holding the Buffalo Springfield album in my hand as I look into her eyes. Her blond hair is draped down to her shoulders. "Do you want to listen to this record sometime? I have it at home."

And that's how it started between Sarah and me. She was someone I could talk to. Someone who cared about me, at a time when I thought no one ever could. Someone who……

The pain! The pain!

"I'm just replacing your foley catheter." There's a searing pain in my loins, like my groin is on fire and I need to pee at the same time, but there's something blocking the flow. Why the hell can I feel pain and yet not be able to move? I try to move my legs, but with all my effort, I feel only the movement of a few toes. Stop it! Stop it! Stop it! God! Motherfucker! Why are you doing this to me? Why is this happening? Something's in my penis! Something's in my penis! The pain subsides suddenly, but the experience puts me on edge.

A dark brown, rounded face appears above my tube with friendly eyes, dark freckles and full lips. She smiles, her teeth perfectly aligned. "We needed to change your Foley catheter, honey. You were growing bacteria."

What a beautiful face! And the words were said so lovingly. I've never been with a black woman before. I feel like putty and wish she'd stay around to adjust anything she needed to, my tube, my IV, or maybe a massage…Swedish or maybe Thai. Where did you go? Her beautiful face has disappeared. Come back! I need a friend, especially now, when my only source of entertainment is counting the holes in this ceiling.

Friends? Jon and Jeff moved away after high school, so did Phil and Damian after college. Marriage brought friends, but those friends were lost when we ceased being a family. There were work buddies, but over the years the people who worked with me got younger and I became their supervisor. My only friend now is Ray. I wonder if he knows I'm here. He's probably calling my home right now, trying to find out when we're next going to head off to

Vegas or Laughlin. Vegas? That last trip was a doozy and I haven't felt right since. Two years ago Ray moved to Thousand Oaks, which might as well be Nebraska for all intents and purposes.

Shoot, for the most part I've been alone the last 2 years, writing and rewriting my book, secluded within the condo. My only meaningful human contacts were the brief words with my neighbors and the conversations with employees at the Blockbuster on Sawtelle. There was that Sheila, who was sort of cute, and would always tell me about her favorite movies and there was that guy, Jason, with the pockmarks on his face, and his brown greasy hair and dry skin. He would always appear nervous, scared, an easy target for criticism. I wonder if they'll wonder where I went.

I'm terribly cold, like somebody has taken the blankets off and a cold wind is blowing directly on my body. Boy, I'm cold. The blue tube is still there along with the ceiling with the perfectly aligned holes. Could someone turn on a heater or something? I want to just lie on my side, curl my arms and legs toward my chest, but all I can move is a toe. I'm shivering, feeling tired, my head feeling as if it's being compressed in a vise. Can someone get me a blanket? Aren't I in a hospital? Does anyone care? My eyes close again and I'm comforted by the darkness.

I feel hot and nauseous. Sort of like I'm in a tropical climate, sensing the perspiration on my face; the beads of sweat feel like tickling ants on my chest and back. I'm burning up. It reminds me of that trip a long time ago to Hawaii with Jacob and Sarah. Dad gave us the money for the trip, knowing we needed time together after the miscarriage. Jacob must have been eight, July 1980, and we had two weeks on the main island. But all I can remember now is that hike, near Waikiki. After eating one of those large Hawaiian buffets, we felt heavy and somewhat bored, so I asked the woman at the front desk of the motel if there was anything fun to do off the beaten path.

"Well there's always the rain forest. That's real nice and they have a waterfall there," she said. We stopped the car at a state park in the hills and after walking around aimlessly for a bit, I noticed a sign that said "Waterfall" and an arrow pointing up a forested path.

12

A stream trickled slowly alongside the trail. "Let's go!" I don't know what got into me, but I started running up that hill. Jacob, caught up in the excitement, chased after me and Sarah tailed behind. There were no markers on that trail so there was no telling where the waterfall would be. That path meandered up the mountain, and around each corner I looked and listened for some evidence of falling water. I couldn't seem to get enough oxygen, but I didn't care and kept trudging ahead, thinking this hike would be good for Jacob, make him less of a momma's boy, make him stop whining about every little thing. Yet the more I tried to encourage him, the more he would whine. I can hear him whining now. "Dad, when are we going to get to the waterfall?" "Dad let's turn around." "Dad, I want to go back to the motel." "Dad, I don't see any waterfall. Can we go back?"

"Quit your whining, Jacob! You can make it." Drops of perspiration drip down my face. Inhaling the thick air I say, "Don't be so lazy!" He has stopped walking and is looking at me defiantly. I can see him with his shorts, a T-shirt with the bold letters "Hawaii 80" on the front, his shoes and his drooping white socks. The boy needs to be motivated. He's been such a sourpuss the entire trip, not wanting to do anything except watch TV in the motel room and eat ice cream. Not giving a shit that both Sarah and I were suffering after the miscarriage. "Jacob, get your rear moving!" I gesticulate with my arms.

Jacob's face turns red, his eyes fill with anger as he looks up at me. "I hate you. I hate you."

"Why do you hate me? I'm just trying to make you a better man. You know, we're almost there," I wheeze.

"He's right, Paul. This was a bad idea. Let's go back." Why does she continually undermine my relationship with Jacob? I can see her look of disappointment. Forget her. She babies that boy too much. How is he ever going to be a man?

"We're not going back."

"Paul, you're being stubborn."

"Sometimes you have to work hard to get what you want," I proselytize. "Not everything is going to be handed to you." I need to take a stand, need to elevate our family to something better than it is, better than our mundane jobs, better than our mediocrity. This is not the life I wanted, not the life I chose. I never wanted to be an average Joe. I'm not going to turn around and I'm going to push my family forward.

I'm feeling short of breath. That respiratory therapist better stop smoking and come here and clear this tube. Something feels stuck down there and it makes me want to cough.

Yeah, I remember convincing them into going further and how they believed they could make it to the waterfall. I remember being happy for taking a stand. After hiking an hour we ran into a couple walking down the hill.

"How much further to the waterfall," I asked.

"Five more minutes," the man responded.

We came to the end of the trail. The trail headed a little downhill and ended at a pool of murky water. One hundred feet above were small sprays of water that fell off a cliff and landed below as a mild mist. We stood and watched while mosquitoes bit our legs. It was not the waterfall I'd imagined. It was deflating and my attempts at inflation were useless. We argued all the way back to the car and we never talked again about the hike to the waterfall. Funny, when you look back, the entire episode seemed like a great story with Sarah, Jacob and me as actors following a script. I wish we could all sit together and laugh about it now.

It feels so hot and yet I feel cold too, burning up, but at the same time wanting a blanket. I really can't breathe either. There's something stuck in this tube in my throat, and I try to cough, but am unable to. The machine is beeping again and the noise is mind-shattering. BEEEEEEP! BEEEEEP! BEEEEP! I feel like I'm in hell, with Satan stuffing cotton candy into my lungs. The redheaded nurse comes in. I think her name is Tracy.

"What have you done now?" She quickly goes to the blue tube and for a second my breathing is completely blocked until I hear a suctioning sound and then my breathing is a little bit better. But now I feel a cold sweat and shivers throughout my body. A few moments later I smell cigarettes and although I can't see him I think it is the respiratory therapist fixing my tube.

"Tracy, I think the man's in heart failure or has pneumonia. I'm going to get a blood gas."

"Probably pneumonia. He's got a fever and purulent secretions."

14

"His O$_2$ Sats are dropping."

"And he's a full code. I'm waiting for Dr. Gellman to call me back."

Son of bitch, that hurts.

"I didn't know this guy could move," the man says.

"Yeah, he's been moving his toes and fingers a little on the right side," Tracy answers.

"Well, I was able to get enough blood for a blood gas. I'm going to put this on ice."

"OK, be back soon. Did anybody page Dr. Gellman?" Tracy yells.

"He's on the phone now," a distant voice answers.

In the distance I can hear Tracy's voice, but can't hear everything she's saying. "His blood pressure's dropping to the 80's and his oxygen saturation is..." Oh, I don't feel well, feel like vomiting. There's food coming up, although I don't remember eating anything. They must have been force feeding me. What the hell! I don't want to be force fed, especially now. Suddenly all the contents in my stomach are motioned upward and I desperately want to lean over the side of the bed and puke, but I can't and it all fills up the back of my mouth. I gag and am not able to breathe. The horrible beeping resonates as a constant, high-pitched sound in my head. "Beep! Beep! Beep!" It's awful and it won't stop. I want to die. Please, God, let me die! Why must I go through this? Aren't I pretty much dead already?

Now there are multiple beeping machines that are not synchronized, two are high-pitched beats and one lower pitched. I'm lightheaded and heavy. Oh, this is it! Drifting off, sinking into the ground. The earth is going to swallow me up. I just want quiet now, to lie down by the grass here and sleep for a little while. The warmth of the sun feels nice and the grass on my back is cool. Oh there are butterflies fluttering their wings above me! I look up at the blue sky, the butterflies, the birds darting back and forth, the leaves of the trees, the...

"What the hell happened here? Call a Code Blue. Shit, call respiratory."

"Code Blue ICU, Code Blue ICU."

Sarah is above me, her dirty blond hair touching my face. Speckles of sun and shade run through her hair. She's like a wild animal liberated from some unseen captivity. Her lips are full and pink as she bends down to kiss me. She loves me. She really loves me. She's saved me from despair, when my life had no meaning, when I had no direction. I feel her breasts upon my chest as I embrace her. She feels so soft and the grass is our bed. I close my eyes and am now solely sensate, a tactile individual, accepting her lips, drunken by love. Oh I love you, Sarah. I'll always love you. She rests her head on my chest as I wrap my arms around her. I look up at sky. "I'm tired now Sarah. I think I'm going to sleep for a while."

"Mom, is that you?" Mom's loving face is above me, looking down at me, her most precious baby. She's holding me, caressing my face and hair, kissing me on my forehead, making me smile and coo, feeling so loved. I nestle my head into her breasts and her warmth comes over me. Next to her is Dad, clean-shaven, looking young and vital. He tickles my belly as I fall back into my mother's bosom. Oh Mommy, Daddy, I missed you so much. I never want to leave you. I want to stay with you forever. Why did I forget you?

Ouch! Ouch! Someone is jumping on my chest in a rhythmic motion. How cruel! "Mom, Dad, tell them to stop." I want to cry out to them, but I can't. I can't make a sound. The whole world is black, with only a circle of red in the center and no sign of Mom or Dad. Where have they gone? I want to be with them. Get off my chest! Stop this! I don't want this!

"One, two, three, four, five, breathe, one, two, three, four, five, breathe."

It keeps repeating. My chest gets pushed in five times, and then a force of air is jetted into my lungs. I feel there must be at least ten people around me.

"I have a radial pulse," one yells.

"He's in sinus rhythm," boasts another. The thumping on my chest has stopped.

"We need to establish a central line and an arterial line," an authoritarian man calls out. "Call pulmonary, he needs to be bronched."

16

It all sounds bad. I'm back in the hospital, but I don't want to be. Dr. Gellman said I had no chance. Do I have a chance? Ouch! Someone's sticking a hot spear into my leg. Get the hell off me! Another person is sticking a knife into my right arm. Tortured and ripped apart by animals, all my appendages, all my faculties, are being taken away from me. I want to give up. I don't feel anything now.

And the cat's in the cradle and the silver spoon
Little Boy Blue and the Man on the Moon
When you coming home, Dad?
I don't know when. But we'll get together then, son.
You know we'll have a good time then.

The music is coming from Jacob's room. His door's closed, so I take a deep breath and knock.

"Who's there?"

"It's your dad." The door opens. Jacob walks away from me as I enter the room.

"I was just lifting weights, Dad, so if you don't mind, I'd like to be alone," Jacob says as he picks up his weights next to a full-length mirror. He's without his shirt and he's pumping iron to the music, trying his best to ignore me as I stand next to him. I notice that his hair is becoming curly and that there are reddish inflamed pimples on his face and back. He's just a little bit shorter than I and has only a little muscular definition, but is working hard to change that. Thirteen years old. These will be awkward years for him, especially with the divorce. I have second thoughts about the divorce when I look at him, but the divorce is an inevitability, one that neither Sarah nor I can change. The arguments and the yelling have become a daily affair, and it's left us all unhappy. What began with so much hope was fizzling out in despair.

"Son, I would like to have a word with you." I sit on a chair next to him. He's still lifting weights, curling each of the weights up to his shoulders, ignoring me. The twang of the music corresponds to Jacob's rhythmic arm movements and I find it annoying. "Son, I'd like to have a word with you."

17

"And what word would that be Dad?" He waits. "Retarded?" A little smile appears on his face. How can I expect him to understand?

"Listen to me, Jacob. I want to explain."

"Listen to me, Paul. I don't want to hear your explanation. I've already heard enough explanations from Mom and it all sounds like bullshit. You lied to me." He puts the weights down and sits on his bed with his arms crossed over his chest.

"I haven't lied to you."

"You lied!"

"Well, what is it I've lied about?"

"You said you loved Mom, but you don't"

"I did love your Mom, Jacob, and probably still do. I just want to say that sometimes…"

"Sometimes, what?"

"I know you're angry with me and you have every right to be. It's just that you have to realize that your mother and I are people, just like you."

"So?"

"So, each one of us has our needs and we're unable to fill each other's needs. We're both unhappy with our situation. We've tried to work it out and we do still love each other, but it turns out that our differences are too great to reconcile. We're two different people." I sit next to him on the bed and try to put my arm around him.

"I want to be alone," Jacob says as he stands up and returns in earnest to his weights, curling them up toward his shoulders. He's clearly disappointed, but he'll have to get over it.

"This has nothing to do with you, Jake. You're a great kid. This is between your mother and me. I'll still be there for your Little League games and the apartment I'm renting is only mile away from here. You can ride your bike over any time and I will always be your father, if you let me." He is turned away from me. I come closer to him and put my hand on his shoulder. I want him to understand that I love him, but the move seems to backfire as I feel his muscles tense up beneath my hand.

"Why don't you just get out!" He drops his weights as the music ends. He walks over to turn over the record.

18

"We'll still see each other on weekends, and I'll come over for Thanksgiving."

"Just get out, you loser," he yells in a squeaky voice. "I want to be alone."

"Listen, Son! I just want to still be friends. Don't be that way with me." Will he ever forgive me? All is black.

"He is in V. fib. He's hypotensive again," a woman yells.

Darkness is all I see. Soft, heavy, Mother Earth is sinking me in. My face, all the years of expressions, the smiles, the fake smiles, the frowns, the looks of interest, the looks of lust, the tears held back, everything falls into the ground. Oh, God, I am ready. I just feel so tired of this thing, this life. I've lived enough. The waves of the ocean are below and I fall slowly down as if off a cliff and plunge into the warm, turbulent water. May the tide take me where it will. I'm being pummeled by the waves, thrashed about, as if I were laundry needing to be cleansed, having no ability to resist the onslaught of the waves. Then, after a while, the tide turns softer and gentle and I submerge slowly underneath the surface. The tide spins me slowly now and my white arms are spinning, too, as they cut through the water. The sun is shining and I see that my expanding arms are filled with multiple glimmering lights, circling as I am circling. As I look distinctly I see that the arms are filled with thousands of small fish, swimming in a circle, with the sun reflecting its glorious light off their iridescent bodies. As I spin the congregation of minnows spreads wider so that my arms appear more like the sails of a boat. The warm water floods into my mouth and ebbs through my body. Above me the sun filters through the water and all is a beautiful hazy light. I feel hope. What am I? What was I? Much of my life had been a distraction that led me away from that question.

The minnows race forward and I see that between each one is a dark space. I look to that dark empty space and the darkness consumes me; not a thought, not an idea, just the darkness. I have looked for an eternity, when I realize that all is dark except for the minnows, who appear more as stars. I am floating slowly along in this space. I have no emotion. I have no pain. I have no breath. Wonderful!

"360 Joules"

"Clear"

"V tach, no palpable pulse"

"360 Joules"

"Clear"

A large gathering of people is above me, but they're all indistinct in the bright light.

"Blood pressure is 85/40"

"Start 10 micrograms of Dopamine"

I sense that people are frantically, mechanically moving, adjusting instruments, playing with wires and talking what sounds like a medical lingo. After some time the voices and the movement die down. I start to open my eyes and through the blinding light I can make out the shapes of these people.

"Welcome back, Mr. Mathews," says what I believe to be a young man. He seems to be very happy, which is nice to hear.

"Did somebody get in touch with his family?" he asks.

"We have a number here for his son, but it doesn't work," a woman replies.

"Who's his primary doctor? Did somebody notify him?" the young man's voice questions.

"We've called him."

"This patient needs to have his code status clarified."

All of this seems so silly, all these words. I feel so much peace now. Why even bother to follow the meaning of their words? I breathe in harmony with the machine. The hazy light now turns to black. I feel no pain.

Chapter 2

What am I supposed to do?

I'm looking at Yosemite Falls, the sprays of water falling from gargantuan heights, falling from the grey rock, with the deep dark blue sky as background. Dad puts his arm around me. "Isn't it amazing?" he says. There's no question about it. It is amazing, this natural world, with the rustle of the trees, the chirping of the birds, the sound of the water hitting the rocks and sharing this with Mom and Dad. I take a good look at Dad's features as he's talking, his brownish-grey gelled hair pulled back, the wrinkles around his eyes, his reddened skin, his dry lips, the cigarette in his mouth, and the smile on his face as he looks up at the waterfall. The man smiled rarely. Mom always said it was because of World War II and all the death he saw, so this is a happy occasion, and rare, to see Dad's smile. "Do you know, Paul, this valley has been here for millions of years; that it will still be here even after we're dead and gone? It is nice to know that something so beautiful will never die."

"I can see people at the top of the waterfall," I say, looking through my binoculars.

"Let me take a look." He grabs the binoculars and focuses them on the top of the waterfall. "You're right, Paul. I count four people up there."

"You want to try to go up there?"

"I would love to," he says, removing the binoculars from his eyes, "but you know how my knees are. I'd be lucky to make it half way up and then I'd have a hard time coming down. Or you'd have to carry me."

"Come on. Let's go."

"I left my knees in Germany."

"Come on."

"You know what? I'm pretty content just standing here with my family in one of the most beautiful places on earth."

Ouch! Someone has pricked my finger and it pulsates with pain. I open my eyes. "Just checking your blood sugar, honey." Breathe in, breathe out. Dad? My old man. He was always distant. Kept me at arm's length, but that trip to Yosemite was one moment where he brought me closer. Only other times were at ballgames and at the store. He loved jewelry, sort of got me into it too with how to sort out the good cuts in a diamond. I thought it was so cool how those diamonds sparkled, emanating the shades of the rainbow. I loved emeralds, green and shiny. Mom said it was my birthstone.

There was a time I used to want to be like him, but somewhere in my college years I saw him and his life as dull and uninspiring; just another average Joe, trying to make a buck. I don't think he thought too much of my life, either, or my desire to change the world. Seems like neither one of us changed the world, did he? Yosemite…

I took Jacob to Yosemite once, but I don't think he appreciated it like I did. I doubt if we'll ever see it again together. He's older now, thirty-two. The last time we saw each other was at his wedding, two years ago in Sacramento. That was sort of weird. I remember the reception and dancing with Melissa, overly cognizant of the ghastly white of her painted face. She didn't talk much, didn't impress me much, appeared somewhat homely, and I couldn't say more than, "I'm happy for the both of you." But, as I was dancing with Melissa, regretting my son's choice of a wife, I remember looking over at Jacob, with a beer in his hand, surrounded by his friends. He seemed happy, which made me happy. I can see him there, standing with his brown hair disorganized, his ruddy face, his eyes looking down at his beer and I remember thinking, "he's my son and I want the best for him and if this is what made him happy, so be it." But something in the back of my head worried that all the joys of the wedding day were just a façade and that the reality of marriage would rear its ugly head. I thought about my wedding and what must have been going through Dad's head. He must have had the same worries. I'm sure Sarah's parents did. Or maybe Dad was just glad that his son finally got married, that his son had some direction in life. I don't know.

Jacob's wedding was also the last time I saw Sarah. We talked about her life in Santa Maria and my pending retirement, and all the while I was trying to be positive about the reunion of our family. "We did good, Sarah. Through it all we did good." I told Sarah that I was planning on finishing my book after the retirement.

"You're still working on that same book," she said.

"Yeah, the same book."

"So did Edward Winter ever find his way to Los Angeles?"

"Let's say he never realized that he was already there."

"Huh?"

"I'm revising it for the last time. You'll get it, when you read it."

"So what'll you do when it's done?"

"I don't know. I hadn't thought about it. I guess I'll celebrate."

"Don't celebrate too hard. You know you're no spring chicken. Is your heart OK?"

"The heart's fine. Thanks for calling me in the hospital. It meant a lot to me."

"I was worried about you. You should be taking care of yourself," she said to me as if she were my mother.

"And how are you doing?" Sarah had actually lost weight and seemed happy.

"Oh fine. It's much slower living in Santa Maria, but I like it. Found some good people, caring people. Oh, there's Ken. Ken! Ken!"

She was with her husband. Ken's first wife died of leukemia. He seemed like a nice guy, a little too religious for my taste, but still pleasant. "Isn't it wonderful how God brings his children together? You must be really proud of your son." He was one of those "Let us hold hands and pray" kind of religious folk, but he made Sarah happy. I remember Sarah and Ken dancing close together on the dance floor and my feelings of inadequacy for my lack of a partner; how that feeling of inadequacy would continue at the brunch the following day. Jacob did tell me that it would be a casual affair so, hell, I wore my Hawaiian shirt and my loafers. It took me some time to realize that Jacob's friends and the in-laws were laughing at me, laughing at me because I didn't wear a Polo shirt, a stupid necktie or polished Florsheim shoes. Jacob pulled me aside later.

"Jacob, you told me this would be casual."

"Dad, this is Sacramento, not Waikiki."

I felt like a derelict that happened upon the wrong party. Sure, maybe to others I was a loser who couldn't fit in. But so what? I'm still his father. He should at least have some degree of respect for me. I haven't seen Jacob since.........

"Hi, Mr. Mathews, I'm Dr. Johnson, the Infectious Disease doctor. Mr. Mathews, Mr. Mathews, Mr. Mathews." Somebody's grinding their knuckles into my chest, but while feeling the pain, the pain itself doesn't bother me, as if I'm busy with something else and don't have to acknowledge or seem to mind the pain. OK man, I'll wake up. The ethereal light blinds me and it takes some time to distinguish this man with a beard. He appears to be an older guy, probably in his sixties. "Mr. Mathews, I'm Dr. Johnson. Are you in any pain? Mr. Mathews, can you hear me?" Yes man, I can hear you. "Mr. Mathews, you've had a large stroke. I was consulted to see you because you have a severe case of pneumonia. Mr. Mathews, do you understand?"

Ouch! Hey, stop grinding your boney knuckles in my chest! I can hear you fine!

"You're connected to a respirator and you're getting feeding through a vein in your arm." He stops his grinding and pauses. I can see him clearer. He's looking directly into my eyes. "Mr. Mathews, your chance of regaining any significant use of your left arm and leg is poor. Your chance of survival without artificial means is also poor." What are you saying, man? I'm looking up at the ceiling. What do you mean by "artificial means"? Who are you kidding! I've survived my whole life by artificial means, having a car for transportation, never growing or killing my own food, subsisting on television, isolating myself from the natural world, taking medication for my heart, using air conditioning when it was hot, a heater when it was cold, a toilet when I needed to defecate, and a beer when I needed to relax. Artificial means? Man, what you should be saying is that my chance of surviving without 'more than normal' artificial means is poor. Besides—what's an infectious disease guy telling me this for? Isn't he supposed to think about germs?

"Mr. Mathews, do you understand what I'm saying?"

24

Buddy, I can't tell anybody anything. What do you want from me? Do with me what you must.

Do you have any idea how I'm feeling? So what if I die? Nobody really cares about me anyway. I don't care anymore......haven't cared in a long time. I'm looking at the doctor again, and although my vision is poor, I can see he's sincere and wants the best for me. He turns his head away.

"Does anyone have a number for a relative?"

"We have a number for a son in Duarte, but they say he moved two years ago," a female voice answers. Shit! Why didn't I give Dr. Gellman Jacob's new phone number? They still have the old number.

"We have a name, right?"

"His son's? Jacob Mathews."

"Well, did anybody ever think that maybe Mr. Mathews has his son's phone number in his home? Has Social Services looked into that?" His voice raises, "Or have they looked into finding another family member?"

"They said they were looking into it," the nurse says defensively. "I don't have a lot of control over what Social Services does."

"If they'd put any energy into thinking, they'd have found the son by now. This man's been here for two weeks! How hard did they look? All it takes is going through his house and locating the man's telephone book or his phone records." Dr. Johnson's tough, and he's not letting it drop. "I'm going to talk to those idiots. All they're good for is discharging patients."

My condo! They'll get a hold of Jacob or maybe Ray......or maybe Sarah. Maybe they'll find my book! Will they like it?

"Well, Dr. Gellman made the consult," she says sheepishly.

"As he should have. But, we need to follow through. This patient's going to be set up for a G-tube, and a tracheostomy and a state of prolonged incapacity. I don't know if he wants this. Would you want this? We need to find his son and get an idea of his wishes. Either that, or make him a ward of the state, but they would keep him alive forever. I'm going to talk to Social Services. Something needs to be done." He walks away.

What a performance! Bravo! Bravo! A man of moral action! It still exists, this moral sense and it has piqued my interest in what this man is going to do. He walks away and I'm still feeling the sting of chest pain from his knuckles.

It gets dark and there is the distant sound of someone talking and it isn't Dr. Johnson.

"All of this is absurd." Is that Stephen Petry? Haven't thought about him for a while, my former neighbor. Strange he should come into my head. He was filled with this messianic energy that the boy couldn't keep inside, ranting to me about the problems of humanity and what he called "our current society." He reminded me of myself when I was in college, the rebellious part of me I thought was gone, the individual spirit that defied convention. He wanted to change the world, make it a better place, doing stuff like volunteering most all his extra time at the church, the hospital, his old high school. Sunday afternoons were the only times I saw him, the only time he took for himself.

There was something about those eyes of his though, something unafraid and completely willing to share from the man's soul. I can see him again, watering some potted plants with a hose, while I'm waxing the Mustang next to the garage.

"Can't you see it is absurd?"

"What's absurd, Stephen?"

"This whole world we've created."

"No kidding! What's your point?"

"Look, the world's a place of creation, death and regeneration." Stephen points to the plant he's finished watering. "Yet while a plant works within the confines of its environment, only growing where water, earth and sun will allow it, we humans have created our own environment, taming our nature, creating processed human beings."

"Devoid of all natural flavors or colors?"

"Seriously, we have created this human world with freeways, streets, lights, billboards and that world has a feeling of permanence. Skyscrapers replace mountains, ceilings replace the sky, the shower replaces the spring and it all makes us oblivious to this process of life and death."

"Here you go again!"

26

"What?"

"You're preaching again."

"I can't help myself," he smiles. "I mean look at how we die. How natural is that? We place ourselves in coffins, lined with satin and comfortable pillows, closing ourselves off from nature's decomposition of us, and then plunk on a tombstone as a monument to our permanence. Shouldn't we be smart enough to know we're not permanent? What is worse are those people that cremate themselves, so that they pollute the air."

"What are we supposed to do Stephen? In many ways we need to be protected from nature. Where would we be without sanitation? What would happen if people died and didn't get buried? Where would we be without vaccines or antibiotics?"

"OK. But do we go for those things at any cost?" He smacks the back of his hand into the palm of the other. "Our hearts and our minds are separated from the process of life. We have all these benefits so we don't see the grotesque portion of life; the pestilence, the killing of animals for food, the death."

"Blah! Blah! Blah! Don't leave out the killing of plants. Just because they don't complain doesn't mean they like it. And I myself like to sit in a warm bathtub, listen to music on the radio and have a beer. Without 'our current society' I wouldn't have hot water, I wouldn't have recorded music, I wouldn't have a beer and I would not have a bathtub. I don't know if I want to give up these conveniences to live a life in nature and so what if it makes me less of an animal within nature?" It sounds as if there are a hundred birds in the tree next to us, but it's difficult to see them all. The noise of the birds is drowned out by a passing car with a bad muffler, and then the noise returns. Stephen walks up to the Mustang and while he's a tall man, there's something so pure and childlike about him.

"I understand what you're saying, but how long can we keep doing this?"

"Doing what?"

"Living like this."

"Nothing's forever. It'll end when it ends, and probably end badly. Still? You can't change the world, Stephen. This is what it is. I tried to change the world a long time ago, when I was in

27

college and for sometime afterward, but I couldn't, for this world is all I know. I'm part of it; I'm part of what needs to be changed. Who am I to say how the world should be?"

"You're right! You can't change the world, but you can change yourself. We have a choice. Each day we have a choice, an ability to either interact with our natural world or stay sequestered within our cubicle and within our apartments watching our TV."

"Get real! Look around you! The whole country lives like this. There's only so much one individual can do."

"I don't agree. There is so much more a person can do. He can teach, be a mentor, give a helping a hand for someone in need. We don't have to live these selfish, consumptive lives separated from one another." I put down my towel and stand facing him.

"The more you stand up against society, the harder society will work against you, bud. Take it from me. I've tried it, Stephen, and it doesn't work and my fight has left me with no desire to fight any more. The only fight I've left is my book. If you don't follow the rules of society, you don't get the benefits that come with society.

"The benefits? They're dangled in front of us and this society knows we become slaves to them. As much as seedlings will compete for the best soil and the best light, so we too will struggle for our place in this world."

"It's all in our biology."

"Yeah, maybe what our society is doing is actually wholly natural." He starts to laugh.

Stephen's face is fading away into black, the silhouette of his curly hair and the tree in the background is all I see. His voice fades into some other thought, some other rant. The man drove me up a wall sometimes, but I loved it when he went on a tear. It reminded me of me, hectoring my elders. I open my eyes.

The tube still levitates above my head, and air is still being pumped in and out of my lungs. I still can't move any body part, only able to look around and think of Stephen's words. Is what our society doing, natural? This place sure doesn't feel natural. Maybe I'll close my eyes and think, or dream, of something natural.

Standing at the top of a mountain, I'm looking at clouds as they journey toward the horizon. The large cumulus clouds are traveling like ships off to battle. The blue sky is the inverted sea that supports them. The wind is traveling behind me, parting my hair and running around my outstretched arms. I'm flying off the mountain carried by the wind, floating along, being propelled by the air. My head is light, my body is light, my feet are light. In fact I feel that there's no humanly form to me; an observer, floating with the clouds, now peering down at the mountainous desert below me, the wind now blowing in my eyes and causing tears to drop toward the arid land. The tears come down happily.

I'm floating above this beautiful earth. There are the tops of green pine below me and an alpine lake shimmering with the reflected rays of the sun. I want to look closer at this beauty, so I descend. Hovering over the edge of the lake I see water bugs gliding over the surface and down below them the patient trout. Propelling my body past the lake, I move along to a light green meadow, dip low and spread my arms wide so they touch the blades of grass, causing birds to dart away. A small stream cuts through the meadow and the sound of the rippling water softens my mind. Butterflies and flies skirt back and forth at the edge of the stream. The grey-rock mountains surround me like fatherly sentinels, their permanence keeping guard over the lake and meadow. Oh, how grand it is! I glide to the base of one of these spires and look up to pay homage to this giant, wanting to ascend to its peak. A sound disturbs my reverie and I look to my left and see something moving. What could that be? I come by slowly, creeping around a boulder and see a beautiful, tan mountain lion digging its face deep into the belly of a deer. The deer, fallen on its left side, looks up and cries, but the cry is halfhearted, as if to say, "Help! Help! ...Oh what does it matter! I'm a goner anyway." The sad bleating continues as the mountain lion rips away more meat from under the open fur. The crying stops. It's all so horrible and yet so beautiful, exciting and perfect. The mountain lion looks up at me. "This is what I am supposed to do," he says. I ponder that. What am I supposed to do?

"Paul! Paul!" Someone's rubbing my chest. The rocks, the meadow, the mountain lion and his dead partner are fading away.

"Paul! It's Dr. Gellman."

"He is starting to come around again," a woman's voice says.

29

"Paul!" Oh man! A flood of light blinds me and after some time I can make out the grey, curly hair of Dr. Gellman, the reddish hue of his face, the scaly lips, the double chin, the steel blue eyes behind his glasses. He looks a little frightening. He has me at my weakest moment, and his whim could be my adventure through hell. He could sedate me, stick needles in me like some voodoo doll, or do things to me that I never would want done. His steel-blue eyes peer down.

"Paul, can you hear me? Paul I want you to squeeze my fingers with your hand." His two fingers are in my right hand and I try my hardest to squeeze his fingers, wanting him to know that I can understand him.

"That's good, Paul. I can see your fingers moving." He seems genuinely pleased. "Now, try it with your left hand." I'm trying my hardest now to squeeze my left hand, but there's no movement. He's looking intently at my left hand, but he appears tired, almost straining in his attempt at being hopeful. Gellman's been my doctor for the last 15 years. He has a wife and kids, but I know little else about him. It's strange because I always envisioned a doctor like some kind of wise man who knew everyone in town, a guy you could invite over for dinner, who would take care of your ailments, whom you could trust, someone who was an integral part of your world. We are not in that world. Wish I had known him better, been a better patient, listened to him when he lectured me about my bad habits. Wish I could tell him I was sorry. Looks like he feels sorry, too; sorry for my current predicament and maybe sorry for his inability to help me. Maybe just sorry to be here. He's looking down at my left hand.

"Paul, you've been on the ventilator for more than 2 weeks now. We're unable to remove the ventilator because you've bad lung disease and I don't think you can protect your airway, so we may need to make a hole in your airway through your trachea and place the breathing tube over that hole, so you can breathe. We'll also need to place a tube in your stomach to continue your feeding. You're on antibiotics for pneumonia now and this is getting better. Do you understand?"

I can't even nod my head to say yes, man! He moves out of my field of vision, but his voice is in the distance.

30

"Angela, have we heard anything from Social Services?"

"They found a number for his ex-wife."

"But doesn't he also have a son?"

"Yes, Doc. His son moved to Sacramento, and we got his phone number too." Angela answers.

"Could you get me the number? I'd like to talk to him."

Jacob! They found him! Hallelujah! Jake! This may be my last shot to make up with him. Hopefully, he'll forgive me for all my transgressions and get them to let me die in peace, not attached to these machines. The machines are beeping again. Fuck it! I don't care. To hell with these machines! To hell with this way of living! What's hell anyway? Locked down by paralysis, unable to defecate, urinate, breath or eat for myself, is a good description of hell and with the end of my life I will be lifted out of this inferno. Jacob! My boy's coming! The machine beeps and I'm coughing uncontrollably. "Beep! Beep! Beep!"

"Angela, give him two of Ativan," Dr. Gellman orders. In a few moments, Angela comes across my left side and leans over my groin. I see the back of Angela's head, with her smooth black Asian hair, leaning over my midsection. She appears to be trying to fix something, but I really don't care because the image of her is arousing. I'd love to grab her, stroke her hair, make mad passionate love to her, but I may frighten her with all my tubes and my inability to stay continent. What do I look like to her? She leaves and my half-closed eyes look at the empty space. I've not been with a woman in so long. It must have been four years ago. The beeping stops. Her name was Joyce. Ray set me up with her. "She's just what you need, Pauley, something nice and steady." I wanted a relationship again and was willing to compromise my standards. Joyce had a nice face, but her body was soft and she had those scaly lesions on her back and arms. Her mouth also spewed an incessant stream of half-interesting conversation. After a couple of months of intermittent dating, we drove up the coast in the Mustang for a nice dinner and came back to watch a rented film, and that's when we attempted fornication on the sofa. It took some time until we both had our clothes off, the light of the television exposing our not so beautiful bodies. She was underneath me on the couch, her body was soft, almost doughy, and we kissed and

31

embraced. As time passed I became bored, frustrated, and felt an urgency to complete my task. We kept repositioning ourselves so as to copulate, but it was fruitless. "Maybe you could try Viagra." I couldn't get a very good erection, but I smoked a cigarette afterward and that was the last I saw of Joyce. I really wasn't into her. I smell the respiratory therapist. "Hey, buddy, can I bum a cigarette off you?" I joke to myself, sleepily. The world goes to black.

A saguaro cactus towers above me. It's dusk and the moon rises over the desert mountains. Faint stars are interspersed between high wispy clouds and a plane cuts through this night sky with its lights blinking; all those people on the plane, going to their destinations, watching their in-flight movie, unaware of those down below, unaware of me and my plight. The saguaro's arms creeping upward, praying to the gods above. The horizon has an orange hue and a dry warm wind forces its way through my hair. I bring a cigarette to my mouth, inhale deeply and softly blow out the smoke. It's calm here, quiet, the sounds of city replaced by silence. No Sarah. No Jacob. No conflict. Just quiet. Sarah was more than happy to see me go. No goodbye kiss, just simply "Bye" as she left for work. It seems like lately everything is a competition, like adversaries wanting to claim complete victory, never wanting compromise.

Mom moved to Tucson after Dad died, following many of her friends who had left Southern California to live in Arizona. Walking back inside her adobe home I notice a big dream catcher above her fireplace, the large feathers of some bird hanging down at the bottom. On a table behind one of her couches sits a bronze statue of a Plains Indian on horseback with a spear in hand, chasing down a buffalo. A multicolored Mexican rug's spread on the floor in front of Mom, who sits in a wooden rocking chair knitting a sweater. Maybe the sweater is for me. There's a fake ficus tree, looking real, standing behind her.

"Paul, come sit. You've been pacing around the house since you got here. Come, sit on the couch," Mom says, lifting her head up and pointing her knitting needles at the couch in front of her.

"OK." I sit. There's a book on Anasazi art on the coffee table. I open it to a page that has figures of men and deer etched in red rock.

"It's nice you came to see me." Mom puts down her knitting.

"It's nice to be here. I love the quiet of this place."

"The quiet is the best part. The last time I saw you in Tucson this place wasn't even decorated."

"I like what you've done."

She's thinking of something to say. With her alpaca sweater, her turquoise necklace and her grey hair pulled back in a bun, she has the appearance of a wise elder who gives council to those in need.

"It's become a comfortable home. But it can get lonely."

"I'm sorry, Mom. I…"

"Don't worry about it, Paul. I know. We all get so busy with our own lives." She looks down at her knitting and then looks up at me. "Is something troubling you?"

"Troubling me? No, everything's fine."

"You don't seem happy. Something's wrong. Is everything fine between you and Sarah?"

"Everything's fine," I browse through the picture of cliff dwellings, avoiding her gaze.

"So why did you come alone? Why not bring Jacob and Sarah?"

"Sarah had to work and Jacob is in school. I really just needed some time away, needed to clear my head."

"Of what?"

"I guess I've been a little stressed about losing the money and sometimes just everything. I just can't seem to find time to relax at home. There's always something to do and Sarah……Sarah's all over me about everything."

"How's Sarah doing?"

"Crazy. Crazy Sarah. I don't think she's still over the miscarriage and she's becoming more and more religious."

"What's wrong with that?"

"She looks at me strange."

"Strange?"

"Like I'm a sinner. She talks about God all the time now and keeps a Bible on the nightstand and she wears a cross. She's lost it, Mom. Lost it!"

33

"There's nothing wrong with the Bible. Maybe it's her way of dealing with the miscarriage."

"The miscarriage was three years ago."

"Religion…"

"Religion is damaging our marriage!"

"All marriages have difficulties."

"We need to see a therapist or something."

"Do you want me to talk to her?"

"Could you? I don't know if it would help."

"Paul, marriage is like dancing. Each person normally dances to their own tune, but when they come together the partnership needs to have a coordinated movement: One, two, three, one, two, three, one, two, three." She mimics the dance with her hands.

"Sarah and I don't dance," I half jest.

"Stop joking. I'm trying to teach you something. OK?

"OK."

"So, like in dancing, a marriage at times will have a misstep, a snafu……like Sarah's miscarriage." She claps her hands. "Then the dance loses its smoothness and it's up to the couple to regain their composure and dance again. Sometimes, you have to compromise some of yourself for your partner. Sometimes, you have to lose something that you believe is an integral part of you, so you can gain something that is much greater than you." Mom's been reading too many self-help books. It must be the Southwest.

"Mom, I've already made so many compromises in my life. It's just not how I envisioned my life: my writing career, marriage, Reagan, my boring job. You know, I was initially happy selling stereos, happy to be making money but now I feel stuck with that job."

"How about writing for the paper again?"

"I would have to quit Watson's to have the time to do serious reporting. But serious reporting doesn't matter anyway. Last time I tried the editor said my writing was biased and overly harsh."

"Have you tried to tone it down?"

"How can you tone down Chevron's illegal dumping in the Santa Monica Bay?"

"I don't know. Find something else. Do something else, Paul."

"I got an idea for a book."

34

"Wonderful. Write a book. You've always been a good writer."

"It's too much, Mom. The job, the family, the house, the car…It's too much and I have a gnawing sensation that my life is slipping away and now Sarah and I are having difficulties. I won't lie to you."

"Then don't lie to me. You know, your father and I had difficulties, too. I wanted to live in smaller town, where people knew each other, where there was a real connection to the past. But Los Angeles?" Mom looks down shaking her head. "Your father wanted to make a name for himself in L.A., be a jeweler to the wealthy. I would always nag him about leaving the city and moving to a small town."

"I miss Dad. I can't believe he's gone."

"I miss him, too." She looks up at me, reflecting for a moment. "But, Paul what I'm trying to say is that your father and I had our differences. We had to make compromises that incorporated, to some degree, each of our dreams, and this is the funny thing about dreams, as life changes one's dreams change."

"And it sounds like the compromises you made meant neither of you got what you wanted."

"Maybe. But that doesn't mean we got nothing of value. Our compromises allowed us to lead a shared life, one in which I felt like I was part of a community in Los Angeles and your father felt like a success in his jewelry business. It was a dance. Each one of us had our part." I see a tear come to her eye. "And our dance allowed us to fulfill a shared dream of raising a child. We had to make compromises all the time when we were raising you." What a guilt trip.

"Mom, Sarah and I have some differences that are beyond compromise." I need to get up. "Like religion, like the last presidential election." I'm walking toward the bathroom. "Like sports, like turning my son into a choir-boy sissy." Looking into the toilet, talking to myself, "Like nearly every conceivable topic."

When I return, I reopen the book to a picture of cliff dwellings with the caption, **What happened to the Anasazi?** They disappeared from the face of the earth. Why? Mom clears her throat. "Paul, in all life, there's work. People today expect that somehow they will live happily ever after, and are disappointed that it turned out differently."

"I'm aware of that, Mom."

"Are you?" Mom's never been one to lecture me. She usually left that up to Dad. "Who knows if things will work out like you planned?"

"OK Mom. Enough lecturing! Do you have a TV?"

"I gave it away."

"Why?"

"I don't know, just don't need it. It doesn't seem real."

"What's real anymore?"

"Well, not the TV. We sure didn't have TV when I was a kid and I think I'm happier for it."

"But when I was a kid you had no qualms with TV."

"I know and I'm sorry." She looks down, and her words come out methodically. "But when you go from one movie, one sitcom, to the next, you see resolutions easily made and then you hurry off to the next story. You're just an observer. Instead of the work of your own life, you watch others work out the conflicts of life. You don't deal with those conflicts yourself. It's just entertainment and it makes people irresponsible."

"Do you think I'm irresponsible?" She looks down at her hands and then slowly raises her wrinkled face to look at me. After a while, a smile appears.

"At one time I did, with your crazy notions of the world, and your long hair, but now I don't. You're all grown up. You have a wife and child, Paul, and the maintenance of that family takes work. Take it from me. While that work may seem to get easier over time, it never ends." I look above her at a picture of an Indian chief with a headdress of colorful feathers, reddened, wrinkled skin and serene eyes peering down over the earth. It's good to see Mom again. Mom…Mom?

"Mr. Mathews, we're doing a portable chest X-ray. Mr. Mathews can you hear me? I'm going to turn you on your side and put a plate on your bed for the X-ray. OK, here we go, one, two, three!" I'm being moved on my side and he's grunting as he holds me while at the same time placing a cold, hard object behind me. He turns me on top of this cold flat object. "OK, X-ray in the room," he announces to I don't know whom. "One, Two, Three." A high-pitched alien-like sound comes from the X-ray machine. He's moving me again to my side, the hard object is removed and then he turns me again to my back to look up at the ceiling with the neatly arranged holes. My butt hurts. There's a stinging there, more like a painful itch, and I want to scratch it. I wish I could scratch it. It's maddening! Focus on your breathing man. The rhythmic oscillations of air are gliding me away from the pain. The blue tube hovers on my left side and underneath the blue tube there's a wall with blue tile; a light blue tile that gives the room an aseptic, lifeless appearance. I need to close my eyes and focus on something else. I can hear the television. It has some strange demonic organ music and then a sermonic voice.

"Jesus will save you!" My instinct is to change the channel. "Yield from this material world and come into the arms of love. He has not forgotten you." Must be Sunday television. At least I know what day of the week it is.

"God spoke unto Timothy and said that the goal of life is not the acquisition of material wealth; that material wealth will trap you, it will shield you from the true nature of the world, it will make you blind to His laws. I see the pain this causes." "Amen!" the audience replies. "I see it every day, and I know that you, too, see it, and maybe some of you have experienced this pain. Amen! I see the disconnection, the separation of God's children from His laws. Follow the way of the righteous and feel the love of the Lord. Amen! Don't run away from Him. Don't be afraid. He will guide you. Timothy asked God, 'How can I avoid this path of materialism?'" He's waiting, like he's waiting for someone in the audience to answer. The silence is discomforting.

"And Jesus said, 'You will avoid the path of gaudy materialism, if you listen and follow my laws.'"

Oh man! It's one thing to philosophize about the meaning of existence and our place in the world, but it's entirely another thing when one's told to follow dogma. Jesus was a good man and said good things. But he's not the only good man and the Bible is not the only good book out there. Trying to explain that to Sarah was like talking to a wall. The church killed our marriage.

"Listen to the word of Jesus. It will save you."

37

Jesus. Son of God. Man has created God in a human form, his words to live by. But why should I pay homage to a past human form? Why would I listen to Jesus more than my contemporaries? Sarah was brainwashing Jacob with that stuff. What choice did I have, but to counter her so Jacob wouldn't blindly accept the church's way of life?

I'm clueless as to why I'm here, what the meaning of existence is, or as to what, if anything, is the meaning of my suffering with this tube in my lungs, looking at a ceiling with perfectly aligned holes, with a complete inability to move anything, except my bowels. Clueless... Clueless... Clueless. The point is, is that there is no meaning.

"Timothy was lured not only by the idea of material wealth, but by the idea of distraction. It is this distraction that shelters us away from the true meaning of our lives and of God's laws. To follow the path of the Lord is difficult for there are many paths that will lead you astray. Amen! It is so easy to follow another path, a distraction, whether it is the distraction of gossip, the distraction of shopping, the distraction of alcohol, tobacco, drugs, the distraction of adultery, the distraction of—"

Someone has changed the channel. The voice is gone, replaced by another voice. "Third and five at the Philadelphia thirty-yard line. Carter is in the shotgun, split receivers. Carter is chased out of the pocket, looking downfield, fakes a pass and takes off, and is tackled down at the Philadephia twenty-six. Fourth and one." There's someone else in the room, watching the TV.

"Come on, Dallas. You've got to go for it," a man's voice calls out.

"They're bringing the field goal unit in. This will be a forty-three-yard field goal."

"Ah, come on, coach, you got to go for it. Don't be a pussy." The announcer's voice returns.

"He missed his last field goal of thirty-eight yards. Here we go. The set, the kick, it's long enough, but to the right. So Dallas squanders away another opportunity."

"Damn," he says, walking away.

"This is not your average beer. Cool and fresh with one third less calories than regular beers." The ceiling appears to be getting darker and darker. Now it's black. Darkness is all I see and darkness is all I want to see. The sounds of the TV and the voices around the hallway are disappearing. The question that comes to mind is, 'Why struggle at all?' Why worry about the world and its absurdity? The past is done and there's no way to change it and in my present situation...... there's nothing I can do about the present situation. Quiet darkness is all I desire now and a heavy sleep to befall me.

"Sarah, I'm home." My old apartment in Culver City. It must have been before we got married.

"I've got dinner cooking."

Sarah's in the kitchen, pulling baked chicken out of the oven; the homemaker looking pretty in her dress! I come behind her, wrap my arms around her belly, kiss her neck, feel her nestling back into me. She turns her head toward me and we kiss heavily. My hands reach down to her upper thighs, but she pulls away.

"Come on now. Let me finish with dinner."

"OK, OK. I'll help you set the table. Hey! You made corn."

"I know how you like corn."

"I like everything about this. I could really get used to this type of living."

"What are you trying to say?"

"I'm trying to say I'm a lucky man."

"I'm lucky, too." It feels so homey, comfortable, eating together in my small apartment, drinking a beer at the kitchen table. She's smiling at me at the other side of the table.

"Why are you smiling? What's going on?'

"I read that poem 'The Song of the Open Road.' I really liked it."

"I told you it was good."

"It makes you feel like anything's possible."

"The Open Road."

I bite into the chicken and lick the barbeque sauce off my lips. Sarah bites into the corn. She's wearing her white dress with flowers with a V-neck that displays a hint of her cleavage. She puts down the corn and looks up at me in a loving way. *"I give you my hand! I give you my love, more precious than money. I give you*

39

myself, before preaching or law. Will you give me yourself? Will you come travel with me? Shall we stick by each other as long as we live?"

"You memorized it?"

"It's such a wonderful poem. I can see why you love Whitman so much."

"Did you know he was bisexual?"

"No! Do you mean he had sex with other men?"

"I think so. I'm not saying that's why I like him, but it's interesting. I remember when I first read Whitman and realized how free life could be without the constraints of society, school, my parents."

"Could you show me more books?"

"Yeah. Sure."

"I'd love to read more, learn more, maybe go to college. There's so much I don't understand."

"Books can help, but you have to be the one to open your mind to them."

"Have you thought any more about finishing your English degree?"

"Why do you ask?"

"Well it's just that you'd be such a great teacher."

"Would you want to be in my class?"

"Sure."

"No, the degree would be nice, but the school year's already started and frankly I'm not too excited about going back to school."

"Why not?"

"I'd rather be a reporter. Open up people's minds to the world around them."

"You've certainly opened my mind, Paul... and my heart." She looks at me and then at her plate, blushing, trying to avoid my gaze. "Anyway, I wouldn't want to share you with all those female students."

"You'll always be my favorite student. And my best." We continue eating quietly, pausing only to look at each other and smile.

"You know, this time with you has been the best time of my life."

"Same with me."

We look at each for a while and I have a feeling that Sarah wants to say something.

"Paul."

"Yeah?"

"I worry about all the things you've done in the past. Things I've never done: the drugs, the protesting, Vietnam, and then there was that girl you were with there."

A moment of despair! Vulnerable, talking about that stupid war, my mouth had the runs. Her name was Hanh and I was only with her once.

"Honey, it didn't mean anything. I was desperate and lonely in that godforsaken country."

"But you didn't need to sleep with her."

"I needed female companionship. I needed to feel loved." How can I ever tell her about the other women I've been with?

"Is that what you call sex? And the drugs?"

"You know I stopped the drugs after Vietnam, after I met you."

"But, how will I know…"

"Well, how will I know? I mean, why are you hanging out with me? Seriously? On a beauty scale you definitely outflank me and you're just so much younger than I am. Don't you want to be with someone your own age?"

"I want to be with you and nobody else. I believe in you." She smiles at me. "And you are beautiful, you just don't always feel like you are."

"You're wonderful Sarah. I'd be lucky to spend the rest of my life with you."

"Paul."

"No, I mean it. I want to get married."

"Paul?"

"We'll get married at the beach, outside with our family and friends."

"On the beach?

"Yeah, think about it, the beach with the sun setting."

"I always thought I would get married in a church."

"Church?"

"I know it's silly."

"Nothing is more spiritual then the ocean with the sun setting. I've spent many days looking out at that ocean, realizing that I was so small, and wanting one day to be something more than being small."

"I love you for who you are. Paul Mathews and nothing more."

"That's sweet."

"Anyway, I know I'd be happier married at the beach during sunset; much better than a church, and be as we are in front of God and Nature."

"You said it."

"And if God is everywhere around us, then it doesn't matter where we get married, as long as there's love."

"Amen."

"Would you like another beer?"

"No, I'm completely content."

"So what would you like for dessert?" She smiles a mischievous little smile.

"I don't know? What did you have in mind?" She puts her foot on my lap and rubs it into my crouch. My member elevates as if on cue.

"I think our last course is in the bedroom," she says in a corny and awkward way. She stands and is leading me down the hall to my bedroom. We are kissing heavily as we stand next to the bed, pressing our chests close, panting heavily as if we're dogs in heat. I'm kissing her neck and feeling her soft hair on my face. She reaches down into my pants. Oh Sarah. Sarah! Breathe in! Breathe out! Breathe in! Breathe out! The machine's bringing me back. Back again to stare at a ceiling, thinking about Sarah.

Her parents were pissed when we told them we were getting married at the beach. They protested that we didn't get married in church, but we ignored them and they had to accept as consolation the fact that we were married by a priest. It was a small wedding……Mom and Dad were there, along with my man Phil and his wife and Ray with some floozy. Everybody took off their shoes to feel the sand upon their feet. The priest did a good ceremony, but the best part was that it culminated with a sunset that made everybody feel that God was watching.

Chapter 3

Jacob

I've been waiting for 30 minutes for Dr. Shields. Where is this guy? Doesn't he realize that other people's time is precious? There's a knock on the door and he finally walks in.

"Hello, Jacob. How are you feeling?"

"I'm fine. Do you have the test results?"

"Let's see if they're back yet." He's walking out of the room. What the hell? He knows I'm here to go over the blood tests and he doesn't even know if he's got the results. I could be dying of cancer! These chest pains, the sweats, the lack of energy… I'm too young to die. Dude, focus on something else. There's a picture of Jennifer Aniston on the cover of *Us*. Why do they call it *Us,* when it is really about *Them.* Doctor Shields walks back into the room.

"Everything looks normal, Mr. Mathews."

"Normal?"

"Your liver tests, kidney tests, thyroid test, blood-cell count and your electrolytes are all normal. Everything looks normal."

"I don't feel normal. What's going on with me?"

"I understand you're not feeling well, Mr. Mathews, but the chest x-ray, EKG and all the labs are normal. I can't find a measurable cause of why you're feeling sick."

"Isn't there some other test we could do?"

"Not that I can think of."

"So what can it be?"

"I don't know. Have your stress levels changed at all?"

"No. Do you think my symptoms are related to stress?"

"Well, you mentioned your wife's pregnant. It can be a stressful time." He's seeming to wait for me to say something, waiting for me to blubber on about the stresses of life. He starts to fill out something in the chart. "Well, we can rest assured that the tests are normal. I would like to see you back here in 3 weeks. In the meantime try to stop the smoking."

"Thanks doctor."

Driving home on I-50, traffic's pretty tight and I get in the fast lane, but no lane is good now. I thought once I moved from LA to Sacramento I'd never see traffic again. So much for expectations! The phone's ringing. It's Melissa.

"Hi, honey."

"Hi, Mel."

"How did it go at the doctors'?"

"Uh…everything turned out fine. He wants me to follow up with him."

"That's good. There's nothing to worry about."

"I just don't know why I feel so awful?"

"I don't know either." She pauses. "You haven't been sleeping well. Are you worried about something?"

"I guess a little bit."

"Are you worried about being a dad?"

"It's not just that. Work's been stressful. I've got that 401K presentation for Sandor Realty on Saturday and I don't want to blow it."

"Jacob, listen to me. You're not going to blow it. They wouldn't be giving you this chance if they didn't trust you."

"It'll be nice when the presentation's done and I can just relax."

"How about I make reservations for Saturday at Il Fornaio?"

"That sounds nice."

"So don't stress so much."

"OK. I'll try not to."

"Honey, I'm going to take a shower. Don't forget to pick up my pre-natal vitamins."

"I won't forget. I love you."

"Love you too."

Waiting in the pharmacy line at Rite-Aid with three people in front of me. I've got nothing to do but listen to the music and focus on the aisle of fiber supplements. My Lord, will I have to take these one day? The line's not moving. At the register there's a woman pleading with the pharmacist to talk to her doctor. She says the doctor's office faxed the prescription today, but the pharmacist says they don't have it. Oh boy! This is going to take a long time. Bono is singing in the background. *"But I still…haven't found…what I'm looking for."* An appropriate song for standing in this line, surrounded by laxatives and listening to this woman argue with the pharmacist about her Vicodin prescription. Cell phone's ringing. Thank God. It's Mom. I wonder what she wants.

"Hello."

"Jacob?"

"Yeah Mom."

"Are you busy?"

"Not really. What's going on?"

"It's your father. He's had a stroke."

"A stroke? No! Is he all right?" Mom doesn't answer. She's sniffling and deeply exhaling. "Mom?"

"From what they told me he's really sick. He's been in the hospital more than two weeks."

"Two weeks! What the hell! Why didn't you tell me sooner?"

"I just found out myself. I don't understand how they got my number and not yours, but that's not important."

"He's going to be all right, Mom. Right?"

"I don't know, Jacob. It's all in the Lord's hands."

"Damn! Damn!" The elderly man in front of me turns his head quickly to look at me. Fuck off, old man! I walk away from the line and slowly meander toward the exit. "Damn! Damn!" I yell thinking about my presentation and Melissa's pregnancy. What a shitty time for this to happen. "Shit!"

"Jacob, stop swearing! It doesn't do you any good." Mom yells over the phone.

"Sorry. This is a horrible time for this to happen."

"Is there ever a good time?"

"I just don't know when I can make it down there. There's so much going on up here." I feel a piercing pain on the left side of my head.

"He's your father, Jacob. Your work will understand."

"It's not just work. It's Melissa's pregnancy too and I'm the only one who can do this presentation on Saturday and it's important for us, especially with…"

"Jacob, that can wait. Your father can't. He has nobody down there."

"He'll have to wait!" I'm yelling.

46

"OK Jacob. I understand. Your job's important to you, I know. Look, I'm going to drive down tomorrow to see your father."

"Tomorrow?"

"Yes Jacob, tomorrow."

"Well, can you tell me how he's doing?"

"Of course."

"I'm sorry I can't go and meet you, but I'll go later. I promise."

"I understand. You've got your family to think about. Is Melissa doing OK?"

"She's fine. Mom, could you tell Dad that I love him and I'll be there as soon as I'm able? Don't tell him Melissa's pregnant. I want to tell him."

"Sure. I gave the hospital your cell phone number. They should be calling you soon. They were mentioning doing some procedure on him, for him to breathe better."

"What are they going to do?"

"I don't really know."

"Mom?"

"Don't worry Jacob. Christ will look after him. The Lord will be with him." That does not comfort me. I'm sure it doesn't comfort Dad. It's starting to feel chilly. "Jacob?"

"Yes, Mom."

"Everything will be all right. I'll call you tomorrow." I put the phone back in the holster, staring at the sun receding on the horizon, mechanically making my way to the car. Everything's going to be alright.

I drive home with no music, no sound but the rev of the engine. What am I supposed to do? Here's the house. Here's the driveway. Home... Three months in this house and now a baby and now this shit with Dad. I need Melissa. I need a drink. I walk into the house and make a beeline to the kitchen. Melissa's at the stove, focused on the bubbling pot of stew in front of her.

"You get my vitamins?"

"Oh, shit! I forgot. I went to the pharmacy and..."

"And what?"

"My father's in the hospital."

She puts down the ladle and walks up to me. "Is he going to be OK?"

"I don't know. He's had a stroke." Dad… God dammit, Dad! You can't pull this shit now! Melissa wraps her arms around me and holds me tight. Her belly rubs on my side and I'm feeling nauseous and weak in the knees. She pulls away from me and tries to look into my eyes, but I can't look at her.

"Jake, go sit on the couch. I'll turn down the stove and meet you there." She walks away, giving me the opportunity to walk over to the cupboard, pick up a glass and grab some ice from the freezer. I need a drink; Maker's Mark and a little water. It's time to take your medicine, Jake. The bourbon burns smoothly in the back of my throat.

Melissa's waiting for me at the couch. I go to her and rest my head in her lap. Melissa's stroking my hair and all I want to do is fall asleep.

"So, how bad is he?"

"I just want to lay here for a second."

"Jake? Come on, you can talk to me."

"I don't know. He's been in the hospital for more than two weeks."

"Two weeks? Why haven't they called you?"

"They didn't have our new phone number."

"When are you going down there?"

I need to sit up. "Do you want to come?" She doesn't say anything, and looking at her face I'm not going to wait for an answer. "You know what? It's probably not a good idea with the baby and all."

"I could come."

"Don't worry about it. The only thing is that I have to do this presentation on Saturday." I take another sip of the Maker's.

"Is the presentation that important?"

"You know it is. It will bring in maybe a hundred new 401K accounts and they're counting on me."

"Won't there be other accounts?" Doesn't she understand the kind of expense we're about to have?

"Not on the horizon. Not that I can count on." I need to stand up to think. OK, the first thing is to get everything set up with the prospectus forms, the power point slides and sign people up. Then, I'll fly down to L.A., deal with the mess down there without losing my marbles, come back here Monday evening and input the customer information.

Melissa's rubbing my back, distracting me from my thoughts. I turn to look at her face, her pink cheeks, and her look of devotion to me. My hand is over her enlarging belly, feeling our future. She nestles her head into my chest and my face drops down into her soft hair, my lips touch the top of her head.

"So, how bad is he?"

"I don't know. I don't know anything."

"You haven't talked to anyone from the hospital? Do you have the number for the hospital?"

"No, I'll have to call my mom back. She must have it. "

Mom gives me the number and I ring over to St. Luke's, where Dad went when he had his heart attack. And now a stroke. The man is the antithesis of health, smoking, drinking, and no concept of exercise. The hospital gives me the number of Dr. Masterson, the doctor taking care of Dad in the hospital. The operator for Dr. Masterson's office says that Dr. Masterson is not on call tonight, but that I can leave him a message at his office. Before I go to bed I take an Ambien.

Sitting in my office, waiting for the call, comparing the expense ratios for the Royce funds and the phone finally rings.

"Hello, Mr. Mathews?"

"Yes"

"I'm Dr. Masterson, the pulmonologist attending your dad."

"What's happened to him?"

"Your father's had a severe stroke. It caused bleeding and swelling in his brain. He's been on the ventilator for 17 days."

"17 days on a breathing machine?"

"He showed little signs of brain activity until about a week ago, and now there're some signs he's coming back. He's opening his eyes and moving his fingers on the right side."

"Coming back?"

"Waking up."

"So he's going to make it?"

"Well, he also has had pneumonia, coded, and had to be shocked. He's had some mild dysfunction of his kidneys."

"Is he going to make it?"

"He is improving, but slowly. Whether he'll make it, in the sense of survive? I'm not sure. Whether he'll make it, to recover fully enough to resume his life? That's pretty doubtful."

How can he say this so calmly?

"Mr. Mathews, we need to discuss a couple of procedures your father is going to need. The first one is called a tracheostomy. Right now your dad is breathing from a tube that goes into his mouth and ends in his lungs. The problem is the longer that tube is in there, the more chance he has of getting an infection and that's why he needs a tracheostomy."

"What's a trachy, uh tracheotomy?"

"A tracheostomy is where we make an opening in the front of the neck and then attach the ventilator to that opening."

"And he has pneumonia?"

"Yes, and we're treating it with antibiotics and...and...that sort of brings me to the next point. Your dad's nutritional level is pretty low. We're unable to feed him after his pneumonia, so he's been getting some nutrition through a vein in his arm, but it's not enough."

What's going on with my heart? Not again. Friggin' palpitations, that squeeze in the chest, and that vise around the head. It all sounds awful. "I thought you said he was getting better."

"He's improving, but he needs nutrition. He'll need a feeding tube placed through his skin into his stomach, if he's going to survive. Without nutrition he'll probably die."

This is not happening. "Just do what you need to, Doctor. You're the doctor. You know best."

"Mr. Mathews, did your dad ever mention his wishes if something like this were to happen to him?"

"No, he didn't."

"Do you think he wanted to be kept alive like this?"

"Why are you asking me this?"

"Well, the other option, instead of doing these procedures, is to keep him comfortable and see how he does."

"Comfortable. You mean pulling the plug."

"Not exactly. It's just that your father has had a large stroke and a period of time without oxygen and while he's recovering somewhat, he'll need to be maintained on artificial means, for probably a very long time, to be kept alive. It's important for us to know whether your father wants that."

Almost certainly. "This is my father, Doc."

"I know."

"Have you tried to talk to him about what he wants?"

"I'm not sure he could give us a clear answer."

"What if this were your father? I told you to do whatever you have to do. Don't give up on him."

"We're not giving up on him."

"OK, then! We're on the same page."

"Well, then we'll proceed with the tracheostomy and the gastric tube, as we've planned."

"OK. OK…Will he be in any pain?"

"He'll be sedated for these procedures."

"The trach… How do you pronounce that again?"

"Tracheostomy. It's a hole in the front part of his neck where we will connect the ventilator."

"I got that. When are you going to do it?"

"I think we are looking at Dr. Gold performing that operation tomorrow. We're going to need your approval for the procedure, in writing. Do you have a fax?"

"Yes, I do at work."

"If you'll give my office the number, they'll fax over the consent form."

"Thanks, doctor."

"Are you going to be coming to see your father?"

"I have to make arrangements, but I don't think I can make it down there until Sunday."

"Sunday? I'm not going to be in the hospital on Sunday, but I'll be there on Monday. I'll see you then."

Sitting in my office for I don't know how long, looking blankly at the computer. Get motivated Jake! I need to finish the paperwork on these last two annuities. The 401K presentation is in three days and I'm a wreck. Dad! Your life of abuse! This is my big chance. This is what I've worked for. Shoot, I have to better coordinate my lines with the PowerPoint; need to appear competent and unfaltering. Come on, Jake, you can do it!

51

Melissa's at her parents, so the home is empty. I get a drink and go outside for a smoke. I got to relax, sit down in one of these patio chairs from IKEA, take a puff from the cigarette, watch the moon suspended in the sky, but it's no use. Maybe I should just go down there and forget the presentation.

Dad... I haven't seen him for two years. Who the hell was this man? He tried to be some kind of rebel, always railing about the failures of government, like when I was seven and we went to that Japanese internment camp. "Fear your government, Jake. It's so easy for liberty to be taken away," he said when we were driving away. But the man was all American when it came to sports; took me to baseball games as a kid, watched them with me at home, took me to play T-ball and Little League. It was an obsession, like how he loved to read me stories. He was a good father, took Mom and me to Disneyland and the beach and how we'd all drive with the top down in his Mustang. That was fun, listening to music with the top down. But something changed along the way and he became no fun at all.

Closing my eyes, I try to recall the man of my youth: lanky, serious, and always somewhat distant like he was above it all. Maybe, I never really understood who he was. He loved me, but he could be so damn critical of me for just being me. It seemed like nothing I did measured up to his lofty demands. Like I failed because I couldn't be the son he wanted me to be, his Sixties drugged-out hippie love-child.

How could he criticize me? So damn hypocritical! Look how he fucked up his life! What kind of career did he have? He was a failed writer. He thought he was some kind of rebel, but in the end he was a just a manager for a second-rate stereo store who got lucky buying a house when property values were low, lucky that Grandpa Josh helped support his rear; and he almost lost all of Grandpa's money on that stupid real estate LLC. He didn't know Jack about handling money.

And then there was how he treated mom, always arguing with her, needling her into arguments. What kind of marriage did he have? Pushed us both away! He always thought he knew the right answers and still thinks that way, always disappointed I went after the things I wanted and not what he wanted. He doesn't come out and say it, but I can hear it in his voice and can see it in his face. He put down my career, always bringing it up by snidely asking, "So how's Wall Street?" No wonder I don't talk to him anymore.

I haven't even told him that Melissa's pregnant. Shit... I sip some more of the Maker's and slide back comfortably in the chair. Criticize me? What did he ever do with his life?

Chapter 4

What Are We Going to Do With Him?

"Mr. Mathews. Mr. Mathews." There's a grey haired man with a moustache peering over the blue tube and down at me. He's seems younger than his salt-and-pepper hair.

"Mr. Mathews, I'm Dr. Masterson, the lung doctor. Mr. Mathews, do you understand me?" Sure man, I understand. He's pausing for a second, looking at my eyes. "We've been following you for some time in the hospital and I think you should know what we've been doing lately. Mr. Mathews, contents from your stomach came up and you swallowed them into your lungs. We had to go into your airways to suction out all that material. We have you on antibiotics and you're doing much better, but the problem is you've had the tube in your lungs for more than two weeks. Do you understand?"

Dude, I can't even respond to you. My lips are too dry to move and even if they could move I've got this massive tube between my dry lips. I'm a monster, a deformed, disgusting mass, unable to fall under the definition of human being, but desiring to feel human again. I understand what you're saying, Doctor. I understand what you're saying. How can I make you comprehend my ability to comprehend? He's making eye contact with me as if he's trying to understand me.

"Mr. Mathews, can you do something for me? I want you to blink twice if you understand me. Can you do that for me now?"

It seems simple enough. My eyes are open now. All I have to do is close them, open them, and then close them again. Can I do this? There's a look of impatience in his eyes. OK, I'm going to do it. I'm closing my eyes and the figure in front of me disappears. OK, so now I'll reopen my eyes and there is the good doctor looking intently at me. Well now, what were the directions? Blink twice? Did I blink twice already? I can remember opening and closing my eyes, but I think I only did that once. I probably should do it again, just in case. Closing my eyes again the image of Dr. Masterson disappears and reappears when they open again.

"That's good Mr. Mathews. Really good!" He clears his throat. "Mr. Mathews, I know you can't talk, but I want to make sure you are OK with what we've done so far."

"Hi, Joseph," a voice calls out from somewhere on the other side of the room.

Dr. Masterson looks up. "Hello, Marvin."

There's somebody is on my right side that I can't see.

"Hey Marv, I think he's coming around a bit. He blinked on my command."

"I don't see why he can't do that." Marvin says. "His stroke was right fronto-parietal."

"Well, he's much better than before."

"So the pneumonia looks better on X-ray."

"Yeah, I saw it today."

"I'd keep him on Cefipime and Vanco for another 7 days." A bearded man appears above the blue tube. "Hi, Mr. Mathews it's Dr. Johnson." I remember you. You're the infection guy. He turns his head to the other doctor.

"Is he going to get a tracheostomy?" Dr. Johnson questions.

"That's the plan. Dr. Gold is going to do it tomorrow."

"Did Social Services get in touch with his son?"

"They did and I talked to his son and his ex-wife."

"What did his son say?"

"About?"

"About what he wants us to do?"

"He said, 'Do everything you can to keep him alive.'"

"What a surprise. Maybe he'll feel different when he sees his father. When's he coming down?"

"Sunday"

"Sunday!" Dr. Johnson lifts up his eyebrows and drops his jaw in disbelief. "Are you serious? Didn't you explain his father's condition?"

"Yes, I did. He said that he had obligations to attend to, so we're going to do the tracheostomy tomorrow with his permission." Dr. Masterson sounds defiant. "How about we move away from the bedside?"

They've both stepped away, but not far enough, for I still hear them.

"You know as well as I that the quality of this man's life is poor and that keeping him alive like this will do him more harm than good," Dr. Johnson fires.

"More harm? I can't be the judge of one's quality of life, or one's desire to live, no matter how bad their lot might be. His son wants him to stay alive. There must be a reason."

"Well, have you talked to Bill Gellman about this patient?"

"Of course… About what issue specifically?"

"About the issue of a living will, about the issue of what this man wanted at the end of his life."

"Gellman says he doesn't have a living will."

"I'm sorry to belabor the point, but…"

"Marv, my work is critical care and keeping these people alive. It would be nice if he had a living will, but he does have a son who can speak for him and that son wants him alive. The ICU is often a family's last hope of seeing their loved one alive."

"But for how long? How long do you keep a patient alive? Joe, I understand the need for ICU care when a life is salvageable, but I don't understand the need for prolonged ICU care with a ventilator and a gastric tube when the quality of life is so poor."

"Marv, that's not for you to define. And really, this isn't the place to debate it."

"You would think that after his heart attack, Bill Gellman would have approached him about a living will."

Living will? Dr. Gellman never mentioned that to me. Why is Doctor Johnson making such a big deal over this? Doesn't he have other patients to see? I wanted to die before, but now…now I want to wait until Jacob gets here, to see him again, to see his face, and maybe to say goodbye to him. Those two doctors are walking away but Dr. Johnson keeps talking.

"Don't get me wrong. I'm all for saving lives, if those lives are salvageable, but when a person's health is so poor, it's like whipping a dead horse, trying to get it to run again. I don't know, but I don't think this man cared too much about his life to begin with."

Wait a second, buddy! There was a time I really did care about my life. It was the whole fucking system that didn't care about me. Shit! I must have had some stupid, naïve notion about what this

56

place was about, but medicine is just like the whole god damn system! To it I'm just another record number, just an average Joe. Any idea of being an individual, my stories, my family, my favorite baseball team, my religion, or lack of one, does not mean shit in this place. It certainly doesn't mean much to these two doctors.

And did my life ever truly mean anything? No! No! That's the wrong question. Did my life ever truly mean anything to anybody other than me? I think so. I influenced Jacob; put my heart and soul into him. And my life was an important part of my parents' life and Sarah's life. The question really is, do I have any meaning to anybody now or is my significance an idea that's lost somewhere in the past? Is my significance a weathered picture of me with a smiling face? I don't know what to think. If I could, I'd walk out of here, get in my car and visit Jacob and Melissa.

"Dad, they said you were in the hospital and you were very sick."

"I'm better now Jake. I am better now," I say embracing my son. The image fades to black.

"Hey, Mathews, I need your help. One of our choppers barely made it here. Hit by enemy fire while transporting downed soldiers."

"What do you need me to do, sir?"

"I need you and Brady to move the bodies to the transport plane."

"Bodies?"

"The dead soldiers, dipshit."

"Yes, sir."

"The chopper is right next to the airfield so it should be easy to load them on."

"How do we move the bodies, sir?"

"You put the bodies on gurneys. Get the gurneys from medical."

"Yes, sir."

"Don't forget, you still have to take inventory on what you unloaded yesterday."

"I won't forget, sir."

"OK, get going."

57

I walk out of the barracks and find Brady over at the commissary. We walk over to the medical area.

"I need a couple of gurneys with wheels."

"What for?"

"We need to move the dead from a downed chopper."

"You'll need to make sure they're clean when you bring them back."

We walk out. Brady is pushing the gurney forward. "Why do we have to do this crappy job?"

I look at him for a moment as we walk. "Would you rather carry a gun in a swamp, surrounded by hostile fire?"

"No."

"Then shut your mouth and consider yourself lucky."

It takes about five minutes to get over to the helicopter, which is right next to the transport plane. The tree covered hills are in the background. The air lately has felt a little drier and the mosquitoes have not been as active, but I still get bit on the back of my neck. If only I could have kept my hair long, I wouldn't have all these welts back there. The chopper has a big blackened area in the rear within which is a gaping hole. There's a man in front of the chopper smoking a cigarette.

"Are you here to move these men."

"Yes, sir," I respond.

"Well, get them moving then. We need to move these bodies out by 15:00."

There they are, green body bags, I'd guess ten of them in the back of the chopper, some piled on top of each other. The smell is not as foul as I expected.

"Let's get this over with."

I reach in and pull at one of the plastic bags lying on top. It doesn't move. "What the hell are you standing there for? I need your help."

Brady grabs the other end of the bag. I move my arms underneath and leverage them against the lifeless arms within.

"Lift him on the count of three. One, two, three."

I pull my side up and I feel the back of a head rest on my chest, the neck limp and wobbly. We get him on and wheel him over to the other helicopter about fifty yards away and lift him in. We go

58

back and forth between the two choppers. After about the fifth body, I've had enough.

"You're right, this is a crappy job," I say.

"I told you so."

"This is so fucking depressing. Why the hell are we here? Why the hell am I here?"

"You got drafted."

"I know. But I could have gone to Canada. I could have run away."

"It's too late now, man. Come on, we got five more bodies left."

"The whole fucking system. It don't care about me, it don't care about you and it sure don't care about these five godforsaken dead guys."

"Hey, Paul?"

"What?"

Brady smiles, "Why don't you just shut your mouth and consider yourself lucky."

Ouch! That's sharp! Someone's sticking a needle in the front of my neck and it's burning. But now the pain's disappeared. There's a man standing above me with a syringe in his hand. He's wearing a blue gown, glasses, a blue mask covering his lower face, and a blue paper cap.

"His eyes are open. Did you give him sedation?"

"Yes, doctor."

"Where are the gauze pads? I said to get everything at the bedside for the tracheostomy, including gauze pads. I don't have a lot of time here. Get me some gauze now" the man yells out.

"Dr. Gold, there are gauze pads in the tracheostomy kit," a woman's voice answers.

"I know that. Don't you think I know that? I asked for gauze pads," Dr. Gold yells out.

"Well, I thought the gauze pads were in the kit," a quivering female voice responds. "I thought those were the gauze pads you meant."

"I told you to do something and you did not do it. It's not your job to think."

59

This guy doesn't sound very nice to me. Dr. Masterson talked about the tracheostomy, but I didn't think much about it. Isn't a tracheostomy where they put an opening in your neck so you can breathe? I've only seen tracheotomies on TV, where some smoker who was never able to stop would use the opening to inhale from a cigarette.

A familiar Asian woman's face comes into my view. She's doing something to my neck, but I can't see what she's doing. She has this mechanical look about her and after the doctor's tirade she appears glad to be doing something that doesn't take much thought. She pulls open a blue plastic drape and covers my vision with it. I'm now looking at blue; a beautiful dark blue, a peaceful blue filled with multiple little squares. The sounds of my breathing are in unison with the respirator and I'm feeling an ease that I don't think I should be feeling. They're putting a frickin hole in my neck! Why are they doing that? There's pressure at the front of my neck. There are the sounds and the sensations of crunching and popping, as they open up this space in my neck.

"I don't know which stereo to get. Do you prefer the Ban Sonic or the Panasonic? The Ban Sonic is much cheaper." In front of me is an elderly Asian man, with no accent, wearing gold-rimmed glasses. He has grayish-black hair and a thin face with wrinkles on the outer edge of his eyes. He's tall for an Asian, as tall as I am.

"Ban Sonic is a newer company. Their products are made cheaper, but I haven't had any complaints with them. The Panasonic's record player, though, has a real smooth sound I believe sells the product. For me, it would be worth the difference. Would you like to listen?"

"Yes, I would." We walk to the stereos.

"What would you like to listen to?" I hold up records of Chicago, Seals and Croft, Three Dog Night, Gustav Holst and Beethoven. He looks the records over.

"Could you play "Venus" on the *Planets* record?" He smiles as if remembering a moment.

"Sure thing, you're going to love this." I put the record on the turntable and the sound from the speakers comes through beautifully. I love Holst's Planets. Mars has a bombastic, destructive style that makes the listener feel the Rapture is upon us and that the Lord himself and all his minions have come to destroy everything, but then comes the sad plaintive Venus as if to say, 'What have we done? Why have we destroyed something so beautiful?' I can see Venus looking there through the ashes, the carcasses of plant and animal life returned to their elemental carbon forms, hoping to find some blade of grass, some little flower, some sign of life, and it is to this life she is singing to, this cute, innocent, playful life, trying to bring it to full bloom.

The Asian man smiles and while I feel pressured to sell, I listen too. The music makes me think of little Jacob, springing through life following the tune of his singing Venus, who he believes watches the moments of his life. It's a sad day when one realizes that nobody is watching and that you're all alone. The song finishes with a whimsical note of early life.

"That's beautiful. It's amazing how clear the sound is," he says. He wears a collared yellow, short sleeved shirt and long slacks that run down to his brown shoes.

"It sure is. Holst really runs the emotional gamut."

"Do you want to listen to Mars?"

"That would be wonderful." The music plays.

Music means so much to me; truly my escape. I could simply sit and listen to an entire album. Maybe that's why I like working at Watson's and it is steady work, unlike the income from my journalistic career which is inconsistent, and I sure don't want to work for Dad. I've always been good at selling things. Now if only I could sell my writing…

"Robert, I'm over here." The old man has called out to a younger version of himself. The man walking toward the elder man is in middle age, also wearing gold-rimmed glasses. He places his arm around his father, so his hand sits perched upon his shoulder.

"Robert, I think I am going to buy the Panasonic. Wouldn't it be great to sit on the porch and listen to Holst or Mahler or Gershwin?"

"That sounds great," the son replies.

61

"I'm going to sit on my porch and listen to music!" he says to both of us. The son and father seem so comfortable with one another.

"Well don't forget the speakers also. The one's you're listening to now are without any vibration. Do you here how clear that sounds?" They both listen on cue until the old man's son speaks.

"Dad, I'm going to get the kids. They're back at the aquarium."

"I'll see you back here then."

"Do you want to listen to the Ban Sonic?"

"I don't think I need to," the old man smiles.

The son leaves and I go to get the Panasonic and the speakers from stock. We meet at the counter. The man has a contented smile on his face, seeming so at peace, making me want to ask him how I too can find peace; a peace that alludes me at work, at home, when I'm with Sarah, even when I'm simply sitting, doing nothing .

"How many children do you have?" I ask tangentially.

"I have four, but I only have two here in Los Angeles."

"Your son seems very close to you. I have a son. He's four."

"A wonderful age."

"I hope that when I'm older I can have as good a relationship with my son as you do with yours." What the hell just came out my mouth? He looks puzzled and it takes him a while to speak.

"Yes, we have a good relationship now, but the relationship has been a difficult one and, as with anything in life, it was not easy." What made their relationship so difficult? He answers my inquisitive stare. "We were in a Japanese internment camp in the Owens Valley for two years."

"Oh yeah, I heard about those internment camps when I was in college and I heard about that book *Farewell to...Farewell to...* ".

"*Manzanar*"

"Yeah, Manzanar. That's awful! Your son was with you?"

"Yes, Robert was only ten at the time and my youngest was only two. It was not easy. All we had was each other."

"I can't even imagine."

"One good thing, though, was that it brought us closer together and made us appreciate life. Sometimes when life is too easy one can neglect the vital things."

"I've never met anyone who was in an internment camp. Um...I do some writing for the Santa Monica *Outlook*. Could I interview you for a piece?" This may be a good story.

I'm walking to his house in Culver City. Bamboo lines both sides of the property. There's a lawn in front and a concrete walkway leading straight to a white Spanish-style house with a red roof and a wooden door. Daniel Aoyama opens the door and walks me to his back yard. He beckons me to sit at a table on his wooden porch. His wife, a full-faced Japanese woman looking younger than what I guess must be her age, brings us glasses of lemonade. The yard has lemon, orange and fig trees and has a pebble walkway that meanders along both sides of the backyard. Two Japanese maples, with their baby green leaves, stand next to the porch.

"This is beautiful."

"Yes, it is nice" he says. "It's my own little world."

"Did you make this garden yourself?"

"Me and the wife." He points to inside the house.

"I've never met anyone from a Japanese internment camp. Could you tell me more about them." I start the tape recorder and remove a pen and paper.

"There were many internment camps, but I only really know about the one our family was at."

"Well, tell me your story."

"I was working for Hughes aircraft as an engineer, living with my wife and four children, not far from here, in Culver City. My parents were retired and lived close to us. They would come over on many days during the week to play with the children."

My story will begin with a placid existence, sort of like the calm before the storm. This is going to be good. I instinctively reach for my shirt pocket to fetch my Marlboros.

"Do you mind if I smoke?"

"I'm sorry, the smoke bothers me," he answers. The cigarettes slide back into my pocket.

"So tell me how it was like here in Los Angeles?"

"It was different then, not as crowded, and people were friendly. We knew everyone who lived on our block. Our children went to school and we would celebrate Christmas, Easter and the Fourth of

July with our neighbors. My parents were from Japan, but my wife and I were born in America and we thought of ourselves as Americans."

"But not everyone thought of you as Americans? You looked different right?"

"We tried our best to fit in, but there were always some people though who didn't care that we knew the Pledge of Allegiance, that we played baseball, that we listened to jazz, that we believed in Roosevelt and his ability to get us out of the Depression. They saw themselves as the sole proprietors of America, and while they rarely said it to our faces they felt that we Japanese Americans should never integrate into their society."

"And then Pearl Harbor happened." He puts his arms up in the air. "What was Japan thinking? Attack the most powerful country in the world, just when they were realizing that they were the most powerful country in the world. Like waking a sleeping lion! No good! So stupid! Our lives changed after Pearl Harbor. We suddenly became ostracized, outcasts with slanted eyes. In the beginning there was a great silence around us except for some men, women and children who would find it quite easy to yell, 'Go home, Jap!' A few months later I was fired from Hughes Aircraft, along with other Japanese workers."

"So how did you survive?"

"Soon people would not sell us groceries. We could only get food from Japanese farmers. Life began to spiral beyond our control. My ten-year-old son would get beaten up by boys in his school and we felt powerless to do anything about it except take our children out of school. We then began hearing of Japanese people's homes being vandalized. Soon people came to our house throwing beer bottles and destroying our lawn. Our neighbors no longer spoke to us and gave us disapproving looks. We were afraid to socialize with other Japanese people for fear we would be implicated in a conspiracy against the United States. So, we maintained this level of fear for six months, fearful, not only of the government but of the people around us. Our lives were desperate and we did not feel like we were people in the land of the free and the home of the brave. Then the government surprisingly came to our rescue and sent us to the Manzanar Relocation Center. We were only allowed to take a certain amount of items with us."

"Wait a second. What do you mean that the government came to your rescue?"

"It's funny how much anti-government sentiment there is today."

"For good reason."

"And what has the government done to you?"

"Shipped me off to Vietnam."

"That was not a good war."

"No, it wasn't. I was lucky not to be on the front lines. No, no…I have no love for the government."

"Speaking only for my family, we were more afraid of the people around us than of the government. The government saved us. We were afraid that we would be killed because the people were so angry at us. I tried to say to those Americans that it was not I who attacked them. But they wanted some form of retribution and we looked like the enemy, so I was glad to leave, although I did not know where I was being taken."

"They took you to Manzanar. Wasn't that in the desert?"

"Manzanar is in the middle of the Owens Valley, in the middle of nowhere."

"Was it hot?"

"Hot in the summer and cold in the winter, and dry all the time. About four hours north of here. When we arrived, there were army personnel to greet us. They wanted us to sign a declaration that we were only citizens of the United States and that we would rescind all ties with Japan. This was easy for me, but much more difficult for my parents, who were born in Japan. But we all signed." He looks down with a pensive expression, takes a deep breath, then gets up slowly to walk to the fig tree, picks two figs, then sits back, placing a fig in front of me.

"So what was camp like, at Manzanar?"

"The facilities were surrounded by barbed wire and were still being constructed when we arrived. They had made these large barracks that were a football field long and there were multiple families sleeping in one of these barracks. I remember the bathrooms. The funny thing about the bathrooms is that they had no partitions. You were sitting on a toilet, relieving yourself and trying not to look at Jim Tanaka who was doing the same. And I never could get used to going to the communal showers."

"So your family stayed together?"

"I was with my wife and four children in one of these barracks. We tried to develop a routine and a world for ourselves and for our children. We built a school and all the children would go to school. I worked in a camouflage net factory and my wife planted crops. Yet within our routine we were observed by 'Americans' in watchtowers."

"Tell me more about the factory."

"Anyone could work at the camouflage net factory, if he were an American citizen. We were placed on a quota system and we had to produce so many nets for the army. The work was grueling and the workers, who were both men and women, would be exhausted by the end of the day. We worked in a building with poor ventilation in unbearable heat; the evaporated sweat of our bodies gave the place an unusually high humidity. And a very bitter smell. The working conditions became more difficult with time and the army officers would yell at us. 'No slacking,' they said. They never hit us, but we always had fear of what these officers would do to us, so we kept doing what we were told."

"Didn't you get angry? They enslaved you and then they make you work for the army?"

"We were prisoners of war." He looks away for an instant.

"In a way." Not according to the Geneva Convention, but I had to let that go. This was his story, not mine. "But I would still be angry."

"We were angry, but it took some time for our fomenting anger to become a unifying voice. We pleaded with the army officers to make better working conditions, but it all fell on deaf ears, and then one day, one of the workers just stopped working after being berated by a white army officer. 'I will not work for you. I am an American, just like you,' he said turning toward the guard. He stood facing that guard as we all watched. The guard, not wanting to lose his authority, pulled out his baton and hit the worker on the side of the head, causing him to fall to the ground. Then one worker after the next stopped working. We began yelling at the guard. 'Who gives you the right to hit us? We are Americans' and many more things that I don't remember. We all stopped working and the white guards did not know what to do, since we outnumbered them. They ran out of that metal building, yelling that there was a riot. They then brought army reinforcements who began clubbing us with their batons and then I remember some gunshots and seeing some of my coworkers fall to the ground. One person died and many of us were injured. The camouflage net factory then ceased to exist." He looks off in the distance. This is a hell of a story.

"Were you hurt?"

"Some cuts on my hands and face, but that was from tripping and falling when I was running away." I look at his face, but I don't see any scars.

"So, what else did do you there besides building the nets?"

"We got very little news about the war, so we didn't know the progress being made in the Pacific or how long we'd be at Manzanar. We built a school, a hospital, a clothing shop, a picnic area and a post office. We had fields where we grew vegetables and we had pens to keep farm animals; plenty of chicken and pigs, but not many cattle. Everyone contributed and there was a certain sense of closeness that developed among us Japanese Americans in this desert landscape; a closeness of community, a closeness of non-individuality."

I think I understand his meaning, sort of. "What do you mean by non-individuality?"

He takes a bite of the fig, slowly chewing the fruit, swallowing, and then clearing seeds and pulp between his teeth and cheek with his tongue. His eyes turn toward me, they size me up and I feel I'm being judged. "After some time of being in this community, where each one of us, man, woman and child, did something to improve the situation, our individuality became a dwindling phenomenon and only could be defined in relation to the group. It was as if we were all falling and did not have anything safe to hold on to except our society of Japanese Americans. Today, we are so busy being individuals, but our individuality is an illusion, *sansari*, providing a sense of importance that really has no substance. Without the focus on the self, you are more likely to listen and interact with your community and the natural world. I'm sorry, I digress."

"That's OK. I like your rant. Don't stop. Keep going. I want to know more." He smiles and I notice a piece of fig on his upper tooth.

"So, after about a year of internment, the same army that imprisoned us asked us to join the ranks and fight in Europe. Some of the young men joined and some of the young men in our community died."

"I didn't know that? How could they do that? They were treated rotten by the government and then they were going to fight for them?" The stupid propaganda machine could make anyone follow its wishes.

"It sounds strange, doesn't it?" he laughs.

"Disturbing is the word that comes to mind. How could you let that happen?"

"Not disturbing. They chose to go. Was I somehow to stop them?"

He pauses and looks at me with a kind of curiosity. I feel like an idiot.

Mercifully, he goes on. "We were able to live a peaceable life. We were being protected by the government. I should be sure you understand: we did not have a great fear that the government would harm us. Not once we were settled. I think many of us, who were older, realized that we were being treated quite well compared to the customs of other countries. If we were the enemy in those countries we would have had a quite different fate. If we were in Germany we would have been gassed, if in Russia, China, and, even Japan, we would have been shot. In comparison, the United States treated us with some degree of respect. I think they finally realized we were its citizens too and Manzanar was not so bad. Even after the internment ended some of the people wanted to stay, fearful more of the outside world, but that did not last."

"Don't you hold some resentment toward the country that imprisoned you?"

"Some resentment, but actually very little anger. What I remember most is the closeness I felt with my family, going to my son's baseball games, helping my children with their homework. I remember moments of meditation, sitting at the edge of a pond that the community had made and looking up at the grand Sierra Nevadas with their jagged rocks, their stillness and my own stillness; watching the sun's rays peering between the mountains down into the valley, the magical glow of waning light, the birds and bats hovering about, feeding on the wealth of flying insects, the warmth of the desert, the love I felt for nature's process, the happiness of being able to reflect, reflecting that I, too, was part of that process, that my children were the tiny sprigs of grass that nature had sprouted, that I would cultivate them with this love, the love for the sky, the earth, the living things and those things that were once living. To be sitting there quiet with all these thoughts, I realize now that I will never know a more peaceful time in my life."

His eyes are wide behind his thick glasses. He takes a deep breath in, holds it for a second, then exhales, allowing his shoulders and neck to relax. I'm not sure what else to say. As a reporter I should be asking more questions, but he pretty much did the interview himself. I stop the tape recorder.

"I'll call you if this gets printed."

This is a good story, better than the story of the old woman who fed the hundreds of rats in her house. He walks me to the front of his house and I thank him for the opportunity to hear his story. He leaves me with some parting words.

"If you are looking for a good relationship with your children, you have to open your heart to them, you have to hold them higher than any lofty career goal and you have to give of yourself, until the border of what is you and what is them becomes a faded line."

Sounds too stern to me, too much like Dad. Yet it makes sense. Bright light is flooding into my eyes and I'm back in the hospital room. The sounds of the television slowly fade into my consciousness, as do the sounds of the respirator, which follow the rhythm of my breathing. But something is different. There's no tube obstructing my vision and I can actually see, fully, the ceiling with the perfectly aligned holes. Do those holes somehow allow for better ventilation or are they just decorative? The blue tube is now in the front of my neck and it must be connected to the respirator. My lips are finally touching each other again.

Daniel Aoyama. How old would he be now? He'd probably be a hundred. It wouldn't surprise me if he's still alive and taking care of that garden. The story I wrote was pretty much a verbatim transcription of our conversation and Gino published it right away in the *Outlook*. Gino was a good guy for an editor and I know he wanted me to do well. I never thanked him when he forwarded my story to *L.A. Times*. I remember the picture in the *Times* article. Daniel Aoyama, his wife, his children and his many grandchildren posed in the desert, with great mountains behind them. Mr. Aoyama had a boyish smile and his arms around two of his children.

Those fifteen milliseconds of fame were totally unexpected. The pride I saw in Mom and Dad's face the day we came over with the article was unforgettable. Dad put his arm around me. "That was a great story, beautifully written Paul." Afterward we left Jacob at their house and drove up the coast in the Mustang to celebrate. Maybe I let that little bit of success get to my head, because looking at the Malibu beach houses and the houses up on the cliffs, I thought loftily that one day maybe we'd live in such a house, among the powerful, and those worries about money and the future would cease. Success was right around the corner. After a shiftless existence, an undirected apprenticeship, I thought my time had come. We had a candlelight dinner at Alice's Restaurant on the pier in Malibu; a moment of freedom from Jacob, a moment of intimacy. We were holding each other on the pier after dinner, looking at the crescent moon as it set into the ocean, hearing the tumble of the waves and kissing. "I'm proud of you, Paul. You really did it." It could never get better than that. It never would.

Chapter 5

Disquiet

"Chuck, tell her what's behind the curtain."

"A Brand-New Car!"

A woman's screaming hysterically, seeming unable to stop. For the love of God, she's actually sobbing, taking deep breaths to try and maintain her composure.

"The 2004 Geo Prism, with automatic transmission, plush interior, adjustable seats, cruise control, AM/FM stereo, automatic locks and air conditioning. An ultimate driving experience for today's driver."

"Carol, Carol, let me tell you how to play this game. This is the over-or-under game. You have to tell me if the price under the domestic item is over or under the actual retail price. Now Carol do you understand?"

"Yes I do." She's practically gasping for air.

Bob Barker mentions the price ($4.59) for Palmolive Liquid Detergent and the poor woman has to decide if the price of the product is too high or too low. I used to watch this show all the time at work and during retirement, finding this game difficult, because there could be a huge variation in the price of the product, depending on where you bought the product and if it was on sale.

"Manufacturer's suggested retail price: four dollars ninety-five cents. Carol you have just won the car!" Carol lets out an emotional flood, sounding as though she's suffering, being disemboweled, giving birth or, as in the case of some women, having an orgasm. It's overdone, yet part of me feels happy for Carol. She deserves it. It's been a long, weary life for her and she sure deserves some hope that the universe does not turn a blind eye to her. That she too is special. Yeah, I had my moment as well. The "Price is Right" theme with its happy horn is playing.

What happened to my old friends, the ones I've lost touch with, the ones I'll never see again? I'm so alone, no one to talk to, no one to relate to my predicament; just like I'm in a box, having no contact with the outside world. It would be nice to see Ray Livorno again. "What do you say man? They're extending happy hour until eight at Whiskey's. Let's get shit-faced tonight." This is the type of loneliness before New Year's and sometimes Christmas, when I often would just watch movies or drive, maybe go to a strip joint if I was really desperate. These holidays of forced group activities were like a death sentence if you were alone and so isolated you would give anything for some form of human contact. We are social animals. We need each other. Damn! I wish I'd not been so stubborn and pushed people away for the consolation of a solitary life, for speaking to my imaginary alter ego, for writing that book; a book that will be read by nobody. Why have I done this to myself? My self-righteousness is biting me in the ass! I'm going to die alone! I'm going to die! I see to the front of the room and the sliding glass doors with an empty hallway behind. Nobody's around me. It's just me! I don't want to be alone. I'm crying. How do I wipe these tears from my face? The most I can do is move my right wrist a small amount. I'm choking. One of machines is dutifully beeping. Help! This is such a pitiful state. Someone please help me! Please help me! Does anybody care? I'm coughing.

"What's going on here?" A figure's passing on my left. She's hovering above me, looking down at my neck and now looking at me. It's the black nurse, Marge. She's looking at my eyes and her eyes reflect the sadness that I feel. She gives a thin smile and her eyes wrinkle up. There are many dark freckles below her lower eyelids. She places her hand on my forehead.

"You poor thing, you must have had a bad dream." She's touching my forehead. Her hand is soft and it runs into my hair, parting my hair. Her nails sensitize my scalp as she croons, "Everything is going to be OK. Everything is going to be OK." Shoot, I forgot I had hair and it feels nice to notice this semblance of my humanity. My breath slows and I'm feeling calmer. Everything will be all right. It's not a solitary existence. Mother Earth will always be there to welcome me back into her arms. The aloneness I feel may be only a temporary thing.

Marge is so nice to me, giving me love and I don't care for what reason. "Don't you worry. Don't you worry." The tears are coming down again. The more I try to stop from crying the more my body convulses. I know I shouldn't worry. There's really nothing I can do. A tear drops from Marge's eye and I wonder if I remind her of anyone. Her attentiveness to me sort of reminds me of when I first met Sarah. How she doted over me. She stops caressing my hair. "Try to relax now. Everything's going to be OK. Nobody should have to go through this, but it's all going to be OK," she says with a smile and she bends down, disappearing below my field of vision. She walks behind me, spending a moment back there and then walks out of the room. The room becomes dark. Thank God for nurses.

"Paul, you are not listening to me!" It's Sarah. What happened to Marge? Boy, Sarah looks angry. What the hell have I done? Her nostrils flare, her eyebrows point down, her forehead wrinkles, her arms are crossed and covering her breasts. Women can look so ugly when they're angry. Jacob and I are sitting on the couch watching the World Series, Dodgers versus Yankees, 1978, but we can't see the television due to this angry female.

"Sarah, keep your voice down, the neighbors will hear you." Reggie Jackson's up in the ninth inning, one of the greatest home run hitters of all time, yet one of the best at missing the ball with his bat. Bob Welch is pitching. The tension is mounting and we're hoping for a strikeout against our most hated rival, the Yankees.

Regaining some composure, Sarah tries to talk to me in the same reasonable, maternal way she reserves for Jacob, but the tension is still in her posture. "Paul, we're going to visit my mom and dad tomorrow. You know this and we've discussed it! Now, we have to get ready for tomorrow. We are going to be there for four days and you guys are not even packed yet and you said you were going to try to fix the stove before we left. Ever since I came home, you've both been watching this baseball game."

"Honey, this is the ninth inning. I'll do what I said when the game is over."

She turns around and turns the TV off.

"Mom, the game's almost over." Jacob whines.

"Sarah, turn the TV on, now!"

73

"Jacob, it's past your bedtime. We need to get you to bed." Sarah walks over to the couch. "Come on now. Let's go." She pulls at his hand.

"I'm not going." He arches his head back and dives backward into the couch.

"Jacob, we're going to go to Grandma Carol's and Grandpa Joe's house tomorrow. We have to wake up early to get there, and you still need to pack."

"I don't want to go." Jacob says, not realizing the gravity of his words. I'm trying not to smile, because I don't want to go either.

"You don't mean that," Sarah says. "You loved it last time we went fishing there."

"Honey, it is sort of boring for a kid." Whoops! She darts me hell-fire look. I don't care. Sarah's parents are boring, stale, bible-thumpers to the core and they're always judging me for my "liberal" views. The most interesting thing about going to their house is going fishing.

"Fine, Paul, you go take Jacob to his room and start packing his things."

There's nothing I can do. The World Series... Doesn't she know how important this is? I'm looking at her and know that I'm up against an irrational, immovable force, so I take Jacob to his room as he's bawling.

"It's not fair! I want to watch the game! It's not fair."

"Mommy's right. We need to pack and you need to go to bed. Reggie's probably already struck out." I help Jacob pack his clothes and get his baseball mitt, a baseball and a few comic books he likes. I read him a story, get him to bed and turn out the light. Fixing the stove will be easy. It's just a simple problem of the pilot going out because there's not enough gas going to it. So I take a wire brush and clean out the gas line and *voilà*, gas goes to the pilot, light the pilot and the problem is over. That crazy woman! I go to the television quickly, turn it on, but the game is over. Well, I'll have to read about it tomorrow. I slowly make my way to the bedroom, unrealistically hoping to avoid another argument. Sarah's sitting on the edge of the bed, looking frayed. Her head and neck are lowered as she rests her forehead on her hand.

74

"Is everything OK, honey?" I timidly ask, as I sit next to her. She begins to cry and lays her head with its blond hair on my lap. I stroke her hair lovingly, while at the same time feeling somewhat aroused by the presence of her face breathing heavily into my lap. It's been a long time since her head has been down there. She picks up her head and looks at me, choking on the words as her bottom lip turns downward.

"Do you understand why I was so angry?"

Why *she* was so angry? When is it my turn to be angry?

"I think so," I hear myself say.

Sarah sits up and looks at me with her reddened eyes. "I was angry at you because I asked you to do something and you told me you were going to do it, and you didn't do it. You had the whole day off! Then you make me look like the bad guy in front of Jacob."

"I was going to, but I realized that I had not paid the mortgage bill nor the gas bill, and then I had to go back to work to collect my paycheck, and then deposit my paycheck, then I promised myself that I'd write a bit, then I had to pick Jacob up from school, then Jacob and I played some catch, then I thought 'Oh the World Series is on tonight. It won't take long to pack and I can spend some quality time with my son.' I put a couple of Swanson's meals in the oven and we sat and watched the game. I was explaining to him all the nuances of the game and we were both getting in to it and then you came in."

"Honey, I'm sorry, but when I came home and saw you sitting on the couch, doing nothing, I got angry."

"You sure did. And it wasn't as if I was doing nothing."

"And you were out late last night. What time did you get home?"

"About 1:00."

"You were asleep when I left the house this morning."

"Ray and I needed to blow off some steam, play some pool, shoot some darts." She looks disappointed.

"You stunk of cigarettes and beer. Come on Paul! You know this always happens when you hang out with Ray." And I broke the cardinal rule by smoking pot last night and I liked it.

"I know you don't like Ray, but he's been a good friend."

"Friend? Ray is your escape from reality."

"What's wrong with that?"

"It's not just Ray. You know, it just seems that things aren't getting done around here. Our house is a mess. We're not working as a team."

"Yeah I know. It's been tough lately," I say looking down at my lap. Glad we have something we agree on.

She puts her hand through my hair and then sits on the bed with her legs crossed.

"I feel like we don't know each other anymore. We're both working and I feel like we're losing track of what's important. Like we're losing our soul."

"Our soul?"

"Our spirituality, our love, our connection to God and to one another."

"Cause you, you light up my life. You give me hope, to carry on."

"Very funny!"

"I know how you like that song."

"Sometimes I wonder if you really know anything about me."

"Come on, we've been married eight years. I know something about you. You're hard working, kind and quite principled."

"I don't know. I guess I just feel kind of stuck." Maybe she's right. Maybe we are losing our soul. She pulls me close. "So, how do you feel?" she says, wrapping her arms lazily around me.

I haven't really stopped to look at her in a long time, the woman I vowed to spend the rest of my life with. I've ignored her and she's ignored me. Looking at her, I remember our wedding at the beach and the excitement we had about our future, and now the future seems bleak and filled with routine. My lips tremble. "I don't know. I feel as if I've lost something."

"What have you lost?" She's caressing my neck, coaxing me to talk. "Tell me honey. What have you lost?"

"You remember when you were younger and the world was filled with new experiences, like the world was this great expansive thing and anything was possible?

"Yes."

"Well, I feel that world has somehow closed and that nothing new will ever happen."

"So you feel stuck too?"

"Yeah, I guess."

"Maybe we've been too afraid of change."

"Maybe." We're gazing into each other's eyes and I'm feeling a connection to her that I've not felt for a long time. Sarah's eyes are wet with tears. Maybe she's been hiding her fears with a smile and has tried to ignore the problems. Maybe she too is suffering and is bored with her life.

"Sarah, it's going to be OK. We're going to get through this." My arms wrap around her and bring her head to my chest, her warm tears soaking through my shirt and her heavy breath warming me. Where did it go wrong and was it ever right? As a child did I believe in an illusory future and, now as an adult, do I believe in some illusory past? The future with its endless possibilities, the past with its placid and facile existence, and the present moment, a place I never wanted to be.

"I don't know if we can make it, Paul. I sometimes don't feel like we can make it. You're becoming more and more bitter, and I know it's been frustrating with the newspaper not printing your articles, but you're letting it get to you. Just because they don't want to publish your stories doesn't make you a failure. It just means you have to try other places and other stories." She's looking at me to see if this is hitting home. "It's just more and more difficult to be around you."

"It's not easy to be around you either. You never seem to be satisfied with anything I do, especially when it pertains to Jacob."

She pulls away from me. "Jacob's very impressionable."

"And you don't like the impression I give him."

"Paul, it's you that's not satisfied. You get home from work, you sit on the couch with your beer, you watch television and then you tell me you've had a hard day."

"Sarah, that's not true. I work five to six days a week, making the bulk of the money to live in this house," I say pointing up to the ceiling. "I mow the lawn, help Jake with his homework and on top of that I'm trying to write a book."

77

"Your book? The one about the two friends who get lost on their way to Los Angeles?"

"Yeah, my book!"

"I rarely see you working on your book, Paul."

"So that means I'm not working on it? I don't see you cut hair, either."

"You see a paycheck from that."

"So that's the issue with my book? No money comes from it?"

"Oh come on, Paul!"

"What?"

"Instead of writing, much of your time is spent sitting outside having a cigarette or inside having a beer and watching sports." She's becoming overwrought, and nearly shrieks the next question. "What in our Lord's name is so important about sports anyway? Who cares if the Dodgers win? Who cares about the Lakers? How is this going to change your life?"

"Sarah, please speak to me nicely or I'm leaving this room."

She decreases the volume. "Sorry, maybe I do nag you too much, but I'm trying to help you and I'm trying to help our family. You have so much, a house, a good job, a wife and child and you're not enjoying your life."

"Again, I'm telling you it's not a problem of what I have. It's that I have nothing to look forward to."

"You can look forward to your son growing up."

"That's his life, it's not mine. I know it sounds selfish, but what's left for me? My writing career is stagnant, the only paper that is printing my stuff has a readership of 100 people and while it's great that I'm now manager of the store, I can see nothing ahead that's better than that. I wanted to make a difference in this world. I never wanted to be an average Joe."

"Average Joe?"

"Just another cog in the wheel."

"What are you talking about?"

"I wanted to be something special."

"You are something special."

"A manager of a stereo store?"

"And what about me, Paul? You think it was my dream to be a hairdresser? No. But you know what? I actually like it. I like talking to people and hearing about their lives. I don't like the attitude of some of them, but for the most part, they make me feel special. So, right now being a hairdresser is my lot in life, and I make the best of it. That's what being an adult is! But you won't accept that. So you're never satisfied with anything in your life."

She's right. I despondently look down at my hands.

"Paul, do you love me?"

If I had a tail it would hide under my legs. Love? Love comes and goes, just like hate, jealousy, lust, and calm are temporary phenomena.

"Paul, it's a simple question. Do you love me?"

"Sure, it's a simple question. Not all simple questions have simple answers.......Yes, I love you, honey." I don't know what's wrong with me; running my life by fear, afraid of Sarah's anger, afraid of letting go. Why am I not happy? Happiness is there, but I can't see it. Somehow, in this simple life of work, wife and son, there is bliss, but I will not allow myself to feel it. But I don't want to be content with bliss. I don't want to settle. Sure, many other men would be happy to be in my situation and if I were one of them then maybe I'd be happy.

"What are you thinking?" Sarah pulls her head toward my chest and the warmth of her body is turning me on like it used to.

"I was thinking it's been some time since we made love." Sarah's looking lovingly at me. Paul, she's still a beautiful woman and she still loves you. I'm holding her closely, wrapping my arms around her, kissing her smooth neck, touching my lips to hers, our soft sensate flesh gliding past each other. She holds me tightly and I'm feeling sad for the way I've neglected her, the way I've treated her.

"I'm so sorry if I've made you unhappy." My face dives into to her soft chest and she gently strokes the back of my head.

"Paul, I love you and right now I am very happy. We have to remember to love one another. I want...... I want us always to be happy."

Sarah's right. My state of self-loathing due to my unfulfilled dreams has pushed me away from her. Those dreams have enveloped me in a thick haze. I must not forget that she and Jacob are the most important things in my life. Sarah and I cling to each other in the night, two souls lost within this ritual, this dance, sheltered from the surrounding entropy.

"I'll always love you, Paul."

Not too much later we found out Sarah was pregnant with our girl.

I smell cigarettes. Hmmm? Sarah never likes to smoke after sex. My eyes open to see the respiratory therapist fiddling with something below my view. The man is gaunt, well-tanned but has pock marks on his face and he's got these deep depressions at the temples. His hair is a blondish-white which is somewhat spiked at the top and he's got a thick moustache. There are multiple veins below his eyes. His lips are dry. His whole being appears dry. In fact, he's the flesh-and-blood manifestation of a cigarette. Dude must smoke 2 packs per day.

Man's adjusting something I can't see, but I believe is at the front of my neck, since I'm feeling pressure there. There's an annoying suctioning sound, like those devices at the dentist's office that suck away your saliva. It intermittently stops, like something is caught in the suctioning device and then the slurping sounds return and then I cannot breath. Why can't I breathe? He dude, I can't breathe. Something's stuck in my throat. I need to cough to get it out, but it's not working. Dude, I need some help here. My mouth's moving up and down, trying to get breath in and I look around for some help but all I'm seeing are the ceiling and the spiked hair of the Marlboro Man. The suctioning sound returns and suddenly I can breathe again. I forgot the breathing tube is in my neck now. It boggles the mind, breathing through my neck and not through my mouth. Thinking about it, my mouth has no function. I'm not speaking through it, I'm not eating with it, I'm not breathing through it and yet, I'm still alive.

"Thanks Ed."

"No problem, Tracy. How have things been? You seem a little stressed."

"OK, but I've been having troubles with my daughter. She's sixteen now."

"Sweet Sixteen?"

"Ha! Ain't nothing sweet about it. She thinks she knows everything. She has a boyfriend all of a sudden. You know how that is. Always talking on the phone, staying out late on the weekends doing God knows what." Tracy pauses for a while, waiting for Ed's response.

"I'm sorry to hear that."

"Girls…They're so easy until they're thirteen, then all hell breaks loose. I don't know what to do with her. Her grades are coming down. She doesn't listen to a word I say and she talks to me like she hates me. You know it's difficult being an ICU nurse, but I get no sympathy from her and no respect. All I'm getting from her is the results of her bad behavior."

"Well, I hope it's just a phase."

"Me too. So how are you doing, Ed?"

"Not bad." Marlboro Man seems to be one of those strong silent types. Tracy comes now to the left side of the bed, with her round, red, chubby face, her wide neck, and her large rounded shoulders. She's wearing purple surgical scrubs in which her wide, freckled arms pop through, and she has a stethoscope around her neck.

"This guy seems to be waking up a bit," Ed says.

"Slowly," Tracy replies. "Really slow… Are you done there?"

"Yeah, he's all cleaned out." Ed's head pops up on my right side. Ed's wearing a white coat over a tan T-shirt.

"That's good because I need to turn him on his side and look for bed sores."

"Do you need help?"

"No, Paula said she'd help me."

"OK then, I'll be seeing you. And don't worry about your daughter. She'll come around."

"I hope so," Tracy sighs. "Thanks."

The quiet permits me to hear the TV, blaring something about Michael Jackson and a court trial. Michael Jackson. What the hell happened to that man?

"Now to the case of Terri Schiavo, the 43-year-old woman who has been in a persistent vegetative state for the last 14 years." I'm following the sounds of the TV to my right and there, in the corner of my vision, is a video of a woman and her mother trying to say something to her, but the woman's not responding. Wait a second!

I can see the TV! I can see the TV! What month are we in? December? There must be a basketball game tonight. Oh, I'd love to watch a Lakers game, watch Kobe and Shaq win another. How the hell do I tell the nurses to change the channel to the basketball game? Tracy's blocking the view of the television with her plump face.

"Paul we have to turn you on your side to look for bed sores." Wait a second woman, I want to talk to you about changing the channel. She doesn't care. She's turning me on my side and there's the sink again and the blue tile. There are hands touching my buttocks and I simultaneously feel violated and aroused, but now I'm feeling pain. Ouch! Stop that! It feels like someone is removing the skin on the lowest portion of my back with sandpaper. The stinging is amazing. I wish I could cry out, but the best I can do is a make a strange guttural sound from my neck as if I'm bringing up a big loogie.

"Sorry, Paul, if this hurts you," Tracy yells out. The pain dies down a bit and I need to close my eyes for a second. What the hell is going on back there?

"Paula, I see a couple there on his sacrum. I've cleaned them off, but I believe both are between stage one and stage 2. What do you think?"

"Looks like stage two to me. When was his last bowel movement?"

"I think it was five days ago. I'd have to check the chart. He's getting TPN, so no bowel movements. And as far as I'm concerned that's fine."

What are they talking about? Stage one, stage two, TPN; all that damn medical jargon. Paula's arms are on my back as she's standing next to my chest. The side of her body is covered in light blue scrubs and I can just make out the curvature of her lower back, leading to her elevated toned rear. Boy, that's beautiful! They turn me on my back again and these two women are now looking down at me, Tracy with her strong yet plump body and her heavily made up face, and Paula with her young tanned face and body oozing youth. The look on their faces is of utter pity. I know they pity my sorry behind and my sorry state. They're not saying anything to one other, but are just looking at me and this look of pity makes me feel unworthy of living. I need to close my eyes and blot out their faces.

I'm feeling disquiet now, not quiet, not at peace. Disquiet? I've heard that word somewhere before, but where was it? Oh come on brain, think now. Forget Tracy's and Paula's voices. In the darkness of your head is the answer. Follow those multiple lights and shapes. The lights and shapes are moving in and out of my vision, having no desire to stay, having no desire to be identified, quantified or defined in any way. I'm feeling quiet now. My breathing is softer and the lights and shapes are gone.

"Is it the disquiet of the human race or is it the disquiet of all life?" The disquiet: What did he mean by that? Stephen's sitting in his condo, having dinner with me on a Sunday night. It was good to have a friend again, someone I could talk to about life, its meaning and its absurdity. With Ray it was almost always the absurdity. Stephen's in a T-shirt, sitting at his table eating the dinner he made for us. It sort of looks like dinner; a plate of Tofu, broccoli and rice. Not my normal fare. Between bites Steven's exhaling thoughtful conversation.

"The disquiet of the human race is the disquiet of the rational mind. Life is not the problem. Somewhere in the past man made a conscious decision to relinquish the peace of his organic being and attempted to become a rational being."

"It's not just man. Patty's dog next door keeps chasing his tail. I'd make the assumption that he's not at peace. Isn't disquiet the state of all life whether it's rational or not?"

"I guess so. I'm not saying rationality is a bad thing, but it often places us in a world of should-be and could-be and not the way the world actually is. It's rationality that led to some of the greatest ideas, like, 'turn the other cheek,' 'all men are created equal' and 'all life is suffering.'"

"You seem to be feeling some disquiet right now."

"Yeah, I guess I am."

"What about?"

"I was volunteering at the hospital last night and found out that a man I was talking to only the night before had died. He was my age and had leukemia." He rests his chin on his hand and looks toward the window.

"It somehow doesn't seem fair when people die young. Think about all those people who died in Vietnam, some of whom I met."

"That must have been hard. I could never fight in war."

"Neither could I. I was just one of the guys who distributed supplies, way back from the lines, happy to never have to fight. So what disturbed you about this guy who died?"

"It was just strange last night to see his dead, motionless body and I realized how utterly base life is. That one day I'll be dead, too, and the world will still turn and nothing will really change. The sky won't open up." He looks upward.

"Maybe you should stop volunteering."

"Why?"

"It seems like it gets to you."

"It does sometimes, but it also feels good to help; to pledge your life to others."

"Is that your form of rationality?"

"I guess." Steven has a soft spot for religion.

"And isn't religion just another one of man's rationalities?"

"Sure it is. Religion at its core has this rational idea of a force greater than us; something we as individuals are subordinate to, in awe of, and something we are trying to understand. It's not a bad thought, right? The problem is that the rationality of religious thought competes with our genetic, organic desire to be powerful, and there's no way to escape it. Religion then can become a hierarchical institution that manipulates."

"Rationality leads to manipulation?"

"Sort of."

"Well you can't be totally pure Stephen. We have needs, like our need for food, water, sleep, our need for comfort, companionship… children. I think though we can be led on tangents that remove us from our biological needs and I think that while rationality can be used to fulfill our needs it can also be used to justify our tangents."

"Tangents?" Stephen laughs as if he's had a revelation.

"Yes, tangents"

"Do you mean our excesses?" He rubs his hand upon his chin.

84

"Tangents, excesses, diversions are the current human way of life. Excesses may be a good word, like someone who overeats to satiate an unfulfilled desire."

"And rationality can lead to excess? Do you think these excesses can modify biology? You mention someone overeating to satisfy an unfulfilled need. So what happens to these people? These people who love to eat? They eat more and more until they become fat, then their biology changes such that these now fat people need to eat more to maintain their body type."

I'm starting to resemble the hypothetical person in that statement. "Why stop there, Steve? Think about people who are excessive about exercise, drugs, work, hobbies, music, or people who are so excessive about organizing their perfect life."

"Yeah, these excessive or may I say disquieted people appear to be following an ever diverging tangent, but when viewed subjectively these people are fulfilling a basic need."

"Society breeds disquieted people." Hell I'm one of them.

"Maybe disquieted people breed society."

"Two sides to everything, I guess."

Stephen leans forward to grab a piece of watermelon with his fork. He places the fruit on his plate, takes a cut piece of lime and squeezes the juice on the melon. His actions have a focused, manly intent. He places a piece of watermelon in his mouth and thoroughly enjoys it. This is too much for me so I have to grab a piece with my hand and shove it directly to my mouth. The crunchy watery fruit tastes surprisingly good.

"How old are you, Paul? 50?"

"51, punk. I'm getting to be an old man. How about yourself?"

"36," Stephen looks toward the kitchen. He walks over to the kitchen and brings back two open bottles, places one down in front of me and sits down sipping his own cold beer. "I think I need to follow a new mythology." He says taking another drink.

"I've a difficult time understanding what our current mythology is."

"I think our American society is still based on the principles of Christianity and the big problem with the myths of Christianity is that the protagonist dies at the age of 33 and society reveres his memory. When you grow up, as I grew up, learning the ways of

85

Jesus Christ and revering his peaceful way of life, loving his equanimity and valuing his strength, you desire to become like him. He's a role model and little boys, like I was, desire to be like him; a perfect human. The only problem is that he was sacrificed at the age of 33. So, if a little boy takes Jesus as his role model and comes to age 33, what are his options? What's he supposed to do? His protagonist is now younger than him and the story is no longer about the aging man, but about youth." Stephen takes another gulp of beer and looks questioningly at the ceiling.

"I understand what you're trying to say, Stephen. You're 36 years old, have done everything in a morally conscious way and society is telling you that you have outlived your usefulness."

"No, I don't think that society is telling me I'm no longer useful. I think, though, the mythology of our society implies that I must pay reverence to the younger generation and that my worth is only as good as what I leave for the next generation. Actually it's not a bad myth for raising children"

"Rationality"

"I guess so."

"Amen to that brother. It seems like we all want to be the thing we worshipped. I worshipped baseball players, rock stars, actors, politicians who died young: John Kennedy, Jimi Hendrix, Martin Luther King, Sandy Koufax, James Dean, but I'm none of these people. So what do I do at 51? What are my options?"

"You finish writing your book and become a literary star?"

"And you become a priest and teach the world about Jesus?"

He stands up and looks out the window at a couple of finches. "I guess the youth do inherit the earth." He pauses a moment focusing out the window. "So what do I do? What am I to do? I've tried so hard to be this helpful servant of God, but how do I lead my life now? Is it just survival at this point? What do I tell my future children?" He walks toward me. "What do you tell your son? Jacob? What do you tell him?"

"Don't ask me. Jacob's just finishing college and doesn't want advice from his old man."

"Yeah, I think I know what you mean. I would always turn a deaf ear to my dad."

"That doesn't sound like you."

86

"He wasn't happy when I chose a less lucrative existence, for a more spiritual one."

"Sounds like my dad. He couldn't understand why I dropped out of college."

"So what would you tell Jacob if you could?"

"I really don't know what to say to Jacob. I just don't feel close to him anymore."

"When was the last time you talked to him?"

"About a month ago"

"A month ago! Is he away somewhere?"

"No, he's going to college in Pomona."

"Pomona? You should call him."

I don't want to talk about the failures of my relationship with Jacob. I walk over to the television, but there's no television, so I walk to the window and watch the finches fly, stepping their talons onto the platform of a bird feeder, peck, peck, pecking at the seeds and then flying away to allow another finch to do the same. Last time I saw Jacob was two months ago. We went to the batting cage and he was hitting the baseball from a machine that fired the ball at 80 miles per hour. He hit the ball well, when he hit it. Much better than his Old Man who stuck to the 50 mph machine and sometimes caught good aluminum on the ball. That was fun, but definitely awkward, filled with moments of silence.

"Yeah, I know. I should call him."

"Who am I to say? But, life is short, it's good not to let the bad feelings fester." Stephen was a good friend. Things would have been different if he had stayed.

The room is somewhat dark, except for the comforting glow of something behind me; all the machines keeping me alive. I should have called Jacob more. I could have tried harder, instead of letting us gradually separate like ships sailing toward different shores. After Sarah took custody of him, I only got to see him every other weekend and when I took him to his Little League games. But each visit was a reminder of my failure and somehow, our failure. We were walking on eggshells with each other, such that our conversations were forced and full of an anxiety that only ended when we parted.

We had our moments though, like the time when he was sixteen and we drove up to San Francisco in the Mustang with the top down and how I let him drive the Mustang on the way back. He loved that car. We really connected on that trip seeing the redwoods, catching a game at Candlestick Park, eating Chinese food in Chinatown. But then we had to come back and get back to our old lives. What I remember is that Mexican restaurant in San Luis Obispo with the monster burritos and how Jacob stood up to his Old Man.

"How's the book going, Dad?"

"Still working on it"

"You've been working on that book for a long time."

"Ten years."

"Ever since I was a kid."

"Yeah, I'd write after you went to bed."

"Ten years and it's still not finished."

"It's not an easy story. It's about dreams and how a dream is sustained when it is unfulfilled."

"And how a dream is unfulfilled when you smoke pot and drink beer."

"Smoke pot? What do you mean?"

"I'm 16 years old, Dad. I know you do it. I've smelled on your clothes."

"I'm sorry. I quit for a long time, but then…"

"Why do you do it?"

"I don't know. It helps me relax. Maybe, it helps me write my book."

"Maybe not. Anyway, writing books doesn't seem like a good way of making money."

"Well, there's more to life than money."

Jacob sips his Coke, and gives me an incredulous look, that turns into a smile and then a giggle. "What? Why are you laughing?"

"Nothing"

"Come on, tell me."

"I have a crazy teacher who also says, 'There's more to life than money'."

"What does she teach?"

88

"English."

"And why is she crazy?"

"She keeps saying for us not to worry about our grades or about money or what she calls superficial things."

"That's not so crazy."

"Oh yeah? So I decided not to worry about my grade and she gave me a C. My only C in high school. If I had worried a little bit more I could have a gotten a B or an A."

"I know, Jacob. But I think that's your teacher's point, right? You can worry about your grade, maybe get an A. Good thing. But maybe there's more to life, too." I take sip of my Coke.

"But I want to get the A, you know?"

"Sure. That's the system."

Jacob rolls his eyes. "Why do you always go back to the system?"

"What?"

"I mean, 'the system this,' 'the system that,' 'the government this,' 'the government that.' You've been talking about the system my whole life."

"The system is what it is. I just live in it. As for the government, well, if you went through what I went through, trusting your world, then seeing your President assassinated, seeing riots happen, going to war for imperialistic interests and then watching as the conformists succeeded, and the idealists failed, you would understand."

"Dad, come on."

"Come on what?"

"The war? You talk about the war like you were napalming villages. You weren't even in action, Dad."

Where's this shit coming from? "I hope they never make you go to war."

"Stop blaming the system. Look at yourself."

"All I was trying to say before is that grades and money aren't everything."

"Grades and money and stuff like that count in this world, whether you like it or not. You should know that."

"At this age the most important thing is to have the experiences that you'll always remember."

Jake's not listening to me, but is immersed in his massive burrito. His tan face has only the slight remnants of adolescent acne and is showing a manly appearance. He's turning out to be a good-looking kid. He's looking up at me again and gives me a contemptuous smile before he talks again. "But you know what? When I'm a dad I'm not going to worry about money, because I'll have it and I'm not going to waste my time blaming the system."

"Let's hope that wish comes true."

"It's not a wish. I'm gonna make it happen. That's the difference between us."

Jake! The machine's beeping at me again. Breathe Paul! Breathe! At 16, Jacob really didn't need his old man anymore and his old man had a hard time accepting him for whom he was; a hard time accepting that he couldn't change who he was. I didn't want him to take the straight and narrow path, but wanted him to be more like me. Shoot, maybe I was an example of what not to do. Maybe I became a derelict and liked it that way.

Someone's touching my arm. There's a woman with long black hair leaning over my right arm. "It's OK, honey. I am just taking blood from your PICC line to send to the lab." Her head turns upward. My benefactor is a beautiful dark-skinned, thin-faced woman, with hazel eyes, a slender neck, wearing a white coat that contrasts with her brown skin. Her voice has a little accent, not African-American, but African. She's labeling the tubes of blood and now she walks away. My eyes turn up toward the ceiling with the perfectly aligned holes. Why the hell do they have holes? The question will torment me until the end.

There's mild pressure on my left shoulder like someone's pushing down on it with their hand. I guess it was nothing because now I don't feel it. There are voices in the background and it's comforting to hear them, the sounds of the television.

"In Iraq today, four servicemen were killed when their Humvee hit a land mine. The identities of the casualties have not been released." I forgot that we're at war. It never really felt like war, but maybe that's the way the government wants it. Numb the masses and bloody the world.

90

"Hi Paul, it's Dr. Gellman. How you doing?" Dr. Gellman's blotchy face is next to mine and his hand is on my chest. I'm moving my lips a little, trying to say something. Dr. Gellman's hovering over me, intently trying to discern what I'm saying. I keep repeating, "My son. My son," but I don't think he understands me. He's getting close enough so that I can see the grey of his nose hairs.

"Your son?"

You understand me! I can talk!

"Your son will be here in three days."

Jake!

"But Paul, your protein levels are low. We've been trying to feed you intravenously, but it's not enough. We need to do a swallowing evaluation to see if you can eat. I spoke to your son, Jacob, and he knows everything that's going on. Hang in there, Paul."

I'm trying to say something like, "Just keep me alive until my son gets here," but all I can repetitively say is a hoarse, "Hust." It's so damn exhausting to talk. Gellman puts his stethoscope in his ears and puts the other end to my chest and listens. He takes the stethoscope off, feels my belly and looks at my legs and touches them, which causes a little pain. He puts his hand on my shoulder, says "Take care," and walks away.

Swallowing evaluation? That sounds disgusting, but I guess I must be doing better if they're giving me food to try and eat. What if I make it out of this? Will I be able to go home? The future is a fog of uncertainty and it will probably be better to just take it one step at a time. But what if I'm never able to free myself from this medical system? I've never thought of myself as severely debilitated. Even after the heart attack, where I knew I'd make a full recovery, I didn't think that there'd ever be a day so near where I could be crippled and unable to take care of myself. Maybe I will get better, but how much better? There's a pressure again on my left shoulder. Is Gellman still here? I don't see him. The pressure is gone and now there's darkness.

"I just don't understand, Paul. You can't drop out now. You're going into your senior year."

91

"Dad, I don't want to talk about this now."

"You have only one more year and then you'll have your degree."

"Dad!"

"Paul, this is your future."

I'll try not to listen. It's just another one of his motivational speeches at the kitchen table. "I'd rather focus on the present, Dad, like baseball and Sandy Koufax's no hitter." I lift up the paper to show him. He takes a quick glance at the paper.

"Paul, listen to me. You're smart, smarter than either your mom or I. Don't waste it. You're lucky enough to go to college. Your mom and I never had that opportunity." I'm doing my best to ignore him, looking at the sports section when suddenly the paper is pulled away from me, inadvertently knocking over my cup of coffee, which shatters on the floor. Dude!

"Now look at what you've done!"

"I'm sorry."

"I liked that cup. Mom, I'm going to need some help here!"

"I'll help you clean it up," Dad offers.

"This is the problem with your generation, Dad. You've just made a mess of everything."

"And what will your generation do, Paul."

"Fix your mess," I say, wiping the floor. Mom comes into the kitchen.

"What happened here?" she says.

"Ask Dad."

"Mary, it was an accident. Did Paul tell you he's dropping out of college?"

"Yes, and I don't know what to say. Paul, don't you understand you can do so much with a college degree? Don't you know that?" She gets a dustpan and a broom and sweeps up the broken cup.

"I know. I know it's important. But I need time away from it."

"And this cockamamie idea of writing for a 'free speech' paper?" Dad's raising his voice to a hoarse cough. "This is not going to get you anywhere."

"Where is it I need to go, Dad? Why should I be part of the rat-race?"

"Just because you have to repeat that one class doesn't mean you have to quit."

"It's not because of that one class, Dad."

"I thought you were going to be a journalist," Mom chimes in.

"I'm going to be a journalist, but I want to fight for the truth though, not the lies that are being perpetuated by this country."

"What the hell are you talking about, Paul?"

"I'm talking about experiencing the truth, knowing who I am, instead of living a lie. It's not good to live a lie Dad."

"You're sounding like a crazy person, a downright Beatnik."

"Most definitely, Dad! I'm off my rocker. The insane people are the only sane ones in this insane world. Can't you see the whole friggin' country is off its rocker. They killed the President in broad daylight, for Christ's sake. They're making more and more nuclear bombs and now this Vietnam thing. What the hell are we doing there anyway?" They're quiet now, trying to digest the truth. Dad raises his head from contemplation, looking much shorter, smaller than the man of my youth.

"What does this have to do with college?"

"I'm not learning anything in college, except how to fit into the system. It's all rote, boring and my teachers are as mechanical as robots."

"I know the system isn't perfect, Paul, but the only way you change it is by working in the system," Mom reasons. Now they're both standing next to me and I feel so much taller, more powerful, than either of them. When did they get so short? "Paul, are you listening to me?"

"Yeah, Mom."

"I'm worried about you, Paul."

"Don't worry about me."

My mother steps closer to me. "Don't worry about me? I'm your mom and I'll always worry about you."

"Leave me be."

"You're not doing well in school, you're letting your hair grow long and now," she's raising her voice, "you want to drop out of college. What's going on with you? Are you drinking?"

"Get off my case."

"Well, just tell me then. You know your grandfather was ruined by alcohol."

"I know. It's not like that. I've been just hanging out with my friends after work and yeah, we sometimes have a beer or go to the bar and watch the ballgame. It's nothing more than that." Watching an occasional baseball game and drinking alcohol were true, but I forgot to mention something. Drugs!!!! Getting high! Pot! LSD! Owsley Acid! Good times! Women! Rock and Roll! Liberation!

"Paul, I've a suspicion you're doing more than just drinking."

"What do you mean Dad?"

"Well look at you. Are you smoking marijuana?"

"What's wrong with marijuana?" I sound sort of like LBJ.

"That stuff will kill your brain, Paul. We used to call that stuff 'LOCOWEED'."

"You're such a slave!" Dad grabs me by the shirt pulling me toward him.

"Listen to me, kid. You talk about my generation, but you'd better take a long hard look at your generation."

Mom pulls us apart. "That's enough! Both of you calm down!" We separate to opposite sides of the kitchen with Mom, the referee, in the middle.

"Mary, the boy thinks everything will be handed to him in life!"

"I don't want anything you're handing out."

Mom comes toward me. "Paul, what's wrong with you? You have no right to talk to your father like that. He's paid your way up till now." So it comes down to the Almighty Dollar.

"I have enough money! I don't need his money!"

"Paul!"

"I'm working and I can pay my own way." Hell, I don't need them. I'm out of here, out the front door and out of this house.

"Come back, Paul," Mom's saying, but for some reason I feel like a bird whose time it is to leave the nest, never to come back. "Come back, Paul. You haven't finished your breakfast." I don't need them. "We still love you Paul." Mom's voice trails off.

Breathe in. Breathe out. The soothing movement of the air. Breathe in. Breathe out. Soft red light bathes the room, an indication that it may be sunrise or sunset. Mom and Dad! They tried to control me, but I wouldn't have it. I had it made, sharing an

94

apartment with Phil in Westwood, working at Keenan's Record Store and making pretty good money selling music. And on campus a revolution was happening, people signing my petitions against the Vietnam War, against the poor treatment of farm workers, and for any cause I could find. We were like a tribe. The Free Speakers! Phil, Billy, Damian, Winston, Craig and Nicole. All we needed was a microphone connected to a portable speaker and every Friday at twelve we'd find someplace on campus and allow anybody to come and speak about anything they wanted to. Freedom and free speech! We were there to open people's minds to the truth of the absurdity of the world......and it was a good way to meet women. Young college women, sequestered within the world of their parents, who desired liberation, would see me as their liberator and I was happy to oblige, be the rebellious symbol that brought them out of their sheltered world.

I wish I stayed in touch with Phil. He was such a cool guy, always mellow, always fun and what was he, like in his sixth year of college when I moved in with him? He took only one or two classes a semester. His parents had a shit-load of money so he was never short of cash or drugs and he put in the majority of the money for the *Free Speech Newsletter.* That little paper was so much fun. It was more editorials than true journalism, but I took it seriously; gave a copy of it to anyone who came in to the store whether they wanted it or not. It was so easy to write about the hypocrisies of government, the lies told to the people, the inequalities of our world. There was so much of it to write about that I was never short of material.

My role at that time was of the dissatisfied, disgruntled youth forsaken by his country. It was a role that worked well for me, especially with Anita and Nicole who tried placating my suffering with sex. When I got morose, Phil would always be the hopeful one, putting a smile to my cynicism. "Things will work out, Paul. They always do. Hey, I have a novel idea! Let's get high!" and we would. All the time. We would head to the beach, drop acid, do prayers to sun and moon gods, lose all sense of self, write poetry and get into the reality of the here and now.

I'd tell people I was taking time off from college to find out who I was. My plan was to eventually finish college, but for some reason, maybe the fear of being part of a corrupt system, I never found the motivation to return. At times I yearned for direction and felt that life was going nowhere, that I had to do something like live on a commune or become a Hare Krishna. But for two years life consisted of working at Keenan's, writing for the *Newsletter*, doing drugs, listening to music, having sex and watching sports on Phil's new TV, watching the Bruins win the championship in '67, '68 and '69. **Turn on, tune in, drop out.** It was like a nice purgatory until I was drafted and that life disappeared. Man, I should have left the country or feigned illness, but I had to have a chip on my shoulder. Maybe I wanted to show the old man that I could do my time, too. Maybe be a martyr. Like my death would show him how fucked up our society was or maybe death would be my escape from a normal life.

Phil and Anita threw me a party the night before leaving so I was still pretty high when Mom and Dad saw me off for basic training at Fort Ord. Mom was crying, Dad was stoic as ever and I didn't show either of them how scared shitless I was, not believing that I was going off to war; a war I was protesting. On the bus to Fort Ord was where I first met Ray. Cocky, loud and didn't give a fuck what people thought of him. "Pauley, I heard the women in Vietnam will do anything you want. How about that? I mean anything. Hey, don't look at me like that! You gotta take what the good Lord gives you…Remember to stay in touch with me. Share stories about the war, drink a beer or maybe two."

Share stories about the war? When we got to Fort Ord the chicken in me came out and I abandoned any notions of being a martyr. Hell, I just wanted to live. I was lucky Sergeant McClinton saw that I had no talent or desire for fighting and commissioned me to work at the commissary, handing out food, supplies, beer and anything else the soldiers needed, like cleaning the latrines and I was damn glad to do it. Seeing those poor deluded soldiers filing off to their deaths, thinking they were fighting for something of substance, toward an enemy they didn't even know, and for a cause that was utterly vague. It was good to be disillusioned with the world before I left for 'Nam, for 'Nam did nothing worse to me than reinforce my disillusionment. It was simply the same government bullshit, but in a warmer climate. Was I going to stand

96

up to the government there? Hell no! I put on a good face, took orders and did my job well, because if I didn't, I'd be placed on the front lines and I had no desire for that. "Yes, sir! No problem, sir!" I remember chain-smoking cigarettes, watching the sunset in An Khe fearing that we would be under attack, or that I would be sent to the front lines. Jacob will never know that fear. Ray told me about the shit he saw in combat. I wasn't going to die for that stupid war; glad the pride that made me go to Vietnam did not bring me in contact with the enemy. Jacob had no idea what I went through. Sure, I didn't fight, but I didn't want to fight.

Shoot! Then coming back to LA…not knowing what to do with myself. Phil finished his college degree and was lucky to get a 4F. He moved back up to the Bay Area, settled down with a girl and settled into his dad's winery business. Damian, Nicole, Anita, and all the Free Speakers had left and there was no way to contact them. It didn't matter anyway. College was gone, that time was done. Walking on campus in 1971, at the age of 26, I felt old and out place. I went to a few protest rallies, but it was never the same. The wood had already burned and there was nothing left to make a fire.

I barely got squat for reporting for the *Outlook*, so I had to work at Turntables, selling records again, staying in that rundown apartment in Culver City, feeling thoroughly alone. And most of the reporting for the *Outlook* was on local issues and none of it was very exciting, like the stories about the city's plan to extend the pier, the Christmas celebration at the mall or about the local art fairs. Dad wanted me to work at the store, but that wasn't my thing. "Then go back to college and finish your degree," he said. Degree? What the hell was that going to do for me?

The only solace was watching sports on a black-and-white television and drinking beer. For six months I subsisted in this shiftless, uninspired state, sort of lost and unhappy until that day Sarah walked into Turntables and then suddenly life had direction. Suddenly, I wanted to fit in. "Paging Dr. Levy. Dr. James Levy, please call the operator." Lying in this bed, unable to move, unable to speak, did I somehow deserve this? Is this retribution for leading a bad life? Someone is sticking my right index finger with a needle. "Sorry about that Mr. Mathews. We're just testing your blood sugar."

Chapter 6

Sarah?

I dreamt something, something pleasant about a voluptuous woman in a room of white. The holey ceiling is reminding me that it was all a dream. Wait a minute. Someone's holding my left hand. It's a pleasant, soft, loving touch upon the dead weight of my limb. Who's touching my left hand? If I just turn my head a little, move my neck a little, I can see her. It's her. She came! You came! Sarah! Sarah! "Sarah!" I'm trying to say, but what keeps coming out is "Sa," "Sa," "Sa." Help me Sarah!

"It's OK Paul. It's OK." She puts her index finger to my lips. "You don't have to talk." Her eyes are filled with tears. Her hand is on my forehead, and her fingers pass through my hair. Sarah, I'm so sorry. "Don't talk, Paul. Don't talk, you poor thing. I'm so sorry." I want to be closer to her, trying to move my head toward her, wanting to recapture the past, but failing to lift from this bed. "I'm so sorry, Paul." She's convulsively sobbing. Oh darn it Sarah! Don't cry now! I'm starting to breathe heavier, deep breaths that hurt my entire body and my crying is making Sarah's face blurry. Fourteen years together, sleeping in the same bed, raising a child and having emotions, both good and bad, that I haven't felt since. How did it get away?

She's walking away. Where's she going? Come back Sarah! Come back! I'm sorry! I won't cry.

There you are! She's back on my left side, rubbing life into my dead arm. "Paul, I'm sorry it took me so long to get down here. Jacob and I just found out yesterday." She looks at me trying to smile. "Paul. Paul! I can't believe this has happened...... or what you must be feeling." Her lip curls again as if she is about to cry. "I wish there was something I could do."

She's looking down at my hand and when she looks back up at me, she reminds of when we were first married; totally devoted to me.

"Are you in any pain?" I'm shaking my head from side to side. "Jacob's worried about you. The whole thing caught him off guard.

He'll be here on Sunday to see you. Melissa's…Melissa's not feeling well, so she won't be coming along." A machine is beeping behind me.

Sunday? What day is it today? Someone's speaking to Sarah. It sounds like Marge, the one with the pretty eyes. "Excuse me, Miss, I think I'm going to need to clear his tracheal tube. There's a little mucous there. Let me suction it out." Marge's face is now in profile and is focused on my neck. Slurping sounds come from my neck and my airway clears and my breathing eases. "I think he wants to tell you something."

"Thank you," Sarah says. She's moving closer to me. "Paul, do you have anything you want to say to me?" There's a chain around her neck connected to a silver cross and I feel like giving confession.

This is it, Paul. You may never see her again. I'm trying to slowly mouth the words, "I miss you," sounding like a frog waiting for a kiss from my heroine, to turn me into a prince.

She's stroking my temple and cheek in a loving way. "I miss you too. I miss our life together; how everything was new, how you were like a teacher to me and read me poetry. You were the love of my life and I still love you."

It sounds like she's reciting a eulogy to a person who will never exist again. There's nothing I can do. No way that we can go back to that time. She has a husband and I have a nurse.

Sarah! Her hair's greyer, her skin's become a little more wrinkled, and her eyes look heavy, the signs of age in her face. That girl I loved is now older and getting closer to death than to birth. I wish things had worked out better for her, wished she had put her money on a better horse, one that ran with all the other horses around the track, instead of the one that hid in the stable. I wish there were some way I could make things better.

I need to speak. I need to tell her. My lips slap together, slowly saying, "I love you, too." She takes her hands, placing them on both my cheeks and is smiling at me, a sweet smile and a sad smile. Coming closer, I'm feeling the warmth of her lips on my forehead. Dear God! Don't go Sarah! Stay with me! I'm sorry. "I'm sorry."

"No, I could have been more supportive, Paul. I could have been better, especially when the newspaper didn't print your stories, especially when those stories meant so much to you."

"Boooook! Booooook!" I have to tell her about the book. It may be the last thing I can give this God-forsaken world. "My, my, my, my, booooooook."

"I know! I know! I criticized you too much about your book, didn't give you enough praise. I could have been better." Are you wanting my forgiveness? Don't say this, Sarah. Don't patronize me. You never took my writing seriously, never understood how it tormented me, never understood that I wanted to make a difference with my words. It was what it was. And I was no angel also. I don't remember ever giving you a ton of praise. We tried Sarah, but it didn't work out. End of story. But my book is finished. "I wish we could have been friends after the divorce." She's looking down at her clasped hands. "Foolish pride, I guess. I was just so angry; angry at you, angry at myself, angry that things didn't work out as I planned, angry that you cheated on me...and then that silly couples therapy. Like the therapy was going to make it all better?"

"I'm sor. I'm sor." I want to say I'm sorry for it all.

"I am not angry anymore, because I've found God. He's forgiven me, and in him I have found love. He made me realize how much you were suffering too."

God made you realize that? Sarah, why did you become a Bible thumper like your parents? We used to make fun of them and all their piousness, but maybe it was just me making fun of the pictures from the Bible and the pictures of Christ in their house. I must have been deluded; deluded to think I could change you. You fled to religion when things got bad, because it is what you grew up with. It's like a bad dream and a dream of my own creation. I'm shaking my head, even though I'm probably only moving it an inch from side to side.

"Paul, it's not like you think. When you realize that you are one of God's creatures and there is love in the universe, the world opens up for you." She's looking up to the ceiling with the multiple holes as if it were a manifestation of God. "God loves all of His children and when you feel His love you feel like a child; the world then becomes a great mystery." She looks at me. "You used to say there is no such thing as God. But God exists and God loves you, too. Open your heart to Him."

"Sarah."

"He forgives you."

"Sarah."

"He loves you."

I'm on my deathbed and you say this shit! Which God do you speak of? The old white man with a long beard, whose enemy is the evil Satan, whose child is the blond-haired Jesus? The old man who inseminated Mary and drowned Pharaoh's army, told Abraham to kill his son and allowed a ninety-something-year-old Sarah to give birth to Isaac? If this is the God you speak of, the one that ruined our marriage, the one you ran to when our unborn daughter died, the one you became celibate for, then I'll tune out. If you're talking about the spiritual, nebulous, unknown universe and call this God and have opened your heart to this thing......but maybe...maybe this is the God you're talking about.

"Religion is not as bad as you think. Ken and I have been volunteering at homeless shelters for the church and we help others in the church when times are tough. They help us too. There's a sense of community in the church, a sense of love, of belonging."

They've been married six years now, living in Santa Maria, in what I imagine is small town life; Sarah must still be doing hairdressing, and Ken was doing physical therapy for children. And what is that I feel? A sting of jealousy when she mentions his name, feeling the loss of something that was once mine, but the obvious truth is that Ken is much better fit for Sarah than I was. That truth is an obvious presence as we look at each other, not able to say anything more.

"Are you Mrs. Mathews?" There's the lung doctor, Dr. Masterson.

"I go by Leeds now."

"Are you related to Mr. Mathews?"

"Well, sort of... I'm his ex-wife."

"Nice to meet you. I'm Dr. Masterson, the Intensivist taking care of Mr. Mathews in the ICU. Maybe I can give you an update on what has transpired here in the hospital."

"Thank you."

102

"Paul, do you mind if I talk to Mrs. Leeds about your condition?"

"Suuure." I think he was going to talk to Sarah with my okay or without it.

"Mrs. Leeds, Paul has suffered a stroke on the right side of his brain. This was created by an abnormality in his heart called atrial fibrillation, which made his heart throw a clot to his brain. The stroke caused bleeding into the brain that left him paralyzed on his left side."

"Oh my God."

"I'm sorry. I know it's not easy to hear this. We've had him on a ventilator for almost three weeks and have placed the tracheostomy for long-term ventilation. The remarkable thing was that after we placed the tube you see in his neck, his breathing dramatically improved. We're now thinking of taking him off the ventilator and seeing how he breathes without it, but this may take a few days. He may need to be on oxygen afterward, though, because of his lung disease."

"Because of the smoking?"

"I believe so. The other issue with him is his nutritional status. We were feeding him before with a tube that went from his nose into his stomach, but after he vomited and aspirated the contents into his lungs and developed pneumonia we had to stop. He's currently getting intravenous nutrition, but it's not enough."

"He's getting better though?"

"Slowly better. It is going to be a long process." Dr. Masterson's looking down at me, his salt-and-pepper hair contrasting with his youthful face. He's garbed in a white coat and has a stethoscope hanging across the back of his neck. The man is really tall. He's towering over me and it's taking him some time to lean down to bring his face close to mine. "Paul, how are you doing today?"

"Ooooooh…keeeeeeh".

"Good. You seem to be better, Paul." He looks like he's thinking of the next words to say, and, by the look on his face, is trying to put what he wants to say delicately. "Paul, we have to start you eating. Your protein levels in your blood are low and it's causing your arms and legs to swell. You're going to see a speech therapist today to see if you can swallow for yourself." He pulls off

103

the stethoscope from around his neck and intently uses it to listen to my chest. After twenty seconds he commands, "Breathe, breathe, breathe." Each time he says "breathe" I oblige and take in a deep breath with the help of the respirator. He's feeling around my stomach and now he's lifting up the blanket, exposing my legs, uncovering and humiliating me in front of Sarah. Hell, my pride's gone anyway. Dr. Masterson covers me, walks away and his tall frame moves toward Sarah, blocking her out of my vision. They're speaking privately and I'm envious of their intimacy.

"I think we have to keep the tracheostomy and the respirator for now. Regarding his nutritional status, if he fails the swallowing evaluation and is unable to eat, I would suggest a gastrostomy tube."

"What's a gastrostomy tube?" Sarah's echoing my thought.

"A gastrostomy tube is a tube that's placed through the skin and into the stomach. The tube can be used as a conduit for food and liquids."

"What kind of food?"

"Protein shakes like Ensure, but because of his Diabetes we would have to use something different."

"Did you talk to his son about this?"

"Yes, and he wanted us to do everything to keep him alive."

This is pitiful, like a sinking ship with the old captain looking on realizing that his vessel will never sail again.

"Well, if that is what my son wants, that's how it should be. It's all in the Lord's hands anyway."

"Yes, it is."

"Have you talked to Paul about the feeding tube?" Sarah asks.

"He hasn't been very responsive, until now."

"Well, why don't you ask him now?"

"OK"

Dr. Masterson walks over to me and bends down. "Paul, I'm going to ask you a question. Paul, do you understand what I'm saying"

"Yes." I whisper with all my energy. It is very difficult to speak, each word draining my breath and energy.

"Paul, if you are unable to swallow, we may have to put a tube into your stomach to feed you. Would it be OK if we did that?"

What do I say? Place a tube in my stomach for feeding? That is creepy! Putting the tube in may keep me alive, alive enough to see Jacob, but what will be my quality of life? Huh! What's the right course of action? If they put this tube into me, I may improve, gain strength, leave the hospital, but then again I may stay just the same and this tube will keep me like I am now. If I say no, then it may be bye, bye Paul. I don't know. Dr. Masterson is looking thoughtfully, though a little impatiently, for an answer. His steel blue eyes are focused like the eyes of a crane waiting for a fish; a good looking man. I wish I were that good looking. I think my life would have turned out differently. People may have listened to me more.

"Paul, do you understand?"

I'm nodding, but can't say anything. There was a question about a tube in my stomach, but I don't know what to say. After some time Dr. Masterson looks down and then walks toward Sarah. "I'll try again with him tomorrow."

"Thank you, Dr. Masterson," Sarah says. Dr. Masterson's gone. Sarah's standing in front of me, dressed in a dark blue dress suit, one she may wear on Sundays to church, her gray hair coming down to her shoulders, her hands holding one another in front of her chest, her breasts hidden behind her jacket, her love forever gone from me. There's something very distant about her, like she doesn't want to stay much longer, but she can find no good way to leave her ill ex-husband. She stands there for a while and then walks to my right side and puts her hand through my hair, stroking my hair softly, rekindling the love we had for one another. Sarah's faintly singing a song that she used to sing when we were both younger, when I was her teacher and she my student who slept with me in her apartment, rejuvenating me at a time when I had little hope, in the years after dropping out of college and returning from Nam. She was that youthful innocence, the small town girl, the idealism I longed to return to. She was so beautiful, so loving and she was so in love with me. We would lie together snuggling in her small bed. I would plunge my head onto her soft chest as she caressed my face and she would sing from her heart, like she's doing now.

"It is the evening of the day…ay…ay…ay. I sit and watch the children play…ay…a…ay. Smiling faces I can see, but not for me. I sit and watch as tears go bye…i…i…i." She always had a beautiful voice. She sings and for a while the world is filled with warmth.

"Sarah, we have to buy now. Brad says the time is right."

"I don't think we should."

"But, this could be our nest egg."

"The money from your father's will is our nest egg."

"Come on Sarah, if we make consistent money off this deal, you won't have to work. You could spend more time with the kids. We won't have to go through daycare again." I wrap my arms around her and feel her protruding belly in the way. She looks up at me.

"I don't know, Paul. You don't know anything about real estate. How can you trust them to run this shopping mall for you?"

"Brad says it's a sure thing."

"Brad? What does Brad know?"

"He's the CPA who's organizing the deal and he's organized others and made a lot of money."

"There's something about him I don't trust. This is someone you went to high school with?"

"He's smart. He knows what he's talking about."

"He seems conniving, both him and his wife with her fake breasts."

"That's a horrible thing to say." Judy did show them off. No doubt they were fake, but nice in that black dress.

"They don't seem to care about anyone. All they care about is money."

"They care about enjoying their life. Look, I don't want to be that extravagant, but I want some breathing room. I want to be happy."

"What? We're not happy?"

"Well, not always." I feel her body pulling away from mine. "I'm sorry. I know money doesn't bring happiness, but it sure makes things easier and in some ways better."

"They are luring you in Paul."

"So?"

106

"Don't listen to them. The path toward Jesus, toward love, has nothing to do with money." For God sakes, she looks like she's praying.

"I'll remember that the next time your church asks me for a donation."

"Why can't you listen to me?"

"Because, all of your religious wisdom has nothing to do with everyday life."

"It has everything to do with everyday life." She curls her lip thinking. After some time she points her finger at me. "'What shall it profit a man if he gains the whole world but loses his soul?'"

"OK. One of many good things Jesus said. But, my soul is stifled here in this world of middle class bullshit. This everyday living is destructive, rotting our souls, packaging our freedom."

"'Rotting our souls, packaging our freedom?' You wrote that?"

"Yeah."

"It's good. But can't you see that's what I am concerned about too? Our souls? Our freedom?" She brings her body close to mine and I look into her face, puffed out from the pregnancy, looking totally unlike when I first met her; looking more like her mother, a little chunky and hell-bent religious. I feel her belly with my hand half-expecting some kick from my child, but I know it's too early for that.

"I'm concerned about our well-being, too. This is the world we have to navigate, an unfair world, where economic well-being is the only power an individual has." I caress her belly. "I don't want us to pander to anyone."

"It would be nice not to work. It would be easier to take care of the house and the children. Maybe we could buy a farm."

"Are you serious? A farm?"

She kisses my neck and, as I bring my head down to look at her, I notice her face. She looks like she's about to cry.

"What's wrong? Don't cry."

"No Paul, I'm just a little scared." She wipes her face and looks back up at me. "...and a little pregnant. My emotions are getting the best of me." She smiles, her eyes still with tears.

"Don't worry Sarah. We're in good hands. Valencia is about to boom. If we can put money in to this investment, soon we'll collect money from rent and just wait as the property appreciates. We can live in a larger house in a nicer area." She sits down on the sofa and looks up at me.

"OK Paul. I wasn't really expecting this money from your father."

"I know. I wasn't thinking he would die."

"If this is what you want to do with the money, then so be it."

My breath is being pushed through, back and forth. I don't know if I'm doing the pushing or if the machine is doing it for me. Brad? That motherfucker! The problem was that the loan was too much for the group of investors to pay and it went into default, only to be picked up by Brad and another group of investors. I lost eighty thousand dollars. Now he sits somewhere in a lavish existence, pocketing the profits. Sarah was right. I couldn't see it. She knew what she was talking about and she didn't even care about the money; her pure, holy self. And she kept shoving it into my face. That I didn't research the deal enough, that I spent too much time in front of the TV, that I wasn't focused, that I was cajoled by a good-looking devil. Basically, saying to me, that I was a fuck-up. And so what if I was a fuck-up, she's supposed to support me.

The ceiling comes in to focus and the sounds of the television pervade the room.

"Where have you been?" a female voice says.

"I…I just went for a walk," stutters a male voice.

"Where did you go?" she pursues.

"Am I on trial here? I just wanted to come home for some peace and quiet and instead I get your accusations." No doubt he's done something wrong.

"I'm not accusing you of anything. Not yet."

The tone shifts. Happy music is playing in the background and my eye turns toward the TV. There's a grinning woman in a sideways profile, holding out the waistband of pants that are much too large for her. "Jenny Craig has helped millions of people lose weight and keep it off," an optimistic sounding female announcer says. Another cheery woman says, "I never thought it was possible. I've tried all types of weight loss plans, but nothing kept the weight off. But Jenny's plan was easy to follow and I've lost fifty pounds and have kept it off." "We both did Jenny's plan and lost over 40 pounds," a man says sitting next to his wife. "We feel better, more active and excited about life. Thanks, Jenny." The music's volume increases. The female announcer gleefully announces, "Don't wait. Call or visit us at our website and take charge of your life."

A woman is now talking about diapers and someone is pouring blue water into a diaper to show how much pee it could hold. Where did Sarah go? My eyes rove from right to left, but she's nowhere to be found. Maybe if I move a little, but all I can do is elevate my head a little and barely move my right leg. Maybe she's at the front of the room on the other side of the half-opened sliding glass window, but instead there are nurses, doctors, and cleaning ladies walking past the sliding glass window, oblivious to my predicament.

"With Byron out of the way, there's nobody who can take my rightful spot as heir to the Crawford Estate."

"What do you mean 'with Byron out of the way'?"

"Let's just say that Byron does not know the trap he will soon fall into."

"You're devious."

"Thank you."

Could someone turn off the goddam TV? There's a red button on a rail that goes along the right side of my bed. That must be the button to get the nurse. Come on, Paul! Push the button! Sarah may be gone forever! Use every ounce of your strength to raise your right arm. You can do it. Now move your finger to that red button on the side rail. My hand is going up, but it's not moving laterally toward the side rail, so I decide to fling my entire arm toward the right edge of the bed. After multiple attempts of flinging my right arm at the railing, the hand finally arrives at the red button. I look at my hand, fat and swollen, and my forearm with an IV tube attached to someplace behind my vision. My hand and arm look grotesque, like they would burst with fluid if someone had a needle. What does my face look like? Maybe that's why Sarah left. My middle finger pushes on the red button. Nothing happens. I push it again and nothing happens. What the fuck is going on here? They call this a hospital? Where's the service? I could be dying here, pressing this button as my last dying act and no one would even know. Marge, where are you? Holy shit, can someone come here and tell me where Sarah is? I keep pressing the button and nothing is happening.

I'm lying in bed, waiting, listening to the television telling me that five out of six dentists prefer Trident chewing gum. They've been passing me that line for the last twenty years. Who the hell are these dentists and how can it be that year in and year out the same exact percentage of dentists prefer Trident over some other brand of chewing gum? Who the hell does these studies? This whole fucking, manipulating, capitalistic system sucks! Where's my nurse. One of the machines is loudly beeping and it's more annoying than the television. There's a tightening in my chest and my left shoulder.

"Beep. Beep. Beep. Beep." A monotonous, low-pitched sound separated by about three seconds of silence. A youngish looking, dark-haired, dark-skinned Asian woman walks in on my left and looks up at the monitor. She looks toward me.

"Your nurse is off on a lunch break, I'm covering for her. Are you doing all right?" as she moves her hair behind her ears. I point to the nurse's button on the side rail and await an explanation.

She points to the side rail. "That button won't call us. She lifts up a speaker the size of my hand that provides the sound to the television. She points toward the red button below the speaker that has the figure of a nurse's head with a nurse's cap. "You have to press this button for one of us to come."

What the hell is the other red button for?

"My wife, my wife," I try to say, but it comes out all garbled. Her hand lightly presses upon my chest.

"I can't understand you," she says. "I'm going to have to call the Doctor though. Your pulse rate is fast." She disappears behind me, doing something to make the beeping stop. She's walking out of the room now.

"On the Channel Four news at 12:00: two teenagers have been picked up in Hawthorne in connection with the shooting of a middle-aged woman, and a new breakthrough in breast cancer treatment. Stay tuned for the Channel Four news at 12:00." The pressure on my chest is getting worse and I'm feeling short of

110

breath. Where did Sarah go? She's probably driving back to Ken and her cozy life in Santa Maria. I don't know if I'll ever see her again.

But, maybe I deserve to be alone. I really did mess things up. My chest tightens further, my shoulder hurts and I'm feeling very hot and this inability to breathe is becoming worse. It feels like when I had my heart attack. Holy shit! Am I having another heart attack? Oh hell! Are you kidding me? Not before Jacob comes.

Calm down, Paul! Calm down! Find that call button the nurse just showed me, the one with the speaker box. There's the red button on the side-rail. Why the fuck would they make them both red? Sadists. The beeping goes off again and runs in syncopation to my level of distress. The nurse runs in on my left and moves behind my vision and the beeping stops. She's brought in a machine.

"Mr. Mathews, we're going to do an EKG of your heart and give you medication to slow down your heart rate." She removes the blanket from my body, places something on my chest, my arms and legs, and attaches wires to each of these locations. She rips a piece of paper from the machine next to her, appears to read what the paper says, and then walks away, leaving me attached to these wires. The chest pain is crushing as if the air is being sucked out of my chest. A sour taste develops in the back of my throat. I need to focus on something else. This is not happening! Not before Jacob gets here. The television is mocking my suffering.

"Why do you skirt around the issue? You know you don't love me." A woman's voice accuses.

"Of course I love you. I wouldn't have married you if I didn't love you," a male voice pleads.

"Really? Or did you marry me for my family and their money?"

"This is ridiculous."

The beeping restarts and it won't go away. Waves of nausea overcome me and there's a crushing pain in my chest, radiating into my neck and left shoulder. The nurse comes in. She appears on my right side, rushing to put a syringe of fluid into the tube in my right arm. She is focused, hurried. She injects the fluid and then opens up something contained in plastic; that something is a bag that has fluid inside with a tube connected to the bottom of the

111

bag. What the hell's going on? She adeptly connects the tube to the IV line in my arm, takes the bag behind me and I hear her fiddling with something. Suddenly I'm lightheaded, like I am going to pass out, and there's a headache coming on, but the pressure in my left shoulder starts to relax. The machine starts to beep again.

"Shit," the nurse says. "I have to turn down the nitro." It's a little disconcerting to hear the nurse say, "shit." Shit does not sound good. "Nitro" she said. She must be giving me nitroglycerin and this must mean I'm having a heart attack. Heart attack! For the love of God! What have I done to you, God? Give me a friggin' heart attack before Jacob gets here. God has to be the malevolent entity of the Old Testament that takes pleasure in teaching his children painful lessons. I can see him way up high with his disciples, like some kind of teacher showing his students the story of Paul Mathews, that poor soul who didn't follow the ways of the Lord. "Well, he sure got his lesson," I faintly hear one of his young disciples say.

Damn nitro headache! The chest pain has lightened a little so it is somewhat less than crushing, which is how I'd describe my headache. My eyes open to an unfocused world, but I think I see Marge walking in with the other nurse, and they both look at something behind me.

"You call the cardiologist?" Marge asks.

"I did. He said he'd be here right away and that we'd probably have to send him to the Cath Lab. The EKG showed ST elevations in the anterolateral leads and I've already pulled the blood for enzymes."

"I should call his son. Damn, the sad part about it was that he was getting better." Her steps are trailing off outside the room. The other nurse is still in the room and I see her blurred figure coming closer to me.

"Mr. Mathews, are you in any pain?" I'm feeling too much fatigue to answer. I sort of want to slip away quietly and end this experience, but I need to see Jacob one last time. If it weren't for Jake, I'd probably give up the ghost and just croak. My eyes close, but the pain in my head and chest keeps me awake.

"Mr. Mathews, I am Dr. Schwartz, your cardiologist." My eyes open to see a blurry representation of a man with disorganized hair, chubby face and eyebrows that join together. Oh yeah, I remember you. You saw me in the hospital the last time I had a heart attack.

"We're going to take you to the Cath Lab. Looking at your EKG, a large portion of your heart is being compromised. We have to do a catheterization to see what's going on with the arteries that give blood to your heart. Do you understand?" His manner implies that he's not going to wait around for an answer. I'm trying to nod to give some form of consent to do the procedure, but don't know if I'm successful. "I am going to call your son to get consent." He walks away. Marge comes along on my left side.

"Paul, you're going to be OK." Before I know it my whole bed is being moved and I see Marge on my right pushing the bed, looking forward. There's also someone at the front of my bed pulling the bed forward, a Hispanic man with dark hair, a moustache and blue scrubs. He pushes a button and we wait to go in the elevator. Trying to forget the pain, my eyes shift to the left and see plain-clothed people walking up and down the hallway and wonder what they're thinking when they look at me in all my suffering. Not long ago, I was one of those people just walking down the hall, part of another world of interaction. Can I ever be part of that other world again?

The elevator is here. They wheel me head first inside the elevator. At my feet is still the Hispanic man and to my right is Marge and to my left there's a young doctor, bald, without his white coat, a stethoscope adorning his neck, looking down and fiddling with his little phone, closing it and then looking toward me. He seems to be sizing up my situation, looking at everything including my eyes, violating me with his curiosity. The door of the elevator opens and the young doctor walks out quickly. There is a metal lattice of squares at the top of the elevator and behind the squares there's an ethereal white light. How do the hands of man create this? It's amazing. The squares disappear and I'm being moved out of the elevator and into a corridor and now wheeled into a large room with bright, blinding light; a good place to die.

"We'll have to lift him from the bed and onto the table," a gruff voice calls out. "Let's put the slideboard under his body so we can pull him up onto the table." I'm being turned to my right side and feel something, I'd guess the slideboard, being placed behind me.

113

They turn me again on my back and onto the board. Two other people come along side me.

"On the count of three, we move him," the gruff man's voice says. "Can you two pull his upper back, Martha and Jenny pull his lower back and I'll help with his legs. OK, One, Two, Three." Slow down! I'm going to fall. My body's heaved up onto something harder than my bed. There's a warm bright light, whose heat floods my face and chest, sort of like I'm basking in the Southern California sun at my condo's pool, inebriated by the sun, reflecting on nothing in particular. My head and chest pain have lessened in the warmth of the light. Marge is along side of me. She touches my shoulder.

"You take care Mr. Mathews. You'll be feeling better real soon."

Many people are surrounding me and are attaching multiple devices to my body. There is the beep of my heart from a machine behind me. It sounds fast at times and irregular.

"What's his name?" a woman inquires.

"Paul Mathews."

There's a woman with a blue mask and cap walking up to me on my right side.

"Mr. Mathews, we're going to clean the right side of your groin area before doing this procedure." In another context those words would be quite arousing. She disappears and whatever was covering the right side of my lower body is being pulled away. "We are going to have to shave off the hair in this area, Mr. Mathews." A hand is touching my right groin and someone is shaving me down there, but it sure doesn't feel like I thought it would. "We're going to put some iodine over the area." Cool fluid runs down my leg. A man arrives on my right side decked out in a blue robe, with a blue cap and wearing a blue mask.

"Hi, Mr. Mathews, it's Dr. Schwartz again. We're going to open up that blockage in your heart now." As if this should allay my fears! He did do the same procedure three years ago, an angioplasty, and afterward I was given four medications and did return home after two days, but I don't think I'll be returning home anytime soon. Schwartz has always been nice to me and his peppy spirit had given me hope in the past that my health would get better.

There's a sharp, stinging pain in my right groin. "Paul, we are placing the anesthetic now. You shouldn't feel anything in a couple seconds." On cue the pain has vanished. "Here we go!" Lying there in the warm light, I'm looking up between the large bulbs to see the ceiling with the rows of perfectly aligned holes; straight and perfect holes. There is the beep, beep, beep of my heart, but it more sounds like beep…beepbeepbeep…beep, beep…beep…beepbeepbeepbeepbeep. The warm light is making me tired and I got to close my eyes, but when they close, all I can think about is Sarah in the hospital standing at my bedside in all her piousness. How could it be that the woman I married changed so drastically? She used to love to listen to poetry, listen to the Beatles and lie naked with me through the night. It all changed when we had Jacob and then that miscarriage threw her over the deep end. She was twenty weeks pregnant when it happened and she cried for days uncontrollably, "My daughter! My daughter! God, why have you taken my daughter?" I could have done more. I know that now, but I was afraid; afraid of feeling her pain, afraid of feeling my own sorrow at losing my little girl. She left to be with her parents and I should never have let her go. It was only a week, but they brainwashed her, made her so god-damn pious I couldn't recognize her. She cut her hair short, became totally controlling, saying grace every time we sat at the table. She stopped having sex and looked at me like I was the devil. Devil! Maybe I did like to play that part.

Sarah's standing at the door of our house, wearing a dark blue jacket and skirt and is ready for Sunday church. Her hair is cut short, sort of like Sandy Duncan. I hate Sandy Duncan! She's looking at me while I have my rear plastered to the couch. Jacob's with her, wearing a similar haircut and is cloaked in slacks and a collared shirt. "Why don't you come with us Paul?"

"It goes against my religious beliefs."

"A little Sunday church never hurt anybody," Sarah is looking into her purse for her keys.

"Look what it did to Jesus." Sarah looks up from her purse.

"Very funny. And what's wrong with Jesus?"

Like it or not, I've just started another argument.

"Mom, let's go." Jacob is pulling at Sarah's blue skirt.

"We will go in a minute, Jake. I just want to talk to your dad." She turns back to me and draws a deep breath.

I reflexively turn to the television. The Redskins are playing the Cowboys.

"Paul, I'm talking to you."

I turn back to Sarah. "I just think you're taking this religion thing a little too far. It is one thing to celebrate Christmas and Easter, but going to church two or three days a week is too much."

"Well, I think watching football every Sunday is too much," she carefully counters.

"I don't watch football every Sunday."

"If not Sunday, then you are watching it on Saturday. What happened to your reporting? It used to mean so much to you.

"I told you. I'm going to focus my attention on writing the book."

"So?"

"So?"

"So focus already. Write your book. 'Going to'? What does that mean?"

"It means I will write when I'm inspired to write."

"What happened to you Paul?"

"What happened to you, Sarah? You told me that never wanted to be like your parents, but lo and behold you have turned into them... A Bible-Thumper."

"I love my parents and at least I care about something that has value. All you care about now is your car, your beer and those god forsaken sports. Oh, and a book you never write. Don't you see how this is damning your soul?"

"Oh! I guess I'm going to hell then."

"Maybe. But you're making your life hell, and ours along with it."

"You're off your rocker."

"Dad, stop bothering Mom." Jacob yells.

"Your Mom and I are having a discussion. That's all. It's normal for adults to argue. Always remember Jacob, you can turn the other cheek, but always watch out for the left hook."

"Paul!"

Jacob frowns and turns to Sarah, but he's still looking at me through the corner of his eye, like I'm some mangy mutt. "Mom, I want to go. We don't need him."

"Jacob, that's not nice to say about your dad. We do need him." She turns to me. "Daddy just needs some time alone."

"That's right. Daddy needs some time alone," I mock.

She walks to the door and I watch her and Jacob leave the house.

The image of the closed door is in my head. All I can see is the closed door and the empty room. The quiet is not at all peaceful and I wish they'd come back. Then again I wish it were me leaving the house and them staying inside. The couch envelops me and I'm unable to turn my head from the closed door and the ceiling and the brown floor tile. I need to be free of this, this room, this house, this life. Somebody get me out of here. Is there nobody to help me? Can they ever forgive me for what I've done?

My chest! My chest! Ouch! I can't breathe. Something bad is happening. My chest can't open up. Something is squeezing it tighter and tighter. My heart! My heart! Oh, this must be the big one! Goodbye! Somewhere there's a big band playing some farewell tune as I wave good-bye to it all. The trumpets play in unison as I sit on the back of a ship, waving goodbye. Goodbye!

"I can't get my catheter through this LAD lesion."

"Dr. Schwartz, his pulse is in the 150's."

"Give him twenty milligrams of IV Diltiazem," Dr. Schwartz anxiously calls out. "If I can just open up this lesion we can stop the progression of the infarct." I've heard that word before, 'infarct', in relation to my heart attack. Infarct meant the dying of heart muscle. Oh, God!

"Twenty milligrams Diltiazem given," a female nurse calls out.

I'm lightheaded and the warm glow of light above me is getting darker with each passing beep of the monitor. My eyes close and I can't breathe. I need to cough and try to stop it, but I don't care about coughing. In fact, I don't care about anything. Let me die! Let me be!

"I have to stop" Dr. Schwartz says. "I'm irritating the heart even more. OK, I'm pulling the catheter out. We will have to medically manage him and allow him to complete his infarct. Let's give him Lovenox, Metoprolol drip and IV Enalapril and send him to the floor."

The world goes to black and I know this is the end. Jacob!

"DADA!! DADA!!" Jake! Little Jacob, in his pajamas, runs toward me in the early morning, slapping his feet on our hard wood floors.

"Shhhh! Mommy's sleeping. Don't wake her up."

"DADA!! DADA!!" Jake's excited to see me.

"What's going on buddy?" I need to bend down to find out what this two-year-old boy wants. I want him to go through life ecstatically happy and looking at him, with his rosy cheeks, his excited hazel eyes, I can see that's all he wants too. He pulls my hand, slapping his feet on the hardwood floor, pulling me toward the couch in front of the television.

"DADA SIT!!" I oblige him and he sits on my lap looking forward at the dark TV screen. We sit there for twenty seconds or so, and then he looks up at me and points his finger at the TV.

"What? Is there something little Jakey wants?" Clever one... He planned on getting Dada to sit with him on the couch, watch TV while sitting on his lap and maybe having juice or milk. Not a bad plan, except the television is not on, a fact that has caused him bewilderment as to the inability of the world to follow this simple plan.

"DADA, TV ON!!"

"I have to turn down the sound, because Mommy is sleeping."

"OK"

It's good to see Jacob talking more, unlike that floppy, grunting infant. I pull him off my lap, and turn on the power to the RCA and shift the channel to 28 on the UHF. A hazy picture appears, with an irregular broken line in the middle of the screen, distorting Big Bird into a yellow mass of feathers, his bill and eyes peering down at the meandering shape of his body. I just have to move around

118

the antennae atop the television a little and *voila*, Big Bird is back to one piece, surrounded by inner-city New York. He's singing a sad song about the color yellow, a song about himself that makes you feel for this overgrown bird. I sit back down with Jacob sitting on my lap.

The back of Jacob's head rests on my chest and my arms surround him around his waist. It doesn't matter to me what we're watching, but it's peculiar to see how the Cookie Monster eats a pile of chocolate chip cookies without ever swallowing them. Everything to him is cookies, which he says with a guttural sound, "Cooookiiie," similar to a wino asking for change to load up again; an addicted, pathologic, blue creature that subsists on nothing but cookies. Even though he's lovable, maybe he's not a good example for Jacob.

My focus shifts behind me through the window and into the street on a quiet, sunny morning in the Southland. I convince Jacob to leave the Cookie Monster and we walk outside of the house on a warm winter morning where the haze has departed and the sky is a deep blue. The Santa Ana Winds have come to bless the angels in us all. Jacob's hand embraces my index and middle fingers and I wrap my palm over the back of his hand as we stroll down the sidewalk in Culver City; a deliciously clear day that holds me in a trance, satisfied in simply placing one foot in front of the next. The street is quiet, cars parked in front of their houses, owners inside shutting out the sparkling day. The bees are already awake, navigating between the fragrant flowers. The smell of jasmine and the hope of a day of leisure invigorate me. I take a deep inhale from my cigarette.

"Dada, butterfly," Jacob says excitedly, points and repeats, "Dada, butterfly." There's an orange and black butterfly, fluttering in arcs seemingly without a destination, its movements totally random. Jacob lets go of my finger, jumping up and down. "Butterfly! Butterfly!"

"Are you a butterfly Jacob?" I put my cigarette in my mouth and mock the movement of the butterfly. He laughs.

"No, Dada, butterfly," and he spreads his own arms, flapping his imaginary wings. We both start laughing as we circle around each other flapping our wings. Jacob! We were so happy! The memory is receding in a deep cave, darkened from my view.

Chapter 7

Little Boy Blue

The cell phone's ringing. It's Mom.

"Jacob?"

"Yes."

"I just saw your father."

"And."

"Well, he…he…umm…umm."

"Mom!"

"He doesn't look very good. He can talk a little bit, but he's all connected to tubes and his face is drooping and he just doesn't look good."

"What are you telling me, Mom?"

"I don't know, Jacob. I don't know if he is going to make it through this." Mom's crying at the other end. I sip my drink and stare at the hovering moon. "I feel so bad for your dad. I just don't want to see him suffer."

"He'll make it through this. He's strong."

"I pray for him, Jacob. I pray that your father will find his way."

"He's got to make it."

"But I worry…"

"I want him to see my daughter!" I look down. Our little girl may never know her grandfather, like I knew my grandfathers, and it's so sad and empty. I start to cry, but stop myself. "I can't believe this has happened. I mean—"

"It's happening, Jacob. I know you're wondering why it had to happen now, but everything has a purpose. Everything… We have to trust in Jesus. He'll make everything right."

"I'll be there on Sunday. Maybe Dad will want to get better when he sees me and I tell him he's about to be a grandfather."

"I'm sure you're right. I just don't want to see him suffer."

I hang up and notice there's a voicemail message.

"Mr. Mathews, this is Dr. Schwartz of Cardiology, your father is having a heart attack. We are going to need to do an emergency

121

angioplasty to stop the heart attack. I was hoping to get consent to do the procedure, but we don't have time to wait."

Oh, my God! I got to call the hospital.

"Can I speak to the doctor taking care of Paul Mathews? I forgot his name—he's in Cardiology."

"The doctor's not here, but his nurse is right next to me. Her name is Angela. I'll give you to her."

"Hello."

"Yes, this is Jacob Mathews, Paul Mathews' son. Dr., I think its Schwartz, called me about my father having a heart attack."

"He had a heart attack earlier today and is in heart failure, but he's currently stable on medication."

"Stable?"

"He's on medication to keep the fluid out of his lungs."

"His heart is failing? Is he going to die?"

"His blood pressure and oxygen levels are a little on the low side, but he's stable."

"Is he awake?"

"No, I think he's still sedated from the procedure."

"Did the procedure fix the problem?"

"I don't think it was successful."

"What?"

"It would be better to speak to the doctor about that. I don't want to give you wrong information."

"Can I speak to the doctor now?"

"The doctor is not here now."

What else can I say?

"Mr. Mathews?"

"Yeah."

"I'll have the doctors call you first thing tomorrow." I can't breathe. My heart's palpitating and sweat is pouring down from the top of my head. I feel like I'm the one having the heart attack.

"OK, thank you."

"I'm sorry about your father."

I sit paralyzed, the phone loose in my hand. This whole thing seems unreal. Is this it? Is he going to die? I have to still do the presentation. I need those accounts.

The next day I'm at work when my cell rings. "Hello."

"Mr. Mathews?"

"Yes."

"This is Dr. Gellman, your father's internist. Your father has had a heart attack."

"I know. How is he?"

"He's stable now, but a considerable part of his heart was damaged."

"Oh God!"

"Dr. Schwartz, the cardiologist, tried to open the blocked blood vessel, but couldn't do it. Your father has had some heart failure since that time and there's now fluid in his lungs. He is more stable now, but he had a difficult night."

"Do you think he'll pull through?"

"I'm not sure. When are you going to come down?" I'm looking out the window of my office at some birds in a tree. "Mr. Mathews?"

"Sunday. I would have come down there sooner, but this all caught me by surprise."

"We're glad we got in touch with you." Should I go down there now?

"Please do everything you can for him, Doctor."

"We will." His tone though makes it sound like Dad may be gone by Sunday. He hangs up the phone. I'm staring through the window at a pretty evergreen. Dad seems so far away now. He's always seemed far away. There's a sound from behind me and I swing my chair around to face the door. Jimmy's standing at the entrance.

"What's going on, Jake? Your father's doing better?"

"No, Jimmy. He had a heart attack yesterday."

"Man, I'm sorry to hear that. What are you doing here? You should go down there."

Christ. Not him, too. "I can't. I'll go down after this 401K account is done."

He's looking at me like I'm loco. "There will be other accounts, Jake."

"I know, but I've already done all the legwork on this one. I got the house and the kid on the way and I need the money. I just hope I can pull it off."

"Just stay calm. You'll do fine."

"Yeah, I hope so."

"You know what helps me sometimes is a small dose of Xanax."

"Xanax?"

Jimmy gave me one of his Xanax, which I took before the 401K presentation and the whole thing went off without a hitch. Sandor is a large realty firm with offices throughout Sacramento and the northern San Joaquin Valley. This was their big yearly meeting held in the Hyatt Downtown. I got up in front of 400 people, talked for maybe an hour, felt fine, and in the end, all I had to do was show the historical averages of the best performing mutual funds, speak a little bit about more conservative portfolios to prevent large losses, like what happened after 9/11 and the dot.com bust, and then show the graphs. The graphs really do the work. When those realtors, and all the people who work for them, saw the graphs and the amount of money they could make in the future, it didn't take long for them to sign up. That day alone 40 new accounts came in and I knew more would be calling me.

"I'm so proud of you!"

"Thanks, Mel, but now I got to deal with my dad."

"I know you can't really celebrate, but I want you to know I'm proud of you." She snuggles up close, puts her arms over my shoulders and gives me a warm kiss, making my lips tingle and making me feel weak in the knees. I'm lucky to have her, to know that no matter what happens in Los Angeles, I'll still have a home to come back to. "Good luck with everything, honey."

Flying over the sprawl of Los Angeles, my home for 30 years, I peer down at the rows of houses, buildings, cars. The lights of the city glow with life. All those people down there, unaware of my existence, hovering high above them. What are all those people doing on a Saturday night? My father's one of those people, somewhere down there, alone in his hospital room. The last time I saw him was up in Sacramento for my wedding. He was there at the Sunday brunch after the wedding, wearing this oversized Hawaiian shirt. Talk about standing out in the crowd, his tallish figure, his protuberant belly and that Hawaiian shirt with the parrots on it. I remember my friend Andy saying, "Your father looks like he got off the wrong plane." And, there he was, my self-righteous father with his slicked back graying hair, his loafers and his I'm-miles-away expression. He didn't even know how pitiful he looked. Shoot! Him and his Sixties Generation are getting old and the time has caught up with them whether they like it or not. As I look at the lights of the city end at the ocean, I think, it is my time now. It's my time now. I'm the man. I feel so anxious though and I wish I had something to calm me down, maybe a cigarette. Maybe another Xanax. The possibility of Dad dying is still inconceivable.

I'm off the plane and make my way outside to catch a taxi. "Where you going?" an Indian man asks.

"Best Western on Sepulveda." The taxi drives quickly from the airport and I arrive at the hotel at about 11 pm. When I get in the room I instinctively turn on the television and am somehow comforted by the ESPN announcers. No matter what happens they will always be there. I need to put away my clothes, my slacks and my nice shirt to wear in front of the doctors. I take a shower, brush my teeth and prop myself up in the bed to watch some sports coverage.

"Now to Kobe Bryant. Bryant has come into the season with new focus. The question will no longer be his focus on basketball, since the rape charges against him have been dropped. Kobe scored 60 points against The Raptors Friday night and could have had more." It's no use. I'm not interested in this shit. I'm just waiting for the big day tomorrow. I turn off the lights, turn off the T.V. and stare up at the ceiling. I'm the one responsible for my father, the old man. This mess he has made, I now get to clean up. I know I can do it, much better than he could, and I'm going to show him that he was wrong about me, that I have more integrity than he ever could.

I awake feeling not refreshed. The last few days have taken a toll on me and I do not want to move. My head aches, my eyes pain... Where the hell am I? Oh God, I don't feel well. The bed is wet with sweat. Slowly I struggle toward the bathroom, turn on the light and take a leak. I walk over to the sink and rinse my face with cold water, look at myself, and the way I look is the way I feel. My hair is graying and is unruly. There's stubble on my face. Can I start the day over again? I shit, shower and then put on clothes while watching the television. The Patriots are playing at the Colts today. What a game that would be! More important things to do. OK man, get the hell out of here. I walk down to the main desk and partake of the continental breakfast, a croissant and coffee. Boy, do I need coffee for my aching head. A man and woman with two young children, a boy and girl, are sitting a couple of tables away from me. The parents are pleading with the boy to eat his cereal, but the boy, who must be four or five, doesn't want the Cheerios. He wants the Fruit Loops. The parents finally cave in. The little girl has left her seat and is walking around the tables.

The little boy complains. "Why does she get to walk around?"

"Because she ate all of her breakfast," the mother answers. The little girl has made her way toward me. She is sucking her thumb and holding a little blanket. She looks up at me. What a cute little girl. I smile at her and she shyly turns her head away toward her shoulder, but she still looks at me. She takes her thumb out of her mouth and gives me a silly smile. I have now made a friend.

"Michelle, stop bothering the man." This emboldens the little girl and she toddles up to my leg, puts her little blanket on my lap and looks up at me. She smiles and I smile back. It will be nice to have a little girl. Her mom comes over and pulls the little girl away from me. "I told you to stop bothering the man. I'm sorry, sir."

"That's OK. She's really cute."

"She's really a handful."

I finish the croissant and coffee and wait for the taxi outside; an opportune time to smoke a cigarette. The hazy day reminds me of so many days I spent here in Los Angeles, playing football or baseball with friends. Days that seem so far away, so distant, a past that only can be seen through a thick haze. The cab arrives.

"Where you going, man?"

"St. Luke's Hospital." We pull out of the driveway and onto Sepulveda. Out the window is a sprawl of coffee houses, liquor stores and every kind of low-end retail imaginable. I'm feeling scared going over to see Dad. I hope he can at least talk, say something to me.

126

"Where you from?" the taxi driver asks.

"Originally from here, but I'm living in Sacramento now. I'm coming here to see my dad in the hospital."

"I'm sorry about that. Is it bad?"

"Pretty bad." He doesn't say anything more so after some time I feel I have to chime in. "I just hope he makes it."

"It's hard when someone in your family's sick."

"Yeah." That same tightness is back in my chest. Could it all be anxiety? I wish I had a Xanax now. I wonder how it was for Dad when he was younger. Did he stress out like this? Maybe that's why he drank and smoked pot. We pull in front of the hospital, into a driveway. The meter on the taxi reads $14.20. I pull 15 dollars out of my wallet.

"I hope the best for your dad?"

"Thanks." I hand him the money, step out of the taxi and walk toward the entrance of the hospital. There is a statue of St. Luke out front, with his long hair and robe. I walk past him and stop at the front desk. There's a plump woman sitting beneath a sign that says. "Admissions."

"I'm looking for Paul Mathews."

"Are you related?"

"I'm his son." She types the name into a computer.

"Mr. Mathews is in room 428 in the ICU." She points behind me. "Just take the elevator to the fourth floor."

"Thank you."

I walk toward the elevator. My heart's pounding, remembering the last time Dad was in the hospital. How he smiled at me and said that everything would be all right, even though he had just had a heart attack. He didn't look so bad that time, but this sounds worse. My poor father! I sort of feel bad for him. Yeah, he could have been a better dad. Maybe I could have been a better son. I could have listened to him more. He wasn't a bad father; just not a great one and then he just stopped being a father at all.

I push the Up button at the elevator.

He did give me everything I ever needed, helped pay my way through college, went to all my baseball games and even helped pay for the wedding. I could have been nicer to him. The elevator door opens and I step in. My chest tightens, and I feel that I can't

127

get a deep breath into it. I try taking shallower breaths, which helps a little, but it's making me lightheaded. The elevator reaches the fourth floor and the doors slide open. I'm walking out the elevator and down a hallway painted light blue, coming to a closed door with a phone on the side. Above the phone is a little plastic plaque. "Pick up phone for entrance. No entrance from 7:00 to 8:00 AM and from 7:00 to 8:00 PM." I look at my watch. It's 10:15. I pick up the phone and hear it ring.

"ICU."

"I'm here to see Paul Mathews in room 428. I'm his son."

The door buzzes and I pull it open. The air feels different inside. I'm walking down a hallway with multiple rooms, more like alcoves, on one side. Each of the alcoves has a sliding-glass front that allows me to see in. My heart's palpitating out of my chest. The hallway and the rooms are painted light blue and the floor is colored bluish-gray. There are the sounds of beeping machines in different pitches and cadences all around which may mean that someone's not doing well. Where's my father? In the room directly in front of me there's an older woman lying flat in a bed with a breathing tube going into her mouth. The room number says room 412.

"Do you need some help, sir?" The woman is dressed in blue scrubs.

"I'm...I'm looking for 428," I weakly say.

She points to my right.

Mechanically, on its own, my head turns that direction.

"Just down the hall. I think Marge is the nurse today, if you see her." I'm slowly making my way down the hall. My legs are like jelly and the pressure in my chest works its way up my neck, making it difficult to swallow. Each of the rooms on my left has a person inside and some of them look like they're not too bad, and some look like crap. Some of these people have tubes coming out of their mouth and their eyes are closed. Even the tubes are blue.

My poor dad. There were those times I was with him and Mom walking on the beach, riding on his shoulders. We were so happy then. I've got to get him out of here. He can't die here. I won't let it happen. This is not the way it's supposed to be. I want him to know how much I love him. Oh Jesus. Oh Jesus. Please give me

128

strength. I stand for some time in front of room 428 looking at the figure in the bed.

"Are you his son?" a voice behind me says.

"Yes, I am." I turn around to face a short man with dark skin in a white jacket. Dude seems a little young to be a doctor.

"I'm Dr. Patel, the internist taking care of your father this weekend."

"Where's Dr. Gellman?"

"He's off this weekend and I'm covering his hospital patients. Have you seen him yet?" He motions his head toward the room behind me.

"No, I just got here. How is he?"

"I saw him earlier today. He's over the heart attack. His heart failure has been stabilized and his kidney tests have improved."

"How long is he going to be on the respirator?"

"I think for some time. Your father has emphysema and still needs a good amount of ventilatory support."

Dr. Patel keeps talking, but my focus is on a bearded man I see out of the corner of my eye, walking toward us. Dr. Patel stops talking and we both turn to look at this older man, who looks a little bit angry.

"Mr. Mathews this is Dr. Johnson. He's the Infectious disease doctor."

"Hi." He extends his hand out to me and we shake. "I'm really not on the case anymore. Your dad's pneumonia has resolved and he's on the right antibiotics."

"Thanks for your help."

"Mr. Mathews, I want to be frank with you. Your father has multiple medical problems: diabetes, heart failure, emphysema and a large stroke. He also has coded twice, meaning there was a good amount of time when his brain did not have oxygen."

"OK."

"What I'm trying to say is that he may never get off the respirator and that he most probably will never lead an independent life."

"Most probably? What percentage chance does he have?"

"I can't give you a percentage."

"Then how can you be so sure? I mean, you don't even know who my dad is, I mean the kind of person he is."

"You're right, I don't know him, but I've been working in this hospital for more than thirty years, have seen birth and death and much of what falls in between."

"Dr. Patel, do you agree?" I look toward the short Indian man.

"In some ways I do, but since I've only seen him for the last two days, I'm not the best person to make that assessment."

"Mr. Mathews, you have to think about what your father wants." Dr. Johnson points into the room. "Do you think he wants this?"

"I don't know what he wants. He never told me. Have you asked him?"

"I've tried to talk to him, but he's been asleep or has not responded."

"Well if he can't give you an answer, then neither can I."

"I understand that. But you may eventually have to, as his closest relative. Would you want this?"

"I'd want anything to make me better." He looks at me with an irritated expression. Boy, this guy's a prick!

"Are you sure?"

"You know, I haven't even seen my father yet. Do you mind?"

"I didn't know you hadn't seen him."

"So, now you know!"

"I just wanted to say my piece. I'm actually coming off the case as he has no further infectious disease issues." His look disarms me. His eyes crinkle up in a look of concern. "I hope for the best for you and your father."

"Thank you."

He turns away and walks down the hall, stopping in front of another patient's room. I look down at Dr. Patel. "I don't like that guy," I say.

"I know he can be pretty abrasive, but he means well. There's no better doctor in this hospital."

"Wonderful bedside manner."

"Well, I've got to go. Dr. Gellman will be coming by tomorrow."

"OK."

I turn back to the room. Dad's lying in the bed, his eyes closed. The left side of his face is drooping. The area around his eyes is swollen and his lower face his swollen. His scant grey hair is messed up. Hanging behind him are multiple bags with fluid connected to tubes that are going into his right arm. He has a blue tube coming out of his neck and it is connected to a machine. His chest heaves up and down. My poor dad! Oh, I'm so sorry! I'll take care of you. I'll take care of you.

Chapter 8

Is that you, Jacob?

What's going on? Where did the blue sky go, and what is this ceiling I'm staring at with these perfectly aligned holes? It looks familiar. Something's wrong with my breathing, like it's not me that's breathing. I need to control this, take a deep breath in. I got to fight this machine, but I can't and my chest is collapsing down against my control. Oh my head! Am I being drugged? Everything is spinning and I feel like I'm going to vomit.

And why the hell can't I breathe? My chest feels like it's expanding too much. God! Give me some independence from this machine. Maybe if I breathe faster and get some of this air out of my lungs I will have control over this machine. But hell, breathing faster is taking a lot of effort and I'm feeling increasingly lightheaded. Breathe, Paul! Or just let the machine breathe for you.

I need to try not to think about my breathing, divert my attention to the ceiling, or think about the itch on the right side of my head that I can't scratch. My body's in a state of lethargy and my mind's equally lethargic. What the hell happened to me? There are voices in the distance, a constant drone that is simultaneously comforting and annoying. This doesn't make sense. For some reason nothing makes sense, so I got to return back to my breathing, which adds to my anxiety. A chill runs up my spine and now there's a pain in my butt and now a perpetual desire to urinate and now a mild pain in my chest. Ahhhhhh! God, why do I have to go through this? Why me?

There must be some way to alleviate my suffering, take away the itch on my forehead, fix my breathing, extinguish the pain in my ass and overcome my lethargy. The drugged nausea is overwhelming bringing acidity in my throat that makes me want to salivate, but my mouth's so dry and my tongue is beef jerky. "Beep, Beep, Beep," the chastising alarm sounds. The beeping suddenly reminds of the respirator, the machine giving me life. My breath is stuttering and I don't know if I am inhaling or exhaling.

There's a woman above me wearing nurse's scrubs. She has white skin, short brown hair that's spiked in the front, wears glasses and looks at me, then looks below me, then looks at my face. What a funny-looking woman. She looks more like a bird. Where did you go, funny woman? Please come back. She looks like someone I'd normally pass in the street and not even notice, but now I'd die just to see her face. The beeping continues, getting maddening. The spike-haired nurse returns on my right side.

"Just a little something to calm you down," she says. The bird-woman bends down over my right arm and all I can see is the top of her spiked head with the spaces between the gelled spikes showing a pink scalp. I marvel at the architecture.

She looks at me, while rubbing my chest. "You'll be OK in a couple of minutes." Her look is kind, attentive and hopeful. Thank you for the distraction from my pain, for your reassuring voice, for considering a job of alleviating people's suffering. The bird-woman looks above me at something, maybe a fish for the eating, and then walks away. The beeping has stopped and my breathing is more relaxed...relaxed...relaxed. Oh, so this is reeeeeeeeeeelaaaaaaaaxed. Oh yeah! Did you ever think you would be President? No, I never thought that. Why not, you're pretty smart? Why would I want to be President? Because the country needs a level-headed guy like you. Why be President when I can be a writer? You're still young. You can change the course of your life. You know what, you're right. I can change things. After this vacation, I am really going to focus on changing my life. First thing I am going to do is...well, I'm going to...Jacob...and there is my condo, maybe I should sell it and use the money to finance...my book... What book is that? Well, let me tell you. It's a story about the migration to Southern California of two friends, guys from a small town in Pennsylvania, who never make it to their destination, never fulfill their dreams, keeping their dreams completely intact and inviolate for years and years. I guess the moral of the story is "never dream." Sounds good. Yeah, I think it is good. It's finished? Yeah it is. It would make your mom and dad so proud. Yeah, it would. So do it, man. Publish it! Yeah. Just think of how jealous Sarah would be if you did it... Sarah?...Jacob. Jacob would really look up to his old man, the writer. I'm not old, you're old. No, you are. No, I'm not. Sleep? Oh yeah, man, I'm tired. Long day it's been. Tomorrow is a new day. Sun will come out tomorrow. Hey, there's the sun and there's the ocean and there's a young man.

"Jacob, Jacob is that you?" Jacob looks younger than I remember. We're sitting on a sandy beach, watching the waves coming in, curling then flattening; the foamy water advancing up the beach, then receding to its origin. The rays of the sun peer up from the ocean's horizon and the thinly clouded sky is drenched in a soft, slowly burning red which light up Jacob's face and make his hair a dusty brown as he calmly watches the sea. His reddish features contrast with the dark blue sky behind him. He is so beautiful at this moment. "Jacob." He looks toward me and while he looks like he is twenty his eyes shine with a wisdom I could never know.

"Yeah."

"What are you thinking about?"

"I was thinking about how beautiful this time is, the sunset."

"It is beautiful."

"It makes me a little sad, though. It lasts such a short time. You know, I feel like I can sit in this light forever, but then the moment is over and I'm left looking at darkness. It makes me kind of sad."

"Darkness is not here yet, Jacob."

"I know, but it's just around the corner. It is always around the corner."

"It's always around the corner. But why focus on something that's not here?"

"What do you mean?

"I mean, why worry about something we probably can't understand?

Jacob looks down at his hands, which grab and contain grains of sand. He turns his fists over, fingers down, slowly releasing the grains of sand and looks up at me. His face has changed, less angular and more rounded, like the face of a twelve-year-old, lit by the dying rays of the sun. His body is thin and small as I look down at him. I must be dreaming. My son! My young, confused son! He speaks in a high-pitched whiny voice, but his manner and speech are thoughtful, deliberate.

"I don't know, Dad. I guess I worry about the darkness, because it comes before I can make any sense out of the light. That I'll never make sense out of this life and that death will come and leave me wondering why I ever had to fulfill the obligation of living. Why do I have to do anything? Why did you bring me into this world?" He looks up with sensitive eyes and I don't know what to say. I place my hand on his brown hair, brush it back, and give him my best version of the truth.

"I don't know, Jacob. I don't know why we brought you in this world. Maybe it was for selfish reasons. Maybe I had a plan in my head of having a job, getting married and raising a child. Maybe you were just part of that plan, but I also think maybe I believed I could show you the beauty and wonder of this life, like watching the sunset on the beach, like those quiet times we've played catch. Help you learn for yourself that life's worth living, although it is beautifully absurd." I draw my hand away. Sitting there in a trance, I look out at the sunset, its inviting fiery glow diminishing on the horizon, and think about how the revolution of the earth can bring about such amazing changes in the sky. I look back toward Jacob and the little boy who sat there is gone, replaced by a confident looking man, older and less fresh, like a man in his thirties. He lies on his back, content to simply look up at the sky and possibly pondering my last words. What's he thinking? He sits up, crosses his hairy legs and looks at the horizon.

"Was life worth living? Your life seemed pretty miserable at times to me."

"I know. I could have been a better example."

"I forgive you. I understand better now. Our lives are often distant, seductive, and unknown, like the sunset on the horizon. We're never able to reach it, handle it, control it. Doesn't the sunset make you feel a little sad?" I turn my head away and look to the orange glow. It is sort of sad and lovely, this culmination of the day.

"I do feel a little sad, but it is not a bad feeling."

"No, not a bad feeling," he says in a crackly voice. I look toward the crackly voice and see my son's face is old and wrinkled, yet beautiful in the fading light, his hair receding and gray, his eyelids drooping, his lips dry and cracking. My son is an old man and I mourn the loss of his youth. He looks forward, smiling, and hoarsely says, "The sun rises and we run to see it. The sun is up and we shield our eyes from it. The sun is gone and we chase after it with all our strength." My son's elderly face becomes darker and darker until his silhouette is all I see, and then his silhouette is lost in darkness.

I look up at the ceiling with the multiple squares filled in with rows of holes. The light is fluorescent. The respirator is giving me breath. A computerized beep runs to the beat of my heart. What a strange dream that was. Was it a dream? Or a memory? In the distance I hear someone saying something, but it is faint and I have to separate that voice from the sounds of my heart and the sounds of the respirator. What is the person saying? It sounds like he's saying "Dad." I look over to my left hand side and sitting there is the old Jacob, the old man of my dream, wrinkled, covered in age spots, his cheeks sunken in due to the loss of his teeth and he looks at me. Jake's a wizened man who has seen everything that life has to offer. The fluorescent light gives his features an unnatural brightness. He's trying to say something, repeating a sentence I can't understand through the sounds of the respirator and the beeping.

"What are you trying to say Jacob? What do you want to tell me?" I say, amazed at my ability to speak.

He points to me and then moves his arms, head and eyes in a circular motion, encompassing the hospital room we are in. "Dad," he turns his gaze to me. "Dad, this is not you. *This is not you!*" He repeats this several more times, more quietly with each repetition, as if it were some mantra. I imagine I'm looking at myself lying in the hospital bed with a respirator at my bedside, a monitor over my head, with my little boy holding my hand, then my little Jacob walks away and I'm left alone lying there.

OUCH! There's a sharp pain in my right arm. My eyes crawl over to see the top of a woman's head, black hair pulled back in a bun. "Just a morning blood draw, Mr. Mathews. We had to do it because your PICC line is clotted," she says in an accent that sounds melodious, like she's singing a song. I don't see the face of my benefactor and before I know it, she's gone. There are sounds in the distance and it is a welcoming distraction.

136

"This is going to be a great match-up of two NFC East Powerhouses, the Indianapolis Colts and the New England Patriots; one team a Super Bowl Champion and the other team wanting respect. Each team is led by great quarterbacks; Peyton Manning, one of the most prolific passers in the game and Tom Brady, a quarterback who knows what it takes to win, guiding his team to the promised land two times in the last three years. Stay tuned for interviews with Colt's running back Edgerrin James on how he believes this year will be the year the Colts take a Super Bowl title home to Indianapolis." The deep voice of the announcer stops and is replaced by a hyper one. "Bring all the gang over for Pizza. Two large pepperoni pizzas, two thirty-two-ounce Cokes and tasty deep-fried breaded cheese, all for fourteen ninety-nine! Now, until the end of the year, you can get all this for fourteen ninety-nine! Don't miss out on Domino's Deals to kick off the game!" Budweiser's espousing the virtue of "fresh" beer. I need to tune out and focus on the sound of my breathing. For some reason breathing has become more comfortable. I want to sleep.

"Mr. Mathews?" Dude, I'm sleeping here! "Mr. Mathews? Mr. Mathews?" Man has a hint of an Indian accent. Is this an Ashram? He has dark skin, a full head of black hair, a chubby face with a hint of a smile. He seems young, no more than thirty.

"Mr. Mathews, I am Doctor Patel. I am covering this weekend for Dr. Gellman. Everything seems to be going smoothly and I have heard that your son should be coming today." He pulls the stethoscope from around his neck, puts on the earpieces and says, "I am going to listen to your heart and lungs." He pulls off the blanket covering me. His head hovers over my chest as he listens with his stethoscope. He makes his way down to my belly, pushing on it for a while, and then he looks at my legs, touching my right leg hard and my first impulse is to jump because of the pain, but I'm barely moving. He puts the blanket over me. "Take care, Mr. Mathews."

Take care? Something is wrong here. I'm staring at this ceiling and for God knows what reason, I feel relaxed......comfortable. The facts are that I feel only minimal sensation on the whole left side of body, that I'm on a respirator with a tube coming out of my neck, that I'm being fed artificially, and that I'm having trouble remembering all these things, but it doesn't seem to bother me. I feel a great love for this benign universe and wish that somehow I could share this love. I even feel love for the ceiling, each hole in a line of perfection. It is truly amazing, what man can do. No other mammal makes such perfectly aligned holes. Who came up with that idea? I marvel at the species.

"The ball is on the twenty-four-yard line, second down and seven. Manning calls an audible. He drops back to pass, throws it over the middle and completes it to Harrison. First down. The New England defense broke down there, Jack. The Colts have a big opportunity to score here on their first drive of the game. First and ten, Indianapolis on the New England thirty-five-yard line. Manning is behind center, hands off to James, who barrels forward to the New England thirty-two-yard line. You would think, Marv, that the Colts would continue to pass there, but they opted for the run. I agree, Mel, with key injuries to New England's secondary, I would look to establish a strong passing game to allow the defense to open up for Edgerrin James."

They seem to take this game so seriously. Shit, I used to take this game seriously. It was part of my life. I loved it. Football on Sundays was a ritual for me, like going to Church was for Sarah. Not that I'm condemning myself. I'm tired of condemning myself. This is the life I led, but laying here it seems the whole thing was sort of funny and somewhat absurd; beautifully absurd. Each player, each team, multiple scenarios, the physical grace of a well-toned athlete making a remarkable play, rooting for one team and vilifying the next, basketball, baseball, football, tennis, hockey, golf, year in and year out, was like opening another page in a long book called *Life Through the Eyes of an Athlete*. A distraction! I think I've finished that book.

My breathing is calm and there is no sound, except the sound of my breathing. There's a weird pain in my lower back, a pain I didn't notice before, a gnawing, itchy pain and it makes me want to scratch it, but I can't move. I close my eyes. Shapes emerge out of the darkness, images of people and characters from the past, Mom and Dad, both old and withered, Dad's blue eyes sunken into his wrinkled face, his white hair having only slightly less color than that of his face. A younger version of Dad, wearing a suit, double-breasted, holding his pocket watch-fob. My mother as I last remember her, wise and calm in the hospital in Tucson, dying of ovarian cancer, waiting for what she said were God's arms; her funeral, long after Sarah and I divorced, and I see myself struggling, trying to bridge the gap that had formed between Sarah, Jacob and me. I see Jacob in a picture holding a bat, dressed in a Little League version of an Oakland A's jersey, his hair long, unruly, dropping down from his cap. Sarah in a flowery dress, young and lovely, crouching next to a tulip. Was that a photo, too? Yes, that was a snapshot of her in Solvang. I don't remember taking it? I see the images and feel a great love for these people of the past. I mourn them.

I think of me. I think of all the pictures of me, the childhood pictures Mom gave me before she died, the college picture of me sitting at Meyerhoff Park at UCLA, smoking a cigarette in the shelter of a group of friends, my wedding pictures, dipping my beautiful bride on the dance-floor, the picture of me at Venice Beach holding Jacob's hand. That person is long gone, replaced by one who you'll not see in a photo album, lying prostrate, looking perpetually upward, vulnerable and unable to resist the outside world. In and out the machine breathes. Why resist it?

"Brady passes to the outside and it is another first down for New England."

"Damn, play some defense why don't you!" a muted voice says. There's someone else in the room. There's a man to my left, holding my lifeless hand. He has brown, wavy hair, pulled back and receding at the corners, a rounded face, but an angular chin and eyes I cannot see because they're looking at the television screen. I want to look at those hazel eyes. Jacob! Jacob, look at me. It's your father. I'm awake. I got to say something, anything, but I can't. Maybe, if I try to move my arm toward him then he'll notice me, but I can only lift it a little. Jacob's here and I thought I'd never see him again. Oh, Jacob! Shoot, a part of me wants to get his attention and a part of me is simply content to look at him. He appears older, a man now in the world, the stubble of a beard covering his cheeks and jaw. His mouth is slightly open as he stares at the TV. I remember holding him as a boy, on my lap.

Now, he's a man who sits over his infirmed father. I search for the boy I remember in this man. Is he trying not to look at me?

Jacob! Jacob! He finally notices me looking at him and his gaze shifts downward and our eyes connect. We're staring at each other, becoming transfixed, dumbfounded by the awe of this reunion; maybe our last. There's a fleeting moment of regret at all my transgressions in life and a desire to confess my sins to my son and humble myself to him. Yet, how can I be more humble than I am now?

Jacob, see what's happened to your proud old man! The vulnerable person disintegrating in this bed is what I've become. I'm trying to convey what I'm thinking and he looks back at me, equally intent on hearing the words of a dying man. Son, realize that your father truly loves you. He rarely showed it, because of his own fear and maybe, when you have your own children, you too will fear the humility of love. Try not to fear pain so much, try to not let the disappointments of the past rule your life. Don't be afraid to try again. I settled for comfort and isolation when my dreams didn't work out. I gave up! Jacob, don't fall into the trap of your own thoughts, of what is bad or good. Don't close yourself within the walls of who you think you are, even though I may have helped build those walls. The past is the past and your old man is on his way to being part of it. Be at peace with me, the good and bad parts.

My mouth's moving, but no words are coming out. Jacob's eyes are swollen, his nose is runny, as he watches me struggle for the words. This is hard on him. There's cheering on the TV and Jake reflexively looks away toward the television.

"Brady throwing to the end-zone… Touchdown Patriots!"

"I tell you, Marv, this New England team is a well-oiled machine. Nothing appears to deter them, not even the most powerful offense in the NFL, from their goal of winning the game."

"I agree with you, Jack, and I believe what you're seeing here reflects on the coach."

Can somebody shut the television off? Television is not living. Jake, look at me! Jacob's not looking at me, but his gaze is upward to an area just below the heavens.

"Veniteri for the extra point, snap down, the kick is good and New England leads 24 to 17." Jacob looks at me again. He appears a little calmer, but somewhat distracted, sitting there with my lifeless hand within his.

"Dad... It's Jacob, Dad. Can you understand me?"

I'm trying to nod, but my head only moves slightly.

He appears to understand. "I'm sorry it took me so long to get here, but they just told me about it a few days ago. Are you in any pain? Are you OK?"

Why the hell am I nodding?

"I spoke to the doctors, Dr. Gellman and Dr. Masterson. They told me what happened and they think you have a good chance of pulling through."

Pulling through? What have these doctors told you, Jake? Pulling through? It sounds as if I am coming out of the birth canal, a perfect new being. I'm shaking my head, barely, managing to move it from side to side. Jacob, I don't think I'm going to make it! I'd be long gone if it were not for these amazing contraptions keeping me alive. This is the end of life, this is saying goodbye. The respirator starts beeping and I'm trying to relax and become one with the respirator, but the beeping continues. Marge comes into the room.

"Is he getting a little agitated?" she says.

"I think he's having a problem with his breathing," Jacob replies.

Marge turns her focus to my neck. After a few seconds there's a sucking sound, like the sucking from a straw at the bottom of a near-empty paper cup, and then my breath is easier. Marge says, "Just tell me if he starts becoming agitated. I can give him medicine to relax," and she leaves the room.

Jacob looks to me, his eyes sincere, but wanting something from me. "Dad, you have to pull through. You have to make it through this. You cannot... Listen. Do you understand me?"

Again I nod. Jacob understands and smiles.

"Dad, Melissa's going to have a baby. She's five months pregnant."

A baby? Jake, you're going to be a father! That's wonderful! I must be smiling, because he's smiling too. Jacob, I'm proud of you. You've persisted, persevered and now you're going to have a kid. He wants to say something else, something that appears meaningful.

"Dad, I want you to see my child."

But, Jacob?

"I want our child to know her grandfather, like I got to know Grandpa Josh and Grandpa Joe."

Jake, look at me, look at my body. I've been hit by a Semi. Jacob! No! I don't think I could have a meaningful relationship with anyone.

"Dad! Dad!"

I don't think any child is going to get a favorable impression of a person covered in tubes, who smells of shit and drools. God, I wish I could talk and try to convey to him what I'm thinking. The boy's looking at me with gentle, loving eyes as if I am a baby bird that has fallen out of a nest. The way he's looking at me makes me wonder if somehow, during my past life, I prevented him from being loving and gentle to me; that somehow I stopped something that should have happened. I may have been too proud and blocked his gifts of kindness, and it is only now when I lie prostrate that I may receive his love. Strange that love has as much to do with receiving as it does with giving.

"You have to stay alive. You can't just give up." The boy's pleading with me, bowing down so I only see the top of his head. There are a few streaks of grey. What do I do? What can I do? Maybe, somehow I can survive, but hell, what kind of life will I lead? I owe it to Jake, though; for all the parts of our relationship I've neglected, I do owe him his wishes. If he wants me to stay alive, I'll stay alive. Who am I kidding! I don't even have a choice! I look up to the ceiling with the perfectly aligned holes and pray that there is some deity to show me a happy ending.

"Manning back to pass. He fires over the middle and it is intercepted by Ty Law at the forty-five-yard line and New England can celebrate another victory over their hated rivals. Indianapolis made a valiant effort, but could not overcome this Patriot team."

142

Jacob's attention is focused on the television. Now he looks down at me. "Dad, I have to go to the bathroom. Too much coffee. I'll be right back."

My eyes close and I feel the breath swelling and receding. Is it right to be kept alive like this? My choices are my current incapacitated state and death. Death...to cease existing...to depart from the concept of me...and I thought it would be difficult, but it's not, especially now that my body's failing. All it takes is just letting go and the only thing stopping me from letting go now is Jacob's request that I stay a little longer. I owe him that. I owe him that. I want to know that he'll be OK.

Would it not cause him less suffering if I did die? He would not have to watch his father in this purgatory. His life is about new life now, coming into the world, not worn-out life going out of it. What's the right answer? I have no concept of what death is and I have no concept about what my life would be like in the future. Maybe I can recover. Maybe I just see things too pessimistically. Then there's my book. I've got to tell Jacob about the book.

"What's this! This is completely gross! Nurse! Nurse!" What's wrong Jake? Jacob's towering over me.

"What's the problem? Is everything alright?" Marge's sweet voice says, but I can't see her.

"My dad is lying in his own shit, for I don't know how long." Jacob says in a nasally way.

"That's strange. We haven't been feeding him. "

"Oh, it smells awful."

"Don't worry, Mr. Mathews. Your father's lost control of his bowels and this happens here a lot in the ICU."

"No shit, but how long does he have to lay in it? How often do you check him?"

"Frequently!"

"What does that mean?"

"Please keep your voice down."

"What kind of facility are you running here?"

"I'm not running the facility. I work in it. If you want to talk to the nurse in charge, I'll be happy to arrange that. We do the best we can. We have responsibilities in other rooms, too."

"That's no excuse."

"Mr. Mathews, I have other patients who're sick, too."

"OK. Fine. I do want to speak to your supervisor."

Jacob, take it easy on them. They're doing fine by me. It does bother me to shit my pants, but they're nice enough to clean it up.

"I checked your father myself ten minutes ago. I will bring in an aide and we'll turn him on his side and clean him up. Meanwhile, I'll inform the desk that you would like to see the nursing supervisor."

Jacob looks irate. Wouldn't perpetuating my life be more stressful for him than my checking out? I need to bring this up with him, get his thinking about it, but all I can do is cough, and I can't seem to stop coughing. This sucks! Jacob, let go of me! The more I'm focusing on stopping the cough the worse the cough gets. The respirator is beeping again and another alarm goes off above my head.

"Your father's getting agitated," Marge says in a calm but annoyed voice. "I think you should leave for a little while. I'll give him medication to calm him down and we'll clean him up. Come back in another thirty minutes." Jacob looks down at me, and then brings his head down to speak into my ear. The heat from his voice reflects the anger of his sentiment.

"Dad, I'll be back and make sure they're taking good care of you. I love you, Dad." You love me? He leaves to the rhythm of the beeping machines and Marge returns to the same music, bringing something to soothe my nerves. She disappears from my view and suddenly the alarms cease. I'm still coughing, but it doesn't seem to bother me as much. What did Jacob say? He wants me to see his child? Jake? I feel tired and heavy, like I'm drugged. I feel nothing. I am nothing. I see nothing. Yet, there is something; something, like a light at the end of a tunnel, a circular light that expands in size, consuming the darkness and flooding me with the light that is Stephen Petry.

Stephen's walking toward me in the front of our condo complex as I'm walking the other way. He's carrying a guitar case and is clothed in a beige wool sweater and blue jeans. Kid's beard has gotten thicker. He stops and smiles at me with a disarming smile. Everything seems to be happening now in slow motion. He opens his mouth, but I can't understand a word he is saying. He seems to be very happy, extremely happy, like psychotically happy. What's making him so happy? It is infectious and while I can't seem to decipher exactly what he's saying, his mannerism and a few choice words like "love," "harmony," "transcendence" also make me happy.

"I'm getting married."

"I've been wondering where you've been."

"We just got back from Santa Fe. I've found the love of my life, man! I'm ready to spend the rest of my life with her."

"Congratulations, Steve." I hope he knows what he's in for.

"So, we're getting married in Santa Barbara. My parents want the wedding there, but it doesn't matter to me. I hope you can make it?"

"What's her name again?"

"Jennifer, Jenny. She's so beautiful, everything I've dreamed about." He looks as if he has just found the Grail, the key to life itself. He appears to be truly happy, but in a certain aspect one could argue that he's insane. Insane ones are the only sane ones in an insane world. He spreads his arms wide. "I feel my mind and body are open to the world and feel love floating in and out of me."

"I'm happy for you, but don't you think you need to come back down to earth?"

"Whatever happens from this point on will be done with an open heart and whatever happens I will allow to happen. Everything is vibrant: the sky, the trees, the birds, even the people and their cars. I've found the love in me and the love within another and now the love within all things."

Now I know the boy is totally off his rocker. I can't believe I'm hearing this kind of thing from a man 38 years old.

"Isn't that the girl you met volunteering in the hospital?"

"Yeah! We're going to go to this commune in Santa Fe and live off of the land. I've been there with Jenny and it is a transcendent, holy place, where the people feed from the land and live in harmony with nature and one another."

"That's great Stephen," I say in a subdued, half-hearted way.

145

"You could come with us." No doubt, the boy needs medication. He stops talking for a second and looks into my eyes as if I'm the one that's crazy. "There's nothing keeping you here, Paul."

"I need to finish my book."

"So write your book in New Mexico! Besides—you've been working on that book for years."

"Meaning?"

"Meaning you may have a better chance of finishing it there."

"Me? Live on a commune?"

"Better than going to Vegas. You were a hippie once. You could be again."

"I've had some good times in Vegas."

"Vegas is a hell hole. Look, you can sell your condo, take the money, but you really don't need much money to live there."

"Are you serious?"

"Paul, you're wasting your life away here. I see you putzing around in your condo all the time watching TV, sometimes writing your book or working on your precious Mustang. Your life isn't over. Change your life, man." He's pleading with me and for some reason I think about Jacob.

"Change my life? I can't start over. There's no forgetting my past."

"You can always change. You can always change your course."

"I wish I met you 25 years ago."

"Why?"

"Because I would have gone, but if I can't find peace in my little space here, I probably never will, no matter where I go."

"That makes sense, but you should think about trying something new."

"I'll think about it, Stephen. But, are you sure you're doing the right thing? What about all the good things you're doing for people right here? All that volunteering? All those people that depend on you?"

Stephen's looking down, reflecting on this. "Maybe I've allowed people to depend on me for too long and not allowed them to depend on themselves. Anyway, everyone volunteers at the commune and everyone gives to each other."

146

"Do you think it is really like that? I hate to bust your egalitarian bubble, but all men are not created equal, so you still will have people depending upon you."

"And I think your problem is you think you were kicked out of the Garden of Eden."

Christ almighty. Here we go again. "What the hell are you talking about?'

"Do you think that humanity was kicked out of the Garden of Eden?"

"No, but remember Stephen, I don't believe in God or religion, so I don't give a flying hoot about the Garden of Eden. It's a story and it doesn't pertain to the here and now."

"We are in Eden! We were never kicked out! There is an Eden and it surrounds us."

"You need a drink."

"Think about it. Think about coming with us to Santa Fe. I gotta go. I'm having dinner with Jenny's parents."

"If we are in Eden then why go to Santa Fe?"

"Eden is really not a place. It's a state of mind. I want to be with people who are of that state of mind. Come with us, Paul."

"I'll think about it." Santa Fe? It's cold up there. Stephen gives me a bear hug and I embrace him like a brother, not wanting to see him go.

"OK, do think about it. Really. We're getting married in three months. May 19th. I'll put an invitation in your mailbox."

He walks away, carrying his guitar, and the light seems to follow him. The big circle of light contracts to the size of a pin surrounded by complete darkness, until the pin of light is gone and there is nothing to see; nothing except the thought of leaving with Stephen to another land to start over again.

The white, holey ceiling comes into focus and there is the acrid odor of cigarettes. It's funny how I can't smell my own shit, but I pick up the lingering smell of a cigarette. I don't see the respiratory therapist, but all I can see is Jacob. Jacob, it's good to have you here. He's on my right, pacing from one end of the room to the other, appearing nervous and a little wired. He eventually notices me looking at him and sits next to me. Jacob, you reek of cigarettes. Have you not learned from your old man that cigarettes are bad for the body? Jacob, look at me now. My health would have been far better had I never smoked. Jacob's following a different train of thought.

"Dad, are you OK?"

I nod reflexively.

"Dad, I can only stay until tomorrow evening. I have to fly back to Sacramento."

That's OK Jacob.

"I would have taken more time, but my work wouldn't allow it. I've been working with different companies on their retirement accounts, trying to get more business and I just did a presentation that will land me a ton of accounts, so I have to be back at the office to get the calls."

Don't you have somebody to do that for you?

"You know, sometimes, though, I don't much like the job. I know that surprises you. You think I'm so gung ho about Wall Street and business, but it can be boring. Six to three every day...Um..." He's looking down for a moment, pondering something. Now he's smiling, shaking his head, tilting his head up toward me. "What can I do? I have a wife and I'm having a kid and a mortgage! I can't really change my job."

Jacob, you can change. Don't use the same excuse that I did. It led me to resent my family. I'm trying to move my lips but the words of caution cannot come out.

"I spoke to Mom yesterday."

Sarah, the young woman I married, a woman I thought I could change. Maybe Jacob's trying to motivate me.

"I know you hate to hear it, but she prays for you." He holds my hand and puts his head close to mine. "Do you remember watching the '81 World Series? Garvey, Cey, Lopes and Russell, and how we jumped up and down when the Dodgers won. I remember it like it was yesterday, one of the happiest moments in my life." I remember that 1981 Dodgers team and how Jacob and I watched all the World Series games. Jacob was nine at the time. We bonded during that series, discussing the strategy of the game, our souls rising and our legitimacy confirmed when the Dodgers won the series. Yet, when I try to remember one moment, all I can seem to remember is the couch, Jacob, the television and us jumping up and down when the Dodgers took the pennant, celebrating with root beer.

"It seems like the Dodgers will have a good team this next year, but living in Sacramento has made me more of Giants fan. I've even gone to a couple of games at Petco Park. Dad, you remember going to Candlestick Park when I was sixteen?"

I smile. Or at least feel as if I'm smiling. I do remember that trip.

"I wish we had gone to more ball games." Regret rears its ugly head. He's looking at me and all I'm able to do is look back and wish that our past relationship had been better. That it had at least continued. We've just had no relationship at all for a long time. I close my eyes. I wish after the divorce we could have spent more time together, but I was too bitter to make a great effort, and he didn't seem to need his old man any more. Even on those weekends that he was over at my place, he'd often spend time with his friends at the pool or watch television and I did little to change that pattern. But I wasn't a bad father. I did go to all his baseball games. I still did that. Maybe somehow I can explain to him that there's nothing we can do about the past; we can sugar-coat it and rewrite its history, but it was what it was. Like my current state of life: *it is what it is*. Jacob touches my chest and I open my eyes. He looks down at me, trying to revive the life back into me.

"Dad, Melissa's just showing. She looks beautiful, round and rosy in her face, like she's glowing. I don't know what's going to happen or how my life will change with a baby, but honestly, I am a little scared. Were you scared?"

I'm nodding in recognition and Jacob begins to smile.

"It's good to know I'm not alone." He puts his hand back on my chest and I feel the warm touch of his hand. Oh Jacob! I'm sorry I'm like this. I wish there was something more I could do. He rubs my chest as he says, "Don't worry, Dad. We're going to get you better." His face is surrounded by darkness, and then his face darkens, to the point I only see its outlines. I see only darkness, but feel the love of my son, the love of the universe. I'm ready to let go. I am ready.

149

Ouch! Someone is stabbing me in my right arm. "It's OK, Mr. Mathews. I'm just drawing blood for the morning." An Indian woman says this in a manner similar to a postal worker delivering mail, just doing her job. Why does she have to take blood from my right arm? I can't feel anything on my left side. Why the hell don't you take blood from my left arm?

"We want to send a happy birthday wish to Joseph Klein of St. Louis, Missouri. Joseph is celebrating one hundred years of life today. He loves playing bingo and watching baseball. You are still a handsome devil, Joe. Congratulations. Now, for the weather." Joe's fifteen milliseconds of fame come at the end of his life. At least he got them. More than some of us can say.

"Now back to the case of Terry Schiavo. A judge has granted Terry's husband the power to remove her feeding tube. A spokesman for Terry's parents has indicated that they will appeal the decision. Some Congressmen have indicated they consider the judge's decision unconstitutional."

Up on the television there's a home video of a woman sitting in a chair with her eyes focused on nothing in particular, looking brain dead. Some guy with a Southern drawl is speaking. "This is a question of euthanasia. Nobody has the right to take life and the motives of Terry's husband in wanting her to die should be looked at. We are going to subpoena Michael Schiavo and have him explain to Congress why he wants to take his wife's life."

Jacob steps between me and the screen, eclipsing the television. "Hi, Dad. I seem to have forgotten about L.A. traffic. I thought Sacramento was bad, but not as bad as L.A. I'm lucky to have made it in time for the meeting." Meeting? What meeting? Jacob's cleanly shaven, his hair perfectly aligned and he wears a blue collared shirt: a good Wall Street boy.

"Dad, I'm going to have a conference today with Dr. Gellman and Dr. Masterson. They want to give me an update about what's going on and where we go from here. I've also spoken to that black nurse's supervisor. She won't be working with you anymore."

What the hell! I like Marge. She's been really nice to me!

"Yeah, she makes me mad, too."

Dammit Jacob! I know you're trying to protect me, but you don't know what this is like. Jacob's hand is in my right hand. I try

150

to squeeze his hand and am able to wrap my fingers around his large hand. Jacob looks down at me.

"Hey, that's great! You're using your right hand." He's smiling at me. "Hey, Dad, I went to your condo yesterday to make sure everything was OK. You don't need to worry about a thing. I found your mortgage statements and your checking accounts so I'll be able to pay your mortgage and your homeowner's dues until you're better. Was there anything else you needed me to do?"

"Boo. Booo." My book. Did you find my book! It's finished!

"I don't understand."

I left it in the bottom drawer of the desk in the living room.

"Booo. Booo." That stupid book. All that wasted time for a protagonist that spends the rest of his life in a trailer park.

"Dad?"

"Booo. Booo" All those years of work and nobody will read it.

"Mr. Mathews?" A voice calls out from somewhere beyond my vision.

"Yes."

"I'm Dr. Gellman." Jacob pulls his hand away.

"Nice to finally meet you Doctor."

"How's he doing today?" Dr. Gellman inquires.

"I just got here, but he seems to be doing OK. He just squeezed my hand."

"Good. I was hoping we could go to the conference room to discuss your father's care."

"Will Dr. Masterson be there?"

"The nurse told me he would join us in about five minutes." Dr. Gellman brings his face close to mine. "Hi, Paul. Is it OK if we speak to Jacob about your condition?"

"Boooo. Boooo."

My book you dumbass! That stupid book has been like a curse, eating up my time, taking me away from living, deluding me with the notion I could change the world with my written word. Jacob's looking down at me with a protective look. "I'll tell you everything we talk about, Dad. Don't worry. I can handle this." Oh you can, can you? How can you be so confident? He's leaving the room, leaving me to lie here, which is all I can do.

151

I'm bored. I need something to stimulate me, but there's nothing, not the television, not the respirator, not my body, that I find stimulating. I crave something else, naked women, fornication, nuclear holocaust, rock and roll, riding into Las Vegas in my Mustang, naked doctors doing CPR, wild animals, a monkey playing with my respirator, anything at all. This is more than just loneliness. This is damn boredom. Maybe there is something on the T.V.

"...poor sleep, decreased desire to see friends, poor attention at work, feeling hopeless. These are signs of depression, but now there is a medication, Lexapro, that has been clinically proven to treat depression. Some people may experience common side effects such as dry mouth and headache. People taking MAOI inhibitors should not take Lexapro. Get out of your rut! Ask your doctor if Lexapro is right for you."

A band starts playing some jazzy music. There's a woman on the screen, dressed in tan pants and a tucked-in pink collared shirt, confidently walking up to her oven. "409 Spray can clean the toughest stains." On cue the woman sprays an array of items including the oven, the range, the microwave and her sink. "Nothing cleans better than 409." As the words 409 are said the spray bottle comes down in full view.

"In the next half hour of the *Today* show, we'll discuss new treatments for menopause and Kathy Brooks will show us tasty delights for the holiday season. We'll begin with Dr. Marianne Sattler, a gynecologist and author of the book 'A Natural Guide to Menopause.' Dr. Sattler, thank you for being with us."

"Thank you, Katie, for having me."

"It's our pleasure. Why is menopause such a big issue these days?"

"Katie, I think the feminist movement and greater female independence have made women more proactive about their health and their bodies. Women have become empowered to act and stop the mood swings, the hot flashes and the other physical changes that occur during menopause."

Did Sarah go through this? The doctor is a blonde woman dressed in a tailored suit, with thin, crossed legs covered in black panty-hose. She has a soft reassuring voice, mentioning different

152

herbal therapies for menopause and it's nice to know that women suffering from this affliction have a solution. Look, a commercial about a car that will "put the fun back into driving" and here's another commercial about a toilet bowl cleaner. Katie's back with some woman, dressed in an apron, standing next to a large stove. They're cooking lamb stew, rice pilaf and pumpkin pie and it looks good, better than the frozen meals I've subsisted on. Through the sounds of the breathing machine and the television are the voices of two people. It sounds like Dr. Gellman and Jacob, but where are they? I can't see them.

"Jacob, did you understand everything."

"Yes, I did."

"So you still want to have the gastric tube placed?"

"The tube in the stomach?"

"Yes, the stomach tube."

"Definitely."

"OK, so Dr. Harkin will place the gastric tube tomorrow and once we see it's working, we can feed him through the tube. If everything works out, we can eventually transfer your father to a long-term nursing facility. There's a consent form in the chart for you to sign for the gastric tube. I just want to reiterate that with your father's stroke, his heart failure and emphysema, the recovery process will be slow and he may never fully recover."

"I understand, Doctor, but we have to give him a chance."

"Jacob, I've been following your dad for the last fifteen years, and I hope he pulls through, but he may not. We'll feed him through the stomach tube and keep him on the respirator as long as necessary."

As long as necessary? How long will that be? I need to say something about all this, but, hell, I can't and I'm afraid even the attempt will lead to multiple alarms sounding.

"Doctor, where is the nursing facility, the one for the transfer?"

"This is a specialized kind of nursing facility, for patients on a ventilator. It is called Venticare. I think it is in Gardena. I've never been there, but Dr. Masterson follows patients there. Well, I've got to go back to the office. I'm running behind. If you have any questions, give me a call there."

"I'll be going back to Sacramento tonight."

153

"OK, so I'll give you a call tomorrow about your father's progress. I think we have your cell phone number?"

"Yes."

"Can you also give a work number to the nurse so we have it on file?"

"I'll do that."

"I'll speak to you tomorrow, then, and I'll get that letter to you today so you can access your father's bank accounts."

"Thank you."

Jacob sits to my side, exhales deeply and smiles benevolently at me. Jacob! Jacob, don't keep me alive like this! I don't want to live like this! I can understand your desire for me to see your future child, but can't you understand that living attached to these machines is miserable? It is miserable. More miserable than anything I have ever experienced and I have no ability to change it. The other issue is how much this is all going to cost. You'll have to sell my condo to pay for this. That's yours and Melissa's money. You can use it to buy a better house. Don't squander it on the last moments of my life. Jacob's touching my hand and his smile has a touch of sadness.

Maybe you don't want the money? I always thought that was your greatest motivation. You may be a more complex individual than the simpleton go-getter I believed you to be. Maybe you heard me when I said there was more to life than money. There is this stillness between us and it's making me feel a little uncomfortable, like I'm being exposed and judged by someone better than I. He looks at me, observing me, as if he were watching a *National Geographic* episode about *Homo sapiens*. A cell phone is ringing. "I'll be right back. It's Melissa." Jacob walks away, but I still hear his voice.

"Hi, honey," Jacob calls out.

"Yeah, he's stable." There's a pause. "Yeah, it is not much different than what Dr. Gellman told me, but he says he has a chance of pulling through." He sounds flippant about my state. I wonder if he's told her everything. "I'll be home tonight." There's a pause. "Um. I know we were planning on going to Tahoe with your parents in 2 weeks, but with how things have happened" Another pause. "But, we saw them last week…and…well…I just

154

don't feel like going. You should go, because I may need to come down again to see my dad. OK, we'll talk about it when I get back home. I love you."

Jacob comes back to me, looking a little uneasy, picking at his fingernails. I don't know what's going on in his mind, but I can see that the wheels are turning. He looks at me uncomfortably. "Dad I... I don't know exactly what to say."

Say whatever you want Jacob, whatever's on your mind.

"It's just that I wish things turned out differently."

I know, Jacob, but don't condemn yourself for what your life is not. I made that mistake and all it led to was self-loathing, isolation and depression.

"I wish that miscarriage had never happened and that you and Mom worked things out."

Me, too. But it's all too distant, Jacob. There's nothing we can do about it.

Jacob looks down at my hand.

"Next on *Oprah*: 'Let's say you are having marital problems. Does marital therapy work? We will have two co-authors of a new study showing the benefits of therapy. Next on *Oprah*.'" Who changed the channels? Jacob sits there quietly. Looking at him, I realize the gap forming between us; me passing into the shadow of...death? And him with a life to lead. I wish there was some way I could say goodbye. I close my eyes feeling a desire for nothing.

"Dad. Dad!" I open my eyes. How much time has passed? I'm looking at a blurry image of Jacob. "The X-ray tech is going to do an X-ray." A tall man...well, I think he's tall, leans over the side of my bed. He has a dark moustache, dark hair and because everything seems blurry that's all I can make out.

"OK, Mr. Mathews, we're going to lay you on your side." He's placing me on my side and my bones are cracking with the movement. "We are going to place this X-ray film under your back." He turns me on my back again on top of a hard flat object. "You must leave the room." He must be talking to Jacob.

"OK. One, Two, Three," a buzzing sound resonates for a second then it's gone. He moves me again to my side, so I can sneak a peek at Jacob's slacks and then I'm returned to lying on my back. Ouch! There's a sharp pain at my butt. I'm so tired of it all. Jacob!

155

I can't stay awake. I feel an overwhelming desire to sleep; soft pillows, warm blankets, no thought...

"That is what our study showed. Marital therapy does improve the quality of the relationship." Marital therapy! That was a joke! Sarah and I and the therapist sitting in a private office, a vision of my past like paintings in a restaurant.

"You'll have to forgive him, Sarah. For your marriage to continue, you'll have to forgive."

"I'll never forgive him. Never!"

My eyes open and look for Jacob, but instead see the blue tile to my right and the edge of the railing of my bed. My eyes turn to my left and see rays of light glimmer on the blue tile on the other side of the room. I look up at the ceiling and then in front of me. Jacob's not here and for some reason I'm relieved. Why do I feel relieved? It was nice to have him here with me and I love my son, but I sense he needs something from me. Something I can't give......at least not now. I close my eyes and hear the voice of Dr. Schwartz distantly.

"I took a look at the X-ray and it shows more pulmonary edema. We'll have to increase his diuretic. Where are his labs for today?" His voice trails off, harmonizing with the mechanical sounds of the respirator, returning me to oblivion.

"Dad! Dad! It's Jacob!" Too much light! The light's burning into my eyes.

"Jacob," I hear myself saying, but it sounds more like the respirator is talking.

"Hey, that was pretty good. Keep trying to talk," Jacob says in an encouraging tone.

"The booo. The boooogh." Was he able to find my book? That damn book! No one will ever read it.

"I don't understand. Keep trying."

Oh, it doesn't matter, Jacob... It really doesn't matter.

"Don't stop. Tell me what you're thinking."

A waste of time it was, writing, passing my time in seclusion writing about Edward Winter's fall from grace, writing about the fall of man, really writing about my own fall, when all that time I could have been living, spending time with you Jacob.

156

Jacob looks uneasy about something. I hope I'm not scaring him. He turns his head away, toward his left so I only see the side of his face as if he's preparing to say something, as if he's looking off toward the horizon, looking to his next destination. His gaze returns to me and his shoulders drop down and his face is close to mine.

"Dad, I have to go. I wish I could stay longer."

"Jake…Jake…" So. This is goodbye. Goodbye, son. I love you. Be at peace. Don't worry about your old man. He's going to be fine. Take care of yourself, Jacob, and take care of that wife of yours. You're going to see how life changes and I wish I could teach you more, but I can't, because life is some distant vision, foreign to me, clouded by the past and beyond my ability to teach. Look at me, Jacob. Your old man's gone. No, no, no… OK, I'll stay alive. I'll stay alive to see your child and if I make it through this, I'll be a much different man.

"Take care of yourself, Dad. I love you. I'm counting on you to be in Sacramento with us as soon as the baby comes." He puts his hand on my chest and I feel the weight and warmth of his hand as I look at his face. I'm proud of you son. My eyes are closing. Jacob looks calm as the world becomes dark, his silhouette outlined within the darkness. I sense that I've lost something. What have I lost?

Chapter 9

I Have Had Enough of It

My eyes open. At least I'm trying to open them, but my eyelashes seem glued together, my vision is obscured by these hairy, sticky projections. The room's dark except for light that shines through a sliding glass door at the front of the room. Looking out of my room, I can make out a beige wall on the other side of the hallway and every once in a while I see a person walking past. It's very quiet now except for the soothing sound of the respirator. I'm so tired, so tired of this drudgery.

Someone's touching my belly, so my eyes open wider, but my eyelashes still feel stuck together. A man's face appears. "Hi, Mr. Mathews, I'm Dr. Harkin, the gastroenterologist," he says quickly. This doctor has an amazing amount of nasal hair, bristles protruding from his nose like uncut grass. It's the only thing to focus on and the only attribute to remember after his face quickly disappears, but I can still hear his voice. "Let's give him two of Versed and fifty of Demerol prior to the procedure."

"Should I give it now?" another man asks.

"Do it before you wheel him down."

"OK."

My eyelids open a bit more when I crinkle my forehead. Everything has a hazy appearance, even the ceiling with its perfectly aligned holes. The respirator causes my chest to rise and fall. There's a persistent need to urinate and while I try to urinate to relieve myself, it doesn't relieve the tingling sensation in my dick. I've got to pee! People are talking on the television and it sounds like an advertisement, one of those commercials that are supposed to be funny if you have all the background information, which I don't. There's a man swinging a golf club in an office cubicle, hitting a golf ball through the office and causing unknown destruction. It looks stupid and a little blurry. There's an itchy burn on my butt and I want to scratch it, but I can't. Motherfucker…what I wouldn't give right now to have the use of my arm just to scratch my ass.

"Hello Mr. Mathews, I'm Rick." Hi Rick, I'm Paul. Can you scratch my ass? To my left, there's a blond man with a full face, hair straight and parted on his left, pinkish skin and a syringe in his hand. He looks at me, then above me and then returns his gaze to me. This guy has a happy demeanor, like he could be, and wants to be, a friend to everyone.

"I'm going to give you something for your eyes. They seem a little infected. Do they hurt?"

I try to shake my head.

"I'm going to give you some medication before your procedure." What procedure? What are they going to do to me? Rick lifts up my left arm and the sad thing is that I only feel the movement in my shoulder; feeling nothing except the separation from my appendage. He injects something into a tube attached to my arm. He smiles at me, while bringing my arm down. "This should take care of it." His friendly face reminds me a little of Phil and the many days we spent in Westwood, tripping on LSD or just hanging out stoned and happy. Just a good guy and those were good times... The best times.

Wait a second here. I'm feeling suddenly so light and everything has an air of levity, the respirator, the ceiling, the television, the people walking past in the hallway. It makes me want to laugh at all of this as if my laugh would break some strange spell in this world. There is laughing. I can hear it. The world is laughing. Ha! Ha! Ha! Huh! Ha! The people in the hallway... I hear them laughing. Ha! Ha! Ha! Ha! Huh! Ha! It's infectious, as if my laugh can bring me in line with humanity. Ha! Haaa! Ha. The holes in the ceiling are dancing, swirling around in circles. There's Jesus, robust and bearded holding hands with others, dancing and laughing. Jacob's holding his left hand and I'm holding his right. We are all laughing.

"Did you unlock the bed?"

"Yeah, it's unlocked. Just let me put the monitor on the bed and we'll be ready to go."

"Did you unlock the ventilator?"

"Yeah."

This is so damn funny. There's a whole audience laughing behind me. Ha! Huh! Huh! We're all laughing.

159

"What did you give this guy? If the left side of his face wasn't drooping he'd be grinning from ear to ear."

"Just a little Versed and Demerol..."

"Got any more?" The laughter is pouring forth. Boy, these guys are funny. One guy is black with a smile on his face and I'm waiting for him to work up another joke, but no joke comes. Come on! You're a funny guy. Tell me another joke. There's an audience laughing behind me and I know I just missed something utterly funny. Shoot. I wait for the black man's response, but he's turned his back to me and is now pulling the bed. The room is gone and we're off on an adventure. The lights above me are a fluorescent, ethereal white, coming and going and then coming again and leaving again. My head is filled with vibrations of light, so bright I can see the light with my eyes closed. The light is blinding. Man, how can light be blinding? Hey! Who stopped the ship? I'm stopped. Hey man, where am I? Above me and to my right there's a painting of a thin, grey-haired man attired in a white doctor's coat. He's standing with his right arm on his bent knee, with his chest, neck and head protruding forward, looking like some sort of politician about to orate his vision of the future. The picture appears to vibrate and the doctor looks like he's confidently smiling with this fucking cocksure attitude, like he's holier than anything on this earth. His name is written on his white coat, but I can't read it and now he's gone.

"The ventilator needs to be pushed more into the elevator. The door's not closing."

"OK, I think we're all in now." The ceiling inside the elevator is a metal lattice of squares with holy light shining through. How beautiful! How perfect! God, are you there? It's me, Paul. I am Paul. You know, Paul. Ha! Ha! I'm having trouble remembering who I am. The audience is laughing. I'm laughing, too. I don't know who I am. Oh my God. God? It is everything.

"Hey Mario, take a look at this guy."

"He's trippin'!! Like he's havin' a flashback!"

"Sure is."

"I bet you he doesn't even know where he is."

"Oh, he knows where he is, it's just not on this planet." Gosh, that's funny! The audience has stopped laughing. Gone is the metal lattice and the light and the world is now somewhat blurry. I've stopped moving.

"Who is this?"

"Mathews, Paul."

There are two people above me dressed in blue with blue caps. One looks down at me, checking me over and touching my arm. That man is not funny! I'm moving down a light blue hall, being moved into a room. The movement has stopped, but I feel as if I'm still moving. There seems to be nobody in this room. A bright yellowish light, like a mid-day sun, hovers above me, surrounded by a sky of white. The environment is clean, cold, impersonal and yet somehow perfect. Is there anybody here? What am I doing here? Air rushes in an out of my chest and it feels nice.

"Let's prep his belly." Very quickly two women in blue scrubs, blue masks and funny blue hats work on my stomach. They pull out of somewhere what appears to be a sea of blue paper sheets, and cover my chest and part of my head with this blue paper. The blue paper consists of many tiny blue squares. Everything is squares! Hey, the whole world is made up squares! Four sides, man! The genius of it all!

"Hey, Mr. Uhhhh, how you doing over there?" The blue paper is pulled back and there is a man behind a blue mask with furry eyebrows. Hello, Mister! I'm fine and how are you?

"So… What's his name again?" the man asks as he fidgets with some instrument.

"Paul Mathews," a woman responds.

"So, Paul," he says as he holds a black, serpentine instrument above my head. "We are going to put a feeding tube into your stomach today. I am first going to put this instrument…" And I see him begin to stuff the head of the black serpentine beast into my open mouth, pushing it through one hand after the next as he says, "in your esophagus." Hey man, get that thing out of my throat! Stop that! Stop it! I'm gagging on this tube and he keeps pushing it in. What the hell?

"OK, I'm at the fundus of the stomach. Do you see the light?"

"Yes."

161

"Let's numb the site." There is a stinging pain in my belly but it quickly goes away. The crazy man holding the snake is above me, but I can only see the side of his body and the bottom of his chin.

"Push the Trocar through." I'm feeling a pressure on my belly and then again a sharp pain that doesn't disappear. Ouch! What are they doing down there? Ah, it doesn't matter. It's sort of nice not to care, nice to have all these people around me, to be part of the interplay of humanity. Without me, none of this would work. You know what? Take my body and do with it what you must. Everything is right and everything will work out in the end. The light… Oh the light. We are all light. *Let the sun shine!* We are all harmony. *Let the sunshine in!* We are all love. *The sun…shine in!* I will cling to nothing. *Let the sun shine. Let the sunshine in. The sun…shine in.* It is what it is. I accept it.

"Hi, Dad!" Dad's at the kitchen table, reading the paper and smoking a cigarette. I can't wait until I'm old enough to smoke. He puts down the paper and looks across the table at me.

"Good morning, Paul."

"Hi, Dad." Maybe I should ask him about the game. Sometimes Dad can be a little scary, especially when he doesn't want to be bothered. "Dad, can we go to Wrigley Field to watch the Angels?" The Angels are my favorite team.

"Paul, the Angels are on the road. They won't be back to L.A. for another week."

"We can see them when they come back."

"If you do your chores, if you do your homework, and only if you eat your breakfast," he says, gesturing to the kitchen with his cigarette in hand.

"Please, please, please!"

"Paul! Enough!" Mom brings Dad and me breakfast and walks back to the kitchen sink. Yummy bacon and eggs. I'm so hungry, I could eat the plate. "For God's sake, Mary. Can you stop working for a second and come sit with us?"

"No, I can't. I got to finish baking this cake for our bridge game. It's Doris's birthday tonight."

"Don't kill yourself for that bunch."

"Dad, you promise to take me to Wrigley Field, right?"

"No, I'm not making a promise. I'm offering you a deal. If you do your chores, do your homework and eat your breakfast, we can go to a game."

"I'll do it. But remember, you promised."

Dad slowly chomps on his bacon, Mom's crispy bacon. I could eat a hundred slices. Dad's thinking as he eats his, thinking something about me because he keeps looking at me, wrinkling the corners of his blue eyes, and revealing the dark circles below.

"Kid, I want you to realize something. I want you to understand how lucky you are. The problem is you don't know how lucky you are. You're given much more than many children in this world." Oh, not another one of his "you don't know how lucky you are" speeches. I better listen, though. The ball game hangs in the balance.

"You know, I've seen many children, during the War, without a mother or father; orphans with no family and no means. You know what an orphan is?"

"Yeah."

"I saw children after the bombing of Dresden who'd lost everything. I've seen their faces, their vacant stares."

"Joshua!"

"Mary, I'm talking!" He slams his hand down on the table. "And I've seen children and adults who've been liberated from concentration camps looking as if they had lost something. I don't think you could understand their lives. What I want you to know is that you should be more thankful for the things you've got, and less inclined to demand things you want; thankful that your mother and father are here, that you never go hungry, that you're able to go to school, that you are healthy, that there's nobody bombing you or torturing you. Think of the things that you have Paul, not just the things you would like to have."

"Joshua, he's only a child. He doesn't understand," Mom calls out.

Dad turns his head to her. "He's got to understand. This world can change in an instant, Mary. The boy has to know that. He has to know that he needs great fortitude to survive in this world, in whatever future it's going to bring him. That his life will not always be so easy and that he can't get everything he wants just because he wants it. His whole generation's growing up with this crazy idea that they're entitled to anything and everything. Do you understand what I am saying?" he asks, now looking toward me.

"Yes, Daddy." I don't know what he's talking about. My whole generation is growing up the way his whole generation is raising us. We hear two things. We have the best life of any kids ever, though we don't deserve it, and our fathers are all heroes who saved the world before we were born, just so we could be here and be so unworthy of their sacrifice. How do they expect us to turn out?

"Good... So, I think next Sunday the Seattle Rainiers will be in town. How would you like to go?"

My eyes light up in excitement as I think about sitting in the stands, eating a hot dog and having some pop. "Yippee." I'm bouncing up and down in my chair, humming and then singing, "Take Me Out to the Ballgame."

My father smiles at me. "Maybe you'll come to the jewelry store on Saturday and I'll show you a wonderful blue sapphire I just got."

"Is it big?"

"As big as your eye......Come on Mary, sit down with us."

"I'm almost finished!"

They keep bickering and I tune out, watching the bees through the window, hovering above the sweet flowers, landing then balancing as the tiny flowers bend down with their weight. The bees are so busy, guided by some purpose, rarely diverting their attention from their goal. Is a bee happy? The images fade to darkness and all I know and all I am is the soft and peaceful darkness. The bees are gone.

The breath comes in and out. There's a sharp sensation in my stomach, like there's a stick or spear lodged in my belly. I don't feel well, like I'm hung over and my head is in a world of pain as the light of the room shoots into my brain. The holes in the ceiling come in to focus, perfectly aligned. Breathe in and breathe out. Breathe in. Breathe out. The movement of air is so rhythmic, my entire body and mind seem to harmonize with it. Breathe in. Breathe out. It becomes easier to forget about all the pain. Each breath blows out the pain, and brings peace to my existence. A

164

tanned woman with dark hair walks toward me. She adjusts something behind me and I hear beeps and then the beeps stop. I feel a pinprick on my right middle finger.

"Checking your blood sugar... Are you doing OK, Mr. Mathews?" She places her hand on my shoulder. I smile at her. "That's good. I'm going to turn the lights off and let you rest. You've had a full day." She's very sweet. She walks away and the lights go off, but it is not completely dark for there is the glow of light from something, maybe the machinery, behind me. The machinery is a nice companion. Breathe in and breathe out. Easy to do. Breathe in and breathe out. Everything becomes dark.

"So what did you think of it?" I put down the book, *The Adventures of Huckleberry Finn* and look down at Jacob who's lying in his bed. "Jake? Did you like it?"

"I liked Huck and Jim... I didn't like Tom."

"No, I didn't like Tom either."

"He played a dirty trick on Jim."

"All for an adventure."

"If he did that to me, or any friend of mine, I would never be friends with him again."

"We'll never know if Huck stays friends with Tom. They will always be boys in the story, never men."

Jacob yawns.

"Well, you better go to sleep." I turn off the lights. "Good night Jacob."

"Good night."

I close the door and walk down the hall, soon arriving at the door of our bedroom. Inside, Sarah's kneeling, her hands at her chest in prayer. She looks out the window. She does look cute wearing her blue pajamas in her short blond hair. I kneel down behind her, wrap my arms around her belly and attempt to kiss her neck. Sarah jumps up, her shoulder hitting my chin and causing me to fall backward to the floor. She looks down at me.

"What do you think you're doing?"

"What do you think I'm doing?"

"It's all about sex, isn't it?"

165

"No, it's not all about sex, but you know, we used to have sex all the time when we first met." I get up to my feet.

"You seduced me."

I come closer to her and she looks up at me with an irritated look. I put my arms around her and my hands rest at the small of her back. "You're still the same person. You know you liked it when I seduced you." I pull her close to me, feeling that maybe this time she'll relent, that maybe the erection that I'm getting won't be for naught. My hands lower to her pajama pants and I squeeze her soft rear. She pulls back and gives me that same irritated look.

"What's wrong?"

"Maybe you could talk to me a little before trying something like that."

"Honey, we haven't had sex in I don't know how long."

"There's more to life than just sex. There's love. There's God."

"Oh, come on, Sarah. You don't even cuddle with me anymore. All I'm asking is for some affection."

"I tried and for you cuddling always leads to sex."

"Can't you just give it up for a second?"

"Paul, I don't want to give it up. I don't want to. Can't you understand that?" She has tears running down her cheeks.

"Well, can you understand that I want to? I know this miscarriage has been hard on us both, but…"

"It's not that."

"Then what is it?"

She just looks at me.

"It is that, isn't it?"

"Don't you understand that God does everything for a purpose? He took our daughter away because of what we did."

"What?"

"We were not being good people."

"This is crazy. Totally crazy!"

"Then why did it happen?"

"Because it happened. Shit happens!"

"S, H, I, T doesn't just happen."

"Look, it would have been nice to have a daughter. She would have been Daddy's little girl, but it didn't happen. I'm not going to run to religion to deal with that."

"Your answer is to not deal with it at all."

"I'm not going to blame myself for the miscarriage, nor should you. I'm going to go on with my life, dammit." I walk to the door. "I'm going to do some writing."

"What are you going to teach people with your book, when you are so lost yourself?"

"Maybe I can help people like you."

At the door, I hear her murmur, "He'll never understand." I head down the hall to the kitchen, pull out my notebook from a drawer, and sit down to write. I think about my protagonist, Edward Winter, and what he had to overcome to try and live out his dreams, and how the world beat him down, like Sarah's beating me down now. He still had his dreams though. But what will happen to him and what will happen to me?

Light floods my vision and it causes my head to swim. Slowly through this cloudy light a head covered in grey hair appears. It looks like Dr. Gellman with a stethoscope in his ears. He has a hand on my chest and a pensive, distracted look. He takes the stethoscope off and looks at me, noticing that I'm looking at him.

"Hi, Paul." He's waiting for me to speak, but hell, no words are coming out of my mouth. He places his fingers in my right palm. "Paul, I know you can't speak, but I want to know if you're in any pain. Blink your eyes if you are in pain. Squeeze my fingers if you are not." He waits and since I'm not feeling any pain, I squeeze his fingers. He leans forward and looks at me. "Paul, I just want to give you an update about what's going on. Your heart tests have normalized and we have you on new medications that are keeping your heart stable. Your pneumonia has cleared and you're breathing fine on the respirator. You have just had a feeding tube placed in your stomach and we've started giving you feeding through the tube. We'll continue this until you can eat for yourself. Dr. Masterson says you're stable to leave the intensive care unit and he suggests that we have you go to a rehabilitation facility for those people who still require ventilator support. Do you understand what I'm saying?"

Why the hell am I nodding? Gellman, I don't have a clue what you are implying. What's going to happen to me Doc?

"Good! I've spoken with your son and he agrees to the transfer to Venticare. Dr. Masterson says he'll follow you there until he can wean you off the ventilator." He's looking downward, appearing to ponder his next words. He looks up and smiles at me. "Take care of yourself, Paul." He puts his hand on my shoulder, then leaves the room.

Take care of myself? How the hell do I do that? Do I have some control over my situation? Maybe I do have control. Maybe, somehow, I can make my situation better. If I focus and really try to maintain hope, maybe I can get better.

But what does Gellman really think? Does he think I could get off this ventilator, walk out of this room and go back to my life in my condo? Does he care if I do? It could be that I'm asking too much of the good Dr. Gellman. Maybe all he wants to do is give me a fighting chance to survive; but how does he know when to stop? All this thinking is blurring my mind when all I really can, and should, do is go with the flow. Don't worry about it, Paul. Breathe in, breathe out. The machine is soothing, bringing me back in touch with my breath and my body. It is what it is.

It's the brightness of the fluorescent light I lie in. It is the ceiling that entertains me. It is the machine that gives me life. It is the compression and release of pressure that massages my right leg, the inability to feel my left side, the dry mouth and a perpetual desire to urinate. It is the television that warbles the ever-changing song of humanity. It is the doctors, nurses, the people who draw my blood, the chain-smoking respiratory therapist, the person on the intercom who pages Dr. So-and-so. It is my complete dependence upon this system. It is me and I am it.

"Zero percent APR financing!" My particular absurdity was that, like it or not, I was always part of the system. The world is dark and I feel that it all no longer matters, if it ever did. Living and dying are the same thing. I have died a thousand times over and did not know it, still clinging to some notion of me; to a sense of self I tried to protect. I protected myself from change and could

168

not see that I, along with everything around me, was changing. Who am I? Dr. Gellman asks me to take care of myself, but what is it I'm taking care of? There is an unshakable sense of calm in this world of darkness that overcomes any sense of self.

"While he yet spoke, behold, a bright cloud overshadowed them." To my right there's a grey-haired priest reading a passage from a worn, Bible in a brown cover. He speaks in a soft, whispering voice as if his voice was like a gentle wind. "...and behold a voice out of the cloud, which said, This is my beloved Son, in whom I am well pleased; hear ye Him. And when the disciples heard it, they fell on their face, and were afraid. And Jesus came and touched them, and said, Arise, and be not afraid. And when they had lifted up their eyes, they saw no man, save Jesus only. And as they came down from the mountain, Jesus charged them, saying, Tell the vision to no man, until the Son of Man be risen again from the dead." He pauses as if to reflect upon this, giving me time to reflect upon him. Is this really a priest? What's a priest doing here? Are these my last rites? Am I dying? I can see only the top of his head as he meanders through the book. He is calm and folds over the pages one at a time, searching for the right passage, looking through page after page for something that would be germane to my life. I wonder if he'll read from that song by the Byrds. "*To everything turn,turn,turn. There is a season turn, turn, turn.*" Yeah......and a "*time to be born, a time to die.*"

He stops turning pages and reads. "'And Christ said, 'For as the lightening cometh out of the east, and shineth even unto the west; so shall also the coming of the Son of Man be. For wheresoever the carcass is there will the eagles be gathered together. Immediately after tribulation of those days shall the sun be darkened, and the moon not give her light, and the stars shall fall from heaven, and the powers of the heavens shall be shaken: and then shall all the tribes of the earth mourn, and they shall see the Son of Man coming in the clouds of heaven with power and great glory. And He shall send His angels with a great sound of a trumpet, and they shall gather together His elect from the four winds, from one end of heaven to the other... But of that day and hour knoweth no man, nor the angels of heaven, but my Father only.'" He stops and waits, praying over the book as if his words would cause some dramatic change. Boy is he going to be disappointed!

He looks up at me, his gaze hitting mine and he's clearly surprised that I've been awake, so he clears his throat and quickly looks back down into his book. I didn't get a good look at his face, but the fact that he's hidden his face makes me want to see it more. He pulls his head up and steadies himself. He puts the Bible to his chest. He points his second and third finger at me and then places these fingers on my forehead. "May the Lord bless you and keep you." He walks away. What a strange man. What was he saying? Something about Jesus being the son of God and something about destruction, resurrection and the coming of the Lord? Oh, gosh! What phooey! It's strange how man can put his face on everything. He can put his face on the heavens with his angels and his own representation of God. How is it that man feels that his life and death would cause the sun and moon to darken and the earth to mourn? The earth doesn't care. God doesn't care. You can hallucinate as much as you want, priest, but the reality is that man attempts to control his universe and man only becomes a God within his realm of control. These fuckers will destroy this earth simply for their desire for control. May I be reincarnated as a maggot to eat off the flesh of men.

"The weather tomorrow will be hazy sunshine with scattered low clouds. A high of 70 degrees Downtown and 65 near the coast. This will be the pattern for the rest of the week going through the weekend. Southlanders will be flocking to Disneyland next year for the amusement park's 50th birthday. Disneyland will celebrate, for the entire year, with an electric light parade and fireworks..."

I have had enough of it. Time...time...it doesn't matter.

"So many nights, I sit by my window, waiting for someone to sing me a song. So many dreams, I've kept deep inside me. Alone in the dark, but now you've come along. And you, you light up my life. You give me hope, to carry on. You light up my days, and fill my nights.........with song." I turn off the radio. I can't stand that song.

"Dad, where did Grandpa Josh go?" Jacob asks. We're driving home from Mom and Dad's house......now, I guess, Mom's house.

170

It seemed so sudden. One day he was alive and the next day, gone; sudden heart attack.

"I don't know where people go when they die, Jake, but I know he'll always be with us in spirit." I can't believe I'll never see Dad again.

"Why did Grandpa Josh have to die?"

"Grandpa's heart was bad and he was getting old. When people get old they die."

"I miss Grandpa Josh."

"Me, too."

"Are you going to die too, Dad?"

"Not for a long time." I look back at Jacob through the rear-view mirror. He is looking out the window.

"I never want you to die."

"Don't worry, Jacob," Sarah adds, "we never really die. God has a place for us high in heaven and that's where Grandpa Josh is at, looking down on us."

"Don't confuse the boy, Sarah!" After a moment of silence, I hear Jacob sniffle. "Jake?"

"Yeah."

"Let's just say that it will be long time until I die."

Chapter 10

Relativity

"I can't believe you cheated on me." Sarah's holding a letter in her hand, sitting at the kitchen table. Oh no, she knows.

"I don't know what you're…"

"Liar! It's all right here." She shoves a letter in my face.

"What's right there?"

"She wrote it all down. Don't play stupid with me."

"It just happened. I don't know what I was thinking. I'm sorry." I put my face in my hands, fearing to look up. She finally did it. Damn girl, Janet. Janet Timpson, a girl in her mid-20s, who worked at the pet store next door to Watsons. She was a transplanted Sixties type, living in the Eighties, who wore flowing, flowery skirts and tied-dyed T-shirts, had curly red hair and freckles, was not extremely pretty, even a little chubby, but was young, rebellious and she reminded me of my lost youth. We met when I was buying some fish for Jacob's aquarium. She was flirtatious, especially when I told her about my life in the Sixties, and she didn't seem to care that I was married. And soon I'd go regularly to visit her at the pet store, not to buy anything, but to talk about our time and our society, about Reagan, about music, about the meaning of life.

"She wants to lay you, man," Rudolfo, my buddy from work said. "You can see it on her face."

When I told Ray about it, he got to egging me on, too, "Dude, you're a man. Sarah's putting you out to pasture and it's not fair. You got to go for it! A man needs to fuck and Pauley, my friend, it would do you good." It was such a great escape from the tedious, mechanical, sexless life I led with Sarah.

And it was not just sex. Janet invited me one day to visit her apartment after work and I remember walking in, nervous with excitement and novel expectations, and later pulling up her flowered dress, feeling her warmth, hearing her moan. Ray was right. It did do me good, but then it left me with this nagging guilt. I kept trying to break it off, but couldn't, so I kept sneaking off to

172

her apartment, telling Sarah that I was going out with Ray. And now after finally breaking it off, the shit really has hit the fan. The crazy girl has written Sarah this letter about her unfaithful husband.

"It was just sex."

"'It was just sex,'" Sarah parodies me. "You're so full of shit."

"Sarah, I still want it to work it out between us."

"No, you don't."

"Yes, I do."

"It will never work again, Paul. This is the last straw! No amount of therapy can fix this."

"I know I've hurt you and I'm sorry."

"You can go to hell!" She stands up, pushing the letter up in my face like it was some kind of weapon. "You'll come to realize how much you needed me. I've always been there for you and this is how I get repaid."

Always been there? We haven't had sex in X years and not even an ounce of affection. That's a wife who's there for her husband? "I'm sorry Sarah."

"You need me, Paul. You'll be lost without me."

"Need you?"

"Yes, need me." She pushes her finger hard into my chest.

"OK! That's it! I've had enough! I don't need you."

"Really?" Sarah scoffs.

"I don't need your Old Time Religion. I don't need your Bible-study friends, your blabbering about work, and I don't need your constant nagging! I'll be much happier away from you!"

"We'll see!"

"I can take care of myself!"

"Right, Paul Mathews, a self-sufficient island." She laughs as her tears drop.

"You don't understand how much you've pushed me away."

"You've pushed everyone away," Sarah screams. "I can't believe I wasted my life on you. Fourteen years of my life!"

"Your life would have been wasted no matter who you were with."

"It's 'whom.'"

"What?"

173

"'Whom you were with.' You're supposed to be a writer and you don't even know that much."

Darkness...I should have realized a long time before that Sarah and I were not right for each other. Now those heated words seem so long ago, the anger within them diffused. That whole life seems so long ago. I've learned this much. I'm not an island, and I wish I could just die and leave it all behind, not open my eyes, not have a thought.

Breathe in, breathe out. The mantra brings me slowly back, looking up at a ceiling broken up into squares. Each of the squares has thin irregular lines cut into the particleboard. Why are the lines there? Do they somehow allow for better ventilation? Loose stool slips out my bottom and my only thought is to ignore my incontinence and slip back into unconsciousness.

I've been turned to my right side, looking at someone lying in a bed next to mine. How the hell did he get here? He looks to be an older man with a blue tube covering my view of his face and that blue tube is attached to a machine about the size and shape of a dishwasher. There's nothing else to see except the walls surrounding this man. Where am I?

"Virginia, we should take a picture of this ulcer." The voices are coming from behind me, close behind me, like at my rear end.

"Yeah, we should. Do you have the Polaroid?"

"Wait here a second. I'll get it." Why are they going to take a picture of my backside?

It's quiet for a moment. All quiet except for a television in the background, advertising Viagra. "It's time to get back in the saddle again."

The other woman comes back. "Here's a picture of the ulcer when he first got here."

"It looks deeper now. We should put Duoderm on this and change it daily. How long has he been here?"

"About three months."

"Has family been around?"

"He has that son who lives in Sacramento. He came by one time, but hasn't been back since."

174

"When was that?"

"Early on."

"Right, they all come at the beginning. They all say, 'Keep him alive... Give him a chance.' Then they rarely come by and when they do they're angry and demanding."

"I'd be angry too if I had to see my family member living like this..."

"At least he has a family, unlike Mr. Brooks over there."

"Don't get me started about Mr. Brooks. That's what happens when you become a ward of the state. You get a conservator who doesn't know you from Adam and all the conservator does is keep you alive. The state can't make the decision to end these people's lives and so they just sit here. How long has Mr. Brooks been here?"

"About five years."

"Five years? I bet that's a Venticare record."

"I think we had a couple of people here for about six."

"How many bowel movements a day has Mr. Mathews had?"

"Usually two."

"OK, let's lay him back down."

I'm turned so that I face the ceiling and see a woman with a plump face and brown hair. She smiles at me. "Mr. Mathews, you're awake! This is the first time I've seen you awake." She comes closer with her plump face and peers at me as if she were looking at an animal. "Hello, Mr. Mathews. I'm Virginia, the nurse practitioner here at Venticare. How you doing?"

Oh, I'm great. Never felt better! Her focus shifts to the other nurse. "This is the first time I've seen him open his eyes."

"I know. He hasn't been interacting at all. He seems like he's in his own world... I'm so tired of this, Virginia. I could sure use a vacation."

"When was your last vacation?"

"Four months ago."

"It's been about that long for me. My last vacation was in Vegas. All I need is fifty dollars, cocktails and a slot machine and I could be entertained all day."

"Fifty dollars? Last time I went to Vegas I lost two hundred. No, this next vacation's gonna be different. I'm not going anywhere and I'm not going to do anything except relax."

"That sounds nice."

"Why don't we take a look at Mr. Brooks and see if we can wake him up from his long hibernation?"

Virginia and Jenny walk away. I see the backside of Jenny as she hovers over Mr. Brooks' bed.

"Jonathan, wake up Jonathan!" Virginia calls out as if Mr. Brooks were on the other side of the Pacific. "Of course, he's still on assist control. Has he ever initiated his own breathing?"

"Not from what I've seen."

"Can you believe that conservator? I told her two years ago that the man was brain dead, had no spontaneous movement, had no ability to breathe for himself and that woman said she couldn't pull the plug on him, that she couldn't kill him. My God, the man's already dead."

"You are preaching to the choir, Virginia."

"I know. I know."

"It's just so frustrating, like this Terry Schiavo case."

"Oh! Can you believe that? Leaving a woman like that alive? But the difference is that her parents are there for her."

"Her parents have only made the situation worse."

"Yeah, I guess you're right."

"No, I told Jim, if this were ever to happen to me, just let me go. I don't need all this drama."

"Virginia, could you look at his G-tube site? It looks a little infected. Here, do you see that redness surrounding the site?"

"It does look infected. I'll run it by Dr. Masterson and probably start him on Keflex."

"So when are you going on vacation?"

"Next month... Jim and I are going to San Diego... Should be relaxing."

"Anywhere but here."

"You said it."

The voices trail off and I'm left alone. Well, sort of alone. Mr. Brooks is still here. But, where the hell am I? I'm not able to talk, not able to move my left arm or leg and I can barely move my right

176

hand. I'm feeling a generalized heaviness like I'm wearing clothes drenched with water and the lethargy plunges me into a sea of darkness.

"The 2005 Cingulair NCAA Tournament begins with UCLA and Texas Tech. This is a story of two great coaches: Bobby Knight of Texas Tech and Ben Howland of UCLA. I'm Dick Stockton along with my partner David Thompson. David, what do you think the key to this game will be?"

"Well Dick the key will be the guard play. Texas Tech has experienced guards that know how to run the floor, while UCLA relies on a freshman backcourt."

How long have I been here? March madness? The NCAA tournament! I wish I could sit up and watch this game, have one of you nurses give me a beer so I could sit inebriated and numb, watching these agile, muscular creatures with opposing jersey colors slash, bump and jump around a basketball court. I'd love to lose myself in this entertainment. Keep quiet Paul! Maybe while you can't see the game, you can still follow it.

"Do you suffer from heartburn? 'Sure doesn't everybody?' Well, it may not just be heartburn. It may be GERD, gastroesophageal reflux disease, and it could be a serious condition. Luckily there is new prescription strength Nexium, the strongest antacid on the market. Nexium has been shown to decrease the symptoms and long-term complications of GERD. Side effects may include diarrhea, G.I. discomfort and rare skin conditions, so consult your doctor. Ask your doctor about Nexium and take control of GERD." God, I hate commercials. Breathe in. Breathe out. There's a pain in my rear, an itchy-like pain that makes me want to scratch off multiple layers of skin, but I'm impotent to do anything about it. Ouch! Breathe in. Breathe out.

"Farmer kicks the ball out to Affallo. Three pointer by Affallo. Good. I tell you these freshman guards for UCLA will be something to watch next year. While Texas Tech is going to win this game, I see a bright future here for these Bruins." The game's over already? What happened? I just started listening. Maybe time is somehow different for me than what it is for the rest of the world. The white ceiling with the irregular lines is getting dark.

177

"Hey man, wake up. Dude, wake up. Oh Paul! What the fuck happened to you." The voice sounds familiar waking me up from some deep, dark sleep into a world of bright light and it is hurting my head. Breathe in, breathe out. A face comes into focus, a man with tanned, wrinkled skin, a blond moustache and crooked yellowish teeth. Oh hell, it's Ray! Ray Livorno! Man, where have you been? "That's right Pauley! Wake up, now. I came here three other times and your fat rear has been asleep. No chance of waking you up." Ray, man, you're a sight for sore eyes. Ray! Ray! Ray! If there was ever a man to play the part of the devil, it was you, man, whether it was training before Vietnam, or hanging out with you after work drinking beers, or being my compatriot in debauchery in Vegas. Sarah used to call you and Julia *heathens*. She hated it when you guys came over, said you were too loud, or too drunk or too loose with your tongues. "Dude, you got to get better. We got to do another trip to Vegas."

Vegas was probably what landed me in here, Ray. The ritual of going off to Vegas in the Mustang, staying at the Stardust at 18 bucks a night, getting loaded while playing the dollar blackjack tables, then going to strip joints, is probably over. The last trip we did, to celebrate my finishing my book, almost killed me, going from one blackjack table to the next, drinking from one casino to the next, getting high, drinking until I blacked out. What I always liked about you man was that you were up for anything and it was a necessary distraction from the writing and my loneliness.

"I called you a few times, but I got a 'not in service' message. 'Like hell,' I said! So I went over to your place and one of your neighbors, that ugly broad in the condo next to you, said you were in the hospital. So I called the hospital and they said you weren't there, but I finally tracked you down, but, shit man, you've been sleeping all the time. What kind of fucking living is this? Has Jake been around? Does he know about the book?" Ray leans over the bed, resting his head on his hand. "Pauley, Pauley, Pauley. Shoot, look what time's done to us, man." Kill me Ray. Don't let me go on like this. "It won't be much longer for me. I know that, and Julia's been drinking too much and don't look too good. Shit, our whole generation will be gone soon. Nam, the Stones, the Dead, the Beatles, the Kennedys, going to the moon, Nixon… It won't mean a thing once we're gone."

Does it mean a thing now? Or did it then? Ray's wrinkled face fades away and darkness is all I see.

"Paul! Buddy! Wake up! What about your book? Shoot Paul, is this it? I know you wanted to do more with your life, but this is the life you were dealt and, if anything, you've always been a good friend. Remember what you said? That we live and die in a meaningless world and that we're just one in six billion, so our lives really don't mean that much anyway. That's right Pauley. It never really mattered, but you mattered a lot to me. I'll come back again, Pauley. And next time I'm staying till you wake up."

"Dr. Masterson, I think we need to transfer him back to the hospital. The antibiotics don't seem to be working. His X-ray looks worse… OK, I'm calling 911." Breathe in. Breathe out. The world is a hazy white and it takes some time to make out shapes.

"What's the name of the patient?" To my right is a rugged looking man with a moustache and a full head of straight brown hair. He looks like your prototypic fireman. Is there a fire?

"Paul Mathews," a woman's voice says.

"What's going on with him?"

"Looks like pneumonia and worsening heart failure. Oxygen saturation in the high 80's."

"Who's the pulmonologist?"

"Masterson."

"Does he agree to the readmission?

"Yeah, I just spoke to him."

"Is he a full code?"

"Yes, he is."

"Hey, what did you get?"

"Blood pressure 92 over 50, oxygen saturation, 90 percent, pulse 130. He's taking Lipitor, Diltiazem XR, Isordil, Metoprolol, Amiodorone, Lasix, Potassium, Lisinopril, Digoxin, Coumadin, Glyburide, Albuterol, Atrovent and Levaquin. No known drug allergies. He has course crackles at both lung bases."

"OK, let's get him on the gurney." The world becomes dark as I'm being moved off the bed. Where the hell are they taking me? The hospital?

I don't feel well. This light is killing my eyes. Breathe in. Breathe out. Breathe in. Breathe out. Breathe in. Breathe out. Somehow my breathing is unnaturally rapid and I can't slow it down. Something's stopping me from fully exhaling and before I'm done breathing out, air rushes in against me. There's pain in my chest, but the inability to breathe right overwhelms this. You need to focus on something else, Paul, like the ceiling. It is made up of multiple squares and each of the squares has multiple holes that are in perfect alignment. Do the holes serve some purpose? There's a voice in the distance and it sounds like a conversation that pertains to me.

"I'm looking for Jacob Mathews... Mr. Mathews, this is Dr. Ashkhani and I'm the admitting doctor at the hospital. This is regarding your father, Paul Mathews. He's suffering from a severe pneumonia and congestive heart failure. He's here in the ICU at Saint Luke's Hospital... Yes, the Intensive Care Unit. We're going to start antibiotics and give him medication to help the heart failure, but I want to get an idea of his code status, because it says here that he is a Full Code. If his heart were to stop beating would you want us to perform a code and CPR, shock him and give him medications to revive his heart?.........You would?............ Well, I think we can pull him through this, but I wonder about the quality of his life after we discharge him from the hospital... Yes we will... We'll take very good care of him, Mr. Mathews, but, from looking at his history, I don't think he'll ever be able to walk, talk or lead an independent life. Are you sure your father would want to be kept alive like this?......... I understand... No, I'm just the admitting doctor... I will not be following him. Dr. Masterson and Dr. Gellman will continue to see him in the hospital. Will you be coming down to see him?... Well, anything is possible. He'll very likely pull through this, but I usually think it a good idea for family members to see the patients in the hospital, to see what they're going through and give us direction when the patient is unable to speak... Oh, I understand. That's great, Mr. Mathews.

When is her due date?…You take care, then, and we will take care of your father."

There's a sharp pain in my right arm and it makes look toward the top of a man's head. He has spiked black hair and when he looks up at me he smiles. "We are just drawing blood for the morning." I see the young, smiling face of my benefactor, who then quickly carries his things and walks away. Breathe in. Breathe out. Calm. Relaxed. There's a big release from my belly and I evacuate a large slippery stool.

"An entire meal for three ninety-nine: a Big Mac, large order of French fries and a large Coca-Cola. And nothing beats the taste of our chicken McNuggets they are MMMMMc-Good!… Today on Dr. Phil we'll talk about healthy food choices for dinner and learning how to savor your food." Boring! There's a yellow light, like a sun, burning bright high above me, the beams of light coming down between the square boards and since my body feels frozen, all I want to do is to get closer to this sun; grunting, grasping, jumping and trying to fly to reach that warmth, not caring that the sun will burn me. At least I'll be warm. And as I'm getting closer to the flames my form's disintegrating, melting the skin and liquefying me into a red mass surrounding my skeleton, becoming nothing except for what I can see and feel. All I see is the sun and all I feel is its warmth. It is all light now and it is all so beautiful.

"He that eateth my flesh and drinketh my blood, dwelleth in me, and I in him." To my right is a man dressed in a black shirt and a white collar. There's something about him that looks familiar. Maybe it's the brownish-grey hair, or the thick scar that goes from his left nostril clear to his left ear or his chapped lips. I know I've seen him before, but don't remember where. The man is smiling at me, speaking to me, "May God give you countenance during this time of transition. May you accept the Lord, Jesus Christ, as your savior, as the One who will lead you through the shadow of death and toward the kingdom of heaven. Only through acceptance can you rid yourself of suffering." The man means well, like he's concerned about the well-being of my soul or something of that nature. He's holding my right hand, closing his eyes to quietly pray. But mister, why do I have to accept Jesus to end my suffering. How can a man who lived two thousand years ago understand my predicament today?

Maybe Jesus is still part of the world I live in and I just have to accept it. Maybe he will end my suffering. But am I suffering? Because it doesn't feel like I'm suffering, but if I were suffering I wouldn't run to the carcass of a two-thousand-year-old man. I'd run to someone I've seen and experienced; someone real, like Stephen Petry. I remember him. I remember him now.

There's a church full of people both sitting and standing. This is Stephen's church, and everyone inside is wearing black. The sounds of crying and running noses permeate inside the edifice. A preacher, dressed in black, stands in front of us. There's an open casket to the preacher's right and there's someone inside, a man dressed in a suit, with curly brown hair, surrounded by flowers.

"One thing rings loud and true in the life of Stephen Petry," the preacher begins. "He was loved, by all those who knew him. Stephen could have done anything in his life. He excelled at school, was captain of his high school baseball team and graduated *cum laude* from Stanford. Yet he chose a different course; a course of giving. It was in Stephen's nature to give and nothing could change that. While he worked at a public park organizing sporting leagues, Stephen also volunteered time at the hospital, talking to the infirmed people and bringing them peace. He also volunteered time at this church, taking the children on field trips to the beach, the mountains or to museums. Some of those children, who are no longer children, are here today. Stephen was also a good friend to me. We'd have lengthy conversations about the difficulties and suffering in this world and what would be the best ways to alleviate them. I will miss our conversations. Before his bicycle accident, Stephen was planning to move to New Mexico with his wife-to-be and live a life of harmony with the land."

The bike accident: Stephen was riding his bicycle to the hospital on a Saturday night when he was hit by a car at an intersection. The driver was never caught. Rachel, being a good neighbor, told me the news, which led me to this funeral service.

"Stephen was just a good guy, through and through," a man whispers next to me. He's a little bit older than I, with grey hair, double chin and a reddened face, damaged by the Southern California sun. He extends a hand out to me. "I'm Chuck Turner."

"Paul Mathews." His grip is strong.

"How did you know Stephen?"

"We were neighbors. How about yourself?

"I was his baseball coach in high school. Great kid! You know, he was so good at baseball, he may have gone pro out of high school, but his darn parents convinced him that Stanford was the way to go. Little did they know that he'd give up not only baseball, but on their aspirations of him of being some kind of high-powered professional. I remember one time he came by my house and talked to me about being a Humanities major. He said that giving to the world gave him meaning, not the money nor the prestige. Stephen didn't give a rat's ass about those things. He had a higher calling." Turner stops and turns his head forward to listen to the preacher's eulogy. Tears run from his eyes, as if Stephen were his own son.

The preacher keeps going. "Stephen was drawn to the spiritual side of being. He said to me that what was wrong with man was his endless waiting for some future day. He urged us to live each day as if it were the day we have been waiting for; that life here and now was more precious than any future prize. I believe Jennifer shares the same enthusiasm for life and while it is sad to see Stephen pass from life we should be thankful for the time we did have with him, and for what he taught us, for he was a special person."

"He sure was," Turner whispers. "Did you know Stephen was an assistant coach at the high school for the last six years? He was a damn good influence on those kids, taught them the fundamentals, but also taught them about just relaxing and having a good time."

I feel it is my turn to say something to eulogize this strange man.

"He was a good neighbor and a good friend," I whisper.

"Stephen's parents want Stephen buried in the same plot as Stephen's grandparents, Liam and Marigold Petry. Our thoughts are with his parents and with Jennifer during this difficult time." The weeping hits a crescendo and the preacher pauses so that all may compose themselves. "A world with more people like Stephen Petry would be a better place. He put others before himself. He put his love for his fellow man before profit. Many in this congregation knew Stephen and knew him to be a good man. May we strive to be like him." The sobs and sniffles drown out any other sound. What will they say at my eulogy? "Now, the Petry family invites anybody who wants to say goodbye to Stephen before he leaves for his final resting place."

I walk down the aisle, waiting in line as each person says goodbye. I take a glance at his wife-to-be who is convulsively crying, burying her head in a man's, I presume her father's, chest, her blond hair drops down to her shoulders and contrasts with her black dress. She didn't cover her hair? She's definitely a beautiful woman and I understand Stephen's excitement about living with her on a commune, but the dream of it may very likely have been better than the reality. At least the man died with hope in his eyes.

There's a couple sitting in the front row, presumably Stephen's parents. The father looks to be a man of breeding, sitting erect like a general, a broad chest, jaw and teeth clenched while tears flow down his cheeks. The mother looks like a nun; a thin, angular face and hair covered by a black bonnet. She clasps her hands as if to pray and looks forward in a hopeful, distant way, not looking at her son, but instead at the image of Christ crucified. I'm now at Stephen's coffin. There's an irony in seeing him there, the absurdity that only comes about with living and dying. I remember his saying that when he died he would like to be consumed by Mother Nature, but instead, here he is dead in a coffin lined with a purplish-velvet fabric, flowers all around, dressed in a suit as if he were getting married. His face is heavily made up—covered—completing the thoroughly unnatural look. Yet his hair appears unchanged, as vibrant as the last time I saw him.

With the many others around me, I stand and reflect on Stephen and the three years he was my neighbor. Why did he care about me? He was a good friend to me at a time when I had nobody to talk with seriously, when I needed a friend. Stephen brought me something more than the mindless hedonism Ray and I shared; he brought me hope that my life could change for the better. He was a giving person and although he didn't die for my sins, he showed

184

me more of the good side of humanity than any religious figure ever could. Well, he's with them now.

I was compelled to go to the gravesite and see the burial; dumbfounded as I saw the coffin placed in the ground, watching the dirt poured over its lid and listening to the weeping. I remember sobbing convulsively with the others, not knowing whether I was crying for Stephen or for the loss of something that could never be recovered.

The priest still holds my hand and sits at my right, praying. "Death, thy servant, is at my door. He has crossed the unknown sea and brought thy call to my home and in my desolate home only my forlorn self will remain as my last offering to thee." He looks at me and I focus on his eyes, which look sincere. I understand your message priest. He stands and places two fingers on my forehead and makes a cross. "Peace be with you," he says and then leaves. I am at peace. I am at peace.

There's a pain in my butt, more like an itch I want to scratch but can't; a painful itch that reminds me of a pimple under the skin, building up pressure, ready to pop. Ouch! The ceiling has multiple squares containing a confusing array of irregular lines and holes. Where am I? My chest expands with a deep breath and then collapses. That's right, I remember. Breathe in. Breathe out. Wait a second. Who am I? What's my name? I need to remember this. It's somehow important. Paul Mathews? Yeah! I've a son... and a wife? and work at... There are other sounds in the room, like they're coming from a television.

"Four more soldiers have died in Iraq, when a roadside bomb detonated under their Humvee. The soldier's names have not been released. This comes at a time of increasing ethnic tension within Iraq. For more on the story we go to NBC's Tom Forrest." I can't see the TV. Who is it for? Are there other people here, watching? "When diarrhea takes control, fight back with longer-lasting Imodium." On second thought, can somebody turn off the television? I need to tune out.

"Dad! Daaaaaad! Wake up Dad! It's, Jacob."
Hey Jake, I'm sleeping. I'll call you when I wake up.

185

"Melissa's had the baby. She's a girl. Come on! Wake up! Wake up!"

Who's had a baby?

"Wake up."

I love you Jake. Goodnight. See you in the morning.

The smell of cigarettes, the harsh, acrid odor, makes me open my eyes. Everything is filled with a milky haze that only clears with frequent blinking. A woman is on my left with dyed yellow hair, a thin face with transparent skin showing multiple small veins and scaly red patches. She looks a little scary. "We're giving you a breathing treatment Mr. Mathews." Her voice is gravelly. She sees me looking at her. "So, how are we doing today?" Fine, and how about yourself? "This is some Albuterol and Atrovent to open up the airways." She fiddles with something on my neck. There is a puffing sound, once and then again. "All done," she says and walks away.

"Millions of Americans will be flying or driving this Thanksgiving holiday, reports the Automobile Association of America, and while the holiday is still three days away, many have taken the opportunity of leaving early." Thanksgiving? The ceiling gets darker and darker.

"First, let's scoot him up in the bed a little. Grab the sheet on your side. One, two, three." I'm thrust backward at the count of three. My eyes open to a world that is a milky white and while I can make out shapes, it takes some time for colors to appear. "Let's turn him on his side and take a look at the decubitus." I'm being turned to my side and see a form in a bed next to mine, with a blue tube coming out of its neck. Ouch! Ouch! Get your hands off my ass!

"That looks like a stage-four ulcer at the sacrum."

Get your hands off my ass!

"All the way to the bone, Jenny."

"Just like Mr. Brooks."

"Shoot, that doesn't look good."

"I don't know what else to do. I've been turning him on his side, but he's had difficulty breathing on his side, so I can't do it. I'm also having a hell of time preventing his loose stools from going into that ulcer."

"How many stools is he having per day?"

"About three… some days four."

"We should put the rectal tube back in, to prevent infection."

"I think it'll be easier when Dr. Masterson removes him from the ventilator."

"He came by?"

"Yesterday, and he said we should start weaning him again. His oxygen saturation is at 95 percent and he's only getting 30 percent oxygen." Are they speaking about me?

"Well, until he is off the ventilator, let's put in the rectal tube and prevent soilage of that wound."

"Are you going anywhere for the holiday?"

"We're going to spend Thanksgiving in Sun City, with Jim's parents. Doesn't that sound exciting?"

"Arizona? It may be fun. It beats being here. I have to work again during the holiday."

"Well, at least you get Christmas off. He's desaturating a little bit. Do you have a rectal tube near? We can put it in now."

"I have one in the utility closet."

"We should get it now." The man in the bed next to me is not moving. All I can make out is a balding-grey head.

"I got the tube and some KY."

"Sounds like a party." They're both laughing and it takes some time for the laughter to die down. Something is entering into my rear. That feels weird, like the time Mom placed a thermometer in my butt when I was sick. Disgusting! Paul, think about something else. Breathe in. Breathe out. The image of the man lying next to me disappears, replaced by the back of my eyelids. What the heck is going on here? Is this a hospital?

Breathe in. Breathe out. Breathe in. Breathe out. Something's on my face. It covers my entire nose and mouth and it sends out a warm mist that makes me want to cough and I am coughing. Mucous is stuck to the back of my throat and I'm doing my best to spit it out, forcefully coughing and exhaling, trying to jettison this massive loogey.

187

"Let's suction the back of his throat," a man orders. It takes some time for my eyes to adjust to the light. There's some kind of hard instrument being stuck in the back of my throat and there's this awful slurping. I want to gag, but before I do, the hard thing is removed. My eyes are watering from the trauma and they focus on the man in front of me with salt-and-pepper hair that contrasts with his youthful face. He wears a white coat and looks somewhat familiar, but I can't remember where I've seen this doctor before.

"Mr. Mathews. Mr. Mathews." There's a sharp pain in my chest. The man is pushing his knuckles into my chest. Hey, man! Could you stop that? It frickin' hurts! He speaks in a very loud voice as if he were talking from the other side of the room. "It's Dr. Masterson, Mr. Mathews. We've removed you from the ventilator and you're breathing on your own now. This mask that's covering your face is giving you oxygen, so you're no longer dependent upon the ventilator. I bet you're glad about that." Huh? OK. Well, it sounds like I'm doing better. But better than what? Why can't I move, Doc? He looks away from me and talks to someone who is on my left. "We'll need to get a swallow evaluation to see if he can eat on his own. Put in a call to speech therapy so they can do an evaluation."

"I'll do it now."

There's a sense of happiness among those around me and I'm cheered by it.

"We also need better debridement of that ulcer. We need to clear all that dead tissue there and place Hydrogel to keep the area moist. What did the wound nurse say?"

"She said that the ulcer should get better once we are able to turn him on his side."

"Is physical therapy seeing him?"

"They do range of motion on his legs and arms, but he's been too lethargic to follow commands."

"OK, I'm going to give his son a call. Let's take a look at Mr. Brooks here." He comes close to me with his boyish face and says in a voice that all can hear. "You take care, Paul." Huh? He walks away, but I can still hear his voice. "So what's going on with Mr. Brooks?"

188

"Same old, same old. He's in a paced rhythm and has gone in to V Tach twice in the last week, but has been shocked out of it by his defibrillator. He's on assist control at eighteen and is getting tube feeds at 70 ccs per hour.

"Poor guy, I don't know what else we can do for him. There is no good way for him to die with a defibrillator and pacemaker in place. It's amazing that his kidneys and liver are still working after six years in this state."

"Is there any way we can get another conservator? Someone who's reasonable?"

"The judge said our opinion is biased since we're the ones taking care of him. The judge ruled he would be better served by someone who was not involved in the case."

"And because of this the state has to pay thousands of dollars each year to keep him alive."

"Yeah, I don't know how much it costs, but regardless it's not our decision."

"Don't you think it should be our decision?"

"We're here to take care of these patients the best we can, but maybe......"

The conversation becomes distant and I can't make out what they're saying. The mask sits warm over my face and it's making me feel a little claustrophobic. Breathe in. Breathe out. It's pretty easy to do. Where am I? How did I get here? What was the last thing I remember? The past is foggy, distant. Maybe if I close my eyes, I can remember.

"Mr. Mathews. Mr. Mathews." A woman's face appears through the milky haze. She has dark hair, a rotund face with acne and past acne scars covered up with make-up. She seems pleasant, helpful and cheery, maybe overly so. "I'm Judy Orozco, the speech therapist." Something is different. I'm sitting up in the bed, no longer looking at the ceiling, but instead am looking at this woman and the wall behind her. This is very exciting. Can I walk? No, I'm not moving, but look, I can see the television. Something's pushing air into my nose, making it feel dry and making me want to pick it. "Mr. Mathews, we're going evaluate your ability to swallow food," the acne faced woman says smiling.

189

I don't understand. Why should I have any problem swallowing? But come to think of it, I don't remember the last time I ate anything. "I'm going to give you some of this apple sauce to start out with." She looks down at an open container of applesauce, places a spoon within the container and pulls out half a tablespoon of this yellowish material. "OK, Mr. Mathews, could you open your mouth?" Open your mouth, Paul. My mouth opens as far as it can. Boy, do I feel stupid. It takes all my effort just to open my mouth. "Here we go." I feel like a child at the dinner table as she puts the material in my mouth. "That's good Paul." The food feels slimy and wet and an overwhelming sweet and tangy taste invades my mouth. I got to use my tongue to maneuver the applesauce to the back of my throat. "Take your time. We are in no hurry," Judy says. Moving my mouth open and closed, trying to simulate the eating process, is taking all my effort and I'm feeling winded. "Whenever you're ready, then try to swallow." OK, here's me swallowing, but damn, I have to stop breathing to swallow and it makes me feels that I'm suffocating. "Keep trying." My neck muscles tense up in an attempt to force the food down the throat. Is it working? The whole experience is tiring me. All I want to do now is go to sleep.

"Let's take a look," Judy, the speech therapist says. "Open your mouth, Mr. Mathews." OK, the mouth is open. Tell me what you see. "You're pooling the food in the back of your mouth. It's going to take some time until you'll be able to eat. Let me suction that out." She takes a long tubular instrument and places it within my mouth. There's a slurping sound that reminds of my dentist and the sound stops when she removes the suctioning device. "Last thing we'll try is how you do with water. I'm going to put a little of this water in your mouth and you try to swallow it. All right, here we go." She puts the cup of water to my mouth and pours the water in. The water runs to the back of my throat like gangbusters, and suddenly there's an overwhelming desire to cough, which I convulsively do. My chest is burning with each cough. After some time, the coughing stops and I close my eyes and breathe heavily. "I guess that won't work," Judy says and everything drifts away.

"Wake up! That's right. Open your eyes, Dad."

190

Jacob? You look so much older. Where am I? And where is your mother?

"They told me you're off the breathing machine and that you're breathing on your own now. I had to come and see it for myself." He looks really tired, but excited. "Can you talk? Can you say something, like hello or just anything."

"Huuu. Huuuu. Huuuuullll."

"Keep trying to talk. Don't stop. The nurses here say you're sleeping all the time."

"Hulllll. Hullllll...lowwwwww." I'll keep trying.

"Wake up." I open my eyes and Jacob smiles at me. "Sorry, Dad."

That's OK.

"I love you, Dad... Dad? Dad? Wake up! Wake up! Ray told me to look for your book and I found it. I found your book, Dad. Remember your book?"

That's good Jake. I'm proud of you. Please turn out the lights for your old man.

"We'll keep you updated on Israeli Prime Minister Ariel Sharon's stroke. To summarize, Ariel Sharon, Israel's Prime Minister has suffered a massive stroke. The Prime Minister has had massive bleeding into his brain, which is currently being drained. We will keep you updated on his status on the Evening News. Now back to our regularly scheduled broadcast."

"What are you planning on doing?"

"I'm planning on exposing him. We'll thwart Jake Ridell's attempts at seizing the Garner Estate. We will fight fire with fire."

"How do you plan on doing that?"

"By finding out what his plans are."

"An insider?"

"We need someone to get close to him and get as much information as we can."

"You're implying that... that someone be me."

"You know that Jake has an insatiable desire for women. All you have to do is seduce him and allow him to become careless."

"What's in it for me?'

191

"Money, and maybe Tom Garner's love when you give him the information that will save his company."

The world is a hazy white light that causes a shooting pain in the back of my head. Oh, I feel like crap. My butt is stinging, a sharp pain that feels like it is in the bone, making me want to move to my side to relieve it, but, hell, I can't. The world slowly comes into focus and faded colors soon become more vibrant colors, but vibrant may not be the right word for the colors of this room. A television hangs down from the ceiling in front of me. Where is that old man? He's not there. That's not Mr. Brooks. Mr. Brooks has been replaced by a much younger man with a full head of black hair, a tube emanating from his neck and his eyes transfixed upon the ceiling. He can't be more than thirty. Poor kid! What the hell happened to him?

The television to my right is on, but the many people who come in and out of the television seem uncoordinated, and it's hard to understand if there's some kind of message behind what they're doing. It all seems sort of silly, making me want to close my eyes.

There's someone moving my right arm up and down and now my right leg is being moved up to my chest and back and then my right foot is being moved up and down. There's a young man in a white coat holding my numbed left leg. My leg looks flaccid, bony, and pale in appearance. The light-skinned man sees me looking at him. "Mr. Mathews, you're awake." Yes I am, Einstein. "Do you feel me moving your leg?" My mouth opens and closes, but no words come out. "How about this? Can you push your toes down on your right side?"

Sure thing, here it goes.

"OK, I saw your toes move a little." He puts a couple of his fingers in my hand. "Can you squeeze my fingers?"

No problem.

"Good. Now let's try the left side... Mr. Mathews, do you feel my fingers here?"

No, I don't... I'm tired, man. Can you come back tomorrow?

"Mr. Mathews? Mr. Mathews?"

192

"Take care, Mr. Mathews." There's a woman smiling at me with dark eyes, light skin and dark hair with streaks of grey. "You're leaving Venticare today, Mr. Mathews. You're going to go to Sea Gardens Nursing Home! You have been a pleasure to take care of and we'll miss you. We called your son and he knows where you'll be." Wait a second, where am I going? I've got to ask her, but all I can do is put my lips together, force air through and say "Puh, Puh."

"That's good Mr. Mathews. Keep trying to talk. We'll get speech therapy to help you at the nursing home. These men are going to transport you to Sea Gardens. So take care and have a wonderful 2006." 2006! I remember 2000 and that fucking election and the 2001 terror attacks, but I can't remember any year beyond that. There are three men standing next to my bed, two on my left and one on my right.

"At the count of three, we'll lift," a man's voice says. "One...Two...Three!" Wow, these guys are strong. I'm being elevated above the bed, held by these three men. "Make sure to get the Foley bag." They place me on a less comfortable bed and there's a sudden stinging pain up my ass. "OK, let's connect him to the portable oxygen." Where are they taking me? I'm moving down some kind of hallway and I'm passing by what looks like hospital rooms which look sort of like the room I was in. Each room has two patients, each with a tube emanating from their neck, attached to a machine. I pass by one room after the next until I'm met by the bright sunshine. It's so bright that I have to close my eyes.

Chapter 11

A Bright Sunshiny Day

"Put him in 204-B. Down the hall and make a right."

"Thanks."

"Leave his paperwork at the nurse's station."

I'm moving into a room with a window, moving past an older man who's sleeping, moving to a corner of the room next to a tinted window that looks outside, onto what looks like an alley. There are buildings on the other side of the alley and some kind of bushes at the edge of the window.

"So who do we have here?" A woman asks in a pleasant, singsong voice.

A man with a gruff voice answers. "This a 61-year-old male, with a history of atrial fibrillation, congestive heart failure, and COPD whose status post hemorrhagic stroke in 2004. He was removed from the ventilator three weeks ago and is getting oxygen by nasal cannula at four liters. He's getting G-tube feeds at a rate of 70 cc's per hour and has a stage four decubitus ulcer on the sacrum."

"Thank you very much. Is his medication list at the front desk?"

"Yes, ma'am."

"Now we'll move him on the count of three. Make sure to get the Foley catheter. One...two...three!" Hey wait a second! My ass cries out in pain as I'm placed awkwardly on top of another bed.

"I think he in pain," a woman says in an accent that sounds like something Asian. "Has he been getting anything for pain?"

"Not that I'm aware of," the man answers.

"Who's his primary care doctor?" the other woman asks.

"Let me look here. Primary is Dr. William Gellman."

"Oh Dr. Gellman! I know him. Good doctor and a very nice man."

"Will you be needing anything else from us?"

"No sir, you guys can go. Just leave his medication list at the nurse's desk." The two men leave the room and the two women come closer to me. One of the women is black. "Hi, Mr. Mathews

194

I'm Connie Smith, the head nurse at Sea Gardens, and this is Lily, who will be your daytime nurse." There's an Asian woman with black hair that's flat and falls to the middle of her neck. She has a nice complexion, bright eyes and a wonderful smile, reminding me of those pretty, delightful women in Vietnam. She's the most beautiful thing I've seen in a long time.

"Hi, Mr. Mathews, I'm Lily. We going take good care of you here. You have pain?" Yes, I'm having pain. I'm moving my head up and down, at least I think I am. "You are having pain. We call your primary doctor and give you pain medication in your stomach tube." She's quite pleasant and, as my eyes gaze outside to the alley, I see a small bird on the branch of a tree, next to the window, but eventually the bird flies away and I wait gazing out the window, waiting for the bird to come back.

"Paul, I going to give you pain medicine. Connie and I look at your bottom afterward. OK. OK, Paul." Lily is fiddling with something, like a tube, hanging out of my stomach and when she's done she turns her head up to smile at me. She pats my head. That's nice.

They're moving me to my side. There's an area of deep blue outside the window. Is that the sky? Shoot, I don't remember the last time I saw the sky and though this is only a small part of the sky between the buildings across the alley, the sky is a view of heaven, a marvelous soft blue color and I gaze longingly at it.

"Stage four ulcer, Lily. Look, you can see it goes right to the bone. They've done a good job cleaning it and I can see some granulation tissue coming in. Lily we are going to have to turn him on his side every two hours. That means alternating sides every two hours to take pressure off the sacrum. We'll clean him with wet dressings and clear the dead tissue away." OUCH! There's a stinging pain in my buttock. "We'll put the hydrogel within the ulcer. That's good, Lily. Now let's pack it with wet gauze and cover the area. All done. We can leave him on his side and turn him in another couple hours." Lily's beautiful face shines in front of me and the thought of pain is now remote.

"You OK Paul?" she says. Yes, I'm OK now, Lily. She puts her hand in my hair and brushes it back, making me feel somewhat like a little boy, a feeling I don't mind. She leaves, leaving me to look up at the small patch of sky. Occasionally a wispy cloud passes through. It's serene and it feels as if I'm drifting off on one of these clouds, soft and easy.

"Martha! Martha! Martha! Martha!" The sounds are coming from my right side. The room is dark and the shapes within are slow to focus. I'm lying on my side staring at a curtain, behind which comes that yelling. "Martha! Martha! Martha!" It doesn't stop and you would think that after receiving no response this man would give up his attempt to locate Martha by yelling at the top of his lungs, but this is not the case and he picks up the beat saying her name faster, "Martha! Martha! Martha!" He stops and then returns again, now spending a longer time with the pronunciation of her name. "Maaaarthaaaaaa! Maaaaarthaaaaa! Maaaaarthaaaaaa!" Who the hell is Martha and why is she not responding to this man? Can you put a lid on it man? I wish there was some way I could talk, to tell you to shut the hell up. "Martha! Maaaarthaaaaa!" It's a guttural sound held deep in the caverns of humanity.

"Mr. Wilson! Mr. Wilson!" a woman answers with a Latino accent.

"Martha! Martha!" Mr. Wilson repeats.

"Martha sleeping Mr. Wilson. Don't wake up Martha."

"Martha?"

"It's nighttime, Mr. Wilson. Martha sleeping."

"Martha! Martha!" he calls, knowing now where she is.

"Try relax, Mr. Wilson."

"Martha! Martha!"

"Why every night like this? You know I give you medication, Mr. Wilson, when you like this. Martha gone, Mr. Wilson. Martha gone."

"Martha! Martha! Maaaaaaarthaaaa!" He strongly yells. He sounds like a forceful man.

"OK we'll have it your way. I going get Haldol! You want me to do that!"

"Martha!"

"I go get it then!"

"Martha! Maaaarthaaaa!" We're both waiting for Martha to come into the room at any moment.

"Here is medication. It will calm you down."

"Ow! Stop that! Martha! Martha! Martha!" For some reason I don't think the medication is working, because the desperate cries keep on. I'm powerless to stop the howling coming from behind the curtain. The flimsy visual barrier does not stop sound. "Martha!" The sounds though are becoming fainter and soon become a whisper. "Martha... Martha."

"The day nurse need to speak to doctor. He need medication every night so this don't happen." She would be more convincing if she had a greater command of English. I wonder where Martha really is. There's so much suffering hidden behind every person and I can't remember if I've ever suffered like Mr. Wilson. I breathe heavily through my mouth. Breathe in. Breathe out.

"Mr. Mathews! Paul! Paul!" There's someone rubbing my face with a warm, wet towel. It's comforting. "Paul, it is Lily. Wake up Paul." Lily? Why am I not wearing any clothes? Modesty inclines me to cover myself, but it also feels sort of nice and airy. The warm towel rubs the skin of my chest and belly and it runs down my right leg. "Wake up, Paul. It is Lily. I am cleaning you, Paul." Slowly Lily comes into focus. She's in a white nurses' uniform with pictures of Mickey Mouse, Minnie Mouse, Bambi and some unknown Disney characters. Her skin has a soft glow, her lips are full and pinkish in color and her eyes are filled with caring as she looks toward me. She is lifting my lifeless left arm, rubbing it with the towel down from my wrist and then ending up at my left armpit. She turns her head toward me while she does this. "Good Morning Paul!" Good morning, Lily. She smiles, happy to see me. I've never met anyone with such a cheery disposition. "All clean Paul. Now I going to turn you to your left side." She leaves and comes back with another nurse with pale skin and orange hair. Boy, I'm glad she's not my nurse. She's hideous! She pulls my right arm and Lily tilts my hip so that I lie on my left side, looking out the window at the building across the alley. Lily's body blocks my view and I wish I could put my arms around her and nestle close to her. Lily, it's you I want. She puts her hand through my

197

hair and it's almost like a sleeping pill, effectively making me drowsy and my ability to stay awake wanes...

Lying on my right side, I'm looking at an older man, sitting in a chair. His hair and moustache are white, and he's got a thick neck and wide shoulders. He's vacantly staring at the television, doing something strange with his mouth, like he's chewing something, but there's nothing going into his mouth. He keeps repeating this, stopping chewing, resuming chewing, chewing without purpose. This is so annoying. Dude, you got to stop that! Something's wrong with that guy! I need to close my eyes, focus on something else.

"Martha! Maaarthaaa! Maaaaaartha!" The moonlight illuminates the alley and the buildings across the way. "Martha! Martha!" The voice changes to one of questioning. "Martha? Martha?" The reflection of a full moon is in one of the windows across the alley. The orb is a glowing distant illumination that sits across the alley and reflects an unknown land. "Martha? Martha?" It would be nice to be under the stars, under a full moon, standing next to the glistening ocean with the Santa Ana winds warming my soul, leaving me with no thought; no thought to be burdened with. "Maaaarthaaa! Marthaaaa! Martha! Martha! Martha!"
"Time for medication, Mr. Wilson."
"Martha?"
"Tranquilo, Mr. Wilson. Here your medication."
"Ow! Ow! Ow!"
"Everything be OK soon," the nurse reassures.
"Ow! Ow!"
"I'll check on you soon." Mr. Wilson stops yelling. Only the corner of the window across the street has the reflection of the moon and then the moon is gone. It's time to go back to sleep.

My eyes turn on their own toward the window and the alley. It's dark and rainy. Through the sounds of rain, meanders the sound of television, a person on the TV discussing how to make a delicious Chicken Marsala. There's an itch-like pain in my butt, sort of maddening, made worse by my inability to move. My nose is dry,

198

made more so by air rushing through it. Some contraption is feeding air into my nose and somehow I wish I could remove it and stick my finger in my nose and pull out a dry booger.

"The most important aspect of a good Chicken Marsala is to sauté the mushrooms first in the white wine sauce, then pan-fry the chicken and keep the lid off. Understand keep the lid off. This will go well with a side of polenta." My ass is in pain and all I have to look at is the pouring rain, cats and dogs, and hear this silly cooking channel. It's depressing.........wish somehow I could just stop breathing, stop living.

"What's wrong, Paul? Are you in pain?" It's Lily. Thank God for giving me Lily. She's a comforting presence and it seems that I've no other friend in the world, no other love, except Lily. She's soothing me with her hand on my forehead, caressing my skin gently, then rubbing her hand through my scant hair. "Poor Paul! Poor Paul! Lily will take care of you. I know you having pain in your butt. I give you medicine." She's rubbing my forehead back and forth, softly, lovingly. The rain's pounding outside and I'm glad to be inside here with Lily.

"Wake up Paul, your son wants to speak to you on the phone." A hard object is placed on my right ear.

"Dad, it's Jacob. I read your book and I was able to send it off to a few literary agents. One of them wants me to send the first three chapters. Isn't that great?"

What? Jacob? A book?

"Come on, Dad, say something. We're exhausted. Emily is keeping us up every night... I wish you were here...I love you."

There's fullness in my belly, an uncomfortable swelling of my abdomen as if someone has inflated it with air. My intestines contract, my belly pulls inward and I expunge a large hard stool along with a large quantity of gas. Oh yes! What a relief! I could care less about the slight smell of excrement, but it does make me open my eyes. Where's Mr. Wilson? His bed is empty.

After some time, Lily walks in the room, erect in posture and with sort of a mechanical walk. She comes up to me, smiles and puts her hand on my face. "You doing better, Paul, but you sleepyhead. You've been sleeping two days." She stops for a second to inhale partially. She smiles, coming close so that her lips are near mine and rubs my cheek with her hand. "You did poo-poo, Paul?" she softly asks. Guilt runs over my broken body, but quickly abates when Lily says, "That's OK, Paul! You have accident. Shit happens." She giggles. She's an angel. I don't know what I'd do without her. "I clean you." and she walks away, leaving me staring at the empty bed.

"Show her how much you love her. Give her the gift that lasts forever." That commercial reminds me of Dad and how he helped pick out Sarah's wedding ring. Sarah?

Lily walks back in the room with a rectangular basin. She walks behind me, out of view. Now her hands are on my buttocks and she's cleaning me back there with something warm and wet caressing my backside. It is a soft touch. The faint smell of excrement is gone, replaced by the distant smell of baby powder and I'm feeling sort of like a baby; helpless, comfortable, being changed by my mother. I can't protest and part of me doesn't want to protest, wanting to acquiesce to my inability to change things, to allow life to fall where it may, to be content with wearing a diaper.

"All clean, Paul." Lily covers me with the blanket. Thank you, Lily. I'm warm now, a soul hidden within the covers of life. My little place resides deep within these covers and I don't want to ever come out.

It's dark, a time when no sane person should be awake. Behind the window, the dark alley is quiet. There's a star in the sky, visible between the buildings and I look lovingly at the fraction of the world I can see. The star shines benignly down and I know the world means me no harm. I'm part of this world and even if I were to be destroyed, disintegrated, separated in to millions of parts, and scattered in all directions, I'd still be part of this world. The world would still take me in, never being isolated even in death and especially in death. Oh star, projecting your light from billions of miles away. Who am I anyway? Does it really matter whether I live or die? The room is silent except for the snoring of Mr. Wilson. Did he get his medication? Must have.

"Ocean Spray Cranberry Juice Cocktail has one third more juice than your conventional brands of cranberry juice. This gives Ocean Spray its special flavor. No other brand comes close."

"Back to the *Today* show. The spread of avian influenza has reached Europe and it will only be a matter of time until this virus advances to the United States, says virologist Dr. Deborah Chung of the Harvard Medical School. Dr. Chung joins us today to discuss this deadly virus. Dr. Chung…"

Mr. Wilson's sitting in a chair, a tray of food in front of him. There's a woman slowly feeding him and coaxing him in a soothing voice to eat. "Dad, this is your favorite, rhubarb pie. I baked it myself. Isn't that good?" I can only make out the side of the woman's face. She wears glasses, has a chubby face, straight orange hair that is cut quite short and she is balancing the rhubarb pie on a fork and putting it front of Mr. Wilson's face. He opens his mouth and the food drops in his mouth. He slowly chews, and it's really bugging me to watch him take so long to swallow this little bit of pie.

"Good," he softly says. She methodically gives him one piece after the next, only stopping to wipe off the crumbs from his moustache. He must have worn that moustache his entire adult life and will probably die with it.

"Dad, you have to stay calm. The nurses say you're yelling at night. You have to stop that."

"I'm not yelling," Mr. Wilson grunts.

"They say you are."

"I'm not!"

"OK, Dad, whatever you say. Next time I come I'll bring Susan and Barry. Would you like that?"

"Sure. We haven't seen them in a long time."

"We?"

The sounds of the television are drowning out the conversation. Who cares about woman's deodorant anyway? I'm feeling sleepy.

"Martha! Martha! Martha!" It's dark out. The portion of the alley that I see is empty. Where am I? Why can't I move? "Martha! Maaaaarthaaaa!" the guttural voice calls out. Who's Martha? She must be someone special, like that girl, that special girl. High School! Leslie! Leslie! Oh Leslie!

Talking with her at lunch, I don't know what to say. She looks at me, as if I'm the one she's been waiting for. The one she'll love forever. Listening to her talk, I notice her straight brown hair, her brown eyes, her freckled sweet face, her pink sweater hiding her firm breasts. Don't mess it by talking, Paul. Jay and Jeff are looking at me at this moment as if I were a God and maybe I'll show them the Valentine's card she sent me with the ending, "Love, Leslie."

Take my hand, take my whole life, too. For I can't help, falling in love with you. Am I going too far? Is she out of my league? I should have told her how I felt about her that day in the cafeteria. Don't walk away, Leslie, in that skirt that sways to the motion of your hips! Glen can't love you! He can't adore you like I adore you. I'll win your love back. I call out her name. "Leslie! Leslie!" Can she hear me? "Come back Leslie! Come back! Leslie! Leslie!"

There's another voice. "Martha! Maaarthaaa!"

No not Martha! It's not Martha I love. "Leslie!" Oh, be with me again. We had lunch in the cafeteria together. You were my Valentine. Didn't that mean something? "Leslie! Leslie!" It's very bright now, like someone turned on a thousand lights.

"What's going on here? Mr. Wilson you have to settle down."

"Martha! Martha!"

"Helen, do you need help?"

"I just need two milligrams of Haldol for this patient. He has a PRN order."

"I thought Mr. Wilson had been doing well. I haven't heard his voice at night. Is something wrong with him?"

"Only thing wrong is that his daughter made us stop his nighttime medicine because it was making him too drowsy."

"Don't look too drowsy now."

"Martha! Martha!"

"What's going on with his neighbor? He looks a little agitated."

"Leslie! Leslie!"

"Mr. Mathews, what's wrong?" A dark-skinned woman with an African-sounding accent questions me. Maybe she can tell Leslie

202

that I love her. She and Leslie must know each other. If I implore her to understand my plight, she can talk to Leslie for me.

"Leslie! Leslie!"

"I don't understand what you're saying Mr. Mathews." You know me! Why are you calling me Mr. Mathews? I'm Paul from high school and I love Leslie.

"Leslie! Leslie!"

"Who is Henry? Mr. Wilson's first name is not Henry. It's Edward."

"Leslie! Leslie!"

"I think that he's going to need some sedation also Helen. Does he have an order?"

"I don't think so."

"We'll have to call the doctor on call, then. Do you know his primary?"

"I think it's in the chart."

"Leslie! Leslie!" The dark-skinned lady comes closer to me, hovering over me. She seems too old to be in high school. Maybe she works at the principal's office.

"Who is Henry? Is Henry a family member?"

What's wrong with this woman? Is she deaf? Another voice calls out but I don't see her. Could that be Leslie? Leslie it's me, Paul. I love you. Let's get married. I know we're young, but I don't care what happens.

"I have the medication here, Helen. Haldol for Mr. Wilson and Ativan for Mr. Mathews. Give the Ativan to Mr. Mathews and I will give the Haldol to Mr. Wilson." The dark-skinned woman is holding a syringe in her hands. Hey! Wait! I'm not into heavy drugs. What will Leslie think? There's a sharp pain in my buttock. I thought you were my friend? There's a strange sense of relaxation, making me ambivalent to everything. No, I really don't want to dance. I think I'm going to just sit here and listen to the music. No, Mom, I don't want to go to sleep. It is not my bedtime yet. "Lily! Lily!"

"The new Aerobicizer will shrink off inches from your belly with very little work. Just ten minutes a day is all you need for a slimmer, trimmer you. Why waste money on large complicated machines? The Aerobicizer can fit into your closet. The design contours to your body and within a few weeks you'll see pounds coming off. Mastercard and Visa accepted. Only seventy-nine ninety-five for a commitment to a new you. Call our toll free number now." Is that the television? My nose and mouth feel dry and I wish for a glass of water. There's air being pushed through my nose, drying it out. I'm lying on my left side, looking out through the window at a sunlit day. The bushes that surround the window have full-wide green leaves with small flowers of purple interspersed. Someone's coming toward me, dressed in a white coat and holding a stethoscope in his right hand. He's rotund in body and face. The skin of his face has multiple red scaly blotches and his light blue eyes are covered in glasses. He appears tired, as if his life was sheer drudgery, and in this manner he places the earpieces of the stethoscope to his ears. He holds one end of the stethoscope in his right hand, leans down and places that end to my chest. What is he hearing? What is he thinking? The doctor looks very familiar, though. I know him. He looks at my face and pulls the earpieces out.

"Hi, Paul," he says with a slight smile. "How are we doing today?"

OK Doc, at least I think I am. He's towering above me and I feel so small in comparison.

"Paul, do you know who I am?" You look familiar Doc, but I seem to be forgetting your name. He realizes my blank stare and looks somewhat surprised and somewhat distressed. "Paul, it's Dr. Gellman." Dr. Gellman... Oh, yeah... I know you. You're that doctor I saw before somewhere. I don't remember where. He spots this recognition and a look of relief comes to his face. "Paul, this is the first time I've seen you awake. You must be doing better." Better than what, Doc? He's pressing on my belly and then he turns away from me. Lily walks up to me looking as pretty as spring grass.

"How does the decubitus ulcer look?" Dr. Gellman questions.

"Looking much better, with turning him on his side. There good tissue underneath. We replace bandages every day," Lily dutifully responds. I only see the side of her face.

204

"Let's take a look at it." Lily disappears. Whatever covering or clothing that is at the bottom of my body is being removed and a moment later there's some mild pain in my buttock.

"That ulcer looks much better," Dr. Gellman says. "It's starting to close around the edges. You've done a good job with it."

"We been turning him on side every two hours for last four months. Problem now is that he get ulcers on hips and legs are getting contracted."

"I can see the contractions. You can't straighten his legs?"

"We try, but knees pull up to chest and we can't pull them down." Ouch! Someone is trying to pull my legs straight causing a sharp pain at the back of my right knee.

"I can see what you mean. Well anyway, the ulcers do look better. Has physical therapy come by?"

"They come and do range of motion, but he always asleep."

"How about speech therapy?"

"The same thing, he always sleeping." There's a moment of no sound and there are hands touching my hind side.

"Where is the trash? I'd like to throw these gloves away."

"The trash is by door, Doctor."

"Have you seen his son?"

"He came by three month ago, but did not stay long."

"I should give him a call to update him on his father's condition." His words sound tentative, waiting for some kind of approval. None comes, instead there is silence. A bird sits on a branch outside my window, warbling a melodic song; some kind of song about love and nature and beauty. The bird sings the song of me. Words hold no significance compared to this song. "Let's check a CBC and lytes on him on Monday, please."

"Place order in chart and we do it," Lily responds. Footsteps recede, leaving me alone with Lily. She caresses my face and my hair and smiles an empathic smile. She's like a mother to me, dutiful and comforting to her child. I love you, Lily. I can't think of anything more perfect than you. "I clean you up, Paul. I change your dressing and give you medicine." She says the words lightly, patting me on the shoulder, not wanting to agitate me. She turns around and I follow her lovely backside, dressed in white scrubs, walking away. Oh, I long for you Lily. Please come back. Looking to the head of the bed, waiting for her to return, I see the top left corner of a television. There are different colors and shapes that appear in this corner.

Lily reappears. Gosh, she's beautiful. Like an angel. "I crush your pill, Paul. I put in tube." She's standing now in front of me and I look at her midsection. She bends down and is fiddling with something at my belly. All I see now is the back of her head, her beautiful straight hair so close to my face I almost feel it. How I would love to embrace her and reciprocate the love she shows me. Lily turns and walks away and my eyes follow her until she disappears. At the corner of the room there's a television with its alternating shapes and colors. The colors blend with the colors of the room and the shapes all blend into an amalgam of colors without borders and then it all turns to black.

"On the five-o'clock news, forty-five Iraqis found dead in makeshift graves as sectarian violence increases, Israel elects a new leader, and can your pet call 911? Hear the story of amazing animals that have saved lives." Who left the television on? There's an empty bed next to me with its covers pulled back. The sounds of the television beckon me to listen as there's nothing else that can give me stimulation, not the empty bed, nor the wallpaper at the other end of the room, grey and striped like a dress shirt. The room is still as if waiting for some movement, for some life, but there's none. Hell, I'm no different than this room, lying motionless here like an inanimate object. The only difference between me and a picture on the wall is my ability to observe this world, but for all intents and purposes I'm just part of the ambiance of this room, placed here by some strange interior designer. Who planned this and is there anything required of me? Am I expected to do something?

My eyes open and I'm facing a window that's framed on both sides by large shrubs of green. Someone's touching my rear. It feels warm. "You had a big poop, Paul," a woman calls out from behind me. She's grunting as she's wiping my backside. "Almost done, Paul," she says as she exhales. I guess I've pooped again. Funny, it doesn't bother me. "I'm going to put zinc ointment on buttocks. First, I throw this away." Footsteps fade away and then return. There are hands touching my anal area putting some kind of cream there. My backside is covered and a blanket is placed over my body. Lily walks toward me. She looks a little hurried and does not make eye contact with me until she brings her face close to mine. She adjusts the prongs that go into my nose and fiddles with something around my ears. She then looks at me, places her hand upon the top of my head and says, "Poor Paul, you do not say anything. Can you say something to me? It is Lily, your friend." My mouth opens, but no sound comes. I don't know what to say to her. I've all these thoughts in my head like where am I and who am I, but I don't think I could comprehend the answer. I need to try anyway for she looks at me expecting me to say something and I wouldn't want to disappoint this lovely woman, waiting with her dark eyes and her beautiful mouth opened in a half-smile. I want to ask her where am I.

"Where?" It is all I can say. "Where? Where?"

"Where is your son, Paul? He be here in two week."

Jacob? Jacob is coming here? How about Sarah? Where have they gone? I haven't seen them in a long time. Lily, can you answer me, for I'm a little confused? She keeps stroking my hair.

"Am I your friend Paul?" She leans over and kisses me on the forehead. "Poor, poor Paul. It is sad to see you like this." Sad? With you stroking my hair, kissing me on the forehead and softly speaking to me, sadness is not the emotion I feel Lily. I feel loved. "It will be nice to see your son, no Paul? He call here every week." She stops caressing me and stands up, revealing her white scrubs that cover her belly. "You look tired. It's OK. You sleep," and I oblige her by closing my eyes. I feel loved. Loved not only by Lily, but the bed I lie in, the air I breathe, the sounds of the television and the darkness that consumes me.

"Martha!!! Martha!!!" The room is dark. I think I'm facing a curtain and on the other side of the curtain is the defiant voice of a man yelling, "Maaaaarthaaaa! Marthaaaa! Martha! Martha!" It's rhythmic and I seem to understand Mr. Wilson's music. "Martha! Martha! Marthaaaaaaa!" He's a bird warbling a tune to turn on his lover and bring her close. The song persists because nobody has accepted his invitation. I start to sing my own song. "Lily!

207

Liiiiiileeeeee! Lily!" What a wonderful woman! "Liiiily! Lilyyyyyyyy!" I love the sound of her name and wish that she will listen to my song and come to my bed and stroke my hair, smile at me and talk with that lovely voice. "Liiiiily! Lily! Lily! Lily!"

"Martha!!! Maarthaaaa!"

"Liiiily! Lilyyyy"

"Marthaaaa! Marthaaa!"

"Lily! Lily! Lily! Lily!" I syncopate.

"What's going on here?"

"Martha?"

"Mr. Wilson, you know we have to give you medication when you act like this." Her song doesn't sound near as beautiful as Mr. Wilson's.

"Lily! Lily!"

"Look, you've agitated your neighbor here." The nurse comes close to me and puts her hand on my head.

"Liiiily! Liiiiily!"

"You know I'm going to have to give you both medication. You both want that?"

"Maaaaarthaaaa! Martha!"

"Leeeeely! Leeeeeeeely!"

"Suit yourselves. You both are going to get medication." The lights of the room turn on revealing a view of a purple curtain with shapes of crescent moons and stars. The shapes and colors are fascinating.

"Here you go, Mr. Wilson. Here be your shot," the nurse says.

"Ouch, that hurts! Martha! Maaaaarthaaaaaa!"

"You calm down, Mr. Wilson. Now it's time to give your friend here, Mr. Mathews, a shot of Ativan." The footsteps are approaching and they are getting louder until they stop at my backside. Ouch! There's a sharp pain in my buttock that disappears quickly. "That should do it."

"Martha!"

"That's enough from you, Mr. Wilson. You be waking up everyone in the nursing home. Try to calm down." The footsteps leave the room. The sounds of Mr. Wilson die off and I'm feeling somewhat drowsy, somewhat drunk. What is the meaning of all the things that I see, my existence, the meaning of this life? It doesn't seem to have an absolute meaning. I've always known this, but what I marvel at, as I stare at this curtain in the darkness, is how beautiful and ordered things are in this meaningless world. I think about Lily's beauty and wait for her to come and see me again. Not now. Now it is time for sleep.

"Lily. Lily," I softly say.

The alley out the window is filled with bright light. Someone's wiping my backside and there are two women talking. "That ulcer looks much better."

"Yes, it look better. He soon be on his back and we get him in chair. He don't talk though. He always sleeping."

"Well, Judy told me he called out your name last night. He had to get Ativan to calm him down." The women are laughing. "Looks like you have yourself a new boyfriend, girl."

"He's better than any man I met." Lily approaches. Her hair is pulled back in a bun, and she wears light blue scrubs in which her muscular dark arms protrude through. She's wiping her hands with a paper towel. She smiles and leans forward so her face is about six inches from mine. "You my boyfriend, Paul? We make good couple, no? I clean you and you don't talk. You make good boyfriend." She strokes my hair and part of me is incredulous at what she's saying, but part of me believes she really does like me and that we do have a relationship of some kind and within that relationship there is love going both ways and I'm a man and she's a woman. I like the sound of that. I'm lucky to have her and will do anything to make her happy. She continues to stroke my hair. "My poor Paul! Poor Paul!" I accept her love as the flower receives a bee. You turn off the lights Lily………

"Dad! Dad!" Someone's mouth is near my ear and that mouth is yelling, "Dad! Dad!" OK, OK, I'm up. Stop your yelling. I'm on my side looking at a white shirt, a belt buckle and beige slacks. The body arches forward and over my bed, revealing only the chest, but not the neck or face of this person. "Dad! Dad!" The person pulls his body back and then bends down to look at me.

Jacob is that you? You look different, familiar, but older and a little haggard. Your hair has grey in it, your hairline is receding and there are large dark semicircles under your eyes. What happened to you, Jacob? Jacob seems rather uncomfortable, fidgeting and darting looks at me, above me, to the left and right of me and below me. He finally sits down in a chair next to the bed and stares at me. Jacob? Where have you been? Is this a dream to have you here?

"It's me, Jacob." I know it's you, Jacob. I haven't forgotten. He walks away and comes back with a chair, sits and leans forward to bring his face next to mine. "They tell me you're doing better. They said also that ulcer on your backside is healing. But Dad, they said that you can't do physical therapy or speech therapy because you're always sleeping. You have to try to get better, Dad. You have to want to live." He's looking at me, squinting his eyes, making a big furrow between his eyebrows, something he did when he was younger. He places his elbow on the bed and rests his forehead upon his hand. He's softly crying. I can't see his face, but his body convulses lightly and it forces his head to bob up and down. Don't be sad, Jacob. I hope nothing bad has happened to you. Where is Sarah? She could help. Hey, can someone get my wife? Jacob raises his head, wipes his eyes and nose with his sleeve and rests his chin upon his hand looking away from me. "I don't know what to do." He turns his reddened eyes and distraught face toward me. "I don't know what to do. Is it OK if I sell your condo to help pay for the nursing home?" He looks distressed and talks a little faster. "The money would be for you, Dad, to help take care of you. I wouldn't think of taking a cent of it."

Condo? I thought we owned a house. Do we have a condo, too? Jacob, of course you can sell the condo. I don't even remember what our condo looks like. Sell it, Jacob, and keep the money for yourself. I don't need it.

"I owe it to you Dad. Melissa said it would be the only decent thing to do. When that money runs out, we can put you on Medi-Cal and you won't have to pay a cent."

Who is Melissa? I don't remember Melissa. I wish I could talk to you Jacob. All I can say is, "Ja... Jay...Jay."

"Yes, Dad?" He brings his ear close to my mouth. "What do you want to say?" I want to say, keep the money. I keep trying to say this, like it's my new mantra. *Keep the money. Keep the money. Keep the money.* "Keeee. Keee. Keeeee. Keeeeep." Don't waste the money on me.

"I don't understand, Dad. I don't understand." He moves his head back and sits back in his chair, appearing tired, as if the interaction with me is killing him. "I'll be right back. I got to go to the bathroom and wash off my face." He pushes the chair back and walks away. This is such strange thing. He looked like he wanted something from me, but what can I give him? Maybe I can do something for him.

He returns looking more refreshed and calm. It's nice to see. He walks in front of my bed and passes the edge of my vision. I hear him breathing and my eyes focus on the empty bed next to me. With one last sigh Jacob returns to his chair and we stare at each other. I need to impart some kind of wisdom to him, play some sort of role of a father to a son. But really, how do I do that when I can't talk?

Jacob pulls his wallet out of his pocket. He opens it and takes something out and puts it in front of my face. It's a picture of a baby girl, wearing a pink sweat suit, sitting in front of a background of baby blue. She looks blankly out at me. Her upper lip is flat and her lower lip is raised to keep her mouth somewhat closed. Her cheeks are pinkish and I see dimples that convey she's smiling. Her scant hair is light brown and her eyes are too far away to make out any color, but they look out hopefully and fearfully; the next generation attempting to assimilate the complexities and the contradictions of the human world. She's beautiful with her blank stare.

"Her name is Emily, Dad."

Emily's a nice name.

"She's my daughter… She is a year old now."

Daughter? That's wonderful! That means I'm a grandfather.

"I didn't want her to come to the nursing home, because she's got a bad cold. We'll bring her soon. She's with Melissa back up in Sacramento now."

211

Who is Melissa? She must be Jacob's wife. When did this happen?

"Isn't she beautiful, Dad?"

She sure is Jacob.

"She is tough, though. It took her a whole year to sleep through the night and I feel exhausted most of the time. She is tough." Jacob turns the picture and looks at it himself. He rests his back in the chair and slumps back. I lay quietly as my breath stops, gazing at my son in reflection of his life, having the pieces of my memory return to me in piecemeal. There was the divorce and Jacob's moving up to Sacramento. "I'm sorry, Dad. I just wanted to show you this picture." He again presses the picture forward. Emily stares again at me. I wonder what she would think of me; how she would feel about my being. Would she be scared, cry and never want to see my face again? The inanity of humanity. Jacob takes the picture away and places it back in his wallet. "Oh, I forgot to tell you. I found a literary agent for your book, 'California Dreaming.' He thinks it has a shot at getting published. Wouldn't that be great?" That's right, I wrote a book. "It's really a good book."

Thanks, Jacob, but I wish I never wrote it.

"I like the part at the end where Edward is at the mobile home park drinking tequila and watching the sunset with Loretta. Where he says, 'I'll always have my dreams darling, nothing can touch my dreams.'"

I wrote that?

"So, don't you want to be around when your book is published? The nurses said they can't feed you, that you're not able to swallow because you're sleeping all the time." Jacob looks up from his wallet and brings his head close to my face. "Shit Dad! You have to want to get better. If you don't try, you'll never get better. You'll never get out of here. Do you want that?" He sounds a little angry. "Are you listening to me? Do you want that?"

Should I be angry too? Jacob why do you care so much now about what happens to me?

"You told me never to give up, that you had to work for the things you want. Are you going to quit, Dad?"

212

What is it that you want, Jacob? I can barely move, I can't talk, I cannot eat, I can't clean myself and I don't care anymore. Why do I have to care? You have to let go of the thought of what I used to be. I can barely remember who I was before, but seeing your face is like a subtle reminder of who I was. Don't worry about me Jacob, I am not unhappy.

Jacob sits and looks. He's got nothing more to say, but appears pensive as if he's debating something or struggling with a thought. He looks a little worn; however, he seems less anxious than how I remember him. He's become a man, dealing with the difficulties of life and somehow trying to maintain a cool head. Grey hair has covered his head and with those dark circles under his eyes, it makes me wonder how old he is now. What year is it now? Jacob's pensive look is replaced by a happy face.

"Well, at least you're awake. The last two times I've come to visit you, you didn't wake up at all. Now you seem awake. Are you having any pain?" My head moves from side to side. Jacob still smiles and is trying to figure out something else to say. "Dodgers seem like they have a good team this year. I still follow them. Remember the games we went to at Chavez Ravine when I was little? Those were the best times I had with you. It was just you and me." He looks down, still smiling, but his smile has a nostalgic sadness that mourns a good memory. He looks up again. "I think I liked those times so much, because you were not being so much father, but more a friend, rooting and watching the same team as I was."

"The problem, Dad, is that you were either too demanding or you were too busy with doing your own thing: your book, your newspaper writing, your old beat up Mustang, your sports, your own idea of right and wrong. I thought it was cool for a while, but then I realized that you thought the whole world revolved around you. I hated your selfishness. I hated... I hated you for always thinking you were better than me, that you knew things better than I did. I hated that you were disappointed in who I was. Yeah, maybe I could have been a better son, but it would be better, Dad, if you could have just sat and listened to me, like you're listening to me now and allowed me to be whoever I wanted to be." He grits his teeth and wipes his hand back and forth over his mouth. "You know, I've been so angry at you…so angry…and I want to let go of that anger. The past is past. We can never return to it or fix it. But, you know what I've learned from the Bible? We also learn from the past. I'm going to be a good father to Emily. You'll not have to worry about that. She is the most important thing in my life and, damn it, she's going to know her grandfather!"

The diatribe over, Jacob leans over the bed and rests his weary head on top of his arms. The boy must be working hard to support his family, suffering, as all in life have suffered. I try to remember my suffering: school, my lost friends, the book, Vietnam, Sarah, Jacob, money, that daughter of ours who was never born, Stephen Petry, those sordid times in Vegas, 9/11, but it's all a distant memory as if I'm reading a book about the course of a human life from beginning to end, which is not my life. Jacob holds my hand and still has his head dropped in his arms. The contact with my son is heartening and it's nice to feel his love. I love you, Jacob. Jacob, are you there? I only can see the top of his head, but feel his deep breathing. The breathing slows and after some time I wonder whether he's asleep. Huh, he must be asleep now, for his breathing has become nasally, like he's snoring lightly. It reminds me of when he was a kid and would fall asleep when we read him stories. There's so much peace with him resting next to me, and I'm happy he has come to visit me, again. My son, we have been through so much together and now we are together again. Life is pretty simple after all. Now you will continue the same plan with your wife and child and the same drama will be played out and your children will do the same thing, and their children will do the same thing and so on and so on.

There are voices in the distance. It sounds like Lily and Jacob.

"Have you been at least trying to wake him up every day?"

"Yes, I do, but he sleep all the time."

"Maybe if you were more attentive he wouldn't be sleeping all the time."

"I take good care of Paul. Don't worry."

"I do worry, because he's not getting any better."

"He wake up some time. He happy some time, sometime I don't know. Maybe Ativan makes sleep."

"I don't follow what you're saying. I call here every week to find out how my dad's doing and I can't understand a word you're saying."

"Sorry Mr. Mathews. I try better."

"I'll keep calling here every week and if you can't give me an understandable explanation of how my dad's doing, I'll have to find another nurse."

No, Jacob! Don't take Lily away. Please don't. Stop it! Stop it! The world is becoming dark and I must run to the darkness.

"Get ready for the fall season on NBC with all new episodes of *The Apprentice*, *Scrubs* and the new reality T.V. show *Wife Exchange*. Keep it tuned to the nation's top network, N.B.C... Iran, how real is the threat? The rhetoric has heated up on both sides as Iran continues to enrich uranium. The White House and President Bush are pressing the U.N. to take sanctions if Iran does not allow UN weapon inspectors to investigate Iran's nuclear facilities. We take you to Jack Strong at the White House."

There are shrubs on either side of the window providing a green border for my view of the alley. I feel heavy, unable to move, but hell, I have no desire to move. There's waning light outside. The end of the day approaches. Is it time for dinner yet? I'm feeling hungry and imagine a large meal, like Thanksgiving dinner, awaiting me. Maybe I'll take a nap before dinner comes.

"Hello, Paul." The voice sounds familiar. Lily's here with her dark hair, dark smooth skin and her bright smile. Something is different. I'm sitting up in my bed, looking at Lily in an upright position, like I'm in a position of power, a king on his throne, as Lily patiently leans forward in her servitude. "You finally awake, Paul. You sleep a lot. You have friend come by yesterday. He call himself Ray. He says you and he go to Las Vegas all the time. He want to take you and me to Vegas when you get better!" She pulls down a blanket from my belly, takes a washcloth and starts cleaning something. I feel coolness on my belly. Lily looks up from my belly. "You still my boyfriend, Paul?" She smiles a coyly. I'm entranced by her every move, waiting for what she'll do next, happy for the recognition and the connection to another entity. Her lips are full, her mouth half open to expose her off-white teeth. Her eyes are dark, surrounded by long eyelashes. She is full of life and I'm the receptive audience to her performance. My legs, arms and mouth are immovable objects that don't allow me to participate, but at least my eyes work and the vision of Lily is a most pleasurable sight. "You stop sleeping so much," Lily says. She touches my chest and rubs her hand from one side of my chest to the other. She moves my arms and legs back and forth in the bed, and while I see my left side move, I don't feel my left side. "I'm going to sing song Paul. Would you like to hear song?" Sure, I would love to hear a song Lily. She clears her throat. "I like this song," she says. "My favorite."

"I can see clearly now the rain is gone. I can see all obstacles in my way. Gone are the dark clouds that had me blind. It's going to be a bright," she turns her head from side to side, *"bright...bright... sunshiny day. I think I can make it now, the pain is gone. All those bad feelings have disappeared. Here is the rainbow I've been praying for. It's going to be a bright...bright...bright...bright...sunshiny day. Look all around there's nothing but blue skies. Look everywhere, nothing but blue ski...i...i...i...es."* She bobs up and down like she is dancing, dancing for me. *"I can see clearly now the rain is gone. I can see all obstacles in my way. Gone are the dark clouds that had me blind. It's going to be bright...bright...bright...bright...sunshiny day. It's going to be a bright.. .bright...bright... bright...sunshiny day. It's going to be a bright...bright...bright...bright...sunshiny day."* She stops singing and is breathing somewhat heavily from the effort. "You like that song, Paul."

Yes, can you sing some more?

"I like it. That my favorite song. No matter how bad I feel, I know there always something in future and always something good here now. When I think about all good things in life, I say to myself 'why worry.' Sky still be there, birds still sing, flowers still there, ocean still there, mountain still there and for now I still here. Why worry Paul? That's what I say. Life too short." She snaps her fingers. "Before you know it we are gone." Her face is filled with sincerity, making me truly believe that life is not so bad. She caresses my face gently. "I like you Paul. You still my boyfriend." As implausible as it may seem, I believe her.

216

She smiles and walks away leaving me staring at the television. The sound's turned low. I can't make out what they're saying on the TV, but I'm entranced by the faces and the interactions. In the television there's a thin man with blond hair and a moustache. He's standing, looking away from the television and talking and the scene shifts between this man to a woman dressed in a black robe who I would assume is a judge. She sits on a chair that is elevated in relationship to the camera. She says something and then the frame returns to the man with the moustache, who looks a little flustered. The judge then reappears, looking harshly down at the camera and then the scene shifts to an obese black woman with braided hair who shakes her head and says something. The female judge points her finger toward her left and admonishes the woman. The black woman bows her head in acknowledgement, but then tries to say something in her defense though it's too late and the camera has shifted back to the judge who continues with her monologue. The judge then points her hand holding the gavel toward her right, shaking the gavel violently. The scene shifts to the thin man and he bows his head, though he seems happy to do so. He has won.

There's a wonderful sense of community in watching the television. I've always been fascinated by the many figures projected behind the screen and their ability to entertain me. And now look! A commercial is showing a woman with a heavenly body in a bikini coming out of a pool. Oh, mama! The scene shifts to this same woman in spandex pants and a sports bra exercising on something that looks like a sit-up contraption. She has a smile on her face as she tenses all of her muscles to use the machine. The scene then shifts to the rippled abdomen of a man, but I'm feeling sleepy and have never been too much into looking at men.

"Lily, we should clean up Mr. Wilson before his daughter arrives? Can you clean off his face and fix up his bed?"

"Sure, Connie. I wonder how he die."

"Probably a heart attack."

"Too bad. Well, he with Martha now."

"Yeah, it's going to get mighty quiet around here."

"He make me think of my dad. He getting old too."

217

"Your dad still over in the Philippines?"

"Yes, he getting old. 75 year old. I need to go visit him. Just sad. Nothing we can do to stop it. So old we become, like Mr. Wilson. Make's me sad."

"Well, honey, we all in it together."

"You're right. I worry too much."

"I worry too. I mean like what does it all mean when we all end up like Mr. Wilson here?"

"I don't know. I better clean him up."

"After you're done with him come to the break room. It's Veronica's birthday and we are having cake."

"Yummy." Connie walks away. I want to stay up and wait for Lily, hearing her on the other side of the curtain, hearing her breathe heavily behind the curtain. "Goodbye, Mr. Wilson. Goodbye." I'm going to wait a little longer for Lily to come and see me. Maybe I'll close my eyes and wait for her.

Wait a second, where am I? And who's that guy sitting upright in the bed next to me? He doesn't look familiar. His left eye is open, his mouth is partially open and his chest heaves up and down with each of his breaths. Someone is touching my backside. "Thank you, Mary, for helping to clean up. I hate to clean him alone." It's Lily's voice.

"Honey, you help me out all the time. It's the least I can do. Did you notice this ulcer on his hip?"

"He got one on other side too. They get better once lay him on back and not on hip."

"I'll help you turn him over."

"Thank you." Hands grab my shoulders and hips and turn me quickly on my back to look up at a ceiling, all white without any holes. A small fly is hovering above me, slowly moving back and forth, seemingly having no purpose and I hope to hell he doesn't land on me, because there's nothing I can do if he did. But here's Lily smiling at me. My eyes gravitate from her face to her chest to see her breasts fall with the force of gravity. She notices me watching her chest and she stands up a little, not showing any sign of embarrassment. "Hi, Paul. It is good to see you awake. You like sit up, watch television." That sounds nice, Lily. Lily is holding

218

what looks like a remote controller. My bed vibrates and the head of the bed moves upward. The front upper corner of the room comes into view, then the television and then the front of my bed with my legs covered by a generic blue blanket.

The sound is turned low on the television, the voices on the screen unintelligible, but I see what looks like a newscaster. There's a picture, to the right of the newscaster, of a dark man in a turban with a thin face covered in a beard. He has a scowling look as he looks askance at something on his right. The newscaster is a white woman with blond hair, in a turtle neck and a blue suit. While she speaks the face above her remains unchanged.

"You like TV, don't you, Paul?" Lily says as she puts her hand on my shoulder. "I like TV too. That how I learn English. My favorite show are *Survivor* and *ER*. What you like?"

Haven't thought about it. What do I like? I think I like sports, but am unsure anymore. I don't think I like the news. The television becomes smaller, simply just a box with tiny faces that peer out and looking at it, it is easy to become disinterested in this device. Lily is stroking my hair and we stare at each other. My breathing becomes slow, calmed within a world of sensory bliss. It is a soft world, a caring world that has always opened its arms to me, embracing me whenever I've allowed it. It is a lullaby that puts you to sleep at night and soon the night envelops you within its dark arms. I accept the darkness and don't fight it. It comforts me and I cannot conjure up any reason not to succumb to the bliss, the softness of this moment. Forgive and forget. Why fight it?

Chapter 12

The Good Doctor

Mom! I'm frantically running down a hallway in the hospital. Where are those guys taking Mom? She's on a rolling stretcher, most of her body covered by a blanket, except for her head and neck. There are two attendants guiding her forward and away from me. I'm running toward them and no matter how fast I run I can't catch them. They're coming to a door that swings open as the lead attendant pushes the door with his hand. I run, yelling for them to stop. "That's my mother!" I meet them at the door and they stop with mother's head at the entrance of the doorway. She's levitated by the gurney and my head tilts down toward her. Mom has her eyes closed. Her hair has whitened, her skin has wrinkled and her mouth is closed. I'm feeling guilty, watching her vulnerable, lifeless form. She has done so much for me and asked for so little in return. Was there something else I could have done? Could I have stopped this? It is too late now, nothing more I can do, nothing more I can say. Someone wraps an arm over my shoulder and comforts me. "It's going to be all right," the voice says, but I am not so sure.

"Doctor! Doctor!" I turn around and look down to see a little girl who looks like Jenny. She has her hair pulled back in a pony-tail and wears a T-shirt that says '**Girls Can Do Anything Boys Can Do, Only Better.**' She holds a stethoscope in her hands and lifts it up to me. "You forgot this, Doctor," she says. Taking the stethoscope from her hands, I feel suddenly empowered. I pat her head and start walking back down the hallway of the hospital.

The early morning light sifts its way into the room, giving the ceiling a reddish color. Morning's here. What was I dreaming about? Jenny looked so pretty and she was holding a stethoscope. I wonder if she'll become a doctor. She's definitely smart enough, but she says she doesn't know yet, but maybe if I nudge her. She's already in her second year of college. She should already have some idea. Maybe I need to nudge her a little.

Barbara's lightly snoring. The clock with the large red numbers reads 6:15. Is it 6:15 already? Oh, hell! I've to get out of this warm bed and into the fray. Just do it slowly, Bill. Don't want to wake up Barbara. Alright, go to the bathroom and close the door. The toilet…Sanctuary! Let's finish the article on osteoporosis that I've been reading for the last two weeks. Why do I bother? I can't finish anything on the toilet anymore. That damn Glucophage and the loose bowel movements it gives me! It keeps my blood sugars low, but cuts down on my toilet time. I walk over to the mirror and look at my naked form, pull the shoulders back, push the chest forward, but it's no good. My eyes still focus on my enormous belly. What happened to you man? You were always a little pudgy, but this is too much. You should really go on a diet.

Those actinic keratosis are coming out on your face again. Maybe it's about time to see David again. You've been trying to freeze these suckers off with the liquid nitrogen in the office, but you're not doing a very good job. You look like a hidden devil with these red blotchy lesions erupting from your pale face and, with your double chin, and your bloated face, you look a lot like your aunt Debbie and a little like Dad! Dad was a good man. Pull back those shoulders, pull that chest forward, straighten that belly and turn on the shower. That water feels good hitting my chest. I wish I didn't have to go to work and could just enjoy this moment. I really don't want to go. I want to stay at home and do nothing.

But they're counting on me. It'll be OK, Bill. It's Friday and you don't have to work this weekend. It'll be all right; just one more day. Tomorrow's Ronnie's Little League game and last time he played he smacked the ball real good and got a triple. Maybe I should stop working on the weekends, or maybe just give up work all together. Shoot, when I was younger I could easily have worked three weeks in a in a row and do call, but now at 57 it's onerous. Dry yourself off butthead. This talk is getting you nowhere. We need the money. There are two more years of tuition for Jenny, and if she wants to go to med school that will be a busload as will Ronnie's college and whatever graduate thing he wants to do, and then there's having enough for a decent retirement.

Barbara walks in making a beeline to the toilet and pulls the door shut. Time to get dressed…Let's see…put on underwear, T-shirt, here are my khaki pants, now which shirt? I like that striped blue one, perfect for a Friday and it goes well with this dark-blue tie. 6:45 and I got to put on my belt and head to the bathroom to put on this tie. Barbara's in the shower, her body being smoothed by the water caressing it. She catches me looking at her, smiling as if I interrupted a thought and quickly she returns to that thought.

In the kitchen, Ronnie's sitting at the kitchen table eating a bowl of cereal, and staring at the television. I get my oatmeal and add a little milk to it before putting it into the microwave. After three long beeps the oatmeal is ready and I join Ronnie at the table. He's staring at the plasma television on the wall, watching the news as he has done for the last month, engrossed by the presidential primaries. The boy has the same political motivations as his mother. The election primary in Missouri is next Tuesday and Hillary Clinton is giving the rallying cry of taking the country back from special interest groups. That's funny. Without special interest groups a politician has no money so this seems a bit hypocritical.

My head pivots toward Ronnie. His glasses reflect the light of the television and his face is scattered with pimples, which he takes Retin-A and Benzamycin to control. Pimples run in the family, only mine were worse. What an awkward age.

"What time is your game tomorrow?"

"10:30"

"You want to play some catch before dinner tonight."

"Sure, but, is your arm all right?"

"It feels much better. How's geometry coming along?"

"I have a test today."

"Have you studied?" Ronnie got a B on his last test. He better do well.

"Yeah, Dad, I know it like the back of my hand."

I don't know the back of my hand very well, but I like the kid's cockiness.

"I wish I could remember some of the geometry I learned in school."

"Don't worry. I'll do fine."

"I know you will." Ronnie gets up from the table, rinses his bowl in the sink, and places it in the dishwasher. The car horn from Ronnie's carpool signals his departure.

"See you later, Dad."

"See you, Ronnie. Good luck today."

Oatmeal and milk…I wish I could have something else for breakfast. Outside the window, the pool glistens, reflecting the early morning light. Barbara walks into the kitchen and pulls out a mug from the cupboard.

"Have you made coffee?" she asks.

"I forgot. I'm sorry."

"That's OK, I was just asking."

On the television, a map of the United States encompasses the entire screen and has multiple suns with smiling faces down in Florida and throughout the western states. The central and eastern portions of the country are covered by grey clouds with drops of rain underneath. There are two-digit numbers throughout the United States and my eyes drop down to the lower left corner and see 74. Why do I bother to look? Barbara's saying something, but I don't hear her.

"What did you say?"

"You haven't been drinking coffee lately."

"I've been trying to stay at one cup a day."

"Why?"

"My prostate's been giving me problems and I think coffee makes it worse. So I cut the coffee to one cup at work."

"Have you talked to somebody about that?"

"I did."

"Well, what did they say?"

"Told me my prostate was a little swollen, but that was a couple of years ago."

"You should make an appointment again."

"Barbara, it's difficult having a colleague shove their finger up my ass."

"And it's OK for me to spread my legs for a Pap smear? Bill, you can't take care of this on your own. You need to see a specialist." Barbara will persist until it drives me crazy.

"I'll make an appointment on a Wednesday. What are we eating tonight?"

"I thought I'd pick up Chinese Food and rent a movie."

"Sounds good. Any movie in mind?"

"No idea. I'll only know when I get there. If you want I can give you a call?"

"That sounds nice." My cell phone and keys are on the counter. Barbara's pouring coffee into her thermos mug. I wait for her to finish, waiting for my goodbye kiss. She looks at me and smiles.

"Cheer up. Don't forget, it's Friday," she says, her beautiful blue eyes conveying her support for me.

"I love you." My arms are around her waist and pull her close to me, but we kiss as if we both know we have other things to do. Leaving quickly, I walk into the garage, open the car door and get inside the Volvo. A voice with an English accent comes from the radio.

"Sri Lanka has been in a bitter civil war, with recurrent bombings, murders and intimidation techniques carried out by the Tamil Tiger rebels. The government has attempted to curtail the rebel activity without success..." Well, so much for the news. How about music? The Eagles are playing on the CD. I turn right and drive west on Santa Monica and hit my destination, the 405 freeway. The traffic is not too bad for this time of the morning.

"They came from everywhere to the great divide, seeking a place to stand or a place to hide." It's 7:30. I better switch it back to the news.

"From NPR news this is Craig Windham. A suicide bomber detonated his explosives at a police station in Basra, killing 12 Iraqi soldiers and injuring 30. NPR correspondent Kian Mazarei reports."

"It is the third such attack over the last two days, raising concerns over instability in the area following British troop withdrawals. Senior leaders in the U.S. military assure that the latest wave of violence will not affect the U.S. troop surge. General Petraeus gave a briefing yesterday attesting that Iraqi troops have been trained and that the internal conflict can be handled by the Iraqi military in the area."

"That was Kian Mazarei reporting from Baghdad. Heavy rains and snow are pelting the Midwest on the first day of spring..."

I turn off the 405 onto Jefferson and make my way toward the hospital. There are two patients there, one of whom I can probably discharge today. I go into the parking lot and easily find a parking

224

space, get out of the car and remove my white coat hanging in the back of the car. Is my stethoscope in my coat pocket? Yeah, it's there. My watch says 7:35. I'm just a bit late. Greeting me at the entrance to the hospital is the statue of St. Luke, an effeminate man dressed in a robe, wearing his hair long. What a flaming hippie! In the elevator, I reflect upon Mrs. Susan Jones, the 91-year-old with pneumonia, who lives alone and who's slow to improve. I don't think she can take care of herself at home after she leaves the hospital.

On the back of the elevator there's a picture of a waterfall with the caption, "God's light touches all who see it." The door opens and I make my way to the nurses' station, pull the chart out for room 572, take it to a desk, log into the computer system and retrieve the labs for Mrs. Jones. She's chronically anemic and her sodium is a little low. It's time to go into the room. The vital signs hang on a clipboard at the door and upon review I notice her oxygen saturation is 93 percent. That looks a bit better. Mrs. Jones is lying down with her eyes closed looking peaceful with her rotund face and her surprisingly smooth skin. She's receiving oxygen by nasal cannula that enters her nose and the tubing wraps around her ears. She's snoring heavily and while I wish I didn't have to wake her, I have a schedule to keep. I'll nudge her a little.

"Mrs. Jones. Mrs. Jones."

She slowly awakens opening and closing her mouth in an attempt to add saliva to replace the dryness from sleep. She swallows and looks up at me. "Good morning, Doctor. How am I doing?"

"You tell me."

"I feel very tired, but thank God I was able to sleep last night."

"That's good. Did you get out of bed yesterday?"

"No, I just felt too tired," she says. She's laboring a little bit with her words.

"We have to get you moving, Susan. The more you lie here, the weaker you're going to get. I'm going to order physical therapy and have the nurses sit you up for your meals." My finger presses the touch control for her bed so that the head of her bed rises up. After putting the stethoscope in my ears, I listen to her heart, which sounds regular, then pull her body forward with my left arm and place the diaphragm of the stethoscope on her back. "Breathe in…breathe in…" She follows my command, the lungs sounding crackly on her right side and a little crackly on the left. Checking her legs, there is some swelling bilaterally. "I'll give a call to your son to tell him what's going on. We'll continue the antibiotics and get some physical therapy. You may need to be placed in a nursing facility for further recovery depending on what the physical therapist says." She listens and says nothing. "Now I won't be here this weekend, but there'll be a doctor covering for me, so I'll see you again on Monday."

"OK, Doctor. Make sure to call my son. He wants to hear from you."

"I will Susan. You take care."

"Thank you, Doctor."

I got to write the vitals in the chart, write a quick progress note and then write orders for the day: Physical therapy evaluation, out of bed to chair three times a day, CBC and BMP in AM tomorrow and D/C IV fluids. Don't forget to call the son.

"Mr. Jones, this is Dr. Gellman."

"Hi, Dr. Gellman. How's my mother doing?" a concerned voice on the other line asks.

"She's doing better. The antibiotics are working, but I'm a little worried about her eventually returning to home. I think she'll need physical therapy and time to recuperate first."

"I'm a little worried about her at home, too. I don't think she can take care of herself."

"I agree. I'll be out of the hospital this weekend and another doctor will cover for me, but I'll give you a call on Monday and if she's doing better we can discharge her from the hospital and place her in a rehabilitation facility."

"Which facility will you send her to?"

"I'm not sure yet. I'll get the discharge planner to work on that."

"Thank you, Doctor."

"You're welcome." OK, put the chart in the orders rack and get to the telemetry unit to see Mr. Bennett. In the monitor room there's a tech looking at the multiple heart rhythms on the monitor.

"Were there any abnormalities in Mr. Bennett's heart rhythm last night?"

226

"Sinus rhythm, completely normal," she says in a cheerful voice. Mr. Bennett's labs are on the computer and they are all normal. No heart attack. Mr. Bennett's reclining in his bed, looking up at the ceiling, seemingly entrenched in thought. Not wanting to interrupt him, I walk over to the clipboard that lists his vital signs. His blood pressure, pulse, temperature are all normal.

"Hi, Dr. Gellman." Mr. Bennett looks over to me.

"Hello, Mr. Bennett. How you doing?"

"I feel better today, but I had some bad chest pain last night."

"How long did it last?"

"About 15 minutes."

"Did they give you nitroglycerin?"

"Yeah, but it didn't seem to help."

Hmmm? "One thing we do know is that you haven't had a heart attack. All your cardiac enzymes have been normal."

"Then, what's causing the chest pressure?" he asks in a pleading voice. Hmmm? He's a thin male, 42 years of age, with short curly brown hair and a pencil neck that rises from a sunken chest to a bearded face. He seems like an anxious guy and his anxiety is probably the cause of his chest pressure, but I sure as hell don't want to get sued, so he's going to get a cardiac stress test to make sure.

"It could still be your heart. The Cardiolite test will tell us if this chest pain is coming from decreased blood flow to your heart."

"Well, what if it's not my heart?"

"Then we'll have to look for other causes for your chest pain." His heart sounds regular and totally unremarkable. Mr. Bennett is unmarried and works in real estate, which may be the reason for his current anxiety. Removing the stethoscope from my ears, I say, "So you'll have the heart test later today and if the results are positive I'll have a cardiologist see you. If they're negative, you can go home today and follow up with me next week for a further work-up of the chest pain."

"What's entailed in that further work-up?"

"Possibly a gastric work-up for chest pain, but first we'll do the heart test and then decide about what other tests we have to do." 8:20: I'm doing OK with time. "Do you have any other questions?" His face reveals a multitude of questions.

"What will the cardiologist do if my test is positive?" he asks.

"Well, I believe they would then do an angiogram to look at the blood vessels around your heart."

"Do you think it's my heart?"

"I'm not sure. We'll know for sure after the test."

"You said there could be a gastric cause for my chest pain. You mean my stomach?"

"Not your stomach itself, but maybe your esophagus; the long tube that goes from your mouth to your stomach. Sometimes spasms of the esophagus can mimic a heart attack. I'm sorry; I have to go, Mr. Bennett. I'll call you after the test is done."

"Please tell me what you find, Dr. Gellman."

"I will." I write my note, put the chart back and take the elevator down to the lobby. 8:35: I'm running late. I walk over to the building next door, take the elevator to the fourth floor, and walk passed a door with a sign on the front saying:

Culver Internal Medicine
Dr. Ronald Sohn
Dr. William Gellman
Dr. Jeffrey Tamashiro
Dr. Joyce Felty
Dr. Robert Smith

The back door is open and I walk in, following a long corridor to my office. I jump into my leather chair and swivel myself toward my desk and turn on the computer. I sit for a moment looking up at my bookshelf with multiple books (some out of date), pictures of my family (also out of date), and a rack piled high with patients' charts. The room is well lit and its multiple windows give me a partial view of the mountains. On my desk there are three messages from this morning. Mrs. Gloria Parks wants antibiotics called to the pharmacy today for a sinus infection, Mr. Edward Hines wants the results of his MRI, and Mr. Hiram Levine wants refills of all his medication. Oh boy, I'm going to need some coffee now.

228

In the break room, there's a congregation of staff surrounding a display of food. Maria, a heavyset, gregarious, medical assistant, greets me.

"Good morning, Dr. Gellman," she says as she bites into a chocolate doughnut. Oh yeah! Chocolate doughnuts and coffee!

"Good morning, Maria. How are you today?"

"Fine, and how about yourself?"

"Not bad."

There's a young man in a grey suit sitting next to a display of bagels, juice, coffee and doughnuts. He has dark hair, tanned skin, and a confident smile as he stands to shake my hand. What's his name again? His name tag has a Merck logo on the top and below this is the man's name, Jeff. We shake hands.

"Good morning, Dr. Gellman. We've brought you some breakfast this morning and a reminder about Januvia for your type-two diabetics; a proven medication to fight diabetes. Are you using a lot of Januvia for your diabetic population?"

"When insurance approves it." I let go of his hand and grab a doughnut and move along to get some Peet's Coffee and put in some cream and sugar. Robert Smith, the youngest doctor in the group, walks into the break room. A man of short stature, tanned skin, shaved short brown hair, and a protuberant chin, Robert always has a knack for creating awkward situations, especially with drug reps.

"Good morning Dr. Smith," Maria says with caffeinated gusto.

"Good morning, Maria," Robert says with a joyful, but somewhat condescending tone. Kid needs to lighten up. He's always getting in our face about what we eat.

"Good morning, Dr. Smith," Jeff, the Merck Rep says. "Would you like some breakfast this morning?" Robert looks over at the display of food and we all know what his response will be to the food Jeff has brought.

"Breakfast? No thanks," Robert says.

"I'd just like to remind you about Januvia for your diabetic population. As I was just about to tell Dr. Gellman here, it's now covered under all insurance plans, so your patients will not have any difficulties getting the most effective medicine for diabetes. Do you prescribe a lot of Januvia?"

"More than I would like." There's a silence in the room as all the medical assistants and I listen to the conversation. Robert's looking at the display of food and, after some time, finally decides to get on his high horse. "Jeff, don't you find it a tad hypocritical that you're selling diabetes medication and bringing doughnuts and bagels for us to eat? Don't you find anything wrong with that?"

"Dr. Smith, I know you guys work hard and I wanted to bring you guys something that would cheer you up." Jeff's a little flustered and while that was the intended effect, Robert is somewhat conciliatory.

"Do we seem depressed? Next time, just bring something healthy; fruit or some eggs or granola, but not something that plays havoc with the pancreas." Robert goes to the cupboard next to the sink, grabs a box of teabags and a cup and starts filling the cup with hot water from the water dispenser.

"Duly noted," Jeff says. The mood in the break room has turned somber and reflective. Jeff sits down next to his display of food as Robert walks out.

"I for one want to thank you for bringing us food, Jeff," I say as I take another doughnut, leaving the room with both my coffee and little treat. "So does my pancreas."

"Thanks, Dr. Gellman."

Betty Tanner is sitting in room 6, reading a novel. She's a seventy-year-old retired librarian with diabetes and a history of heart disease. She's somewhat of a loner, always bringing in a novel, and we always talk about what she's reading. Maybe it provides a distraction, but the distraction is sort of a commonality between us. I glance down at her book. "*Anna Karenina*?"

"For the third time." She smiles. "So I guess that means I like it."

"So how you doing today?"

"My blood sugars are going up and I don't know why. I eat barely anything and they go up." She pauses for a moment. "And my legs are swelling a little more."

"Both legs?"

"Yes, they're fine in the morning, but they balloon up during the day." I glance down to her legs and feet. She's taken her shoes off

230

for me to look at her diabetic feet. I lean forward and place my hand on her thick legs, push in with my thumb, remove my thumb and see a small indentation of the skin. Not enough swelling to get me excited, and with Mrs. Tanner's kidney failure I'm unenthused about increasing her dose of diuretic.

"Not so bad right now."

"It's early in the day. They swell up like balloons by the end of the day," she protests.

"Well, I don't want to give you more of the diuretic, because it'll hurt your kidneys."

"So there's nothing I can do about it," she says in somewhat of an angry tone.

"You could wear tight stockings so the fluid doesn't pool in your legs."

"Those stockings hurt and they're always slipping off."

At the front of her chart is her list of medications.

"Well, we can increase the dose of Lasix for four days, then return to your normal dose. Keep the legs elevated and stay away from salt."

"Can you write that down for me? I usually forget by the time I get home."

I write my instructions for her on a prescription, listen to her heart, check her feet for any ulcerations and look at her previous lab results.

"So Sandra's going to come in to draw your blood. Do you have any questions, Betty?"

"No, nothing else."

"I'd like to see you again in one month to follow your leg swelling."

As I'm walking out of the room I hear Betty's voice, "Thank you, Doctor."

I knock on the door of the next room and open the door to see a young man, who looks familiar, sitting in a robe on the examining table. What is his name again? Look at the chart: Graham Fulton. OK stretch your hand out to him.

"Mr. Fulton, how you doing today?" He extends a powerful arm and wraps his fingers tightly around my hand. My grip reflexively tightens, but then stops when the sensation of pain reaches my consciousness.

"I'm feeling well. Just here for a physical." He has brown hair, bushy eyebrows and long eyelashes that surround blue eyes. He appears to be extremely healthy; a single man who exercises five days a week and who has a balanced diet and a negative review of systems. The physical exam is entirely normal.

"Sandra will come and draw your blood."

"Thank you," he says and I leave the room. At my desk are Mr. Edward Hines's brain MRI results and his phone number. I should call him now.

"Ed, this is Dr. Gellman. Your brain MRI was normal."

"So what's causing the headaches?" the voice asks at the other end.

"Are you still having them?"

"Yeah, but they're getting a little better."

"I'm not sure what's causing the headaches, but it could be related to muscle tension in your neck. Make an appointment to see me." I still have time to call Gloria Parks.

"Mrs. Parks, this is Dr. Gellman. What's going on?"

"I've a cold since yesterday, I'm really congested and feel it in my sinuses. I think I've got a sinus infection."

"Do you have any fever or discolored nasal discharge?"

"I feel a little warm."

"Gloria, I'd have you take Sudafed and Tylenol as needed and if you're not feeling better by next week, then make an appointment to see me."

It's time to see the next patient, Mrs. Morris. I don't remember her. Inside the next room there's a beautiful woman with light skin, dirty blond hair and a nice physique hidden behind the blue gown. "Mrs. Morris, how are you doing today?"

"I think something is wrong with my heart. I feel like it's coming out of my chest at times and it's beating irregular and fast. I'm also having this tightness in my chest. It was so bad last night I almost went to the emergency room."

"When did it start?"

"About three weeks ago." She appears in distress.

"When does it occur? Does it occur when you exert yourself?"

"No, it can occur any time, but it occurs more often at work."

"Are you under more stress at work?"

She looks at me and her eyes begin to tear. "No, work's fine. I did just break up with my boyfriend." Her face contorts and she starts to cry a little. Where is that Kleenex box? Oh, it's right behind me. She takes the tissue from the box. "I just thought that this would be it. I'd get married, settle down, not have to worry about dating or looking. I'm tired of looking."

"I know it's difficult."

"Difficult? In this city, finding a good man is like winning the lottery."

I'll give her some Xanax for her panic attacks and have her follow up with me in three weeks. I'll order an electrocardiogram as a precaution.

In the next room there's a portly 42-year-old woman sitting, reading a book to her daughter. She's here to check her thyroid function. "Mrs. Torino, how are you doing today?"

"Fine, Doctor Gellman. This is my daughter, Brook."

"Hi, Brook."

"Hello."

"What grade are you in?"

"Kindergarten"

"Doctor, I don't know why I'm gaining weight. No matter what I eat or how much I exercise, I seem to keep getting bigger. I wonder if my thyroid's off."

"It could be." Her thyroid gland feels normal. "We'll recheck your thyroid tests. Last time we checked it was a year ago."

Sandra has not checked in the next patient, so I better go back to my desk and see the faxes from pharmacies for medication refills. Refill amlodipine 4 times, refill Ambien one time, refill hydrochlorothiazide, then go to a pile of charts sitting on a shelf next to me, review the labs attached to the chart and call a couple of patients. Mrs. Morris's electrocardiogram is done and looks entirely normal. I give her the information, along with a number for a therapist and walk to the next room. The next patient is, Ben, a 60-year-old smoker.

"Hello, Ben. How you doing?"

233

"I've been feeling all right." He pauses for a second. Ben works as a pool man and has chapped lips and multiple solar keratosis upon his face, a reflection of his outdoor time in the California sun. He has that dried-up appearance many smokers get in their later years. "Actually, I've been a little constipated lately. I normally have a bowel movement every day, but now it's every other day and I have to push quite hard to get it out."

"Any change in your diet?"

"No."

"Any blood in your stools?"

"No"

"How long have you been constipated?"

"About four months."

"When was your last colonoscopy?" I'm shuffling through his chart trying to find the results of his last colonoscopy.

"I've never had a colonoscopy. I had a sigmoidoscopy, but that was about fifteen years ago."

"Well, I think we should do one."

"Are you worried about anything, Doc?"

"No, but I think to be safe we should do a colonoscopy and in the meantime, I'll give you something to help with the constipation. How much are you smoking?"

"About a pack a day."

"And looking through your chart, I see you've been smoking since you were 20."

"I've stopped at times, but I always seem to pick it back up."

Why do I bother? I've asked him many times to stop before, but he has no desire to stop smoking. The physical exam reveals multiple scaly red actinic keratosis on his arms and a normal abdomen.

"I think I want a dermatologist to look at those." I finish the exam, fill out a lab requisition form, fill out referral forms to the gastroenterologist and the dermatologist, write four refill prescriptions for his medicines, order for a chest X-ray and an EKG and bid Ben farewell. Back at my desk, there's a message taped onto the phone. The message reads:

Jacob Mathews
(916) 484-2718
Wants an update on
father's (Paul Mathews) status

What does he want? He calls every 2 months about his father and I never have anything new to say. Paul's still bed-bound, still has a feeding tube, doesn't participate in physical therapy and still doesn't speak and nothing's changed since the last time I saw him. The phone rings multiple times. "You have reached the automatic voice mail system for: Jacob Mathews. At the tone leave your name and message."

"Mr. Mathews, this is Dr. Gellman. I'm giving you a call back regarding your father. I haven't heard of any changes in your father's status. If you have any further questions, please call me back." I should probably call the nursing home. I hang up the phone and finish writing my notes on the five patients I saw this morning. Sandra places Ben's EKG on my desk. It looks normal. Sandra hovers above me at the side of my desk. What does she want? Sandra's a short woman from El Salvador, with a chubby tanned face, curly black hair and a somewhat amorphous body. She's a dutiful nurse and the majority of patients like her, speaks English well, but still has a pretty heavy accent.

"Dr. Gellman, Dr. Sohn is still on vacation. This is the laboratory result on a patient of his. The potassium is very high, but the specimen was hemolyzed."

The lab result shows a potassium is 6.5. "Tell him to come back in today for a stat redraw"

"Thank you Doctor. Your next patient is in room six." I open the door. Oh no! In room six is a spidery-looking lady, thin, pale with dark circles around brown eyes. Her haunting appearance is accentuated by dark blue mascara. She wears a flowing flowery dress and a brown buttoned-up shirt. Mrs. Stein is more than just somewhat creepy and the last time we started her on Remeron, for anxiety and depression.

"How you doing, Mrs. Stein?"

Her eyes open wide and it seems like she's going to jump out of her seat. "I'm feeling great, Doctor. You're a genius. I've never

235

felt better. That medication is working well for me. I haven't had this much energy in a long time. Work is great, my relationships are better, I don't need as much sleep. I just overall feel better, except I think I may need a higher dose of medication."

"Why would that be?"

"There was a day last week where I got really depressed and felt like slashing my wrists, but I'm fine now. I think I'd do better on a higher dose of the anti-depressant." Start writing Bill. You need to document everything she says.

"Did you see the psychiatrist?"

"Doctor, listen to me. I told you before I don't want to see a psychiatrist." She's suddenly angry. "I'm doing so much better now and the last time I saw a psychiatrist, he put me on the wrong medication and it took me a long time to get better again. I won't see a psychiatrist." She gets tearful and I feel obliged to get the tissue box and hand her a tissue. Why the hell did I agree to treat her psychiatric problems? I knew it would be too much for me to handle.

"Like I said before, Mrs. Stein, you would be better served seeing a psychiatrist. I'm worried about you harming yourself."

"You're not listening to me, Dr. Gellman. I'm not seeing a psychiatrist. I told you I'm feeling better and it's not a big deal if I have suicidal thoughts. I've had them many times in the past. It doesn't mean I'll act on it."

Creepy is still the word that comes to mind.

"Well let me give you another referral for a psychiatrist. It's up to you if you want to go. I'll give you psychiatric medication for another month, but if you need more, you'll have to see a psychiatrist."

She looks at me with every ounce of vehemence she can muster. "I knew it. You physicians don't care at all about us. You never listen to us. You never spend time with us."

"But, I told you…"

"Don't interrupt me. I'm talking." The volume of her voice is rising and she points a finger at me.

Why do I have to listen to this? I've not caused her problems. There must be some way to end the appointment but she'll have none of it. This is agony.

"And another thing doctor. I called you three times last week and you never called me back." I feel like Prometheus having my liver eaten by a vulture and the only shackle that holds me is my white coat.

I cannot take it anymore. "Mrs. Stein, I'm going to have to leave. There are other patients waiting for me. I'll continue to give you the medicine, but you need to follow up with a psychiatrist. I want you to follow up with me in a couple weeks." Feeling like an abused child, I leave, needing a moment before the next patient. The bathroom is near and there's a sudden desire to urinate, so I rush quickly, open the bathroom door, walk inside and lock the door behind me. Sanctuary! I pull the toilet seat up, pull my pants down and exhale. The urine flows into the toilet at a rate somewhat above a trickle, making me wait for the last drop of nitrogenous waste to leave my body. I think I'm done. I quickly wash my hands and leave the room.

The next patient waits for me in room five. A young man I've never seen. The name on the chart says, Mr. Maury Rosen.

"Hi, Mr. Rosen, I'm Dr. Gellman. How are you doing today?" He looks a little under the weather.

"I feel terrible. My throat is so sore I can barely swallow and I have a fever." He has an angular jaw, a pockmarked face and dirty blond hair.

"How high a temperature?"

"Up to 102 yesterday and I still have a fever today. Your nurse said she got 101."

"How long has it been going on?"

"Three days, and it hit me like a truck."

His throat is inflamed, with enlarged pustular tonsils. His lymph nodes in his neck are swollen and tender. Probably Strep. It's nice to have something definite and treatable. I swab the back of his throat for a bacterial culture, write a prescription for amoxicillin and tell him to take Tylenol for his fevers.

"Thank you, doctor." Going back to room six, I'm glad Mrs. Stein is no longer there, replaced by an old bald-headed man.

"Hi, Richard, how are you doing today?" Richard Delvin is an 88-year-old with a history of atrial fibrillation, who's been on Coumadin for 20 years.

"I'm fine doctor, and how are you?" He has a thin and very well kept moustache. His skin is dark and surprisingly smooth for his age, making him look more like 68 than 88.

"I'm happy it's Friday."

"Hard week?" he asks.

"Pretty hard. I'm just looking forward to a weekend of not being a doctor."

"I don't know how you doctors do it, day in and day out. It must take its toll."

The Protime result is already in the chart, and it is 2.3, which is right where I want him to be. His heart beats with the irregular rhythm of atrial fibrillation.

"Is there anything else I can help you with?"

"No doctor, I'm fine."

"I'd like for you to then stay on your current dose of Coumadin and follow up with me in a month."

"Sure thing, Doc. Don't you work too hard," he cautions me in a friendly tone. I like Mr. Delvin and wish I had more patients like him.

Outside in the hall is an utterly gorgeous woman, a drug rep, but I'm blanking on what she sells and her name. My focus is on her tight dress shirt that accentuates her protruding breasts and her thigh high skirt that reveals tanned and well-toned legs. Humina, Humina!

"So, Dr. Gellman, how you doing today?"

"Fine and how are you?" This is not fair. She's a few inches shorter than I, so that in looking down I easily notice she's unbuttoned the top three buttons of her shirt, revealing the upper contour of her breasts.

"Excellent! I just stopped by to leave samples of Advair for your asthmatic patients. Do you mind signing for the samples?" She places a piece of paper in front of me and I sign on the bottom line.

"Do you have any plans for the weekend?" she asks.

"Going to my son's baseball game tomorrow...How about yourself?"

"I'm going to try my luck at surfing." She smiles at me as she walks by, leaving me one last glimpse of her thigh high skirt, her long legs and her high-heel shoes. Why do women wear high-heels? Look at those legs! Surfing? Wake up Bill! You have to go back and see patients. Room five must be next. The door's closed. I knock and I walk inside. There's a familiar, young-looking, black man dressed in jeans and a T-shirt.

"Mr. Fields, how are you doing?" He shakes my hand.

"I'm pretty good." He releases my hand and points down to his bare feet. "I think I have an infection on my feet."

"What kind of infection?"

"I think it's a fungus, but I don't know. I've been using all these antifungal creams and they don't work?"

"How long has it been going on?" I sit down on my stool and take a closer look at his feet.

"Three months," he says, clearing his throat. He sits down, too, and rotates his right foot on top of his left knee. There's scaling on the sole of his foot and there's peeling skin between his toes. His foot looks a little swollen and I can see now that it's actually red: a bad fungal infection. I have to write all this down.

"This has been going on three months?"

"Yeah, three months."

"It's been getting worse?"

"Yeah, and they itch like mad."

He's wearing work boots. "What kind of work do you do?" He sits back in his chair.

"I work as a cable operator."

"Do you always wear these shoes?

"Yeah."

Bingo! "I think your infection is made worse by the sweat of your feet. You have to find some other shoes to get your..."

"I use powder in my shoes."

"It doesn't seem to be working. Let me look at your other foot." He lifts up his other foot and rests it on the top of his right knee. It's just as bad, if not worse. "I'm going to give you an antifungal tablet that you have to take for four weeks, but you have to change your shoes."

"I have to wear these shoes for work," he pleads.

"Can you find something that allows your feet to breathe?"

He says he will and I give him the prescription for Lamisil and tell him not to drink alcohol with it. "Follow up in three weeks."

He seems pleased with this. But what will his feet look like in three weeks? There's a patient in room six, whom I somewhat recognize, holding a bloody towel in his right hand.

"I sliced it with a knife at work," he says. There's a laceration, still bleeding, extending from the tip of his index finger down to the DIP joint. I take some gauze and quickly cover the bleeding mess. Sandra has left some Lidocaine to numb up the finger.

"This is going to burn a little." I do three injections of Lidocaine at the base of the finger and walk out of the room as the anesthetic takes time to work. I walk over to the bathroom, deposit some urine and then walk over to my office. There's a pile of messages and medication refill authorization forms organized at the front of my desk. I call Janet Washington about her lab results. She has poorly controlled diabetes. Janet is incredulous about her blood sugar, "Are you sure you have the right results?" and doesn't want to take any more medication. I tell her to make an appointment to see me. I walk back to room six and the patient is sitting down with the now blood-soaked gauze on his index finger. He says the finger is numb and I start cleaning the area with saline and gauze. I put in four stitches into the area, which closes the laceration and stops the bleeding.

"Follow up with me in one week."

I'm getting hungry. My watch reads 11:50. The drug reps will be bringing lunch, hopefully something good. At my desk I sign some more refill authorizations for medication, then sift through the messages and one catches my attention from a Linda Tolbert, complaining about chest pain. The problem is Mrs. Tolbert is always complaining about chest pain. I've studied her up and down with CAT scans, treadmill tests, endoscopy and even a bone scan. Everything has been negative. She answers the phone. We talk about her chest pain and she repeats the story she's been telling me for the last 3 years.

"I don't care what you say, Doctor, I think I'm having a heart attack."

"You should go to the emergency room then," I respond, trying to call her bluff.

"I know what they'll tell me in the emergency room. They'll tell me everything is fine with my heart, but I don't believe them." I really don't have time for this.

"Make an appointment to see me, Linda." I call Greg Alvarado to go over his lab results and when I finish, I notice Sandra is standing at the door to my office.

"You have a patient in room five, doctor."

I quickly stand.

"The drug rep is here."

"Good, cause I'm hungry."

"I think they brought Italian today," she adds. I'm salivating in a Pavlovian manner and go to see my last patient for the morning. I knock on the door and slowly open the door, peak inside and see Mrs. Helen Terry sitting in a chair next to the examining table. She's an obese lady in her sixties with a history of diabetes, hypertension and really bad hips and knees "How you doing Helen?"

"My knees are killing me," she says as she begins to massage both of her knees. "I can barely walk."

"Are you taking anything for pain?"

"Only Tylenol and rarely that Vicodin that you gave me, but I only take that at night when the pain is real bad."

"Do your knees lock up on you, or buckle?"

"No, they don't. They just hurt all the time." Her knees on exam are tender on the joint lines of both sides. Her legs are swollen masses of fat and water, which end in tennis shoes that appear too small to accommodate her swollen feet. Her knee X-ray from six months ago showed severe osteoarthritis of both knees.

"Have you seen the orthopedic doctor?"

"Yes, I've see Dr. Mehta and he recommended physical therapy, which I did and found no change in my pain. He said if there was no improvement then I should have a knee replacement. I'm scared to do that." She seems sad, as if there is a world of emotional pain that needs to be released and her appearance seems so pitiful that it makes me want to help her. "I'm sorry. I am just so scared of surgery."

"Dr. Mehta has done plenty of these surgeries and you've lived with this pain for so many years."

"It's not just that. I just know that David will be no help to me after the surgery. He's still drinking like a fish."

"You have to get this done Judy. You shouldn't be living on pain pills." I write her a referral for Dr. Mehta and give her another course of Vicodin. I take a brief look at my watch and cannot believe it is already 12:37. "I've got to go, Judy."

"Thank you so much doctor for helping me."

"You're welcome. I'll see you before the surgery. Take care."

"God bless you, Doctor." I like being blessed, although I don't know who is blessing me. I drop Judy's chart on my desk. The smells of food invade my nose and remind me of the emptiness of my stomach. There's no doubt it is time to eat and I'm pulled toward the break room. Jeff Tamashiro is coming out of one of the patient rooms, looking cool and composed like always. I've never seen that guy lose his cool, unlike me who has a propensity to launch trash cans with my foot when I'm perturbed.

"Are you going to get some food?" I ask him.

"I still have a couple more patients to see, but I'll stop by after I'm done with them," he says as he smiles at me.

"Well, I'll see you there."

"See you." The break room is full of people, mostly women from the front desk and some of the medical assistants. There's Candace, who's black, and has worked at the front desk for ten years.

"Hi, Dr. Gellman, are you going to be eating?" she asks.

"Most definitely!" There's the drug rep sitting to my right, wearing the typical dress suit that includes a skirt that ends at the middle of her thighs revealing legs contained in dark pantyhose.

"Thanks for coming by, Dr. Gellman." She turns her body away from me and toward the food. "I hope you like Chinese." Chinese food gives me gas, but it sure tastes good.

"I heard we were having Italian food. Well it doesn't matter, Chinese is good." A buffet style includes Kung Pao Chicken, General Tsao's Chicken, beef with broccoli, and fried rice. I grab some of each dish, take a Caffeine Free Diet Coke and sit at the table next to the drug rep. What was her name again? I'm glad she's wearing a badge: Nancy. She has brown hair, hazel eyes, and a somewhat pudgy, soft face. The beef with broccoli is chewy and flavorful. I'm still chewing on the meat when I feel Nancy patting my thigh with her hand.

"So Dr. Gellman, do you need any information about Aricept 23mg?"

Hey woman, be careful where you put your hands! "What information do you have?"

Nancy perks up. She opens a notebook computer and points to graphs that have different colored bars. Biting into the General Tsao's Chicken, I listen to Nancy talk about the side-effect profile of Aricept. The food will raise my blood sugar but I can't help myself. The outside of the meat is sweet and crunchy and I wash it all down with the Diet Coke. I've a few bites of the Kung Pao Chicken which is nice and spicy, knowing full well I'll be regretting this in a couple of hours, but it tastes so good now. She touches my leg again.

"So, Dr. Gellman, can you find any reason not to give Aricept to your Alzheimer's patients?"

I'm still chewing and try to swallow the food quickly, but as I attempt to speak, a silent belch balloons within my mouth and leaks between my closed lips.

"I can't see any reason why not," I answer.

Joyce Felty, the lone female doctor in the group, walks in.

"Hi Joyce"

"Hi Bill."

She joined the group about ten years ago and garnered the female patient market. She's had three kids in that ten-year span and, while she's an effective doctor, Joyce has delineated her priorities. Her fellow doctors are not one of her priorities. She sits down at the other side of the table.

"So, Dr. Felty, Dr. Gellman and I were just talking about Aricept 23 and I was wondering if you have been using Aricept in your Geriatric population?" Nancy casually asks.

"I've a few patients on Aricept," Joyce answers.

"And how's it working?"

"I guess pretty well, but I've seen a lot of nausea and I'm sure to see more at the 23mg dose."

"That's interesting you mention that. Dr. Cano, a neurologist from UCLA, is giving a talk on Aricept at Godfrey's Restaurant.

243

He says that if you start at a quarter of the dose and titrate up you can prevent nausea." Nancy pulls out a sheet of paper. "Here's an invitation to the talk if you'd like to come."

"I have three kids and no time for dinners," Joyce quickly says. "But I was hoping you could tell me now how Aricept compares with the other acetylcholinesterase inhibitors?"

"Pretty well." Nancy fumbles through her notebook. "I don't think I have the data here, but I know it's comparable. If you want I can have the research department mail that information to you."

"That would be good," Joyce says as tries to slurp up a long noodle.

There's paperwork waiting for me. I got to go.

"Thank you, Nancy, for bringing us lunch," I say.

"You're welcome, and let me give this invitation to that dinner at Godfreys."

I leave the break room with the invitation and walk down the hallway toward my office, already feeling the ill effects of the meal that I knew would cause me ill effects. Bloated and tired, all I want to do now is sleep and the last thing I want to do is work, but I must trudge on. The week's almost over and all I've got to do now is go through the motions. My office is pretty well lit from the early afternoon sun. I sit down in my chair and finish writing my notes from the morning, then look at my messages and see a few messages from patients who want their prescriptions refilled and messages from patients who want referrals to specialists and a few messages from patients who want advice about one thing or another and one message from Jacob Mathews returning my call. I pick up the phone and dial the number. After two rings a man answers.

"Hello."

"Mr. Mathews it's Dr. Gellman."

"Dr. Gellman thanks for returning my call. I wanted to ask if you knew how my father's doing?" Are you serious? Your father had a stroke and a heart attack and has been bed bound since, in a somewhat vegetative state with a feeding tube. That's been his status for several years.

"I don't know of any changes in his status."

"Well I was speaking to his nurse, Lily. She said that he's getting bed sores again and that something is wrong with his breathing." Paul's son has always been somewhat annoying, but I'm not going to let it bother me. We had a big argument about removing the feeding tube a year ago. Maybe if I tune out for a little bit. I notice out of the corner of my eye blood test results for Leonard Kim and he has an elevation of his calcium. Why the hell does Leonard Kim have elevated calcium? Cancer? Well I'm not sure exactly what to do about that. Mr. Mathews is still talking and I don't know how to reenter the conversation, so I take the high road.

"I'll go see your father today and find out what's going on," I tell him.

"Could you give me a call after you see him?"

"I sure will, Mr. Mathews."

"Thanks. Dr. Gellman, do you think my dad should be in another nursing home?"

"No, I think he's being well taken care of. Why do you ask?"

"I think Sea Gardens may not be the right place for him. He just doesn't seem to be getting any better and I don't know if the nurses are helping him at all and that Filipino nurse, Lily, can barely speak English. I can never understand what she's saying."

"I really don't know of any better place." He's still talking, but I really don't want to hear about the state of the nursing facility, knowing full well that the facility is not a pretty place, but they do a good job with what they have.

"Well, I was looking at Marina Rehab."

"Mr. Mathews, they're doing the best they can with him."

"I know. You're right, Doctor. It's just that I think sometimes they're not telling me what's going on and sometimes they don't give him enough attention."

"They're doing the best they can, Jacob."

"I'm not so sure, because last time I brought my daughter to see my dad he was covered in his own shit and he could barely keep his eyes open." That's unfortunate.

"I'm sorry about that. I will check up on him today and tell you what's going on."

"Thank you, Dr. Gellman. I appreciate all you've done for my dad. Can you also make sure that none of his medicines are making him sleepy?"

"Dr. Gellman, Line 3 is Dr. Ali. Dr. Gellman, Line 3 is Dr. Ali," the overhead pager announces. Who is Dr. Ali?

"I have to go, Jacob. A doctor's on the other line."

"Talk to you later."

I push line 3.

"Hello," I say.

"Hello Dr. Gellman, this is Dr. Ali, nuclear medicine." The accent corresponds well with the last name. "I have the Cardiolite scan on Mr. Bennett. Everything looks normal."

"Great! Thanks for the call."

"You're welcome." I call the hospital and speak to the nurse for Mr. Bennett. I arrange for his discharge and for his follow-up with me. I guess his chest pain was just anxiety, but I have to delve into that at a later date.

I start signing another batch of medication refills. May Cahilly needs a refill of her Xanax. Justin Debs needs a refill for Lipitor. Jasmine Davis needs a refill of her birth control pills and so on and so forth, until I finish the batch. Oh, God! I'm feeling really tired now. Maybe I should have another cup of coffee. I look again at Mr. Kim's labs. Why the hell is his calcium so high?

Chapter 13

The Home Stretch

"Dr. Gellman, you have patients in rooms 5 and 6," Sandra says. Had I dozed off? I must have. Feeling guiltily refreshed, I head over to room five, where Mathew Biddle sits with his wife. He's a 65-year-old with alcohol-induced cirrhosis, which has been stable since stopping alcohol. He's a happy man who tries his best to make those around him happy.

"Hey Matt, how you doing?"

"No complaints Doc. Feeling pretty well," he says proudly, but his wife is not pleased with his answer.

"Tell him about your nightmares, Matt."

"Oh yeah, Doc…I've been having some strange dreams, which sometimes wake me up. The last one I had was about aliens taking over the planet, except it was hard to tell they were aliens since they looked just like us."

"Sounds strange. How long have you been having those dreams?"

"A couple months now."

"Aliens were taking over the planet?"

He smiles. "It was actually an interesting dream, but it was sort of weird. At times I thought I was one of the aliens."

"You are an alien, Matt," his wife chimes in.

This could have something to do with his cirrhosis.

"I want to check an ammonia level," I say.

"Why do you want to do that?" his wife asks.

"I'm worried that Matt's liver problems are not allowing him to clear ammonia."

"Well, what do you do about that?" Mrs. Biddle probes.

"I would increase the amount of Lactulose he's getting." I have Matt lie down, feel his belly and write a prescription for an increased dose of Lactulose. I need to pee again, so I go to the bathroom, place a scant amount of urine in the toilet, wash my hands and leave the restroom. I walk over to room 6 and pull out the chart for Dolores Rodriguez, who is here for a complete

247

physical. Mrs. Rodriguez sits in a gown; a thin, dark-skinned woman with an angular face, small nose, dark eyes and straight black hair. She looks timid and a little uncomfortable sitting on the examining table.

"Hello, Mrs. Rodriguez, how are you doing today?"

"I'm OK. I'm here for my physical exam. Last time I saw you, you said that I needed a physical exam and here I am."

"Let's start, then. How are you feeling today? Are there any problems?"

"No, I feel fine." I start going through a review of symptoms and find out she has been having recurrent nasal congestion and ear pain. Her nose on examination is severely inflamed, boggy with polyps inside. I feel around her neck, listen to her heart and lungs, feel over her abdomen and check reflexes.

"I'll be back." I leave to find Sandra.

"Sandra, could you help me with a female exam?"

"Sure thing Doctor."

I first do a breast exam. Mrs. Rodriguez is lying down with her hands behind her head. Her breasts have a couple mobile lumps that don't appear cancerous. There are no enlarged lymph nodes.

I proceed to the pelvic exam. Mrs. Rodriguez places her feet in the stirrups and scoots her pelvis to the edge of the examining table. "Now you're going to feel the speculum going inside." The cervix is easily located with the speculum. I finish the exam, fill out the laboratory form, give her a nasal spray for her congestion and go back to 5. Dawn Kelly, seventy-something year old, is sitting in a chair. She's very familiar to me, coming in every month to get her Protime checked.

"Hi, Dawn. How are you doing?"

"Not so well. My stomach's bothering me again. It had been doing well until I went to Las Vegas on a senior tour."

"Vegas will do that to you."

"Yeah, I think I ate something bad from one of the buffets."

"Where does it hurt now?" She points to her upper abdomen. I ask her a few more questions and then examine her.

"Ouch that hurts." She jumps away from my hands.

"I think you have gastritis. I have samples of an antacid pill that will help you." I leave the room and return with little boxes of

Nexium. "Take these for the next three weeks, once a day. Come back in three weeks."

"Thank you so much, Doctor. I am so happy to have such a good doctor."

"Thanks, Dawn. Just doing my job." I leave the room feeling tired again. Can I see another patient without just a little bit of coffee? I really shouldn't do it. It irritates my bladder and makes me have to run to the restroom all the time. I don't need it. I look through the chart for room 6: Steven Little, a forty year old with ulcerative colitis and recurrent diarrhea, both having been stable on medication. He's here for a physical. I walk in the room and Steven is dressed in the blue gown, his hairy white legs hanging over the front of the examining table.

"How you doing, Steven?"

"It's all good, Doc." He's always been a jovial character and no matter how virulent his disease has been, no matter how much pain he has been under, he still has managed to put on a happy face. "I've had another child, a girl."

"Congratulations Steven! How many is that now?"

"Three."

"You are a brave man. I couldn't do more than two." He has a negative review of systems. I start the physical and look at his ears and mouth, feel his neck, listen to his lungs and heart, feel his abdomen and check for swelling in his legs. The last thing I have to do is the prostate check. "OK, Steve, I need you to lie on to your left hand side and bring your knees toward your chest."

"Aren't you going to buy me dinner first, Doc?"

"I'll buy you dinner afterward. I promise." I put on my gloves, open up the tube of KY jelly and slide the jelly all around my finger. I place my finger inside the anal orifice and probe into the rectal vault for the prostate, which is normal in size and has no lumps. I pull my finger out. "Have you eaten today?" I ask Steven as he puts his underwear back on.

"Not since last night."

"Good, then just wait right here and Sandra will be in to do your blood work." I start to leave the room.

"Thanks, Doc."

249

"Good luck with number three." There's nobody inside room five, so I keep walking down the hall to the break room, go inside and pour myself a cup of coffee, adding cream and sugar to the black fluid in the Styrofoam cup. The fluid turns a creamy brown and I bring the cup to my mouth and quickly, greedily, take a sip of coffee. To hell with my bladder! I walk back to my office and look through a couple more handwritten messages. David Maderas has a sinus infection again and wants antibiotics. Serena Michaels needs a refill of an asthma inhaler. I call Mr. Maderas, find out his symptoms, call in his antibiotics to the pharmacy and leave the message for Mrs. Michaels for Sandra to answer.

Oh, gosh! I've had enough. I'm ready to go home. Ok, Bill. You can do it, just five more patients. But……but, I don't want to see any more patients. It shouldn't be any problem for you. Think about Dad, who never seemed to complain a day about his work, and think about Ronnie who looks up to you. I drag my body to 5, which has a chart on the bin by the door. The chart is of David Wu, a 55-year-old with diabetes and high blood pressure and a significant amount of work anxiety. I walk in the exam room. Mr. Wu is sitting in a chair. He looks up from the magazine he's reading. "Hi, Doctor, how are you?"

"I'm fine Mr. Wu, and how about yourself?" I sit down in my chair.

"I'm fine. Just feel a little tired."

"Tired?"

"I'm fine in the morning, but later on in the afternoon, I don't have the energy I used to."

"Are you sleeping OK?"

"No. I'm finding it more difficult to sleep—again—and I'm needing to take Benadryl or Ambien more often." There's a look of shame on Mr. Wu's face.

"Do you have trouble falling asleep or do you wake up in the middle of the night?"

"I do both, but mostly trouble falling asleep."

"Why?"

"Maybe, because I'm worried about my wife. She just had breast cancer and it spread to her lymph nodes. She's been going through chemotherapy for the last two months and the chemo is making her sick."

"I'm sorry.........Does she keep you up?"

"No, but I worry about her. I keep thinking that things are going to get worse." He looks at me and his eyes well with tears. There's a moment of silence. I should try to figure out something wise to say, some magic word that would help Mr. Wu find peace with his life, but I feel somewhat impotent. If anything would happen to Barbara, I'd be lost.

"All you can do is be there for her. Once the chemo is done, things will get better. How often are you taking the sleeping medication?"

"Almost every night," he answers with downcast eyes. I write a prescription for Lunesta.

"Take care of yourself, Mr. Wu, and please follow up with me in two months."

"I will, Doctor. Thank you." I need another hit of the coffee. Yes, that would help. The coffee on my desk has cooled so I put the cup close to my mouth and take two large swallows. What time is it? I look at my watch. 4:00 p.m. Barbara should be at Blockbusters by now. I put the phone to my ear and dial her cell number.

"Hello."

"Hi, honey. How's it going?" It's good to hear her voice.

"Oh, I'm OK. A little frustrated about something at work, but I'll tell you later. So do you want me to order Chinese food for tonight?"

"No, I just ate Chinese for lunch."

"How about some Indian?"

"Too spicy" There's a moment of silence. "How about doing take out from Sunshine Café?"

"That sounds good. I already got a movie for tonight."

"What did you get?"

"It's called *A Lover's Quarrel*. It got good reviews."

"So, I'll see you tonight then."

"See you tonight, Bill. I love you."

"Love you, too." I hang up the phone, get out of my chair and make my way out of the office to the hallway and toward room 6. I pull out the chart from the rack and quickly review the file of Joshua Weller: a forty-seven year-old with a history of high blood pressure, in for back pain. Inside the room, Mr. Weller is standing, leaning over the side of the examining table, grimacing in pain.

"So Mr. Weller, what happened?"

He keeps leaning over the edge of the examining table, but turns his head toward me. "I don't know what happened. I just woke up today and I couldn't move without pain in my lower back. I've pulled it before, but it has never hurt this bad."

"Have you taken anything for the pain?"

"Tylenol, but it doesn't seem to cut it. I took today off work because I can't even sit down for more than five minutes." The mention of his back causes Mr. Weller to have a sudden paroxysm of pain, in which he turns his head away from me and leans his upper body more onto the table. "Do you have a shot, or something, for the pain Doc? This is killing me."

"I'll go get you something." His back feels tight and his lumbar muscles are in spasm. I get out of the room and find Sandra at the nurse's station. "Sandra, can you give Mr. Weller a shot of Toradol?"

"How much do you want?"

"Sixty milligrams would be good."

"Sure thing. Mrs. Shamsi is in 5."

"Thanks." I walk over and open up the chart of Ida Shamsi: sixty-nine years old, and one I've been following for many years. She was diagnosed with breast cancer two years ago and has undergone chemotherapy.

"Hi Ida, how are you doing today?"

"I'm having some trouble with my breathing. I get short of breath during my aerobics class."

"Short of breath? How long has this been going on?"

"About two weeks."

I'm listening to her lungs and here decreased sounds at her left base. "I want to do an X-ray."

I put up the orders for the X-ray and look at my watch. It's almost five o'clock. I'm thirty minutes behind. I have to urinate, but this can wait. I rush to 6 and quickly walk in. Sitting next to the

252

examining table is Donna Thompson, twenty-five. She looks up from some tabloid magazine.

"Miss Thompson, I'm sorry I'm late. How can I help you?" She looks a little annoyed as if she won't tell me what's troubling her. I sit down in the chair next to her.

"I'm having a bladder infection," she says.

"What symptoms are you having?"

"It burns when I pee and I have to pee all the time. My stomach also hurts," she says in a bored, uninterested way.

"How long has it been going on?"

"Three days"

"Did you leave a urine sample?"

"Before I came into the room." I feel over her lower abdomen and she's tender there. I tap over her back and she has no tenderness.

"I'm going to check on your urine. I'll be right back." I need to pee now. I make a beeline to the bathroom, try to open the door, but it's locked. OK, don't just stand around, be useful. I walk over to the nurse's station.

"Sandra, do you have the results of the urine test for Miss Thompson?"

"I paper-clipped it to the front of the chart. Didn't you see it?"

"I'm sorry, I wasn't looking. Thanks." I hurry back over to the restroom and open the door. Sanctuary! I lift up the toilet seat, open the zipper to my pants and allow the flood gates to open. The only problem is that they open only part way and instead of torrent of urine, out comes a soft trickling stream. It takes me a couple minutes to finish. Damn prostate. I finish and return to Miss Thompson. I look at her urine test which shows white blood cells and blood, give her prescription for Cipro and she leaves the room quickly. I go back to my office to review Mrs. Shamsi's X-ray. She has a large effusion of the left side of her chest. Oh Fuck! Fuck! Fucking cancer! I walk back to room 5.

"Ida the X-ray shows fluid on the left side of your chest."

"What?" She puts her hand to her mouth and grits her teeth. "Is it the cancer?"

"We won't know for sure unless we remove the fluid from around your lung."

253

"Oh God! I thought I was cured." She drops her head onto her hand, so that all I see of her is the grey hair on the top of her head; hair that was lost when she had her chemotherapy.

"I'm sorry Ida, but this may not be the cancer. I'm going to give you a referral to Dr. Masterson, the pulmonologist."

I dump her chart in my office and hurry toward my last patient of the day in room 6: Barry Arnett a 55-year old who's been basically healthy. I open the door and focus on a large abrasion on Mr. Arnett's forehead and upon his nose. "What happened to you?"

"I was walking my dog, when he lunged at another dog and I tripped and fell. I face-planted on the concrete."

"When did it happen?"

"Early this morning......I cleaned the area with alcohol and put Neosporin on it." Looking closer at his face, he has a large circular patch on his left forehead where the skin has been removed, exposing a raw undersurface. He has a similar smaller patch on the left side of his nose. The lesions appear clean. I put on gloves and touch around the areas to see if there are any breaks. He's only mildly tender to touch, so probably nothing is broken. He's a good-looking man, so the abrasions stand out more and I become worried about how they'll heal.

"Clean the area daily, continue the Neosporin and watch for any signs of infection." There is not much more I can tell him except to wait for Sandra to give him a tetanus shot. I leave the room to find Sandra. OK, now all I have to do is finish my charts, make my calls and then I can leave.

"Sandra, can you give Mr. Arnett a tetanus shot?"

"Sure, Doctor. Did they tell you about the walk-in patient?" she says shyly.

"No, they didn't."

"I put him in 6. It should be quick, just a sore throat." That's annoying. My watch shows 5:30. No use complaining. You can do this, Bill. I quickly walk over to 6, open the door to see a thirty-year-old man with dark skin. He looks familiar. The chart reads: Robert Singh.

"So what's going on, Mr. Singh?" I hurriedly ask, sitting in my swivel chair next to him.

"I think I have strep throat," he says.

"How long have you been having symptoms?"

"It began about three days ago with a runny nose and mild fever, but then yesterday I developed a real sore throat. I have a one-year-old daughter who was also sick. She, thank God, is getting better."

"Let's take a look." Looking in his mouth, there's redness in the back of the throat. The tonsils look mildly enlarged. His neck has bilateral swelling of his lymph nodes, but this is also mild. It's probably not strep throat, but I'd like to make sure since it is Friday. "Mr. Singh, if you don't mind, I would like to do a rapid strep test to make sure you do not have strep." I leave the room to get the rapid strep kit. I return to the room with the kit, swab his throat and put the solution over the swab. "It takes about ten minutes to get a result, so I'll be back then."

"Thank you, Doctor." Back at my office, I finish writing the notes and filling out the super-bill forms for the patients I saw in the afternoon. Mr. Wu's chart is first. I document his sleep problems and the medication I gave. I reach for the coffee cup and notice a written message attached to my phone. Joseph Lindero, that eighty-year-old patient, is having vertigo and wants me to give him a call.

"Hello," a weak voice answers.

"Hi Joe, it's Dr. Gellman. What's going on?"

"Dr. Gellman thanks for your call. I've been having that vertigo again. The whole room is spinning and I'm afraid to move."

"Have you taken anything for the vertigo?"

"I don't have anything to take."

"Is your daughter at home, Joe?"

"No"

"I want you to give her a call and have her pick a medication called Meclizine."

"Do you mind calling her and telling her for me? I'm having a difficult time getting up and I can't get to a pen and paper to write the name down."

"Give me her number."

I keep it in my head and dial right away.

"Hello"

"Dolores, it's Dr. Gellman. I just spoke to your father and he's having vertigo. I want you to pick up an over-the-counter medication for him called Meclizine. He can take this up to three times a day for his vertigo, but be careful because it can make him drowsy. You should probably stay around him so he doesn't fall."

"Dr. Gellman, why does he keep getting these attacks?"

"Probably an inner ear problem. He should make an appointment to see me."

"Thank you, Doctor."

"You're welcome, Dolores." I hang up and return to room 6. The strep test is negative. "Mr. Singh, I think your sore throat is caused by a virus. What I recommend is lots of fluids and rest. This should be better in a matter of days."

"Thank you, Doctor. While I'm here I have one other problem I would like to discuss." What the hell! You didn't even have an appointment... Suck it up, Bill. It's Friday. It'll be over soon.

"What's going on?"

"My shoulder's been aching. It hurts anytime I raise my hand above my head." I quickly go over and do a cursory examination. It seems like he has a biceps tendonitis. I give him a prescription for an anti-inflammatory medication and tell him to come back if it's no better. I'm about to leave the room when he asks me take a look at a mole on his back.

"Make an appointment for a physical exam and we can take a look at the mole then." The nerve of that guy! Back at my office, I sit down and I've no energy to do anything else, looking at the unfinished charts on my desk and the messages I have to answer. There's also that huge pile of mail that I'll have to open at home, a different form of homework. Why do I do this job? I can't believe that I've been doing this for twenty-five years. Medical school seems so long ago, a time I really felt I could make a difference, could make the world a better place and change the system, but somehow, somewhere along the way, I became a part of that system. I came to see many years ago that there's only so much a man can do and hopefully what he does helps the world. I wouldn't have survived without that realization. Yet, all these thoughts won't take the work off my desk, so turn on the radio and listen to some classical music. Starting in earnest upon the charts, I write the rest of the note about Steven Little's physical exam; nice guy. I continue in a methodical fashion finishing one note after the next until I'm finished. What time is it? 6:15. I'm going to be late coming home. I'll call Barbara as I'm driving to the nursing home.

There are more messages. Mrs. Jane Victorio's Detrol is not covered by her insurance company. The insurance is requiring me to fill out an authorization form for Mrs. Victorio to get her medication and this authorization will probably be denied by her insurance. What was I reading the other day? That the CEO for United Health Care has a billion dollars of stock options in the company? And those are the people that are guiding my decisions? Isn't there something wrong with that? I'm busting my ass day in and day out for twenty-five years trying to help people and I have to take orders from a company that is only interested in making a buck. The next message is from George Harwitt, who has a fever and wants to know what to do. I dial his number.

"Hello?" His voice is stuttering and familiar.

"George, it's Dr. Gellman. What's going on?"

"I don't know, Dr. Gellman. I had a really high fever to about one hundred yesterday, but today I don't have a fever."

"Are you having any other symptoms George?

"No, not really; I did have a bit of a headache two days ago, but my head feels fine now."

"Well, okay, if the fever comes back, I want you to take a Tylenol and if you're still having fevers by Monday, I want you to come into the office."

"OK, Doctor. Do you have any idea what this can be?

"No clue George, maybe a virus."

"OK, Doc, I'll come in Monday if it's still going on."

"Bye, George."

I deal with a couple more messages and look at the clock: 6:30. I got to go. I take off my stethoscope and walk out of the office. All the nurses are gone from the nurse's station. The only person who is still around is Robert Smith, still at his desk, talking to a patient on a headset, looking more like an operator or a customer service representative than a doctor. He sees me and waves. He's a good man, but aren't we all.

At the elevator, I pull out my phone to call Barbara. The phone rings. "Hello"

"Ronnie, it's Dad."

"Hi, Dad."

"Hi… Can you tell Mom I'm running late and probably won't be home until 7:30? If you guys get hungry you can eat earlier." The elevator door opens and I walk in.

"Are we still going to play catch?"

"Maybe after dinner… How did the Geometry test go?" I get out of the elevator and walk toward the parking lot.

"OK, I guess…I made one mistake…It was a stupid mistake." He sounds a little nervous.

"Well don't worry about it, Ronnie. We all make mistakes and the most important thing is that it's over." I take off my white coat and hang it up in the back of my car.

"I'll see you soon, Dad."

"See you, Ronnie." I put the phone away and start the car.

"This is NPR's All Things Considered. I'm Robert Siegal. In our series on alternative fuels, our latest topic is methanol. Noah Adams has the story."

I make my way out of the parking lot and take Lincoln over to Venice. It's dark outside. The traffic is moderate, but it's moving. I turn onto Venice and drive until I see a sign for Sea Gardens Convalescent Center. I turn onto a smaller street next to the nursing home and park, get out of the car, open the rear door, pull out my white coat and walk toward a single-story complex, beige with many windows. There is a familiar smell that pours out from the vent of the laundry room of the nursing home, a mixture of cleaning fluids, urine, stool and death. Nursing homes… You can't live with them, can't live without them. At the nurse's station, I'm greeted by a Filipino whom I recognize. His name plate says Greg.

"Hi, Doc! Who are you here to see?"

"Paul Mathews." He pulls out the chart and places it on a desk and pulls up a chair for me. It's nice to sit. My back's starting to ache. Paul's last labs show him to be mildly anemic, but his weight, blood pressure and pulse are stable. He's been somewhat lumpish here, never really able to participate in any form of therapy, never talking, just lying there staring off into space. He's been back into the hospital for pneumonia a couple of times, but recovered quickly and returned to the nursing home. I sort of don't know what keeps him going. "Greg, who's the nurse working with Mr. Mathews? I need to take a look at his decubitus ulcers."

"His nurse is Lily. I'll go get her for you." He hurriedly walks away and leaves me sitting at the nurse's station. I stand up and walk to the front of the nurse's station and see the halls are empty; all the residents are in their rooms. The place is quiet and the fluorescent light gives the facility an eerie feeling. I don't know what to do. Should I wait here for the nurse or should I just go to Paul's room? I walk down the hallway and pass by room after room, each with two beds and a window and all with human beings in different stages of decrepitude. All the televisions are on and there's something comforting about that. I finally come to room 24, which is dimly lit, and walk inside. In the bed next to the door is an elderly man, bald with red, blotchy skin, in wrist restraints tied to the side of the bed. His sheets have been kicked off. He looks up at me and starts to talk and as he talks his head shakes from side to side.

"Doctor, can you help me. I need to use the bathroom." He pulls his arms in, in an attempt to break the restraints, but his efforts are fruitless.

"Maybe the nurse can help you."

"Just untie me. I need to use the bathroom."

What do I say? Poor guy! "The nurse should be here any moment. I'll talk to her for you."

"Thanks, Doc." He continues to try to pull at the restraint as I walk over to the next bed. Paul is lying with the head of the bed propped up, looking forward, looking like he's focusing on the television on the other side of the room. He's in a blue gown and has a blanket that covers his waist and legs. The television is showing a farmer in a field of corn, showing the viewer that his crop has been infested with locust or grasshoppers, I'm not sure which, but I'm already running late, so I turn on a switch that turns on an overhead light and look closely at Paul. His blank stare advertises that nobody's home, but I try my best to rouse him.

"Paul! Paul! It's Dr. Gellman. Paul! Paul!" He turns his eyes toward me and opens his mouth a little. "Paul! Paul! It's Dr. Gellman. How are you doing Paul?" I yell again.

"Leeeeee... Leeeeee... Leeeeee." It's sad to see. His hair's greyer than I remember, thinning in the front. His face is full, bloated, drooping on the left side and has a little stubble. Shit, I remember him when he wasn't like this, remember telling him all the bad things that could happen with his smoking, uncontrolled Diabetes and high blood pressure, but he didn't seem to care; like he had his own agenda to push the envelope toward self-destruction. Maybe he was unhappy with his life and maybe that was why he was unmotivated to change. I don't know, but it's sort of sad. I pull out my stethoscope, lean over the edge of the bed and listen to his heart and lungs. His breath sounds are barely audible, no doubt the result of his many years of smoking. I pull down the blanket and lift up his gown to take a look at his gastric-tube site. The tube, colored blue due to the color of his formula, enters the left side of his abdomen and there's redness surrounding the tube and a little bit of whitish-yellow pus. I should make sure the nurses are cleaning that daily. There are footsteps coming and I straighten up for it must be the nurse. The Filipina nurse comes in the room and walks toward the head of the bed. I've seen her before, but don't remember her name. She's short, stocky and walks with a little bit of a limp; however, she does have a nice complexion and a contented smile.

"You want see me, Dr. Gellman?" she asks in a high-pitched voice that has a song-like quality.

"His son said that his ulcerations were coming back."

"Yes, I talked to son and told him."

"Can I take a look?" I ask.

"Sure, I turn him on side and you look." She seems happy to accommodate. I look at her name badge. Lily, it says.

"Thanks, Lily."

"You welcome." She walks to the other side of the bed and takes gloves out of drawer next to the bed and hands me a couple. I put on the gloves as Lily places her hands through Paul's grey hair. "Paul...Paul." Paul's eyes turn to her. "Paul. It is Lily." She caresses his face and hair. She smiles at him and he seems pretty content just looking at her. "Paul, we have to turn you. Dr. Gellman, he have to look at your back." She's very loving with him and I don't know how anybody could be so loving to a man who has nothing to give? Maybe she's just a giving person. Maybe? She lowers the head of his bed. She pulls at his right shoulder, pulls at his right buttock and Paul easily turns on his left side so his rear faces me. In a quick motion while holding his right shoulder, she pulls down his pants with her left hand. I help pull down his pants and remove an adhesive tape to open up his diaper. He has a small amount of stool that stays attached to his buttock as I pull away the diaper. The buttocks themselves have atrophied and I try not to focus on this, gazing instead upward toward two square bandages that rest above the crease of his butt. I pull off the bandages and see two shallow based ulcers. They appear to be stage two, which for Paul is not bad.

"Lily, Mr. Mathews had a little accident," I say as I stand back up.

"No problem, Dr. Gellman, I clean him up. Leave him on side. I be back in second."

"Oh I forgot, his neighbor there said he needs to use the bathroom."

"OK"

She leaves hurriedly as I stand at Paul's backside holding the right portion of his pelvis so he doesn't fall onto his back. This is a wonderful position to be in, waiting with Paul's rear facing me. At least the TV is on: *Wheel of Fortune*. A man, dressed in some military uniform, is spinning the wheel and then clapping, hoping for a large amount of money. "Big money! Big money!" he says.

I think about the last time I saw Paul in my office before this stroke.

"Hi Doc, how you doing?"

"Fine, Paul, and you."

"Guess I'm OK. You wanted to talk to me about something?"

"Yes. Paul. The last blood test showed your sugars out of control and that your kidney tests look worse."

"Really?"

"Have you been taking your medication daily?"

"Yeah, but some days I forget and some days I remember."

261

"Did you take your blood pressure medication today? You know your blood pressure's really high today."

"Yeah?"

"Yeah, Paul, it is. I gave you referrals last time to the cardiologist and the Diabetes doctor. Did you see them?"

"I'm sorry, Doc. I know I haven't been the best patient, but I've been real busy."

"But you're retired, Paul?"

"I've been working on my book and I finished it."

"Your book?"

"The one I've been writing, rewriting and editing for the last twenty-five years."

"Well that's great and I hope it does well, but if you keep going the way you're going, you won't be alive to see it published."

"Oh, that doesn't matter a lot, Doc. At least it's finished."

"Paul, you shouldn't be so cavalier about your health. You've already had a heart attack. Are you depressed about something?"

"Depressed? What do I have to be depressed about? I just finished my book. Twenty-five years, Dr. Gellman, and I'm done. All I want to do now is celebrate. Live it up a little. In fact, I'm going to Vegas tomorrow in my Mustang and I'll have the top down, baby, the whole way, listening to music as the world goes by."

"Sounds nice."

"It is nice, Doc. I know I need to change things and I will when I come back. There are a lot of things I need to change."

"OK, Paul, I'm going to get you new referrals to the endocrinologist and the cardiologist. I want you to take your medicines every day, decrease sugar and salt in your diet and see me in three months."

"I will, Doc. Things are going to change for me. You'll see."

Hell, was there anymore I could have done to help him? I look back over at Paul. He's not watching the television, but blankly stares at the window. Looking at the window, I can't see to the outside, but instead see a reflection of me standing over Paul, holding Paul's broken body so he won't fall over. Gosh, I don't want to be here. I look again at the window and can't believe that the reflection on the other side is me; but it is, for whom else could it be?

Lily returns with a wash basin and many towels. "I be real quick," she says and I reflexively look at my watch: 7:10. I want to go home. She pulls off the soiled diaper and with one end of the diaper wipes whatever she can into the diaper, then wipes the sticky brown stool off with wet white towels and discards them into the basin. She then pulls out a clean diaper, wrapping it around Paul's buttocks and pulling it in between his legs. I don't want to stay any longer. I've seen enough.

"Lily, I have to call his son. Could you please place Tegaderm on those ulcers and turn him again from side to side every two hours?" She straightens up dutifully and gives me a smile. "Oh! I forgot. Can you make sure to clean the area around his gastric tube? It's looking a little red."

"Please put orders and I will do," she says.

"Goodbye."

"Goodbye," she says and I leave her to finish her work. I walk out of the room and down the hall to the nurse's station, write my note down and place the orders in the chart, including a CBC in one week. Shoot, I almost forgot to call his son, Jacob. His number is in the front of the chart along with his name: Jacob Mathews. I dial the number and the phone rings and rings and rings until I hear a female voice say, "You have reached the home of Jacob, Melissa and Emily. Please leave a message after the tone," and then I hear a beep.

"Jacob, this is Dr. Gellman. I just saw your father and his status is unchanged. His skin ulcerations are mild and they are being treated. If you want to discuss this further, I'll be in the office on Monday." I hang up the phone, stand up and walk directly out of the nursing facility, glad at the idea I won't have to return for another month. I walk out to the street and to the Volvo, take off my white coat again and hang it in the back of the car, then get in the front and turn on the engine. Techno is blaring on the radio and if I listen to this music any longer it will drive me mad. I push the CD button and am returned to Don Henley singing. I make a U-turn and return to Venice Boulevard going east. I am on my way home.

263

"Who will provide the grand design of what is yours and what is mine? Because there is no more new frontier, we have got to make it here. We satisfy our endless needs, and justify our bloody deeds. In the name of destiny and in the name of God." I turn off the CD and call Barbara.

"Hello," Barbara answers.

"Hi, honey. I'm on my way home"

"What's taking you so long? Ronnie's already eaten and he's waiting to play catch."

Guilt, pure and simple.

"I'm sorry, honey. I had to see a nursing home patient and, well, it took a long time. I'll be home in ten minutes."

"Be safe, Bill. You'll get here when you get here."

"I love you."

"I love you, too."

She hangs up. I drop my cell in the passenger seat, trying to focus on Venice Blvd. My mind is a blur from the day, not remembering what happened, except the last patient I saw, Paul Mathews. That poor guy, lying in that bed day after day, fed from a tube and unable to interact at all with his environment. It was his son's choice to keep him like this. Boy! What kind of life is that, to be a burden to your family, to be a burden to the system? I'd hate for Ronnie and Jenny to see me like that, in all my weakness. The traffic light has changed to red. We all got to go sometime. I really should make some kind of living will; some kind of statement telling my family what I'd want for the end of my life and, for the love of God, what I don't want. It's hard thing to do. Maybe that's why most of the people I've given Advance Directives to, haven't filled them out. And every time I've passed out those Advance Directives to my older patients, I always thought that one day I'd be filling out one of these, but thinking that day was some far flung time in the future. Maybe that day is here. The light turns green and I accelerate, passing under the 405, deciding not to take the Freeway, since it's still probably crowded. I make a left on Sepulveda.

A BMW rushes ahead in the right lane toward a car going slower than I am. I know he wants to cut me off and keep rushing ahead. I let him. It seems that some people just like to drive fast, but they really have nowhere to go. I should fill out a living will. Something to say what I'd want if I were in a grave state. Barbara should fill out one too, but I really don't want to think about it. What about intubation and artificial feeding? I never want to be like Paul Mathews, but if there's a good chance I will survive, well, then I'd want everything to be done, especially now when I'm relatively young. Maybe I can set some kind of limit as to how long I'd want to be placed on a respirator or how long I would want artificial feeding. I need to write this stuff down. I'll do it this weekend sometime, but when? Tonight is shot, tomorrow's Ronnie's baseball game and on Sunday I am going to watch the NCAA tournament. When am I going to find time to do this? Maybe next weekend. Shucks, I'm worrying too much. I have plenty of time.

About the Author

Robert Ashley M.D. is an Internal Medicine physician practicing medicine with the UCLA Medical Group in Santa Monica, California. He is an Associate Clinical Professor of Medicine at UCLA. Like other primary care physicians, Dr. Ashley has seen birth, death and much of what falls in between. The motivation to write *Beautifully Absurd* originates from patients' struggles with death that put in to question the meaning of life.

Synopsis

Paul Mathews never wanted to be an average Joe, so when he became a 9-5 working man, a husband and a father, he rebelled. Living alone 20 years later, a massive stroke leaves him tethered to a ventilator and unable to communicate.

Two weeks after his stroke, Paul awakens to a world of beeping machines, dutiful hospital staff and a television he cannot turn off. Severely debilitated and fearing the end, Paul's greatest wish is to see his son, Jacob, again, and somehow repair their fractured relationship. But the hospital doesn't even have Jacob's nor Paul's ex-wife, Sarah's, phone number, leaving Paul dependent upon his doctors to choose his course of care. With the costly advances in medical care, Paul can be kept alive for years, but he only wants to be kept alive long enough to his son again. Isolated and in this tenuous state Paul is bombarded by the recollections of his life: his days of student protest, Vietnam, his hopeful marriage, his bitter divorce and the solitary existence he chose afterward. He urgently struggles to make sense of his life and find a peace that has eluded him up until now.

The Baby Boomers are getting older and while their health care is a right, death is a fact. Paul's ride through the medical system will hopefully give this generation of Americans the impetus to discuss end of life care with their family and their doctor